Primula Bond is an Oxford-educated mother of three boys and has lived in London and Cairo. She currently lives in Hampshire with her husband and younger sons and works part-time as a legal secretary for criminal defence lawyers as well as writing freelance 'human interest' features for the national press. She has written erotic short stories and novels for various publishers and magazines for twenty years and this is her fourth erotic novel.

Primula also offers a critique service for aspiring erotic and romantic writers through the online Writers Workshop.

Keep up to date with Primula's news by following her on Twitter @PrimulaBond and on her blog primulabond.blogspot.com

28
D1135983

PRIMULA BOND

The Silver Chain

AVON

This novel is entirely a work of fiction.
The names, characters and incidents portrayed in it are
the work of the author's imagination. Any resemblance to
actual persons, living or dead, events or localities is
entirely coincidental.

AVON

A division of HarperCollins*Publishers*
77–85 Fulham Palace Road,
London W6 8JB

www.harpercollins.co.uk

A Paperback Original 2013
1

Copyright © Primula Bond 2013

Primula Bond asserts the moral right to
be identified as the author of this work

A catalogue record for this book is
available from the British Library

ISBN 978-0-00-752417-4

Set in Sabon LT Std by Palimpsest Book Production Limited,
Falkirk, Stirlingshire

Printed bound in Great Britain by Clays Ltd, St Ives plc

All rights reserved. No part of this publication may be
reproduced, stored in a retrieval system, or transmitted,
in any form or by any means, electronic, mechanical,
photocopying, recording or otherwise, without the prior
permission of the publishers.

MIX
Paper from responsible sources
FSC C007454

FSC™ is a non-profit international organisation established to promote
the responsible management of the world's forests. Products carrying the
FSC label are independently certified to assure consumers that they come
from forests that are managed to meet the social, economic and
ecological needs of present and future generations,
and other controlled sources.

Find out more about HarperCollins and the environment at
www.harpercollins.co.uk/green

My thanks to all at Avon for this great opportunity, and in particular to Adam Nevill for his enthusiastic and unwavering support down the years.

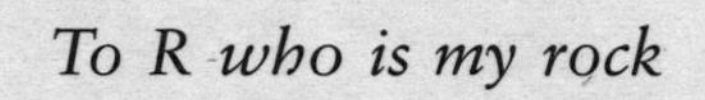
To R who is my rock

ONE

At last. At last. We jolt once, twice, then start to move. The rumbling from the diesel grows louder and more determined as the engine settles into gear. The vibrations under my seat are calmer, but they are doing nothing to quell the churning in my stomach.

The grey paved platform, slippery from the rain driving in from the south west, rolls smoothly alongside as we pull away, but it's still too slow, too slow. I feel like I'm on the run. My hands are shoved under my legs to keep them prisoner. My heart is juddering as if there's still time for someone to slam on the brakes and arrest me. Why do I feel like that? This is as final as it gets. Everything alongside me, soon to be left behind, is finished.

I'm free to go where I like, so why does this feel like the great escape?

I wish I was sitting up front with the driver. Not to talk to him. I only want to perch quietly on a ledge or a stool up front, and stare out at the world.

What a day job a train driver has. He's probably sick to death of it, but what a view he has, all to himself. He clambers up to the cab at the start of every shift, yawning and cursing, carrying his flask of muddy tea, then all day and sometimes all night he's king of the road. The big curving window, smeared with grease and smuts, spattered with rain, sometimes even with blood or guts or bits of animals, is a cinema screen showing the English countryside unfurling between the carved leafy embankments. The gleaming metal tracks converge in the distance just like the parallel lines you draw in art classes to learn perspective.

Why doesn't he step on it? We are still crawling, we still haven't emerged from the canopy roof and ornate bottle-green girders of the station.

The train is wrestling with the wind that blows viciously off the moors no matter what season it is, batting at the station signs as we gather speed. Let other people get off here and feel jolly. Let them think of that breeze as bracing sea air.

Me? I'm turning my back. I can't wait to get out.

The train pulls away fast now, too fast to keep up if you were trying to chase after it, trying to grab the door handles to jump on. Jake isn't trying to stop me. He's not moving at all, in fact. Not that I can see him any more. I'm facing forwards, way past all the drooping heads and shoulders of the other bored passengers.

Usually I like to weave a story around fellow travellers, maybe even catch the eye of an interesting-looking man or woman. I'm not as shy as you'd think, at least not with strangers. I always have something to talk about or show them, my pictures, my work. But this lot are faceless, all anoraks and shopping bags and mobile phones. They don't even glance out of the window at the place they've passed through.

Who can say what they're thinking about behind their laptops and magazines? Work. Warring families. Hospital appointments. Running away. Tonight's supper. Elopement. The car's MOT. Adulterous assignations.

As the distance between us stretches to breaking point the

muscles in my shoulders, my eyebrows, teeth, my jaw, even my hair, all start to let go, relax. The headache hasn't quite gone, but I drank too much last night so I've only myself to blame. I unbutton my new caramel tweed jacket checked with threads of faint blue. It's a little tight because at the last minute I decided to shove my thick white sweater on as well. I smile as my ribcage expands and my breasts rise gently with relief.

I unwrap my oversized royal-blue scarf and run my hand up my warm, slightly sticky neck to release my tangled hair. Horrible how hangovers make you feel. I didn't realise I was still so strung up. Like banging your head on a brick wall. You only know how bad it is when you stop.

I know it isn't fair, but you only get one life. Not fair on Jake, I mean. He looked petrified just now, in the fossilised sense. I've never seen him so angry, or so still. All that fidgeting, the phantom drumming thing he does with imaginary sticks on every available hard surface, the constant foot tapping and knuckle cracking. All stopped.

I didn't want him to come here and see me off. Surely after everything we've said and done he doesn't believe for a second that I'll stay? I have no more energy for any of it. For him. Everything is focused on the future, on selfish little me. Those gleaming metal tracks are carrying me out of here, the big smoke is blooming with promise on the horizon.

How many times can you say goodbye?

Last night, holed up with him in his caravan on the cliff, was dreadful. What was I thinking? Everything had gone so well up until then. All my decisions, plans, all the arguments were over. I was so cool, sorted, strong. And then like an idiot I agreed to meet him for one last drink in his brother's pub. He knew I'd say yes because I wouldn't be able to stand one more night alone in the house. Even though they are finally gone, even though the coldness and the silence, the sneaky feet and surreptitious fists that never left a mark, even though the dead eyes and the lovelessness are all gone, it's still horribly creepy. And now it's deserted as well.

The Black Hat looked jolly and warm enough. Even though it's not Halloween till tomorrow, they'd lit candles and lanterns and draped the beams and light fittings with lacy cobwebs, propped-up broomsticks, carved out grinning pumpkins. One of Jake's many gripes is that I'm buggering off just when the party season is starting. He still doesn't get that I'm done with partying. I'm done with him, with everyone, and certainly with spending any more of my precious time and money in a medieval pub in a dead-end village at the far end of the country.

I have a life to start living.

But I went along for that one last drink, didn't I, persuaded our rag-tag bunch of mates to come along. Hence this hangover. Jake was behind the bar all evening, serving a bubbling punch from a cauldron which was deceptively orange-flavoured and totally lethal. He was ladling out brimming pint glasses for free, and by the time our mates had drifted away, slightly too obviously I thought, I was pissed and careless, and what happened next is that all that coolness, sortedness, strength, it all evaporated. At least physically. Nothing in my mind had changed. My bags were still packed.

I was still the heroine of all those country and western blues you've ever sung along to, about lovers leaving on jet planes.

So there we were, Jake and I, somehow back inside the little tin can that he lives in, and it was midnight. I can only conclude, if there is a jury out there, that it was laziness and familiarity and the remnants of randiness that bore us from the village up the road, along the pitted track, into the muddy field to where the caravan sits, protected from the sheer drop to the fierce sea by massive boulders that look like nightclub bouncers, and purple moss and hard sheep droppings and a broken fence.

That caravan with its moth-eaten pull-down bed and garish seventies orange-flowered curtains, its kettle and booze and stash of chocolate and overflowing ashtrays, it used to be my haven. Once we'd pulled the rickety door closed and bolted it with elastic bands and other flimsy barriers against the world, Jake and I were like babes in the wood in there. We used to cling and whisper together, getting stoned, learning everything together. And I mean everything.

Childhood sweethearts sounds so innocent, doesn't it? But we weren't children. And we were on a mission to shed our innocence.

We both tried to deny we were virgins when we finally found ourselves under that faded duvet. But who else could possibly have got there first? When he passed his driving test and bought the caravan we christened Jake's new toy by deflowering each other.

It's meant to be awful, and painful, the first time, isn't it, but when the fumbling, the probing and the giggling stopped and we became deadly silent and serious, only the sea foam trying to reach up the cliff, only Adele crooning in the background, when we realised that our mouths were made for this different, deep, penetrating kissing, that our bodies were built to fold round and in and out, to become hot and yielding under each other's hands, when I held him balanced in my fingers, long and hard and ready, and he touched me, so soft and wet, and waiting, it was amazing.

Sorry, but it was brilliant. Two fit teenagers hiding away from home, exploring each other in the dark. How could we fail?

I didn't come that first time, or even the second, but boy did he, and my triumph was as explosive as his orgasm. By the third attempt we still weren't always doing it right, or very imaginatively, or with any kind of adult finesse. But we were hooked.

My stomach lurches as the train shoots through a tunnel. Is that a kind of useless death throe of desire kicking me deep inside, or is it excitement about what's ahead? Desire used to be a sharp tugging between my legs or a coiling in my stomach whenever I thought of Jake's angry blue eyes, his hungry mouth, his eager hands, his quiet, rocking caravan. But when the longing slides northwards to the heart, then the brain, by then it's diluted completely and that's when it's platonic. I'm not sure it's even that, now. It can't be. It's over. I keep telling him. I'm gone.

Did I owe it to him, to give him one last night? Payment for keeping me safe when I had nowhere else to go? Did he hope that bringing out all his tricks, all the old words and moves, the guitar strumming that secretly shreds my nerves, did he think that getting me drunkenly naked by the light of his old hurricane lamp would make me chuck all my dreams out of the window and make me stay?

He knows me so well, so how could he not guess last night, once he was on top of me, the usual position, how could he not tell through the limpness of my limbs around him, the tightness of my body resisting him, the difficulty he had pushing in, the way I turned my head away from his desperate kisses so that they missed and slithered instead across my cheek, my half-hearted moaning, how could he not know that I was faking it?

The easiest way for me to explain why I let it happen is that it was sympathy sex. Cruel, I know. But that's how removed I felt from it. From him. I am a bitch, no question, just as he said. How else to excuse the way our fledgling love burned brightly for a while and then just died? Why have I changed so drastically in the space of a couple of years? Almost as if my teens were shackles I was waiting to throw off as soon as I hit twenty. I can't explain it myself. Suggesting that I grew out of my adolescence somehow doesn't cut it.

Just now he slouched out of the shadows as I was heaving my cases and photographic gear into the carriage. And there's the rub. He slouches. I march.

Thank God the train was already there, striking its metal hooves to be off. The guard was waddling along the platform, probably wishing he could slam the doors and wave a flag like in the old days but having to content himself with jabbing at the hissing buttons.

The guard's whistle blew, and there was nothing more to do. I don't even know if Jake saw me. Anyone noticing him standing there, mean and moody and uncomprehending, would think he was a hunk alright. What idiot would kick that out of bed? Some lucky girl, one of the girls in the pub, in the newspaper office, one of the walkers along the cliff, will have him, if they haven't already.

Jake walked to the far end of the platform as the doors folded shut, the end where it slopes down into the nothingness of grass and weeds and rubbish, so that it wouldn't look as if he was going to miss me. His iPod was plugged into his ears, his hands shoved deep into the pockets of his leather jacket. His fingers would have been fiddling and twisting all the items I know he keeps in there. Phone, keys, wine gums, pens, cash, miniature tape recorder. Ripping up the snapshot of me to show that he's over it.

Well, that goes for the two of us. I'm off men now. For good.

The train gathers speed, breathes its huge rumbling sigh of relief as it accelerates out of the station. It rushes with glee through the scruffy outskirts of town, then turns away from the sea, ploughs through the bare, wintry countryside overhung with a heavy blanket of sky, and hurtles towards London.

TWO

I have them in my sights. A ragged crocodile of little witches, snaking their way across the quiet garden square. They seem to know exactly where they are and where they're going, but I am several tube stops away from my flat south of the river and I'm not quite sure where I am. I tell myself that's all part of the fun of being in this city. A mist has descended over London like a ragged curtain and temporarily cowed the commuters who would normally be scurrying home by now.

The leading witch holds a lantern aloft, presumably to guide her gang to some Halloween party round the corner, and it emits a weak glow of eerie orange.

In the middle of the square there's a statue of a man who looks like Robin Hood or someone, maybe Dick Turpin, or Cupid with clothes on. Someone important and athletic, anyway, and yet there is something melancholy in the statue's posture. It even seems, in this dim light, to be turning its head to watch the mini witches pass by beneath it. I count seven in all, maybe six witches and a wizard. I rip my gloves off with my teeth, let them fall onto the spikes of frozen grass, and as the witches pass beneath the statue, its bare toes gripping the edge of its stone plinth, I start to shoot.

'Keep going, my little beauties,' I breathe, stepping silently along the parallel path to keep track of them. 'I've got you exactly where I want you.'

Thank God I've found a focus. One of the many things I didn't anticipate about arriving as a newcomer in London is how quickly, if you have nothing concrete to do, no concrete living to earn, no smart business clothes to wear, you become invisible. Redundant. How busy everyone else is, mouthing into mobile phones, checking watches, filing into tubes and buses, hailing cabs, knocking back coffees. Staying close to people they know. Caring so little about the strangers passing them by.

My mind is teeming with ideas and projects. I'm trained and qualified, ready to sell my soul. I've been prowling the streets all day yesterday and today with my CV, but although I enjoy making contact with each new human being none of them is sealing a deal with me yet, shaking my hand and saying, 'Your work is marvellous, Miss Folkes, and you are going to make millions. I can't believe how lucky we are to have discovered you!'

How quickly the fire and enthusiasm fizzing inside me yesterday, on that train, has faded. Not extinguished. It can't be. I've burned all my bridges coming here. All those bridges the train hurried over and under in its haste to get away from my home town. All burned. I won't go back there in a million years, at least not to stay.

It's not Jake I couldn't face. No-one will believe that, but I can deal with him if I have to. It's the rest of it, the memories, the house on the cliffs, those trapped years stretching on and on with no parole. The person I was, I am, when I'm there. I can never forgive the people who should have guaranteed my happiness, taken notice of my talent. Loved me, just a little.

Even so. I'm in London at last. The end of the rainbow for now. Over painstaking weeks and months I have prepared a sharp, slick portfolio. I have my CV, testimonials, references from my Saturday job bosses and my art tutor Allan Mackenzie. I've even included the catalogue from the exhibition I showed at the local library. Big provincial deal, but still. I'm aiming to kick down the door. No time to fight any encroaching despondency.

The little witches and wizards in their costumes seem to float a few inches above the frosty grass now, some looking down as if contemplating their sins, others gazing up at the night sky like miscast angels. I shoot again, picture after picture. Swap the digital for my old Canon, swap them back again. I'm engrossed, and I'm sure of myself. This is it. This is great. Magical little photogenic beings hovering across my path just when I most needed them.

Suddenly the smallest witch at the back stumbles over her too-long black cloak and lets out a howl. They all, with one fluid movement, swivel round to see what is happening. Another great shot of their sharp white profiles all in a row. They don't help her. They just maintain their positions, wagging black-gloved fingers like disapproving duchesses, shake their heads impatiently, or lift flapping sleeves to adjust their masks until she is upright again and they can continue on their march.

They reach the wrought-iron gate at the northern edge of the square and as they pause to discuss their next move their pointed hats cast triangular shadows over their faces. The leader with her orange lamp gesticulates up the deserted street, away from me, away from the square.

I watch them process towards a tall, grand house on the corner. They slow down. I wonder if they are bravely going to raise their plastic tridents to knock on its double-height black door, maybe wave their baskets about and offer a trick or a treat, risk the wrath of the eccentric rich owner who will open up and yell at them to beat it, leave him alone to his reclusive life. But they obviously think better of it.

All at once, on a silent signal, they break formation like synchronised swimmers, scattering like ducks startled by gunshot, then equally neatly they join forces again and zig-zag briskly onwards. There's the faint scattering of small, impatient feet on the gritty pavement, the tip of the crocodile's tail whisks around the corner. And then they are gone.

'Perfect,' I murmur, following them through the gate. 'My Halloween collection. That'll make a brilliant next series.'

I still have no idea where I am, and they certainly can't help me. But the rumble of traffic is never far away and I'm in no hurry. I could be lost all night and it wouldn't matter. No-one would miss me. I could be lost forever. I lean against the streetlamp to scroll through the latest images.

'Bloody lucky you didn't scare them, creeping about in the dark like that.'

The deep, gravelly voice comes out of nowhere. It gives me such a fright that I bite down on my tongue and taste the iron tang of blood. It's as visceral as if a wild animal has just pounced.

The world has gone very quiet. This great roaring capital is like a graveyard. Where the hell is everybody?

A figure in a long coat, a blood-red scarf wound several times round its neck, steps out of the shadowy square where I have just been. He grasps the gate and it makes a rusty screech as he slams it shut. I don't know whether to cackle or scream. I push my collar and scarf up protectively. I could swear this place was deserted two minutes ago.

'I wasn't creeping about, as you put it.' I line my spine up with the lamp post, straining to make out his features as he approaches. I clear the squeak from my throat. 'Actually I'm working.'

'A voyeur, then. Peeping Tom.'

The overhead lamp seems to glow brighter as he comes nearer, a dimmer switch operating somewhere off stage. All

I can see of him so far is that he's tall. He opens his arms in a wide gesture that looks like a greeting, or a silverback display of ownership. Or maybe he reckons he's right. Then he claps the gloves together for warmth.

The lamp light strikes off the glossy black hair swinging over his forehead as he glances sideways for imaginary interlopers. The shadows stalking him, and the mist separating us, exaggerate his wolfish air, and though it's difficult to gauge his build under the long coat I sense this is a man who could break my neck with one twist of his hands if I was stupid enough to cross him.

As if reading my mind he shoves those same hands in his pockets and moves more thoughtfully, head down, shoulders and body angled slightly sideways as if he's sketching his half of a tango.

He only stops when the toes of his shoes touch mine. Strangers don't usually invade space like this. He's so close I can see the pulse pushing at the pale, oddly vulnerable sliver of skin just visible above his red scarf. But I don't recoil. I can't. I'm blocked in by the lamp post and by the hypnotic way he's looking at me.

My breath is annoyingly damp against my upturned collar but I'm not ready to reveal myself. Happy just to stare him out. His stance, the angle of his gaze, is straight out of a *film noir* publicity still. An assassin lurking in a deserted Montmartre alleyway for his victim. A rejected lover outside his mistress's opulent villa nestled in the hills above Florence, plotting revenge. Both staring down the barrel of a gun. And like the armed assassin, or the vengeful lover serving his dish cold, this guy's in no rush.

I shift my numb feet while I work out how best to extricate myself. As long as he's studying me I'll study him back. First the vital sign beating silently beneath his ear, then the taut jaw line pricked with dark frustrated stubble. Under the smooth plane of cheek I can just see a muscle flickering as if he's grinding his teeth. I can't see his mouth. He could equally be suppressing a smile.

But it's his eyes, black as liquid tar, that keep me pinned down. They have that kind of direct focus which you sometimes see in portraits and makes you wonder what high-octane relationship joined the subject with the artist. Right now it's convincing me that he and I are the only two people in the world. Well, the only two people in London.

Perhaps he's one of those mime artists, the ones who remain immobile for hours. But his eyes are alive, probing mine for the answer to a question he asked long ago.

I fidget with my collar. Hell, I'm not a mind-reader. I'm a photographer, even if the world is apparently indifferent to that fact. My occupation is observing people to the point of rudeness. That's why I'm brazenly returning his gaze out here in the dark, with nobody else about. What's his excuse?

'So what *are* you doing out here?'

He's toned it down but his voice still reverberates deeply, kind of nudges my ear drums. There's a very slight accent. I want him to take off that scarf. It's like the surgical mask of a TV surgeon forced to emote with just his eyes. But what I can see so far is beautiful. I can say that because it's my job. If it wasn't for the pulse going in his neck he could be carved from marble like the statue locked in the square. Steady. Calm. Cold.

The pretentious text beside my portrait of him, hanging in a gallery, would read: *The Stranger in the Square. Here the artist has snatched and translated from life a remote yet idealised masculine aesthetic.*

Except now that the stranger has taken his hands out of his pockets to tug aside the blood-red scarf he's becoming alarmingly human. His mouth parts at the shock of cold air barging in. His lower lip is surprisingly full, blooming with faint colour, and its generous curve is pinched down by the firm line of the upper lip. I was right. He's stifling a smile.

'I told you. I'm working,' I repeat, my voice husky with nerves. My head knocks the lamp post. 'And I must get on.'

His eyes are sucking me in. Get it together, Serena. He's skin, blood and bone, that's all. My fingers grip the edges of my camera. Will he object if I just lift it, like this, take a shot? If I can get the exposure right the shot will be highlighted by the solo, white light above our heads, a shafting beam like the searchlight from a spaceship. The moon dangling down on a string.

Like my little witches he is perfect for Halloween. I wonder if it's deliberate? He's in costume for a party. That explains the looming, vampirical vibe. Even the oversized oval buttons on his coat gleam like beetles' shells. Any minute they're going to scuttle up and down, and rattle.

The straight lines of his thick eyebrows could be inked in. His silky hair is no costume wig, though. It whips across his face in the wind and there's a slight wave where it kinks off the scarf, and in the ocean depths of his eyes I can see myself reflected in miniature, staring and trapped like an effigy inside his pupils. Those snow-piste cheekbones are high, Slavic, and his skin is whiter even than the face paint of those little witches. So white it seems to glow from within.

Yes. A modern-day Dracula. A swarthy Edward Cullen, the Hollywood vampire's less melancholy, more muscular older brother. But if I come out with that he'll either assume the character and ruin the moment, or smirk sarcastically and walk away.

Let's just get the shot, sublime in its anonymity, then beat a retreat.

I twist my zoom and click softly. My Dracula doesn't budge. I swing away, pretending to focus instead on the picturesque bare branches of the garden trees grasping for the sky, the blocks of dense shadow cast by the tall house up the slope. My pretence places him off centre in the picture, as if he's stumbled into the frame by accident, or he's a demon darting away. That's fine. Anarchic in its imperfection. My Halloween series is taking shape.

'Spying on a group of little girls, all alone, rushing through the dark in their party clothes?'

My camera action has snapped him out of his reverie. He claps his hands together again, then nods up the street in the direction that the crocodile has gone. I'm offered his profile for a moment. A strong straight nose, haughty but not hawk-like. Eyelashes spiking his cheek.

'I'm still not sure about you,' he mutters, looking up the street. 'It's obvious you're–'

'Taking photographs. The clue's in the camera? I'm collecting street scenes. Human life. Halloween scenes.'

I'm relieved yet disorientated that he's taken his eyes off me at last. The moon and the streetlights and now the occasional flash of fireworks scatter diamond chips of light over the deserted square. 'And frankly it's not my fault if kids that age are unaccompanied.'

'I stand corrected. Should we, I wonder, investigate? Make sure they're OK?' He strokes his chin thoughtfully. His eyes flash back at me.

'They're long gone now. I thought they might go trick-or-treating in that haunted-looking mansion up the slope there, but they thought better of it and scurried past. They're probably at some rowdy children's party round the corner.'

As I jerk my head towards the grim town house my Breton beret slips backwards and falls right off. My hair untwists from the loose knot and slowly cascades down over my shoulders, catching in my eyelashes, snagging in my collar.

The man gives an almost theatrical start. To my astonishment he snorts with laughter, tapping his head. His amusement rumbles deep down in his chest. It sounds like pebbles being stirred at the bottom of a pond.

'Well, I'll be damned! Round one to you, *mademoiselle*. I had you down as a scrawny bloke. And I'm rarely wrong about anything.'

His eyes elongate with amusement and lift at the corners. They seem to work harder than other people's. Emote, like those TV surgeons. The rest of his face takes its cue from his eyes as his mood changes. Even his eyebrows relax, become less black. The lines of his face seem to settle, become more human, less of a mask. He rubs at his lower lip with his leather-gloved finger with appealing uncertainty.

'Yeah. Well. Not a peeping Tom after all, see? Just going about my own business.' I bend quickly to pick up my hat. I can't see my own gloves. 'I find these bulky winter clothes are a great disguise. Handy for keeping strangers from pestering me, especially at night.'

'Are you saying I'm pestering you? Because you don't look remotely bothered to me.'

'Should I be?' I put my beret back on, fiddling unnecessarily to set it more rakishly on my head. I like the heaviness of my hair on my shoulders and back. It's comforting and also warm. I glance about for my gloves. My fingers are beginning to stiffen up in the biting cold. 'That didn't come out the way I meant it to. You made me jump, that's all.'

He lifts his shoulders, opening his arms in the multi-layered gesture which now includes frivolous apology. His arms are so big in the coat, the width of his embrace so inviting. What would it feel like if he wrapped those warm sleeves tight around me, carried me off somewhere? He's easily strong enough. Embraced me and held me, kept me safe. Or ravished me?

'I didn't mean to scare you.' He leans one elbow casually on the railings and crosses one foot in front of the other. The wind flips his black hair across his face. 'I should have known you were female. You weren't loping like a man at all then but moving gracefully. Your hips. Women sway their hips when they don't even realise it. Especially when they are at their most fertile, apparently.'

Now I'm certain he's making fun of me. I hope to God that prevents him from reading what's really going on in my mind, because my thoughts are skittering off the scale. I must be more frustrated than I realised. Either way I can't help staring at the way his teeth grate across his lower lip, biting but not piercing the tender skin. The upper lip is harder, less forgiving. Still determined to give nothing away. It's such a dynamic smile. Look how it brings his face to life, smoothes out the tension. Those strong white teeth could really hurt, I'm certain of it, but oh, if you let them graze across your mouth, your neck, your breasts, they could so easily please as well.

'Hmm. Too much information.' Thank God it's dark out here. My whole body is burning hot. I blow on my bare fingers. 'You sound like a wildlife documentary.'

'Too observant for my own good, especially when there are interesting specimens to track.' His hair flips off his brow, making his eyes startling like searchlights. 'I only meant to say that you have much lovelier, longer legs than any male and I should have clocked those. I'm guessing you're an athlete, or used to running over rough terrain.'

'Athlete? No, Mr Attenborough. But rough terrain, yes. I used to live by the sea.' My stiff fingers fiddle with my camera. I'm desperate to study the new images.

'Right. And people who live by the sea don't like being complimented on their legs or any other part of their anatomy?' The stranger tilts his head like an artist at his easel and with his hands starts to sketch the outline of my legs from my feet upwards. He glances mischievously at me as he reaches my waist and makes an exaggerated hourglass.

We both know that's daft because tonight I'm shapeless in my jacket. 'Or are you really a mermaid?'

'Nothing mythical ever materialises in my neck of the woods. Not that it's my neck of the woods any more.' I have to smile, partly because that is such a good thought. 'You're obviously used to charming the birds off the trees, mister, but my being female still doesn't give you *carte blanche* to comment on my hips or legs or fertility, or speculate about my natural habitat.'

He shrugs cheerfully. 'I'm no Neanderthal, *mademoiselle*. Just as keen an observer as you are.'

I've only ever seen strong white teeth like that in America, or on television. Over here such fine teeth belong only to the very famous or very rich. In the lamplight, which has continued to brighten and is now as strong as a floodlight, his lips and those teeth are glinting as if he's hungry. Or thirsty. His firm lips curl back slightly, and there's that wolfish air again.

You hungry for some comfort, stranger? Because I sure as hell am.

'You are absolutely right, of course,' he concedes. His face straightens as he looks away from me again, up towards the town house. 'And yet again I apologise. I just didn't expect to bump into someone like you tonight, that's all. Ever, in fact.'

'Someone real, you mean? Rather than a ghoulie, or a ghostie, or someone dressed up as a sacrificial virgin?'

He claps his gloved hands. 'Well, I guess you could pass as a woodland nymph, with a better body, more hair, and a louder voice. But actually I just meant someone who doesn't have a clue how stunning she is.'

This doesn't feel wrong. This encounter. This conversation. How could anyone call this pestering? It feels totally right. I keep the camera in front of my face, framing him in my viewfinder. I have no desire to run away. He could be menacing, if I really wanted to dissect it, but so what? Any sensible girl would be beating a retreat by now with some kind of polite excuse, but I'm done with being sensible. Maybe that's why I'm drawn towards him like money to a magnet. So who cares? And where are my bloody gloves?

My cousin Polly, whose chic little riverside flat I'm borrowing while she smashes the glass ceiling in New York, would be that sensible girl. She'd take one look at this tall dark man looming over me, with the black eyes glittering and lively now from the lamplight, and she'd call him a Lothario. Such a great word. So good you can melt it on your tongue. She wouldn't get that I'm a goner now I've seen him smiling. He looks like he would remove every lacy scrap of your underwear with those perfect teeth. She'd declare that proved her point, made him some kind of creep who got his kicks chatting up country bumpkins or scaring the living daylights out of them.

Well, she'd be wrong. Whether he's a Lothario or a Lancelot, I want to find out more. I want to go on standing here with my camera, propped up by this Narnian lamp post, staring at this possibly dangerous, probably harmless, smiling stranger.

'Sorry,' I say, looking down, my boot stirring some little stones sparkling with frost. 'That did sound surly. What I meant was, do you often play spot the difference between men and women?'

'Any entrepreneur worth his gold-plated pension watches people for a living so he can separate the wheat from the chaff.' Those eyes again. Nonchalant stance, maybe, all casual against the railings, but those eyes are boring into me so sharply I'm feeling punctured. 'You know. The sheep from the goats.'

'Same for photographers,' I mumble. 'Those biblical sayings have a point.'

He grins. 'And in the business world, what that means is,

anyone with any nous can spot a success story from fifty paces. Likewise we can sniff out the losers.'

'All sounds a bit Lord Sugar!'

'You better believe it. We're cut from the same cloth. I happen to be an admirer of his, and yes, I do make it my business to hire and fire apprentices.' He rubs his nose scornfully. 'If politicians had half the common sense of people like me and him, we'd all be out of this mess by now.'

'What about personally?' I'm feeling bold now. Brassy. 'Do you observe, do you watch people closely who might come into your private life?'

'Do you mean women?' he asks quietly. 'Am I discerning about the women I want? I could answer that if I wasn't so out of practice. But yes. Perhaps I should identify and stalk my prey like I do in business.'

I realise we've moved closer together again, both leaning on the sharp railings. I'm not interested in coming over all Germaine Greer, though. This man can say whatever he likes, and if it wasn't so cold I'd just stand here all night lapping it up. It's that damn mouth of his, that soft lower lip, that hard upper clamping down. His mouth has a story to tell, I'm certain of it. How can it be amused and sardonic, hard and inviting, all at the same time? It's daring me, or asking me something. It's wide, and confident, but it also desperately needs to know a lot more. About me. About his prey.

Well, I like what I see, too. This man. That mouth. And God help me, if he wasn't so goddamn superior the devil in me would just go ahead, decide to really shock him, and kiss it.

'Well, you got it spectacularly wrong in my case, didn't you?'

'You got me.' He holds his gloves up in surrender. 'Not a peeping Tom at all. A Thomasina.'

'Not peeping at anything. I told you, I'm working.' I shake my head. 'And it's Serena. That's my name.'

There's another pause. My heart thumps in my ears. *Why did I tell him that, for God's sake*?

The city surrounding us, this garden square, this lamp post, this man, and me, it all shrinks, closing in on us, pushing us together. The steam of our breath curls delicately in the freezing air between us. His deep black eyes pull me in. I can see the tiny flare of his nostrils as he breathes, the twitch of his kissable mouth as he ponders.

He takes my hand, the one not holding the camera, pulls it away from where I'm still instinctively, defensively, using it to shield my body, enfolds it in the creaking leather of his glove, holds it tight for a moment, then gives it a formal shake.

'And my name's Gustav. Gustav Levi.'

My hand rests so easily in his, like a small pet. 'That would explain the cheekbones. Are you from Transylvania?'

'Smart, as well as stunning,' he chuckles. He must know how cold my fingers are, because he squeezes them. I curl my fingers round his palm, and he puts the other hand on top of it. 'Sort of, as it happens. My family originally came from that area. But they're all gone now. Except me. I'm here, as you can see.'

'My turn to be ridiculously observant.' I give a triumphant punch. 'Because I already have you labelled for my collection as Count Dracula.'

'We can be a little brooding at times, granted.' He laughs again. A little lighter, but still that deep, pebbly chest-stirring sound. 'But if you knew Transylvania, the landscape, the music, you'd know it can be magical. But then the name comes from the Latin word *sylva*, meaning forest.'

'Ah, yes. Forests, mountains, and castles. Like a fairy tale. Not a horror movie at all.'

'That depends on who is in the movie. Who is the wicked witch in the fairy tale.' His fingers are like a vice now. I don't think he realises how tightly he's holding me because he's not looking at me but over my shoulder, his eyes as black as the dark shadows behind me in the square. 'But I'm still drawn to forests and mountains. I don't have a castle, but I do have a chalet in Switzerland. Right on Lake Lugano.'

'Lugano also comes from the word "forest". Did you know? You must have been a wolf in another life, Gustav.'

He closes his eyes for a moment. The lines down his cheeks are etching out some awful thought. I reach up and stroke his cheek, try to iron them out. I expect him to leap away from me but he squeezes my hand more gently now and a rush of heat powers up my arm, fanning under my ribs. I try to breathe. I look up at him again, my eyes resting on his mouth.

'You said my name,' he murmurs, opening his eyes.

'It's a cool name. But you're hurting me.'

He releases my hand and it's my turn. Very slowly I start to pull off his glove. It's a kind of leather ski glove, tighter fitting than I thought, with a small annoying zip, and it takes a couple of seconds, but the rip of the zip, that sound effect of getting naked, sounds so sexy-good it sullies the silence. I peel the glove down from under his sleeve, reveal first his lean forearm streaked with hair, the slim ropes of muscle under the skin, then the flash of pale wrist. His long, strong fingers slide out one by one and while I now own his glove, he claims my bare hand.

The muscle is playing in his jaw again but I'm pretty sure it's not suppressed laughter this time. Is it quicksilver that changes like this, or mercury? If I ever see him again, I'll have to learn to keep up.

I already know these eyes, how black they are, how deep, I've noticed the crackle of yellow streaking round one iris like sunrise edging a cloud. Does he know mine? Some people call them green. Others emerald. After what feels like hours of talking, he's travelling right inside me now.

I imagined his hand would be cold, like the statue, but his skin on mine is dry and warm. There's his pulse again, this time beating in his wrist, beating into my hand. I can feel the heat crackling through the network of veins and arteries like a tidal wave.

'I'd like to see your lake, and your castle. Sorry. Chalet.' My voice is a frog's croak. What am I saying? 'I'd like to go there one day.'

'Who knows? One day perhaps we will.'

He lifts my hand, so small in his, and turns it over. He has one glove on, one glove off. He separates my fingers. I hold my breath.

Did he just say 'we'?

He kisses each finger on the tip, watching me all the while. It's all I can do not to collapse against him. My legs feel weak. My head is heavy and lazy on my neck. The gorgeous, scary mouth I will try to kiss in a minute if I'm not careful is blowing over the palm of my hand now, and just as I lean towards him he presses my hand against his mouth, kisses it with a delicious dampness, then releases it.

'Wow. Is this how the locals introduce themselves in Lake Lugano?'

Gustav Levi just chuckles and sheaths his fingers one by one. Then he claps his sturdy gloves together in what I take to be his hearty, scene-changing gesture. He glances around the square, towards the bright lights. His black hair blows back off his face like a stallion ready to hit the horizon.

'Only the charming locals, and only when they meet beautiful ladies. It's the Italian influence. So. Can I walk you somewhere, Serena? It might be best to come away from this area. Shepherd's Market is just down there. Not dodgy like it used to be, but still, you hear things about the new clubs that have opened up.'

'Shepherd's Market?'

He laughs, re-organising his scarf. To my dismay covers his mouth. 'You really are from out of town. It used to be a red light district. Or at least, very boisterous and of ill repute. That's why they banned the sheep market in the end.'

I don't reply. I'm nearly losing my grip on my camera because my gloveless fingers are so cold. He hooks it safely onto the strap and loops it round my neck. I wait to see what he'll do next and yes, he does it. His gloves brush against my neck as he lifts my hair out of the snagging strap, holds it for a moment, then lets it fall. He's watching me, all the time.

'A party, perhaps? It's Halloween, after all. A gorgeous young woman like you must be in demand?' He steps back suddenly. 'A boyfriend waiting for you. Damn. Of course there is!'

I shake my head as carelessly as I can.

'No. No boyfriend. I'm not going anywhere. I'm too busy. I have to get these pictures edited and use my cousin's printer. I've only just arrived in London, you see. I'm touting my portfolio round the galleries.'

'So you've only just left that desolate seaside you were telling me about?'

'It's all behind me now. I'm in London, now, and that's all that matters.'

'Yes indeed. And lucky London.'

He starts to walk away from me, up the hill where the little witches went. OK. So that was goodbye then. Fine. Goodbye, mister. It's a relief, actually. He's had me dancing on tacks the last few minutes, and I haven't time for this kind of distraction.

I need to find my gloves, because if I don't my fingers will seize up and I won't be able to feed the tube ticket through the machine or unlock my front door, or work Polly's printer, let alone press the shutter on my camera. I hunt around on the ground. Nothing. Try the gate to the square, rattle it, but it appears to be locked. My fingers stick to the iron. I wrench them off before they freeze there permanently. You hear of that happening, don't you? In the Himalayas, or the Arctic. People's tongues stuck to, what, pickaxes? Cups? Spoons? What else in the Arctic would you be licking?

I can feel ridiculous tears crowding into my throat.

'Where am I going to get some new gloves at this time of night, for God's sake?'

My gloves float out of the darkness, right under my nose where I'm hunched over the gate, biting back sobs. The bloody things are waggling and waving at me in thin air. They look solid, filled, as if they have fingers inside them.

'I took them hostage, Serena. I'm so sorry. I was teasing you. I picked them up earlier in the garden.'

Gustav Levi is indeed wearing them, and they look ridiculous, like a child's mittens hanging off his long fingers. My eyes are still heavy and wet with unshed tears, and though I blink furiously to try to hide it, he bends and peers into my face. The new expression there, the softness in his eyes, the self-mocking bat of his thick eyelashes, the teasing lift of his mouth, are all so unexpected that I nearly burst into tears in earnest.

'I'm OK, it's fine, really,' I gulp, blinking back at him like an owl. 'Thank you for my gloves.'

He wipes one leather finger gently along the lower lid of each eye and then hands both gloves back to me.

'Now. Tell me I can't escort you somewhere, Serena. You look a bit, well, undone. Dishevelled? No, that's not the right word. At sixes and sevens. Knackered. Who wouldn't be? This can be an exhausting old town. How about allowing me to buy you a drink if you think you can trust me?'

THREE

It takes me all of three seconds to make up my mind. There's no-one waiting for me. No-one expecting me to check in. No-one who gives a toss.

'Mr Levi? Thank you. I could murder a glass of dry white wine.'

'Gustav. You were OK with it before. It's a formal enough name without your making me feel like a sergeant major.'

'OK, Gustav. And if you're not to be trusted, well, I'm a big girl now. I can look after myself.'

He presses his hand into the small of my back. A signal of agreement, or the commencement of a new journey? Either way it gets me going, like the crank handle on a vintage car. I'm happy for him to keep his hand there, actually. Against all my resolutions, despite my upbeat retorts, I feel right now as if I have no spine, no backbone, that I'll crumple in a heap and give up with no visible means of support.

But to my disappointment he removes it, puts his hands thoughtfully into his pockets, and instead of walking up the hill, as he started to do just now, he leads me away from the dark square, towards the bright lights of what must be

Piccadilly where red buses and black taxis and normal people are going about their business.

Behind me I imagine the shadows in the square staring after us, reluctant to let us go.

We cross the street and like everyone else we walk briskly towards the Ritz Hotel. The famous lights illuminating its name above the colonnade are so inviting. Gustav glances down at me. The amusement I'm becoming familiar with starts in the crinkling of his eyes, the softening of his cheeks, lifts the curve of his argumentative mouth.

'They have a dress code in there, I'm afraid, to go with all that glitzy gilt. They wouldn't let us set foot in this revolving door, let alone contaminate one of their precious seats in the Rivoli Bar.'

I am an urchin, standing in the cold, elbowed aside by the glossy rich visitors in their fur coats and ostentatious jewellery, being fussed into the hotel by pompous-looking doormen.

'No problem. I'd better get home, actually Mr – Gustav. A drink is very tempting, but maybe not such a good idea after all.' I pat my pockets. 'And I'm skint.'

'Pavements not paved with gold yet, eh?' He moves on along the facade of the grand hotel to the corner, and waits. He's staring not back at me but down St James's Street. I wage a little war with myself. He's a stranger, remember.

The newspaper headlines, exaggerated by the time they reach the office of Jake's local rag: *Country girl from the sticks raped and murdered in London by suave conman.*

Even Polly would be wagging her metaphorical finger at me by now. Blaming herself for not being there, looking out for me. But we're out in public here. Lots of people around us. He's charming. He's incredibly attractive. He's got a lovely deep, well spoken voice. And he's an entrepreneur who must be bloody rich if he owns more than one house. What the hell else am I going to do with myself when everyone else is out having fun?

One thing I won't tell him is that my pockets might be empty, but my bank account is full.

'One drink. Then I must get back.'

He doesn't answer or protest, but with a courtly bow he crooks his elbow and escorts me down St James's. We turn right and into the far more subtle splendour of Dukes Hotel.

'Dress code?' I ask nervously, wiping my feet obediently on the huge but welcoming doormat and drifting ahead of him into the smart interior where domed and glassed corridors lead here and there. The foyer smells of mulled wine and candles and entices you to succumb to its perfumed embrace.

'Not as such. It's not whether you're wearing the latest Victoria Beckham or carrying a Hermès that counts in a place like this.' His voice has become more mocking since we stepped out of the cold. He snaps his gloves off.

'As if. I've never even been into the kind of shop that would sell those.'

'Well, don't ever go there. It's a total waste of money. Vanity and greed. And the women who claim their lives aren't worth living if they don't have the latest designer crap are a waste of space too.'

Waves of hostility are coming off him now that we're within spitting distance of others. 'So what does count here?'

'Standing. Class. Breeding. Beauty helps, no matter what people say.' He unwinds his scarf as if it has offended him, then turns at last towards me. The sudden annoyance melts away as quickly as it arrives. He flicks imaginary dust off my shoulder. 'And of course, whether or not you can pay your bar bill.'

'Oh Gustav, I told you I've no money on me.'

'And I told you, not a problem. Your beauty and my wallet

will see us through this evening.' He laughs softly. 'So how about we rearrange you, Serena, undress you a little? How would that be?'

I open my mouth and shut it like a fish. Open it again. 'Undress me?'

'I meant – what did I mean?'

For the first time he stutters. There are streaks of colour in his pale cheeks from our chat in the cold and our brisk walk down here. He brings his big hands up to frame my face. They push against my tender skin and the bones beneath as if he's a blind man moulding clay. It makes me feel small, and young, and clueless. The last time anyone touched me was Jake, but I was always in charge then. The leader.

There's a twist of lust lighting up Gustav's black eyes. He said 'this evening' as if we have all the time in the world. Maybe we'll get a room. The pulse is banging fast in his neck. I'm learning that's his gauge. His meter. Does he want me? Oh God, can I ask him?

'Christ, Serena,' he mutters thickly as the hotel buzzes around us. His licks his mouth as he tries to speak. He must be reading my mind again. 'If things were different. In a heartbeat.'

'What things? How different?'

Silky strands of hair are sticking to his forehead as the overblown heating of the hotel attacks us in our outdoor clothes. He looks as if he's been running or hurdling. I stroke the hair away. He's so close, one little move from me and we will be kissing. But abruptly he presses one finger so hard against my mouth that it folds inwards and catches on my teeth.

'I meant, we should get these things off.'

I got it wrong. Fine. I'm rusty. Clueless. He closes his eyes for a moment, then whips off my beret. The roots of my hair prickle.

Gustav moves slowly behind me and unwinds my blue scarf. So far, so harmless. So brotherly. But then he combs his fingers through my hair, starting at the base of my neck, and I shiver with uncontrollable, unexpected pleasure. He misreads my shivering for cold, or rejection, pauses as if waiting for me to stop him.

'Please, don't stop, Gustav,' I moan quietly.

He has no idea how this has calmed me, like a wild horse. I had no idea how someone stroking my hair would affect me. He stands very close. His tall body lines itself up behind mine, firm and unbending like the lamp post in the square. I push myself back against him. Oh, we fit so well. My bottom is just a little lower than his hips. His fingers go back to work. His hands are circling my throat loosely like a noose. I brush against the hardness in his trousers and it gives him away. My stomach curls over, my body tightening in dark agreement.

Does he know I know? I tilt my head sideways. If I'm too shy to speak, how can I show him what I want, how I want the tips of his fingers to go on combing and stroking me, how I want him to stand nice and tight behind me, set my cold body on fire.

He knows. He strokes my skin. He lifts my hair, unwinding it out of my collar as if it's a magician's endless rope or a charmer's snake.

'You have no idea,' I breathe, my eyes fluttering closed as my hair lifts and curls round his fingers, strokes against my cheek and neck, sends its own minute promises of pleasure down my body, 'how good that feels.'

'My ragged Rapunzel,' he breathes, so hot on the back of my neck. A squeal of excitement bunches in my throat. I bring my hands up to his, try to keep him there, get his warm mouth to press down onto me.

But he steps away, leaving a cool space between us. My hair drops like a curtain.

'Why have you stopped?'

He comes round in front of me and puts his finger on my mouth. 'It's a crime to hide this amazing hair. And the colour, in this candlelight! Rossetti and those pre-Raphaelites would have had a name for it. A glorious Italian-sounding tint. Titian. Tintoretto. Not red. Auburn. Claret. Cinnamon.'

'Five spice?'

'And what about introducing this tangle to a pair of scissors, Calamity Jane?'

I can't help smiling. How has he managed to get under my skin so quickly? Is it because he's taller and older, impossibly attractive with his own unruly hair and steady black eyes? He's unlike anyone I've ever met down there in my dreary old life by the sea. Is it the chameleon way he's simultaneously courteous and mocking? Is it his deep voice or the way his face goes from cold to hot like running water, from dark to light like the changing hours?

'Oh, I know all about scissors, believe me,' I retort.

A single hair he's missed is caught in my eye and when he sees me blinking at it he hooks it away absently, familiarly, before he steps towards the reception desk.

I've been growing it for years, but until I was big enough to fight them off my hair was an unkempt bird's nest because they never understood how to treat it. They didn't understand how to treat me. The night before each new school term they would shove me down on a hard chair as if I was Anne Boleyn being prepared for the block. He would hold me down while she would start chopping at it with a pair of kitchen scissors.

No point wasting money on a hairdresser, it's just ugly, dead material.

I learned to control the impotent tears as she hacked and he shoved and I watched the russet curls, the emerging tendrils struggling to prove themselves, kinking up even when they were only a few inches long. Shorn, limp, kicked about on the dirty floor like withering autumn leaves. Where did I come from? Who in my biological past had, or has, this hair?

'I've stepped over a line. Taken liberties.' These aren't questions. They're statements. Gustav Levi is watching me again, trying to read me. He's not succeeding.

But even through the sudden wretchedness I can still see the way my blue pashmina dangles over his arm like a waiter's napkin as comical.

I shake my head. 'I'm just reminded of things, people, I'd rather forget.'

'You don't like your hair being touched?'

'*Au contraire*,' I sigh. 'I have just discovered that I love it being touched. No-one's ever – it took me by surprise, that's all.'

'I'm continental. Too tactile. And you Anglo-Saxons?' He flips his hands dismissively. 'Ice in your veins.'

'I always think of myself as Celtic. Fire, not ice. But no, Gustav. I'm trying to tell you it felt nice. Lovely. It was just more intimate than I'm used to.'

He raises his eyebrows questioningly.

'I would defy any man not to want to either stroke it or paint pictures of it all day long. Christ, even mammals groom each other, don't they?' He pushes the hair off his face and unbuttons his coat. 'You telling me your mother never brushed it? All that sunset splendour?'

'Brushed it?' I repeat harshly. 'God no. She pulled it when I was naughty, the little baby hairs just in front of my ears, oh, and she chopped it off, as soon as it grew more than a few inches, because she hated it. It wasn't sunset splendour to her. It was ugly and ginger.'

A shadow passes over Gustav's face. A brief cloud, followed by watery sunlight. I wonder if he realises how easy he is to read. The black gleam in his eyes steadies to understanding, as if he's listening to a piece of music he used to play.

'I've never told anyone that before. No-one has ever stood still long enough to listen.'

'My God, Serena,' he says, very softly, his eyes softening. 'You really are a lost soul under all that chutzpah, aren't you?'

'Not lost. Fighting to be heard. I'm fine. You learn to be the cat who walks alone when you're kicked about often enough.'

A small, dark man in an impeccable suit appears soundlessly from behind a huge vase of winter flowers. 'Mr Levi. How very good to see you. Your usual tipple this evening?'

Gustav nods. 'Thank you, Jerome. If you have my favourite seat, too?'

The tinkle of glasses and low murmur of voices start to trickle out of the bar as if we've disturbed birds sleeping on a wire.

'And very sexy they are too.' Gustav takes a step towards the bar.

'What are?'

'Cats. Cold, distant. And you have the eyes, too. Green, slightly slanted. Perfect for Halloween.' Gustav crooks his arm again. 'They sometimes pounce on mice for fun, when no-one's looking, don't they? Don't make that face. I mean it in a good way.'

I toss my jacket and gloves at him, as if he's a servant. His hand shoots out overarm as if he's catching a cricket ball.

'Are we going to have that drink or what?'

He laughs and slaps his leg. Those expressive hands. 'Of course. What would you like?'

'Surprise me. And could you look after my camera, while I freshen up? Guard it with your life.'

'Oh, I will, Serena. Don't you worry about that.'

I know he's watching me, my butt, my supposedly fertile woman's hips, my legs, sketching me all over again in his head as I make my way self-consciously down the airy corridor to the ladies' room. The knowledge that he's watching makes hot sweat spring through my cold skin. I pray I don't trip. I push open the big white door, slip inside. Alone at last.

False pretences. I don't really need the bathroom. I just need a moment. Work out what's going on. Get a grip. I need to, what do those counsellors say? Regroup.

Polly, the only person who looks out for me, would still be nagging me.

You have no idea who this guy is. He could be an axe murderer. He could be twice your age. Get the hell out of there, before something happens.

But I want something to happen! That's precisely why I came to London, isn't it? And it's not as if I've gone down a dark alley with him, is it, tempted as I was, or allowed him to drag me back to his lair.

I start to tremble. I close my eyes and let it take me over. I know what that means. It's my body's reaction to the possibility of danger. Gustav Levi's lair. What would that be like? What would happen there? What would he do to me if I went there with him?

I open my eyes and stare at the girl reflected in the huge mirror. I barely recognise her. In the house on the cliff they used to nail up one or two dusty panes of mirrored glass in the only places where it was absolutely necessary. The bathroom, beside the front door, so the handful of visitors, the priest, the doctor, the undertaker, could check that they looked sane before taking great lungfuls of fresh air on departure.

Only two days ago this girl was still in that house, reflected in those paltry mirrors. Pale, transparent, only catching sight of herself out of the corner of her eye. She was a ghost, not just because the house was deserted, no furniture now, never any ornaments or pictures, no cushions or rugs. Not just because everyone else was dead and gone, burned to a crisp like the tables and chairs and beds. But because in that house she had never had a life.

Even the girl at the railway station yesterday, shoving the beret down on her hair, applying lip gloss to stop her biting her lips, looked drained and anxious as if any minute someone would burst in like it was a Wild West saloon and tell her she would never leave this one-horse town.

This girl, the one who got to London in the end, is loitering in an expensive hotel, about to have a drink with a very attractive vampire, possibly a dangerous stranger, and she's up for it. There. I've said it. I'm going to do whatever the hell I like, wherever the hell it leads me.

This huge mirror is a mirror that invites, that celebrates reflections. Not makes them out to be something vain and sinful. It's almost too brightly lit, as if put there to help Hollywood starlets apply their stage make-up. Pampering and vanity is encouraged in this boudoir with its piles of soft white face towels, its elegant curved taps, its primrose-flavoured, oily, perfumed handwash in crystal bottles attached to the basins so that urchins like me won't nick them.

But the girl in the mirror has altered. It's like the portrait of a different girl. Her face is pale, cheeks flushed with red. Her eyes, her Halloween cat's eyes, are sparking with anticipation. The mouth with its pillowy lips is open, as if I'm out of breath. Those lips earned the nickname *Fishy*, taken up by every bully at school.

Here's my tongue, running along the lower lip, catching on the curve because the surface is so dry.

I giggle into the silence and bite my finger. There's a drip,

drip of water from one of the cubicles. I press my hands on my head to try to calm myself down. It doesn't work. I press my palms against my hollowed cheeks like Edvard Munch's *The Scream*. Do I want to kiss Gustav? Is that it? Do I want him to kiss me? I don't know. Not yet. I'm off men, remember? Too much going on in my head for that. So, no. I just want to get near him. He's deadly, the way he pins you like a butterfly. I've followed him here without question, but what's going to happen next?

You're just lonely. You don't know anyone in town. Sad sack. Any old company will do.

But Gustav Levi is not just any old company. I have the weirdest feeling that he's picked me.

The crazy reflection in the mirror shakes its head, and I bend to wash my hands.

I step smartly into the small bar with its glittering wall of bottles, all brimming with the fuel of adventure. He is sitting on a tall stool, elbow propped on the bar, coat off, jumper slung round his shoulders, his long fingers turning a glass swizzle stick. In the soft lighting his face is sculpted with the rough promise of a piratical beard, so how does he still manage to look like James Bond under cover as an unshaven bandit?

I pull my stomach in. This guy is waiting for me. This cool, sexy, scary guy.

His long legs in dark blue jeans are crossed comfortably, one Italian loafer tapping out a tune on the rung of the bar stool. Those lovely legs. Just now they were standing behind me, pressed against my back as he tried and failed to groom me. My stomach kicks rebelliously at the memory. The hard evidence I felt of his maleness. The proof that being close to me aroused him. He's not made of stone at all, even if it takes hieroglyphics to understand him. I may just be one girl amongst many, but I'm the one who's right here, right now, and it's me he's waiting for.

Look at him. That languid body the dark blue cashmere fits so well, skimming the muscular torso beneath, the run of muscle under his ribs, the subtle flex in his forearm as he twirls his swizzle up and down his fingers like a cheerleader's baton.

I stand at the door. I observe his air of elegant alienation. No Brit by definition can combine the two. Yet he's so restless when he thinks no-one's looking. His tapping foot, his long fingers twisting and clapping and explaining. The muscle in his jaw is going again. His eyes are lowered over his cocktail as if he's a soothsayer examining the entrails of a goat. All I can see from his profile is the fierce jut of his eyelashes.

He turns his head as if he senses a siren call and sees me leaning against the door frame. He nods as if I've just asked him something. His eyes lock onto mine for a moment, dark and persuasive, before moving easily over my mouth, my throat, the barely visible curves deliberately hidden under my sweater. My body tightens and resists my clothing. Something uneasy stirs. There's something final in his study of me, as if this is the last time.

I walk towards him and he pushes himself away from the bar to stand chivalrously as I approach him. I wrap my fingers round the cold glass.

How many mobile phones have broken how many perfect moments? Mine buzzes impatiently into life just then, dancing about on the chrome bar. We both glare at it as if it's a scorpion just scuttled out of a salad.

'This is so rude, Gustav.' I glance down anxiously to see who it is. 'But it's a text from my cousin.'

Surprise! In town 1 nite only. Don't worry, won't invade space, staying with boyf, v late notice but party tonite, come quick here's the address! Costume provided x

A fancy dress party is the last thing I feel like tonight. I glance at Gustav, who is staring at the steamed window. Polly will be gutted if I say no.

'I'm so sorry, Gustav, this has been great, but I have to go.'

I waggle my mobile phone in explanation. I sound far too flippant.

He hands me a cocktail glass with a clear liquid as if he hasn't heard me. Now that his gloves and coat are off, I notice the chunky Rolex slipping on his wrist.

'James Bond drinks in here,' he remarks. His eyes, his face, are very calm.

'You took the words out of my mouth.' I take the glass from him a shade too quickly so the liquid tips in a mini tidal wave. 'That sounds like the kind of code spooks would use at a meet.'

He laughs. The laugh is reined in now, and I suspect that's my fault for wrecking the mood.

I stand beside the bar stool where he's neatly folded my jacket, scarf and beret. I don't sit down on the proffered bar stool. We chink our glasses very carefully. They look so fragile they could shatter with a sneeze. I can't look at him. I'm afraid that if I stare into those pensive eyes I'll never stop. So I stare down into the liquid, and the conversation dries up.

The martini is exquisite. It flurries over my tongue and warms its way down my throat, prising the top off my head, lifting me instantly. I don't want to leave. But I'm equally sure that I must.

'And his tipple of choice is exquisite. I love this place. I feel as if I was born to sit here sipping cocktails. But it turns out a Halloween party does await me, after all.'

'Of course it does. Go trip the light fantastic, Serena.' He turns the stem of his glass and smiles, not at me but at the olive bobbing on the surface of his martini. 'But don't get abducted by the undead, will you?'

I put my glass down and start to struggle with my jacket. My arm gets stuck in the sleeve as I'm halfway in.

'Oh, blow it!' I mutter crossly, my fist punching at the lining.

'Stop struggling. You'll rip it.' When he stands to help me he seems taller than ever. He chuckles, hands me my blue scarf and catches it before I fling it messily round my neck and wraps it slowly round. We're rewinding the earlier scene in the lobby, when he was close up behind me and I felt the swell of his excitement.

'I can do it, thank you Gustav.'

He shakes his head, his black hair falling over his eyes. 'I beg to differ, *signorina*.'

He bends to pick up my gloves from the pile. I stand there like a child, or like the child I would have been if anyone had ever bothered to dress me like this. I stick my fingers out stiffly. He smiles at my hopelessness and edges on the gloves.

'Anything else I can do for you?' he mocks, tugging at his forelock like a servant.

Our laughter dies almost as soon as it starts. I wonder if he, like me, is remembering the quiet shiver of recognition when I pulled his glove off earlier, in the square, to take his bare hand. When he then took mine, and kissed my soft palm.

Now he's holding out my beret. How does this ritual look to the barman, the onlooker?

Well dressed, handsome man settling in for a solitary brooding drink, disturbed by hectic, flushed girl. Rising courteously, dressing her up before bidding farewell. Is it obvious we've just met, or does it come over as the in-joke of a relationship? Any age difference only occurs to me now I can see him in the light. Ten years, maybe fifteen, but no older than an uncle or godfather, though my scruffiness makes me look like a teenager. We're not joshing or familiar enough to be siblings or cousins, but none of the above would put gloves on for you, and all have the whiff of the *verboten*.

What I want to know is, do Gustav Levi and Serena Folkes look like lovers, engaged as we are in this private, apparently perfected little sequence?

'What about your costume?' he asks suddenly, turning my beret over in his hand as if trying to decode a message. 'Can't go to a party without a costume.'

I try to take the beret off him, but he tugs it back and starts to put it on, resting his hands on the top of my head.

'My cousin has something for me to change into when I get there.'

By now one or two people in the bar, as well as the barman, are watching us. Gustav doesn't care, or notice. He tucks my hair behind the exposed ear, his fingers cool on the tender skin behind. My eyes close involuntarily to relish the tremor running through me. Lovers, surely, is how it looks. Ex-lovers? No. I would never let Jake get as close as this.

'Good to go.'

He pulls my hair long on the other side, smoothes the riot of ringlets as best he can, and stands back. I feel like a prize exhibit.

'It's been fun, Serena. Who knows what's in store for you tonight, and beyond? Some incredible times, I'm sure.'

I take another long sip, his eyes on my mouth as it drinks, my throat as it swallows. Then I put the glass down. My hand is shaking.

'Thanks, Gustav. For the drink. For everything. It's been fun meeting you, too.'

Amazing how convincingly detached I sound. I start to back away and suddenly he's in front of me. He's looking down. All I can see is his black hair, the slope of his nose as he takes my hand and pushes a business card into it. Closes my fingers round it. Holding his own warm hand round mine like a cage as he pats it down into my pocket.

'You never know.' His voice is sombre and sad.

I hesitate. I haven't told him the party isn't that far away. I could stay for at least a couple more drinks. Everything in me is straining to stay, but I won't. I might never know if there's something between us. If that spark I felt when his fingers were on my neck, his mouth on my fingers, was real.

What is real is the way he nods at me to go then leans back against the bar, arms crossed over his wide chest, the sleeves rolled up over his wrists. I must depart, otherwise I never will. So with his eyes watching my every move, every bounce of my hair on my back, burning hot under my stranger's gaze as I try to move gracefully, I push out into the foggy cold.

FOUR

My feet are curiously sluggish as I walk down St James's Street, as if there are weights in my boots or a magnet is drawing me backwards. The truth is I don't want to go anywhere. I don't want to leave that warm bar, that half-sipped cocktail. That intriguing tall stranger with the split-screen eyes and a way with his fingers.

But as he lifted his hand in casual farewell just now it was as if he'd already forgotten me.

There's a chain spanning the space between us, a rope between ship and shore; no, more like a jailor's thick chain jangling with keys and handcuffs. Except this is woven thin like a spider's web, so delicate, so invisible it only occasionally catches the light. I don't know which one of us holds it. Which one is caught.

I might not see him again. So what? It was only an hour or so. A chat. He bought me a drink. Dry martini. Period. Why would I even consider missing a party to spend the evening with an older guy who, come to think of it, idiot that I am, oh my God how stupid am I, probably has a beautiful wife waiting for him in his beautiful home, stirring a stunning soup in a designer kitchen.

My phone buzzes again, as if to knock some sense into me. I study the map that Pol has texted, so my eyes are down as I cross Trafalgar Square. The map shows a warren of streets on the other side of Covent Garden, and the venue is in the narrowest street of all.

It feels very quiet out here. I thought there would be more of a party atmosphere, but I guess it's still quite early. A few people are wandering about under Nelson's haughty column, emerging from the tube at Charing Cross Station. They're mostly in costume. The stab of scarlet skirts and fiery masks, the sharp black outlines of stalking skeletons, of horns and tails, pierce the thickening fog, which has simply dropped like a shroud. It dims the circling traffic, the glowing street-lamps, muffles the foot shuffle, like old photographs of the smog in post-war London.

They seem to be gathering by one of the lions. I reach under my scarf to lift the camera from its strap. And I realise it's not there. Icy panic grips me as I scrabble in my bag, my pockets, under my jacket even. As I stand there, going round in circles like a cat with a firework on its tail, I'm vaguely aware of people whispering and jostling around me, a shout, a cackle, but I can't focus on them.

A voice seems to whisper in my ear, the exposed ear, the ear he tucked my hair behind. It's here, it says. Your camera. Both cameras. You left them in the cocktail bar in Dukes Hotel.

I don't know whether to laugh or cry. Without my cameras I might as well have had my eyes put out.

I have to get back there, sharpish, this is too good a photo op to miss. What makes it all the worse is that out of nowhere I think of how Jake would be nagging me to get the picture, how this unfolding scenario would sell brilliantly to a news-paper or YouTube. But I'm crippled without my equipment, and now I can't even move because both my arms are grabbed and pulled out sideways as if I'm in a line dance. It hurts. I'm sure my left shoulder is wrenched out of its socket, but that's exactly what it is, a dance, I'm part of some kind of formation, all the people in their costumes have suddenly organised themselves into a pattern, and then suddenly the intro to 'Thriller' screams out from hidden amplifiers; the crowd starts to dance perfectly in time, jerky and robotic, all crawling and grimacing like the zombies in the video.

I've been caught up in a flash mob in eccentric, crazy Trafalgar Square, on Halloween night. Getting on that train yesterday and coming up to London, and finding myself part of this kind of mass madness was the best thing I could have done.

I'm part of the picture tonight, the subject in front of the lens for a change, not behind. And I know who has my cameras. A sudden calm floods me, like a warm shower. The same sensation as when Gustav Levi put my beret on me just now, hooked my hair behind my ear.

Gustav has everything safe. He'll look after everything. So for tonight, I'll be observed instead of always the observer.

Passersby are laughing and clapping and filming, the front of the National Gallery morphs into a giant cinema screen showing images of Michael Jackson, magical and tragical. The throb of the music makes everyone dance, makes me dance despite myself, and we're all zombies now, stamping and waving and crouching and yelling, intoxicated with madness and music.

Eventually I reach the cobbled alleyway that Polly has directed me to. A trio of grisly vampires with rubber fangs, red paint dripping down their chins, troops past me drinking tiredly from Coke cans. I stop in front of what looks like an antique shop. The whole structure is bowed as if it has the weight of the world on its roof. The window bulges outwards and the doorstep is worn almost through from being crossed by centuries of shoes and boots.

Decapitated mannequins scratch at the greenish glass as if to escape. They have been dressed in strapless ballgowns and pose with diamante tiaras circling their wooden necks, as if the heads where the tiaras once perched have been guillotined. Further inside there are figures, just like my zombie friends, dancing and whooping.

I push open the door and weird, hypnotic, twangy music assaults me. The kind that twines in and out of your psyche. Whales, or dolphins, calling to each other in the deep.

People in period costume are drinking and singing and smoking, but it's difficult to tell the revellers from the displays. The shop is like the Tardis, much bigger inside than its tiny bent facade. Various fringed shades, candles and lamps throw a low, red-tinged light as if we're all in an Edwardian bordello. The air is a mist of sandalwood, patchouli, and sweet dope. Hammered to the walls are enormous glass cases full of skewered black butterflies, beetles and scorpions. Cherrywood cabinets burst with everything under the sun. Watches, jewellery, weapons. Cross-bows, arrows, curved scimitar daggers. Even a row of vicious-looking whips hanging from butcher's hooks.

I push my way through the crowd to find my cousin, and a flock of boas tries to strangle me as I pause before a rail of antique lace dresses.

'One of those will look great on you, petal! I'm so glad you came!'

Polly winds her arms round my neck and nearly squeezes the breath out of me.

'Oh, Pol, it's so good to see you!' I disentangle myself after I've buried my nose in her neck to take in the familiar, overscented smell of her. 'Oh my God, you look like Snow White! I presume that black hair dye is temporary?'

'It's a syrup, actually!' She tweaks it off her narrow head to show the ice-blonde crop beneath.

'And you've lost another stone! Don't they have food over there? Don't people eat in Manhattan?'

'Only on Fridays!' she laughs, and starts to drag me to the back of the shop. She swishes and sways in a scarlet Vivienne Westwood-style ballgown. 'Those gorgeous curves of yours would be totally frowned on, but we're forgetting all that tonight. What do you think of this place?'

'It's incredible! What are we doing here?'

'It's Pierre's. My new boyfriend's. It's his first costumier outlet in London. We're only here for tonight, for this launch party. Not many people will know about this place because mostly he'll be supplying wardrobe departments for theatres and movies and so on. He's here somewhere. Let's get you dressed up first!'

She high-fives and kisses various people on her procession through the guests, but it's impossible to tell what any of them really look like. Even the men are painted with white theatrical make-up, red slashes for mouths. If they're not painted they're wearing masks. Polly looks like a Disney princess. If she's Snow White, I'm Rose Red.

The back wall of the shop consists of a huge glass awning leading out to an enclosed yard, twined with ivy and brambles, and round a bubbling cauldron witches are spiking lumps of bleeding red meat into their mouths with pitchforks, a barbeque of the damned, and fake bats swing on invisible strings from the trees. Even the moon is streaked with red as if bleeding, glowing through shredded clouds streaking the London sky like claw marks.

My long-lost cousin pulls a curtain across the changing cubicle at the back of the shop and hands me a long, fluted glass of champagne. We stand together in front of the full-size, gilt-framed mirror as she chatters on about New York.

Then from a rail she unhooks an ivory lace dress so flimsy it could be made from gossamer feathers.

'You look amazing, Rena. You seem to be on fire, or is that just the cold? What's been going on with you?' she says, holding my hair clear as I struggle out of my clothes.

I get a flash of Gustav Levi's serious face in my mind, uncoiling my hair from my blue scarf in the garden square. Calling me Rapunzel.

'I've just had an extraordinary twenty-four hours, that's all. First proper day in London. I think I've already got enough Halloween shots for an entire exhibition if only I can get someone to show my work.'

'Someone will snap you up. And if they don't, I'll get Pierre on the case. He has contacts all over the planet.' She catches my hand as it goes up in protest. 'I know. You're always so stubborn! Don't need anyone's help. Cat that walks alone. But bear it in mind, cuz. You've struggled enough.'

I fling my arms around her again. 'I never felt alone when you were there. The best bits of that miserable life were when you came to stay.'

'Careful with the taffeta, hon. This dress is the real deal. Anyhow do you really want to go over all that old ground? Those bastards should never have been allowed to keep you, just because they were the ones who found you by that church.'

'Whoever thought foundlings came from fairy tales?'

She balls her hand into a fist and bashes at her chest. 'I wish I'd told my family how foul and neglectful your lot were. Persuaded them to take you in. I'll never forgive myself for failing you like that. But ain't it all dead and buried now?'

She holds out the dress for me to step into. I know her mind is like a firefly. You can never pin her down for long.

'Dead and buried, Pol.'

'Beautiful underwear, by the way, Rena! You always did

have a thing about matching knickers. You saved up every penny from your Saturday jobs to buy it, even when on the outside you were all rags and tatters!'

We giggle feebly, just like we used to when she came down to Devon, trailing glamour and fun and naughtiness from the big bad city. We would run down to the beach and rip open the crisps and fags and bottles of vodka she'd brought with her, and try to put out of our minds the disapproving looks on their faces, watching us from the house on the cliffs. They could never believe, since we weren't related by blood, how Polly Folkes could love me. How we could be so close.

'Yeah. You're right. The new chapter has started.'

I let her do up the tiny buttons at the back of the dress, twist my hair into a loose knot on top of my head. Push sparkling diamante earrings into my lobes to dangle right down to my shoulders. Then she gets to work on the make-up.

'Was it awful, though, leaving? Did Jake give you hell?'

She helps me take everything off and as she brushes thick mascara on my eyelashes I battle with what to say.

'He was upset, of course he was, but I'm not a heartbreaker, Pol. You know that. I tried to make him understand, but I don't think he does. It wasn't just that I had to leave that place. When I got back from Europe I just didn't want him any more. I don't think I want anyone.'

'Well, you cut your teeth on each other. Got to lose your cherry with someone. But you were kids. Maybe he was even more of a kid than you.'

'Too right,' I snort. 'He thought foreplay was the name of an indie band.'

She chuckles. 'You need someone older, wiser now, girl. I reckon you're ripe for a new man. One who's going to teach you stuff you've never dreamed of. Someone who won't be able to believe his luck.'

'You got a crystal ball here somewhere, Pol? Because it needs a good polish. I'm off men at the moment. I don't want the hassle. The mess.'

In the mirror we are so different. White faces, red lips, but her eyes are the pale blue of a Malibu swimming pool. Mine are green, like the sea before it reaches the rocks.

Gustav Levi said my eyes belonged to a Halloween cat. Where is he right now? Is he still in the cocktail bar, or has he picked up a beautiful stranger, vanished into the night with her? Or gone home to the mythical wife who must surely be waiting for him? I have this overpowering sensation, a pulling, tugging desire to find him.

Even with my cousin here, my only family, even in this hot, crowded party full of people, there is a new person missing. There's no point denying it. I wish Gustav Levi was here.

'Well, just for tonight you can be the vestal virgin! Pure as the driven snow. Freeze them all out if you want to, but I'm willing to bet that one of these horny guys will fancy the arse off you before the night is out and carry you off on their charger!'

Someone calls out to Polly and she leaves me alone for a moment. The mirror is tarnished, as if smoke from a steam bath obscures it. I stare at myself. My skin feels tight, like someone has stretched it over my bones. Every little hair stands on end. Maybe it's all the dope in the air, but I feel as if I'm poised on a high ledge, just waiting to open my arms and fly down. My face hangs there, the moon behind the clouds.

Flying? Ledges? The moon? I'm not normally given to flights of fancy. Usually the only place I find poetry is through my viewfinder.

I run my finger down the side of my neck, where the pulse is going. My neck rises like a swan's, extending from the fronds of lace clinging to me like a second skin yet cut into fragments as if someone has tried to rip it off me. Over my clavicle towards my breasts, exposed almost to the nipple in the tight bodice of the dress. And on cue my nipples start to harden, sending a buzz of wicked euphoria through me.

I need to get back to him. Someone older, wiser, who's going to teach you stuff you've never dreamed of. I bend to collect everything, my jacket, beret, scarf, but someone slaps my slender lace rump and grabs hold of me.

'Come on, girl. I want to introduce my vestal virgin! My cousin Serena, everyone!' Polly pulls me into the crowd of Sherlock Holmeses and Jack the Rippers, Miss Havishams and Carmens. She ties a sparkling white mask onto me, fastening it tight with white ribbons. 'Now, you look hot, girl. You get out here and charm the pants off my friends! I already love you, but Pierre will love you forever, too!'

All sound and movement shrinks to the narrowness of the mask's slit, like the helmet of a suit of armour. Everything has a dreamy, surreal air.

'You will remain virginal and masked, until I set you free.' Polly cackles like a pantomime villain, reminding me of her filthy side, and as she moves back into the party she's like a dancing flame around which huge menacing moths flutter in their swirling cloaks and feathered, furry, Venetian, Phantom, lace masks. Polly has put on a mask in the style of Catwoman and her eyes seem to sink back into her head, narrowing into red-glowing slits.

I love my beautiful, borrowed cousin to death. But mixed with the love there's always been jealousy. That she had a family who gave her that confidence, that generosity and style, of the cocksure way she can look down her nose at an admirer so he has no idea if she's going to lick him or lump him one. Someone offers me a tray of devils on horse-back, fiery fruit wrapped in salty bacon, and as I stuff in a handful I realise I'm ravenous. I can't remember when I last ate.

Someone changes the music. It grows louder, and wilder, looping endlessly round the same gypsy spirals. Everyone is dancing like there's no tomorrow in this confined space, knocking over stands, mannequin arms and legs flailing like marionettes, and some, oh my God, are getting frisky now, grabbing at each other's clothes, ripping at dresses and trousers, showing knickerbockers and camisoles, but it all looks directed, like a show, everything looks so choreographed, like a ballet, composed like a mural.

Everyone is so white, some almost transparent so that you can see the blood blue in their veins, painted red on their throats, white arms, white faces bending into each other, kissing, licking, pretending to bite, pretending to be vampires with their false fangs.

Now I do wish I had my camera. It's my disguise. My shield. Normally I'd be prowling the place taking photographs, offering to display them later, sell them for a fee. Or keep them for my own archives.

I am limbless and naked without it.

A violin tests its strings in a kind of screech and the music lurches into another gypsy dance, the kind that makes you want to leap over a camp fire, and suddenly I'm lifted off my feet, tossed across the sea of bodies, hands and faces everywhere, stamping, clapping, whooping.

A man coated in green feathers with a hooked mask bows courteously, but as we start to waltz his hands wander over my dress, lightly resting on my hips or bottom, threatening to move further up, further in, but luckily another figure dressed as a court jester spins me round so he can rock me from behind, but then he pushes himself into my back, getting off on the feel of my buttocks pressed against his groin, ripping my dress a little more. I squeal and wriggle away from him. My breasts are in danger of falling out for all the world to see.

'Hey, babe, you having fun? You're the belle of the ball tonight!'

Polly sweeps past me in the arms of a very tall man in top hat and tails. They look exactly like Ginger Rogers and Fred Astaire. I try to screech at her that actually I want to go, but the music is too loud. I try to veer away from the friendly fingers and hands on me, but there's no point. There are too many of them, big men, slender women, heads bobbing and pecking like birds in their elaborate costumes and sinister masks, all with red-painted mouths, those clever white fangs which look totally real, stabbing at their lips.

Whatever was in those canapés suddenly kicks in and instead of panicky and desperate I now get high. Euphoria must be close to mania, because now I'm laughing as two men wearing cat masks advance on me and throw me back and forth between them.

I know I'm hallucinating mad because as Polly twirls in her partner's arms and Fred Astaire's face appears above her head, I'm convinced that she's dancing with Gustav Levi. Through the mask those eyes are unmistakable, glittering black and boring into my very soul.

I clap my hand to my mouth, my whole body trembling with excitement.

'Gustav!' I shout and wave, trying to push towards him. But he doesn't hear or recognise me, because like an artist's anatomical doll he turns Polly stiffly in his arms and spins away into the shadows.

That jealousy, twisting like a small knife again. If I'm the belle of the ball, Polly is undoubtedly the queen. She always is. She's sorted. She has a job, a flat, a man. There he is, parading her in his arms. And me? Apart from a large inheritance which has come by default from people who would rather have pulled their own eyes out than give me anything, what have I got?

I stagger backwards through the crowd, aiming for the cubicle where my clothes are strewn about on the floor, but the push of the throng sends me crashing out into the back yard instead, and when the doors shut behind me it's blissfully quiet out here. The embers which were heating the cauldron earlier are still glowing, heating up the patio.

I stumble towards a kind of bower in the corner and without checking what or who might be there as well I collapse onto a day bed under a curtain of ivy, spread-eagled across the white calico cushions. All I can see through the curtain of ivy is the orange fuzz of the city sky. No moon. No stars. No clouds.

'Are you OK?' Someone else has got here first.

I heave myself up onto my elbows, irritation prickling through me. 'I thought I was alone out here,' I mutter crossly. 'Who's that?'

I find myself staring into the blank gaze of mirrored Elvis shades. As my eyes move over the interloper I see how totally incongruous those glasses are with the short white toga and laurel wreath he's wearing, shoved on top of impossibly golden curls.

'Friend of Pierre's. Who are you?'

'Cousin of Polly.'

He doesn't move from his Caesar-like pose. I fiddle with my tattered dress, realising that even if I wanted to leave I'd have to take it with me, because I can't get out of it without help.

'Wrong party, huh?' he murmurs in an American accent. 'You look far too pure and innocent to be mingling with these ghoulies and ghosties. Some very decadent people here, you know.'

'Polly dressed me up like this. It's not really me. Her idea of a joke.'

'May be a joke to you, but however dirty you really are you sure look the part in that scrap of a dress. Bit rough with you, were they?' He speaks with a subdued gruffness that makes me glance at him more closely. 'A bit of rape and pillage back there?'

I toss my head in just the way a vestal virgin would. 'All a bit of fun. Actually I've got to go. I've got things to do in the morning.'

'Hey, you don't want to go now. This is where it starts to get interesting. Why should our host and hostess have all the fun?' His hands gesticulate as if they might slice right through me like butter, then he aims them like a couple of pistols to point out my cousin. 'You can tell they've only been dating for a short time. They can't keep their hands off each other!'

It's true. Polly and Pierre are in the doorway. The moon is their spotlight as they sway together, totally oblivious to everyone else.

'She deserves it. New York has always been her goal. She's worked for it.'

He picks up a bottle of wine and hands it to me. 'And you haven't?'

'I'm just starting out. My first day in London.'

I regret it as soon as it's out, like I did earlier when I told Gustav Levi my name, and sure enough those disconcertingly blind shades are still fixed on me, the American mouth grinning as I take a big swig of wine and wipe my mouth with the back of my hand like a navvy.

'How about that! Mine too. Fancy showing me the sights while I'm here? Starting now? Show Princess Polly she's not the only one who can take a city by storm?'

I glance instinctively back towards the party, as if I need to ask permission.

But there's no-one to ask. Certainly not our Polly. She has always encouraged me to go for it. Rebel. Do what the hell I like. In any case, she's not available for comment. Her eyes are closed behind her mask, her arms around Pierre's neck and his mouth is locked down on hers, and they are kissing, hard, I can see their tongues, and their hands are roving, hers going under his tail coat and squeezing his buttocks, his wandering shamelessly between her legs, wrinkling up her red skirt, pushing it up her thighs, his hand and wrist diving in.

Polly's knee lifts and hooks around her boyfriend's leg to steady herself as his hand disappears, touching her where no-one else is allowed, assuming that no-one else can see.

But I *can* see, and so can my companion. I tear my eyes away from my cousin, because the sight of that naked love, or at least lust, is embarrassing to watch. *She's got what you haven't got.* But the jealousy is all grown up now. Emphasising what I'm missing. Who I'm missing.

I squeeze my bare legs together, trying to quell the hint of heat between them, and then I see all too obviously what the sight of my kissing cousin has done to the American. There is a big bulge under his toga. The white cotton is rising in a comical tent over his crotch.

'How about it, Polly's cousin? They're all at it in there, or they will be.'

I blush hotter as he shifts closer along the seat. I move slightly away, but he's reasonably gentlemanly, at least at first. He takes my hands and pulls me closer.

'There's a light in your eyes,' he says quietly, his mouth close to mine now. 'And I can see you're distracted. Who are you thinking about?'

I don't move or say anything. He's right, I am distracted. I can't help thinking about Gustav. I wish he was here, looking at me like a glittering treasure he found in the snow. I'm dying to show Polly, her friends, that I can click my fingers and get anyone. But this all feels like a silly game.

My heart isn't in it. I want to get out of here, back to him. Look into his eyes which will tell me clearly that they like what they see.

'Well, if you're not distracted, I sure as hell am. Look how I'm fixed now.'

The guy takes my silence for consent, and takes my hands. He places them over the rigid shape under the cotton and it jumps in response. He leaves my hands there and strokes my legs, fingers wandering, under my dress. They pause, politely, then move on up my thighs.

My hands are still resting on him. I'm letting him touch me. I should play along. I will myself to want it, enjoy it, but I can't. I shake my head and close my legs against his exploring fingers, and thankfully he pulls away.

In the doorway I can see Pierre's hand working under Polly's skirts. She is half opening her legs to him, wanting us all to see, to know what he's doing to her, but half trying to keep herself hidden for the sake of decency. Her dress has ridden right up and every time he pushes at her, the curve of her butt presses white and flat against the glass door.

What's wrong with me? If I'm aching for something, attention, caresses, then let this guy have his way. No point pining after someone else. Gustav won't be giving me another thought, while this guy is here, he's hard, he's willing and able. So get over it. Show Polly I'm sexy, too, and desired. This guy is up for it, but he's not doing it for me. Just as Jake didn't do it for me, in the end. Maybe if I wait, sit here very still, the ache will subside, or wake up into something more useful.

Or maybe there's nothing in me to wake up. Maybe I'm sitting here on this seat with a good-looking, aroused bloke unable to react because I'm terminally frigid, as Jake shouted yesterday morning (was it as recent as that?); he shouted it after me, standing on the metal step, shivering in the damp dawn as I stumbled across the field, away from his caravan.

Frigid cow, he'd yelled, the new, insulting violence weighting his words to make him feel better. And to punish me for faking it, and then leaving him.

The American starts to sing under his breath. *Hello? Is it me you're looking for?*

He strokes my face. No. It's not him I'm looking for. But there's no harm in letting him touch me like this, is there? It's a party. He's cute enough. Why not test myself? See if I am really frigid?

Are you somewhere feeling lonely? Or is lonely feeling you?

Still looking at Polly, certain that she can see me, I turn my mouth into his stroking hand, flip out my tongue and hook the guy's finger into my mouth. Even though he's still wearing those stupid glasses I can tell from the excited biting down of his teeth that I've suitably surprised him. I nibble further down the finger and start to suck.

His tongue flicks across his slightly open mouth. It's such a quick flick that I can tell what he's thinking. He reckons he's reading my signals loud and clear.

And Polly has noticed, just as I wanted her to. She can see me up close to one of her cute friends. She nudges Pierre to show him, too, but he's talking to someone else and he doesn't turn to look. She puts her thumb up to me, shakes her dress down to cover her legs again, then Pierre's arm comes round her waist and they merge into the crowd.

The music has faded to one plaintive violin, the lowest possible notes probing the emotions. The dancing has slowed.

The American sees that no-one is watching. He's strong, and he pulls me over onto him, to sit right down on his lap. My lace dress floats up round my hips. The hardness grows and jumps under the toga and pokes at my inner thigh, jabbing on the bone, at the tendons up high, trying to impress me, weaken me so that it can get in.

'I need help with this,' he groans, lying back, complacent

in the assumption that he's got me where he wants me. 'I'm sorry, honey, but you caused this boner.'

I look down at him. 'No I didn't. My cousin getting it on with Pierre did that to you.'

'Well, you've kept it going. I'm in trouble if I don't have a woman at least once a day. Polly promised that this would be the place and she's right. Look at you. Sex on a stick, like all the horny English girls. You gotta help me out here. Just with your hand. Your mouth?'

I sit there for another moment, straddling his bare thighs, feeling the hardness pulsing against me under the stupid toga. What a drag that must be for a guy, being attached to that hardness all your life, no control over it, what or who is going to trigger it, or when. Pretty girl wandering round a party on her own in flimsy dress. Get hard. Picture in a magazine. Get hard. Sit on a beach. Listen to sexy music, that disco thump that matches your heart beat. Matches the bump and grind of lovemaking.

But what about me? I may as well be made of stone. My body isn't reacting to him at all. I'm straddling a handsome guy with a thumping erection who will do anything to relieve himself and nothing's happening *in here*. I'm closed up. Dry as dust.

I come to my senses. 'No. No. I'm sorry. I'm not like that. I've got to go.'

I lift my leg and climb off him, tug my dress down, hear the rip of vintage lace, feel the dress slipping.

Frigid. You frigid cow.

'Look, fair enough if you don't want to go with someone you've just met. Choosy's fine. But what about me? Help me out here. Girls like you shouldn't be allowed out looking so goddamn hot!'

He sits up, slams a cushion down on his disobedient groin. I wince.

'I don't blame you for being pissed with me. But I'm not putting out. No.'

He sighs. 'I can tell your head is somewhere else. Who's the lucky guy?'

I fiddle with a loose thread on my dress. 'Don't be nice to me. I just acted like a tease.'

'And I acted like a schmuck. But I still say you owe some responsibility for this situation.' His smile spreads wider. Those amazing straight American teeth. He's obviously relieved that we can talk. And talking like civilised people might just make his hardness subside. 'Cousin Polly's never mentioned you'd be here. She's a great stylist, isn't she? You know some of the studios are looking at her fashion work? She's made you look like something Dracula would happily snack on. I'm not sure you realise.'

'Well, I'm flattered, Elvis. Really.' Emboldened by distance I point playfully at his crotch. 'And flattered that I still have that effect on people. But I'm not the girl for you. Find one who'll want to make use of all that.'

He lifts the pillow off it. The toga is flat, no life under there now. 'Begone, wench. See if I care.'

I lean over him and kiss him on the mouth. There's a shy stirring in me as our lips meet. A shy tugging in the places where he touched me. But it's not him.

Look at me, Gustav.

I put my hands on the boy's shoulders. Make nice with him. Love the one you're with. His tongue flips out hopefully. I hesitate, and pull away. Relief that I'm not frigid, that I can react to a cute guy? Or relief that I've said no?

'So long, toga boy.'

He lifts the wine bottle in weary farewell. I still haven't seen his eyes, and now I never will. The clouds of the night sky drift across the twin mirrors of his glasses.

Polly is waiting for me just inside. She's been watching me.

'You turned Toga Tomas down? Unbelievable. He's got the hots for you. What's up, hon?'

I shrug. 'I'm bushed, that's all.'

'We've got lots of other cute guys around if Tomas doesn't do it for you.'

She winds one arm round my neck and holds me for a long moment. The crowd has dissipated. Pierre is nowhere to be seen. The music has stopped. Empty bottles and glasses and trays have been virtually kicked into a pile in the corner. One or two overhead lights have been switched on in place of the old lamps. Scraps of lace and feather and ribbon are shed on the parquet floor, shining dully like fish scales. Masks have been ripped off and draped jokingly on the mannequins in the shop.

In short, the spell has been broken.

'We're all going up into the piazza for a meal. You coming, hon?'

I shake my head. 'Can we catch up tomorrow?'

'We're leaving first thing. Might not even get any sleep. Might get on the plane dressed like this! Oh, please come with us, Rena? You look a sensation like that. Even more dishevelled than you were before, if that's possible, like Tess of the D'Urbervilles. Like someone's just ravished you, although I know damn well they haven't, you saucy minx!'

'I told you, Polly, and tonight's just proved it. I'm genuinely off men.'

'OK, forget men. Forget sex. I just want to show you off to my friends! Who knows, someone might offer you a photographic commission. Tomas is big in the film industry.'

I hold her tight. Kiss her cheek. I smell Eternity, by Calvin Klein. Just like mine. 'Baby steps, Pol. I'm not a player like you. Not yet, anyway. I want to see if I can make it here in London, first. Come back and check me out in a year's time. Who knows? I might be ready to fly by then!'

'I'll be back sooner than that. OK. Piss off into the night like a little bat, then! Take Pierre's car. It's the incredibly expensive and luxurious red Bentley parked outside. His driver will make sure you get back to the flat safely. And keep the dress. My gift to you. You look magical this evening.'

'That's down to you, Pol. Tomas just mentioned what a great stylist you are.'

'Tonight London, tomorrow the world!' She gives me a little shake, then another huge hug. 'But you know, you're looking so good tonight. Kind of ragged, and feverish. If you really are off men, then celibacy suits you!'

I have left the blinds open in Polly's flat and through the huge plate-glass window the River Thames glints like steel under the night as it slides under Tower Bridge. Fireworks are spattering somewhere over to the east where the Docklands railway will be trundling lethargically around the glittering skyscrapers.

I ease the dress off my shoulders, managing to get enough buttons undone until it sheds like a second skin. My reflection is overlaid by the river, but I can see my body unpeeled in the moonlight, the body hidden in its laddish layers from Gustav Levi. The body that Polly dressed up like her dolly, that Tomas tried half-heartedly to ravish. But neither of them got down to the skin, did they? They didn't see the whole of me.

My breasts, released from the dress and the bra, are high and full. I cup them gently, so heavy and warm, hold them forwards, watch as soon as they make contact with the cold glass how the nipples pinch into dark red points, an answering tightness behind my navel, the bounce of my breasts as my heart expresses its interest.

Jake didn't like my breasts. It was as if he was scared of them. He'd ogle other people's tits, as he called them, or comment on pictures in magazines, but he never touched mine except to give them a brief squeeze and a token rub before we scrabbled out of our clothes and lay down on that narrow bed. I'd push them into his hands. I'd try to kneel up over him and push them at his mouth, but he'd give them a cursory fondle before pushing me onto my back and getting down to what he really wanted.

These buried untried responses are like roses that will shrivel if they are not pruned. A vine that will wither if it's not plucked. Any poetic image you choose. I'm alone tonight, I can set it to music if I want.

When the nipples go hard like this they burn and prick, little beacons, bright cheerleaders waving their pom poms, no, that's a daft simile, they are just a pair of super sensitive buds that set off the train of wanting, the heavy ache pulling down to my centre, travelling towards a really deep, dark desire which I know has never been truly awoken.

What are they all doing now? Polly and her friends, dancing in a hoola round Covent Garden or crossing the Strand and demanding breakfast in the River Room of the Savoy where she is staying with her rich boyfriend. Jake, strumming discordantly on his guitar, cigarette dangling out of his mouth like James Dean, glowering at the sea beneath his caravan.

Gustav – I can't picture him. Maybe he's still sitting up on that high stool, turning the stem of his refilled cocktail in his long fingers while the barman polishes the glasses and tries not to glance pointedly at the clock ticking away at his overtime.

I lie down on Polly's queen-sized bed, just in my knickers, my hands resting on my breasts. In my cousin's walk-in closet is a wardrobe full of cellophane-wrapped dresses and suits and blouses, all for me to borrow, she said. All swaying as if in a breeze, or as if someone has just brushed their hands along them.

One hand trails down my flat stomach and onwards, into my knickers. The images of the last two days stalk across my mind like the credits of a movie. Now there's just me, naked and alone on this low white bed, resisting the warm tugging between my legs, teased into being by all that's happened. Not by Tomas and his tumescent toga. Not by the desire biting in his mouth, the hardness lifting the white cotton.

I'm turned on by the thought of Gustav's wrist when I pulled off his glove in the square. Gustav's finger, hooking my hair behind my ear.

So my fingers trail down, and into my knickers, pull them aside and then right off, stroking and parting myself. I'm too lazy to find anything else to use on myself. I push in a little more, the warmth and wetness, withdrawing, pushing in harder, and what makes me flower brightly under my own probing fingers is no amount of music or poetry or lovely photographs.

I'm not frigid.

As dawn blossoms over my drowsy face, what makes the wetness spring and spark is the wondering of how Gustav Levi's mouth would feel, kissing me right there.

FIVE

I have actually run some of the way to get here. I tell myself it's only because I'm desperate to get my cameras back.

He's told me which way to come and now I'm in a street on the other side of the river, practically next door to the Savoy Hotel in fact. But Polly is long gone.

I didn't wake up until midday. The first thing I did was look for Gustav Levi's business card. And I couldn't find it. I tipped my jacket upside down, inside out, shook it. It was plain white, thick, his name in a thick black Modoni font. I tried to envisage the number across the bottom. I couldn't. I hadn't even read the card. I must have dropped it in the street. At the party. In Pierre's red car.

I slammed my hands down on the bed. Then I forced myself to count to ten and walk to the window and back ten times. My camera. My cameras. Think. My life's work is stored in there.

My mobile phone buzzed on the table beside the bed. I can't think who that is. Please not Jake. And I'll kill Polly if she gave Tomas my number. I don't want to have to find the words to put him off. No. Stay calm. It could be one of those galleries. Number unknown.

'Yes. Serena Folkes here. Hello?'

There was a pause. Then, 'Ah. Serena.'

His voice was even deeper than I remembered, pouring treacle. My knees went from under me and I fell onto the bed.

'Gustav! Mr Levi. Oh my God. You don't know how happy I am to hear from you!'

He chuckled. I could hear low voices and brisk footsteps in the background. He sounded as if he was an echoing room.

'Maybe you could come and show me how happy?'

'How did you find me?'

'The wonders of technology, Serena. I just made a note of your mobile number when you left your phone with me in the bar last evening. If you go to your contacts you'll see I've added myself in there, too. So now we're both armed with vital information. I told you I wanted to see you again, and I meant it.'

I just stared stupidly at the phone.

'You do want your cameras back, don't you?'

Yes I did. I do. And so it was arranged.

This must be it. There's a flight of steps and big glass doors up ahead of me, but before I reach them and check the address I stop to look at the publicity poster attached to the approaching railings.

There's no obvious gallery anywhere nearby, but the poster shows a sepia photograph of a group of comely women reclining on a sofa, with tumbling black hair, plump bodies, and can-can corsets and stockings. They are incredibly dated, girlishly coy, mostly, their backs turned to the camera to show mooning white buttocks and big bovine hips and shoulders, but the eyes gleaming under curled fringes are vacant and old as the hills.

I guess they are from a collection of dirty postcards of *fin-de-siècle* Parisian prostitutes, or a clever reproduction.

They are certainly faded. Patches of the background are missing or cracked where the old processing ink has peeled away from the paper, but the women are intact.

I run my hands over my own rounded hips. I've made a real effort today. After we'd arranged to meet I told myself as I showered and dressed in Polly's glittering white bathroom that today is the day to make some changes.

So I've shed Rena the scruff in her jeans and biker boots, and I'm wearing a dress. Well, he told me that this was business and that I was to come to his office, so businesslike is how I want to be. It won't go amiss for my other appointments, either. So it's not only a dress, but a black jersey dress, flaring on the hips, wrapped tight across the bust, severe yet softened by these shiny black boots. Flat, not heeled. I can't masquerade to that extent, let alone pound the streets of London in heels. And a cropped black Cossack jacket with velvet collar and cuffs and military silver buttons.

At the last minute I pull on the beret for comfort, but this time I wear it low over my forehead Garbo-style.

I continue on up the polished white steps and read the name above the door. It says *The Levi Building*. It's not as phallic as some City buildings. None of the structures along the Embankment reach any higher than Big Ben. But it's no less hulking and impressive for that. The words swim into focus. The Levi Building. So he owns the whole shebang?

The lobby is vast and echoing. There is a chrome shelf, not even a desk, in the middle of the place, and a lady sitting bolt upright behind a switchboard of buttons. She looks like a spooky Mary Poppins. Black hair pulled back into a bun so tight that her face is dragged back with it. A black broderie anglaise blouse pinned with a cameo brooch. She glances up and without speaking pokes out a long plum-painted fingernail to press a button marked *Levi*.

'Is everything around here named after him?' I ask. My

voice hisses across the black marble interior as if I'm in church.

'Penthouse office. Top floor.' Her voice is high, as if holding a top note.

The lift spits me out at the top, and I am dazzled by the blaze of light. It's hard to know where the light comes from, whether I'm facing north or south, even.

'Ah, Serena. How lovely to see you again.'

A pin man appears in the distance, etiolated and thin like an alien just about to step out of the blinding interior of the mother ship. I rub my eyes and step towards him. He seems to be wearing a suit and a white shirt today, but before I can focus properly he takes my hand and shakes it formally. He holds it for an extra moment.

'I'm so glad you took my phone number,' I gibber, as we start to move back towards the light, one of my hands still in his. 'I would be absolutely lost without my cameras!'

'Your head is like a sieve, so it's lucky I'm a magpie. Gloves, cameras–'

How familiar his deep, calm voice is. I only met him yesterday.

There is a cool, tomb-like atmosphere in this place. I still can't see clearly, but I think we are in a corridor. He turns right and leads me into another big space but this is insulated. Not warm, but not cold, either.

He drops my hand and leaves me standing in this vast, warehouse-like space. He walks towards another window but the light in here is less glaring, and finally I can focus. I turn in a full circle. There are more of the French photographs, blown up, on one wall, and others, sepia, black and white, none coloured, but I'm assailed, as any visitor would be, by rolling flesh, and plump women, and vivid nakedness.

'You've brought me to a gallery? This is awesome. A real inspiration. Exactly the kind of venue I've dreamt about.'

'Not just any gallery, Serena.' There's a click. On goes an oversized chrome Anglepoise lamp by his desk and there he is, springing back into my life. Someone who looks just like him, anyway, but this guy is scrubbed and brushed today, those eyes blacker, deeper, more glittering in contrast to the cleanly shaved cheeks. The formal tailoring makes him seem taller and broader, but the fine fabric also restrains him, restrains all that restless energy.

He stands and moves differently, slowly, considerately, the jacket creasing slightly as he bends his arms, the trousers revealing nothing of the long legs I saw in their jeans last night. The body that pressed against me. No hint of the manhood, what lies beneath. He moves almost in slow motion, but not his hands. They are restless as ever. They pluck the middle buttons, doing and undoing. The man I know as Gustav Levi is someone who stalks misty London squares at night, wrapped up warm but unshaven, wild eyes watching.

Apart from a giant vase of lilies in the corner tall enough to bathe in, there is nothing else visible in this space.

As the light snaps on the lively photographs leap away into the shadows cast by the winter afternoon light.

'This is *my* gallery.'

I walk towards the window. Behind him the river flows dark and fast past the London Eye and the South Bank opposite, multi-coloured lights winking off the various bridges spanning the Thames.

'What can I say, Mr Levi? You said you were an entrepreneur, but this? You own this place? This whole building?'

'That's my name on the door. And more besides, Serena. You could say I'm multi-national. London. Paris. New York is currently being conquered.' He takes a pen out of his breast pocket and taps it against his chin. His mouth is hard today. Both lips equally unforgiving. 'I'm a walking, talking, living corporation. Mostly I own and lease galleries. I prefer to try to keep art in my life, but I do own other kinds of industrial space, too.'

'A real tycoon. I should have been nicer to you.'

We stare at each other for a moment. He does indeed look every inch the tycoon. The knot of his dark red tie with a pattern I can't decipher from here is tight up against his Adam's apple. He's so cool, and handsome, all that contained power, but his fine face is etched with a tiredness I didn't see yesterday.

And I was right. He's closer to forty than thirty. As if he knows what I'm thinking he fiddles under the knot of his tie, undoing the top button.

'Meeting you made my day, Serena.'

Oh, the eyes. How they glitter with life.

Look at me again, then, Gustav.

His thumb is poised to punch at the top of his pen as if it's misbehaved. 'But you've changed.'

'So have you.'

'I look like this every working day. But you're all – neat and tidy! What's happened to Calamity Jane?'

'She's still here, but I thought I'd make an effort.' I run my hands over my new, svelte outline. 'My cousin left loads of clothes in the flat and told me to help myself. And I've got a lot to do today. Places to go, people to see.'

'Appointments made?'

'Not new ones, no.' I grip the handle of my portfolio. 'I needed to get my cameras back first.'

He sits on the edge of the desk, swinging one long leg. Shut away from the world this is how a master of the universe looks in the flesh. His eyes are chips of black ice. This intense attention, scrutiny almost, must be part of his business technique. Because it's certainly working.

'The beret. They way you're wearing it today. It's less the

impoverished artist, more the student from the Left Bank. *Très chic*. Who knew you were two different women, rolled into one?'

If it wasn't for the very slight swinging of his foot in its polished black brogue, he could be a waxwork. One of his own exhibits. But the whole room, the whole building vibrates with his aura. And best of all, he is totally zoned in on me. Again I am the only person in his world.

'Who's to say you get either? Look, I shouldn't keep you, Mr Levi. You must have so much to do. So many deals to cut. So many fortunes to make. But thank you for looking after my camera.'

'You told me to guard it with my life, and that's exactly what I did.' He folds his hands on his leg in an effort to keep it still. 'I told you I had a proposition for you, so I'll get straight to the point. I want you to hold all your other appointments. I don't want you to rush off anywhere, Serena, because I've had a look at your work and I like it. I think I can help you. I *want* to help you.'

'My work? How did you take a look?'

'Simple.' He picks up my camera bag, takes out the Lumix. 'You just switch on this little device, press the screen button and presto. Scroll through all the images.'

I laugh at the faux advertising speak. 'I should be very cross with you for invading my privacy, Mr Levi. For all I know you could have copied the lot onto your computer by now, even though they're my intellectual property!'

'Industrial espionage. I like it. But not nearly as much fun as just coming to a good, old-fashioned, *quid pro quo* arrangement, eh?'

There's a brief, easy silence between us. I glance at him, his eyes holding mine, then walk past him towards the light, suddenly exquisitely self-conscious in my dress, aware of my legs, exposed as they swish in their stockings. I'm trying to walk elegantly in the shiny boots. If I feel a fraud dressed like this, I'm a fraud who is about to make something happen.

I sit down on the broad window sill. The light is behind me so he's at a disadvantage now. He's forced to swivel sideways.

'So what did you see on my camera?'

He holds his fingers up and counts them off. 'The little witch at the back of the line falling over. The others all standing there, huffing and puffing till she got up again. The streetlight casting those triangular shadows from their hats. But much more besides. I seem to have got a kind of potted history of your life. Well, your travels anyway. Egypt. Morocco. France.'

'And there's more. Venice, that was my favourite. Here, in my portfolio.'

'Which I will look at, too, if you'll let me. There's so much talent here.' He walks over to the other end of the window sill and wags his finger at me. 'I'm not just saying it. I know how tough it is when you're starting out. And what I can see in front of me is a girl who could use a break.'

'Yes, I could. Of course I could.' I grip the edge of the window sill. 'But I've only just got to London. I've got to give it my best shot. There's lots of places to try before I start taking charity.'

'Who said anything about charity?' He slams his hands down on his knees. What did I say yesterday about crossing him? About those hands being able to twist necks? 'Don't be so stubborn, Serena. Everyone needs a leg-up in life, especially in the arts world. And I'm just the guy you need. I'm not kidding you.' His black eyes are deadly serious now. They are boring into mine, boring into all that misplaced pride, clumsy resistance. They're sucking me in again. 'I'm the answer to your prayers.'

I feel unbalanced, dizzy. Rest my back against the cold

glass as I wait for the prickling goosebumps on my skin to subside.

'You know nothing about me,' I say softly. If we keep talking at least I can stay here a little longer. I wish I could press myself against him again, touch him, have his arms pinning me there, stopping me from leaving.

'That's not strictly true. I learned a lot about you last night. And now I also know you have talent.'

He stands. God he's tall. I get a crick in my neck just staring at him. He comes towards me, fans his fingers under my jaw, pauses, strokes a little further down my neck. 'Last night's chance meeting will prove to be a stroke of luck for both of us.'

'How?'

His black eyes are devouring me again. Glittering, and deep, drawing me further in. Less demonic today. More mesmeric. Something is being drawn out of me. Not my energy. Quite the opposite. It's resistance and anxiety he's taking away. I feel as if I'm being charged up, like I've been plugged into the mains.

His hand rests on my cheek a little longer, then he stands abruptly and goes back to sit behind his desk. Steeples his fingers.

'I'm in danger of losing my concentration,' he says, clearing his throat. His hair finally gives up and falls away from where he's combed it back. 'I'm going to have to come clean and admit that you have an extraordinary effect on me, Serena. I thought you'd walked out of my life yesterday, off to your party.'

'I didn't want to go.'

'Your cousin must have been chuffed you made it. Your friends.' He cuts through me, pushing his hair back. 'But I haven't been able to stop thinking about you since yesterday. So let's start again. Let's turn this into an interview. Please take a seat.'

'All a bit formal?' I laugh, but he waves towards the white leather chair in front of his desk. Obediently I change seats.

'Too right. Now. I have mounted photographic exhibitions many times, as well as fine arts, installations. Even concerts. I've sponsored some very famous names while they were struggling to get a foot on the ladder. So not only can I afford to take a risk with an emerging talent like yours, Serena. I am positively seeking out fresh blood.'

'You make me sound like a rare steak.'

'The rarer and bloodier, the better.' He grins. His face goes light. It's totally unexpected, like a flash of lightning on a sunny day. I'm liking his interview technique. 'Come on. We all have to take leaps into the dark. How else are people going to notice you or your work? I can offer you the venue, the publicity machine, the marketing. The media exposure.'

I sit very still, very quiet. I'm still digesting what he said about being unable to stop thinking about me.

'What's in it for you?'

'Well, firstly it has all the promise of a very lucrative, no, *rewarding* partnership. I'll have priceless modern art on my walls. It's essential to keep one's finger on the pulse, especially with fledgling talent. Maybe I'll even buy some for my private collection at home. And if we work towards a sell-out between now and Christmas, from there on in you'll be able to charge whatever you like for your work.'

'That really is a leap of faith. It all sounds too good to be true, Mr Levi.'

'Gustav.'

'So what's the catch?'

He taps his fingers against his lips. So suave. So scary. His eyes sparking with a kind of mischief now.

'I don't see it as a catch. I see it as something beneficial for both of us. Like I said, a *quid pro quo*. You scratch my back, I'll scratch yours. Because I have seen something daring and brave in you, Serena. I've seen . . . well, I think we get on. Yes?'

The way he's staring at me now. Even behind his desk. Behind his hands. He's doing something to me. I cross my legs, aware of how bare they feel under this dress. Also aware, with an inward gasp, of a softening dampness.

'What's daring and brave got to do with your showcasing my work?'

'Because of how I want this to go. How I propose you repay me.'

This is where Polly would be jumping up and down saying *I'm right, I'm right, watch him, he's after something.*

Yes, yes! I hope he is! I want him to be after something, however reckless that sounds. Because I am after something too.

But what I actually say is, 'Money. We haven't talked about money.'

No, not wet, I'm imagining things. I shift about on the chair. Just warm from the white leather that's sticking to me. I lace my fingers in front of my knee, let it swing. The leg looks quite elegant in the opaque stockings, just like the stockings worn by these *filles de joie* in the Parisian pictures on the walls.

'I'm trying to find the best way to say this.' He folds his arms, looks genuinely awkward for a moment, and with the awkwardness comes an instant lifting of the years, as if dropping the facade of hard businessman is a relief. 'I have in mind something mutual, something which pleases both of us, benefits you, makes me happy, and involves no hard cash whatsoever.'

'I'm not understanding.' I fold my arms, too. 'You want me to give my photos away?'

He shakes his head, presses his hands together like a priest.

'I'm assuming you're living on private means at the moment, Serena? If that's not too intrusive a question?'

I nod as if it's the most normal thing in the world for a girl of twenty to have no visible means of support. 'I've recently inherited a substantial sum of money. And I'll get more when I sell the house.'

He stares at me a moment. I'm aware how cold that sounds. But I'm not an actress. I can't affect sorrow or grief, or even gratitude, where there is none.

'You're alone in the world?'

'I have my cousin, Polly – she's the one who had the party last night, but she's working as a stylist in New York at the moment. I told you I'm living in her flat. But Gustav, my money won't last forever, not once I've bought property and so on. What do they say about paying monkeys with peanuts? I intend to earn a living. If we're going to do this, if I'm ever going to be taken seriously, I need to do it properly. I need to sell these pictures!'

'And you will, my – Serena. You will. Money will exchange hands in the usual way between the gallery and any buyers, commissioners or collectors. And the gallery will then split the sales fifty–fifty with the artist – you – which in itself is unusual. I usually sting my clients for at least eighty–twenty.'

I laugh, but he's looking at me so seriously, as if he's afraid I'll disappear.

'So why give me the preferential treatment?'

'Because I like you, Serena. I don't think you realise what a find you are.' He holds up his hand and starts ticking off points on his fingers. 'Basics. You're beautiful to look at, invigorating to be with, and what makes it even better is that you don't know it. I have a painting in my house by Dante Gabriel Rossetti, and you're in it. No-one's ever told you you're gorgeous, have they?'

I shake my head. He had me at beautiful.

'Not even the boyfriend you've left behind you. Because there's always a boyfriend left behind. First love. But too callow, I'm guessing. Too young, once you'd seen a bit of the world. Too set in his ways and his horizons so much narrower than yours?'

Tears are fighting flattery here. How does he suss all that?

'You're young, and fresh, and undemanding. And like me you're pretty much alone in the world, which gives you that hungry edge. Oh, there's room for refinement. We'll do a little work on you, me and my assistant. Continue what your cousin has started. Wardrobe, hair, make-up. Don't frown at me. I love the waif-and-stray look. But this is a competitive business. You need to present a flawless face to your public, yes?' He spreads out his hands, presenting his findings. 'What do you think?'

'Of your resume? More complimentary than my own profile.'

He taps the portfolio with his long fingers. 'You want professional exposure and although I've never stopped working my personal life has taken a dive. I've been hibernating like a monk for too long.'

'I've never met anyone who looks less like a monk!'

He grimaces. 'I need re-tuning. The personal angle I'm after is pure pleasure. If pleasure can ever be wholly pure.'

I sit bolt upright in my chair, my knuckles white on my knees. He's still a stranger, however mesmeric his eyes. Remember that. 'And this personal pleasure will come from me?'

'I want to be able to call you my own, Serena. For a measurable period. Enough to restore my faith in womankind. Sound odd to you? Well, I've been licking my wounds for too long. I took one look at you stalking those poor little witches yesterday, and I thought, that's the girl to wake me up. I want that one.'

'You thought I was a bloke when you first saw me!'

'Only for a moment, till I got closer.' His narrowed eyes

gleam at the reminder. 'And for once I was delighted to be proved wrong!'

I nod distractedly. 'A measurable period, you said? You mean this doesn't have to go on forever?'

He shakes his head and looks out of the window. I follow his gaze over the rooftops.

'This is a deal. Not a life sentence. I'm suggesting until the very last photograph is sold. Between now and Christmas. I have been dragged down some very crooked, dark paths in the past. I need your company to shine a light. Just by being by my side, especially when the day's graft is at an end. I want to wine and dine you. I want to see you blossom. It won't be particularly chaste. I may as well warn you of that now. But I'm going to enjoy your gratitude.'

'Doesn't that work two ways?'

He laughs. 'Of course. I will be grateful too. Believe me.'

'Still makes me sound like more of an escort.'

He looks back at me and nods slowly. I watch his mouth for signs of a smile. 'I realise how that sounds. And yes. It's come out all wrong, but that is kind of what I mean.'

'With the sex thrown in?'

'I was getting to that. Please, don't look so shocked. I didn't have you down as a prude. Hear me out. There's so much pleasure to be had out there, Serena, if you just know where to look. Do I look satisfied to you?'

'Honestly? No. You look famished. Hungry like the wolf.' I uncross my legs and stamp both feet on the ground. 'But why me? I'm not pure as the driven snow, but I'm not exactly a woman of the world either. I've only had one. One boyfriend I mean. There must be heiresses and models and powerful women up and down the land with all kind of skills who would be delighted to oblige you!'

'Gold diggers, sure.' He gets up and walks away from me, to the corner of the building where it looks out over Westminster

Bridge. Leans his forehead against the glass. 'Cynical, bitter women who pounced as soon as I was single again and thought I'd wave a magic wand to make them comfortable with no effort on their part. I was taken in by my ex-wife. I was stupid. She was the woman with two faces. The face of an angel, the body and soul of the devil.'

I shift uncomfortably at the sudden bitterness in his voice. 'Why didn't you leave her, then?'

He doesn't turn round. Talks to the window. 'Besotted. Blinded. Belittled, in that order. And blamed. But the blame is all on me, because I should have known better.'

'Sounds like a classic case of mental cruelty to me.'

'You have a wise head on those slender shoulders, Serena. But I still need to be absolutely sure that you are the girl I think you are. Because if so, the rewards will be endless.'

'And if not?'

He comes back towards me, stretches out his two hands and separates them as if swimming, or parting the Red Sea.

'Where is she now?'

He sighs. That muscle is going in his jaw again. Either he's the actor I'll never be, or there is a real weight of sadness tugging at him, chaining him under those chalk stripes.

'She's gone. That's all you need to know.'

'So this isn't a Rebecca scenario. The ghostly paragon hovering over our shoulders. The paragon I could never match.'

'There are no paragons in my story. One younger brother. I took care of him all his life. We were thick as thieves until we were estranged. He witnessed things in our house he shouldn't have, but when I tried to fix it, promised to change, she not only seduced him under my nose but succeeded in poisoning his mind.' He laughs caustically. '*Voilà*. The concept of family is irrelevant to me now, just as it is to you.'

'We have that heart of darkness in common, definitely. But do you not see how perverted your suggestion sounds?'

He seems to be growing in stature again. Taller, broader, darker. The exhaustion is scrubbed off his pale face. He flicks his jacket back, shoves his hands in his trouser pockets. I study the tautness of his stomach under the pressed shirt. The way his trousers are tailored beneath his belt. Professionalism personified. Not a hint of what lies beneath.

'And do you realise how prim you sound?'

'*Touché*.' I laugh a little shakily and stand up to hold the back of my chair. 'I am listening, Gustav. I'm not – I'm not saying no. I'm just trying to understand, that's all.'

Polly is screeching *no, no, no, Lothario* like some kind of Greek chorus in my head, but my own voice is saying *yes, yes*. Who is left to stop me?

We move at the same time, right up to each other. Behind us, the darkening gallery with the naughty pictures capering across the walls. In front, the great river and the westering sun casting orange ripples under the boats ploughing home over the river. The London Eye rotating.

'This is my office. My rules. I can lay down whatever warped plan I like. What I want is to be woken up again, but on my own terms. You don't have to accept any of it. You can walk out that door any time you like.'

He laughs softly, and there it is. The soft lower lip, pushing slightly away from the upper. The run of his tongue across it, the glint of those biting, hurting teeth.

'Why don't I just cut the sob story and show you just how carnal I want to be?'

'Should we not discuss terms?' My voice warbles up the scale. 'Sign something?'

'In blood, do you think?' he chuckles, leaning down towards me. I can see that yellow crinkle on the edge of his eye. The calmness of his brow. I can smell a faint, lemony tang of scent. 'Later, perhaps. Let's see how we get on. *Poco a poco*.'

'Baby steps.'

We stare at each other. The mini version of me reflected in his black eyes shimmers against the afternoon light. The bug-eyed girl I can see there is perfectly calm, too. His face relaxes into a smile, the creases at the corners of his eyes showing me it's heartfelt.

I lift my hands up like praying paws but instead of taking them like he did before, kissing them like a courtier, he pulls me roughly and imprisons both wrists behind my back with one hand. Right. So he's not being gentle today. I put up a token fight, try to wrench my hands back, but his tall, firm body is pressed hard against mine and my resistance is shrivelling.

'Trust me, Serena. I'm not going to do anything you won't like. You responded to me yesterday. I love that you're so transparent. You're a frustrated, lovely temptress. You make the blood pump through these weary veins again.' He tightens his grip on my wrists, nearly stopping the pumping of my own blood, but I welcome the pain because it's brought him up close. 'Remember, you're free to leave whenever you wish. But I guarantee by the end of our time together you'll wonder how you ever lived without the attention I'm going to lavish on you.'

The window sill digs into the backs of my legs. His smile fades into seriousness as he examines my face silently, sliding his free hand under my hair. Watching the way my hair curls round his fingers, his eyes sliding back to mine to see how I'm reacting. He already knows how that weakens me. He'll remember, because every time he strokes or tugs or tangles my hair, my eyes will close, my head fall back with surrender. After that I'm a sure thing.

His hand moves down, framing my face, then as it continues on, down my throat, his face is brought so close it's almost blurred. I focus on his mouth. What will it give away about him today? Those teeth are a tiger's barrier to his emotions. They come down hard when he's hesitant or thoughtful, then when some kind of release is allowed the tiny dents in his lip fill out again. It's happening now. How warm his breath is on my cheek as he brushes his lips against my skin. I tilt my face up, move my mouth towards his, but he turns his face sideways, his black hair falling like water against my mouth instead.

The idea that whores don't kiss shoots through me and hits its target. Dark determination twists inside me. We'll see about that.

His hand is over the swell of my breasts now. He closes his eyes. The V of the neckline is very flattering, framing and hoisting them invitingly. The perfect choice for today's encounter. The perfect garment to launch my new, brazenly ambitious self. Keep the red blood boiling in his veins no matter how controlled he thinks he is.

It's as if he's measuring me for something. His hand barely touches, merely brushes. I arch my spine to push my breasts closer to him. If he just moves a little to the left he could untie the wrap fastening with one move and undress me, reveal the black lace I'm wearing underneath.

But his hand travels on, smoothes over my stomach. His grip tightens on my wrists. He half opens his eyes again, watches the exploring progress of his own hand skimming down my body, over the soft rising mound. It doesn't stop. It doesn't stop, and then he's there, down there, between my legs. If his hand goes in through the skirt of my dress he'll know the dampness springing there, oh God, that *is* what he's doing, he's found where the dress wraps over and he's inside, touching the bare skin of my thigh above the stocking.

Instinctively I try to sidle away, close my legs against his hand. Behave like a lady before it's too late.

His fingers rest easily on my thigh. His black eyes are on mine. 'Stay still when I ask. Move when I ask.'

'My mind is whirling, Gustav. This feels good, but it also feels very, very bad.'

My body belies everything I'm saying and thinking. It feels absolutely right that he's touching me and lording it over me. All my life I've struggled to appear strong, never show the damage. Even with Jake I led the way sexually, I always gave the go-ahead, but after a while I wanted more than he could give me.

'Whirling is fine.' Gustav's chuckle is low, almost a growl. 'You telling me there's something wrong about a man who just wants to touch you? Who's wanted you since he set eyes on your scruffy little butt?'

'You didn't give much away yesterday.'

'Well, I'm telling you now. I was being old-fashioned. Respectful.'

'Or slow off the mark?'

He laughs quietly and as always when he laughs his hair falls forward as if it wants to join in. His eyes half-close but they can't hide the want gleaming there, the lust shining through. 'Time to make up for that, then. I want to know if you feel as good as you look today.'

Who am I kidding? I'll never be a lady. Would a lady deliberately put on a low cut, seductive, breast-boosting dress to visit a gentleman? I'll enjoy the ride, and see how far he goes, how far I'll let him go, what this demented arrangement will actually turn out to be, what it will actually feel like.

'Stay still, Serena.' His mouth is hot against my hair now. 'Let me enjoy this.'

My body has made up its own mind already. It's given in, willingly. I'm so tired of arguments or arrangements or agreements. I'm weak with the waiting. His breath heats my hair as he mutters something in a foreign language which sounds dirty and which I know he won't translate for me, but his fingers do the talking instead, stroking in between my thighs and opening me up, as if about to play the harp. My thighs part obediently, and oh God there he is, touching me, treading over the softness.

The scent from the lilies clogs into my nostrils, so heady and thick that it has actual substance, like stuffing my skull with cotton wool. Some kind of barge or boat outside judders into the river bank. I can hear the pilot telling his mate to cast the rope round the bollard on the pier.

One more feeble attempt at decency and decorum. My thighs press together, meaning to stop his hand but instead trapping it there, the tips of his fingers already inside.

He pauses, his mouth pressed against my hair. He remembers what I said last night, knowing that the little hairs which that woman used to yank when she thought I was naughty are rising sensuously like baby feathers under his breath.

'Still time to back out, Serena. You have no idea what you've done to me. So warm. So sweet and fresh. I could play with you all day. But it's not too late. If you don't like it, you're free to leave and we'll say no more about any of this.'

Those words decency, decorum, dignity are like shreds caught on barbed wire. Distant voices tell me he should shove his gallery, along with his twisted suggestions.

But I like the feel of his hand there. My body wants it, him, inside me.

'Not that sweet. Go on, if you dare. Put your fingers in me,' I whisper. 'But look at me while you're doing it.'

He nods, as if I've answered a question correctly. His mouth slides across my cheek, just touches my mouth, then his eyes are there again, locking onto mine and it's like I've always known them, the dark messages burning inside, the pulse pummelling his neck to confirm the urges he's struggling to control. The desire he has to touch me and own me.

He doesn't hurry, though. His self-control is almost

military. He continues softly onwards and upwards, to invade me, smoothly, making all my senses come alive. He keeps his eyes steady on me, his mouth a closed line as he feels underneath me. I squirm in response, shamelessly, close my thighs harder as his hand finds its goal, and I start to ride it.

Shame flees, hands above its head like a horrified spectre. Sense and sensibility flee too, along with every other sensible attribute: chastity, modesty, mystique. I close my eyes, the better to feel his breath now on my neck, under my ear.

'You like that? Of course you do.' He grunts approvingly. 'Remember to stay very still. What I didn't tell you is that if I think you're resisting me or being disobedient, I might get angry.'

'Yes,' I stammer, confused. 'But I thought I was the one who was supposed to – I thought it was your own pleasure you were after?' I open my eyes again. He's doing what I asked. He's still staring at me but it's the deep stare of the hypnotist now. I'm ready to drown in it.

'You're pleasing me already. Look at you. So lovely perched here in front of me, opening your legs for me. So quiet now. Obedient. Willing. Just the way I like it.' He hooks one finger into my knickers, keeping his eyes on mine. 'How could any man not get pleasure from doing this?'

He can feel how wet I am. He strokes me for a moment, his face still so intense. A strand of his black hair has been hooked by one of my curls. There's no-one else in the world except us.

I'm tight under his fingers, but he pushes more insistently, knowing his way, so that everything loosens and opens, and then he groans quietly and changes tempo, and he's being rough and hard with me now and several fingers are up inside me, thrusting into the emptiness, and it's so, so good.

His eyes are burning with triumph. 'This lovely body has

so much to give. So much to learn, too. You can't help showing me, my lovely. Can you?'

I moan incoherently, not really hearing what he's saying, tipping myself up to his fingers.

'You don't want me to stop, do you? You'll never want me to stop.'

He pushes his fingers in harder, moving his arm so I am rocking on his hand. This is what Pierre was doing to Polly last night at the party. She was riding on his hand, right there in front of everybody. It's what caused old Toga Tomas to get so aroused. But there's no-one watching us now. I fall back against the window as my legs lose their strength. Gustav grips my wrists harder to keep me from falling.

His eyes flash. He can sense the build-up of excitement in me just as strongly as I can, I'm certain of it. The last bastions of my resistance give way, no point even pretending to fight, I'm going weak with it, his fingers are doing what he said they'd do, claiming me as I whimper into his shoulder and I surrender and buck against his hand, my honey soaking his fingers.

He leans his forehead on mine and waits for my hysteria to subside. He releases my wrists and wraps one arm around me. His other fingers still possess me. We're breathless, embracing lovers there in the window inflamed by the sunset.

At last he pulls away, leaving me wet and still wanting. He smiles as he holds his hand up to the fading light and one by one he licks his fingers.

'You're mine now, my Serena. That was me, taking possession.'

I nod wordlessly, watching him sucking my juices. He pokes that last finger into my mouth, pushing it between my teeth so that I taste the faint salt-sweet tang of my own arousal.

He holds my face thoughtfully. 'Good girl. So. Are you

ready to do this? You and me, working and playing together?'

'And at Christmas I turn back into a pumpkin?'

He wipes his finger across my mouth and holds it there as he studies me, his black eyes dancing now as if he, too, has been relieved of some massive tension.

Then he steps away to his desk and takes out a sheaf of papers.

'That depends. You are mine until every one of your photographs is sold. Agreed? So I suppose the nicer you are to me, the more we learn about each other, the quicker the photographs will sell, the more successful you'll become, and the sooner you can go back to your old life.'

I'm aching now, pulsing with soreness. He's right. I am his, body and soul. He reached right inside me just now, flicked a switch. Hooked me like a little wriggling fish.

I lean back gingerly against the window sill, aware of the naughty stickiness.

'It's only till Christmas. It's why I came to London, after all. To sell myself. I've nothing to lose and everything to gain.'

He turns back to me, smiling broadly now, as if he can never get enough of looking at me. 'Got it in one. And who knows? By then you might not want to leave.'

'So what's the document?'

'A letter of agreement for you to mull over. I prefer this kind of formula to be signed face to face, on paper, not done by email. If you're happy to sign it, let me know before the end of today. Let's be really dramatic and Cinderella-like and say midnight. If not, just give me a call and we can rip it all up.'

There is a long pause. Big Ben is tolling. It must be about four by now.

Gustav holds the document out towards me, then when I don't respond he puts it back on the desk with a shrug.

'You haven't got much time, granted. But I wanted to make sure you couldn't tackle any other galleries today. And you're not really in a fit state to go touting for business now, are you?'

I look up at him and catch his grin. He really does look like the wolf who has taken a nip at his prey and is relishing the promise of devouring the whole meal very, very soon.

'If you do agree, then make sure you're here tomorrow morning at nine a.m. sharp. Leave your portfolio with me. We can start printing and framing the best once I've had a good look at the whole collection, see if we can't produce various themes to flow from wall to wall. Then I'll convene some meetings with my marketing guys.'

I am going to agree to all of it. Of course I am. Just not yet.

'Give me a moment. I can't think straight. Let's talk about something I do have an opinion on.' I stand up shakily and smooth down my dress. 'Tell me about the show you have on at the moment. Who are they, by the way? Parisian whores?'

He spreads his arms to present the whole display. 'Ah, my bordello show. Yes. Turn of the last century, some of them. Others taken during the occupation of Paris in the Second World War, in the *maisons closes* they kept for Nazi officers. There's a family legend that several of my own relations were involved. Controversial form of collaboration, to say the least. But some of these pictures were taken as recently as the sixties. Gets you in the mood just looking at these ladies of the night, doesn't it? They're so innocent, yet so dirty. So hairy!'

Every hair on my own body prickles in response. I blush and walk over to a picture to study it more closely. I'm sore, but deliciously so. I can't put one foot in front of the other now without remembering his fingers inside me. If he'd shown me these pictures yesterday I'd have taken a purely professional interest, perhaps felt awkward forensically examining these women alongside an attractive stranger. But today it's fun to look at them frankly and easily. Let the subjects of the pictures speak eloquently in all their plump, open nakedness.

Gustav Levi has taken me with his fingers. I don't feel shy any more.

He strides round the gallery pointing out each different picture of each era, his jacket flapping over his hips every time he lifts his arm. The way he taps at each picture like a magician tapping his magic wand at a top hat full of secrets is infectious. I follow him around, start to see more detail in each picture. The awkward way the women have been positioned by the photographer, their large buttocks squashed against a buttoned cushion or a piano stool while their knees tip the other way. But all with a coy smile, all with their legs open, everything on show so untidy, so luxuriant, *au naturel*.

The same place where he just touched me. I look at the plump, naked women, and they look at me, and we are conspirators. We give pleasure naturally and easily. Who cares how we all arrive at the arrangement?

The past is another country, though. These women are another species. How small and neat are their breasts compared with modern breasts. Much smaller than mine. They're even a different shape, curving upwards like flowers meeting the light, nipples by contrast huge and dark on each white cupcake.

'Shame to see them go. I've enjoyed sharing my space with these lovelies.' Gustav has stopped presenting, and is beside me again. 'They're incredibly erotic, no? A study, a celebration of the female form, even when these particular female forms seem crude by today's standards, even when there's no denying they are only there to debase themselves. Talk about sleeping with the enemy!'

One of the pictures in particular strikes me. One from the sixties. A very young woman, my age, maybe, sitting in the middle of a huge sofa, totally alone but for blurred male figures standing about in doorways, on distant stairways, all looking at her. Queuing for her services. But she is oblivious. She's one of the few subjects staring straight at the camera, legs akimbo, arms crossed in a vain attempt to hide her breasts. They are huge, and generous, and rest on her slender arms. Her hair is long, right down to her waist, curling and tangling like jungle vines. And the label underneath the picture? One word. *Rapunzel.*

'She looks just like you, doesn't she? She also looks like the Rossetti I have at home. She's the woman I was thinking about last night, when your beret fell off.' Gustav comes to stand next to me. Our arms touch. 'She could be you.'

'No-one has ever compared me to a pre-Raphaelite painting before.'

'You've been mixing with rude mechanicals then, with no culture.' He snorts and turns to me. 'But you've risen above all that, haven't you, Serena? And maybe one day you'll be taking photographs like these.'

'Oh, you ain't seen nothing yet,' I laugh softly. I'm emboldened by everything that's happened today. 'In a way, I already have. Not prostitutes. Something much, much more kinky!'

His eyes flash with amusement.

'Now I'm itching to see what other work you've done. And by the way that bravado will take you anywhere.'

'That's what my art lecturer used to tell me.'

We seem unable to leave each other's side. Again I get a waft of the sharp, crisp, lemony scent off his cheeks, but I also notice the bristles starting to push their way through his skin as the evening approaches. I try in vain to suppress a sudden, vivid image of Gustav Levi in a vast Italian marble bathroom somewhere this morning, patting on the cologne before he came to work, his face and lean, naked body reflected in a huge, spot-lit mirror.

I force myself to move away from him. The exhibition continues on the walls down the corridor towards the lift, except these are blown-up photographs of Roman frescoes. At first they look as if the subjects are dancing or praying, and I wonder if this is a totally separate theme, but then I see that the men and women are standing, sitting and lying in various positions.

'The *lupanare*,' Gustav says in a low voice behind me, like the commentary of a *son et lumière*. 'From Pompeii. The frescoes should give you a clue what the *lupanare* was.'

Very faint, cracked figures, painted in terracotta and black over ancient bricks. At first they look as if they are dancing, or praying, but no. They are copulating, rutting, humping, in every position under the sun. Here is a tough man gripping a slender girl's thighs while she stretches out gracefully and he takes her from behind. There is a woman with elegant coiled hair straddling a man as he reclines on cushions, her breasts pert and terracotta coloured, the nipples sharp cherries dotted on with the tip of a paintbrush.

'It's like a menu, see? All the services you could get for your *dinarii*,' he whispers into my ear. 'Or perhaps the pictures were just designed to get them horny.'

There is such a heavy silence in the gallery that I am being sucked right into the ancient paintings. Another pair of lovers, or punters, kneel up and go at it face to face, togas slipping to the floor. A man simply poses for his own enjoyment, staring into the middle distance as he displays his thumping erection. A girl solemnly lowers her face into a man's groin. Another woman, naked and with her legs open, sits on the bed with them, staring directly at me. The same attitude as Rapunzel, the Parisian whore with the long red hair.

'Do you think they were still in here when the lava came?' I am leaning against him, now. The etchings are so delicate, yet so businesslike. The theme of giving pleasure for money smoothly reproduced, but going back centuries. 'Were they petrified exactly as it found them, you know, *in flagrante*?'

'Some of them would have been, yes. But what a way to go.' Now both his hands are resting on my hips. He's stepped over the first of a series of lines today. An intricate game of hopscotch. But his fingers have been inside me now. He's taken hold of me. I still ache down there, and I'm aching for much, much more.

I am too turned on by the pictures, by everything that has happened, to stop him. He runs his hands over my hips, down my legs, tugs the soft jersey dress.

'Imagine coming to your favourite whore, paying your usual, getting her to service you every which way on the bed, hot, tangled, no clue what is erupting outside on the mountain, just what is erupting inside these walls, the client lost inside his whore, pumping his life away.'

He runs his fingers up under my dress and sinks them into the soft flesh of my butt cheeks above the stockings, stroking where he stroked me before. I push against him as the shivering starts and yes, there it is, the hardness straining into my back. Gustav Levi wants me.

'They wouldn't have stopped, would they, even if their hearts were clattering with fear?' I dare to bring my hands onto his hips to keep him there as my nipples go rigid inside my dress. 'They would have gone on and on, don't stop until I come, whatever it is can't touch us in here–'

'That's right. Safe inside the *lupanare*.' His voice is a groan as my hand runs over the definite bulge. I fold my fingers lightly round the shape of him. 'Everyone at it like there's no tomorrow.'

'But you and I have tomorrow.' I close my eyes, swallow, squeeze very lightly. I feel the jump and swell of his response. 'And tomorrow you can tell me what you think of my portfolio, Mr Levi.'

'You make that sound so dirty. I've managed to corrupt you in a few short hours. Oh, God, this is like taking a hot meal from a starving prisoner, but not now, Serena.' He pushes me gently away, my dress draping unhappily back into place. 'Not now.'

I turn to look at him and he is standing where I left him, his hands hanging loosely by his sides.

'You'll see I'm not as sweet as you're painting me when you see what's in my portfolio.' I smooth my hands down over my legs, fan them out over the throbbing area where he touched me. 'My work was becoming risqué long before we met! Easily as erotic as these.'

He fiddles his jacket closed as if trying to button up the red-blooded part of him. He takes my arm and leads me down the corridor towards the lift and presses the down button.

'Yet again you've whetted my appetite, Serena. Actually I've seen at least one very sensual picture on your camera. The one of the couple kissing in the rain? Where is that?'

'Pont Neuf in Paris. Not a very original location.'

'But exquisitely romantic nevertheless. His hand right on her backside, pushing her against that lamp post on the bridge? Shocking? No. Sexy? Extremely.'

'Wait until you see my Venice series.'

His eyes flash black fire as he steps towards me. 'Tell me more, you little minx.'

'They are classified until we both sign. Yes? Then my portfolio will be your portfolio.'

I rip open the envelope, take out the one-page contract, skim the contents until I get to the figures *50:50*. He stands there as if his stuffing has been knocked out. I laugh softly and reach into his jacket. What a way to pitch my work. I may as well have thrown a dart directly onto the bull's eye.

I let my hand brush against the smooth Egyptian cotton of his shirt, feel the thumping of Gustav's heart inside his chest, and as he looks down in surprise I reach into his inside pocket and draw out the heavy silver fountain pen he used earlier.

'How did you know?'

'You're not the only one who watches people like a hawk.'

I can't believe my own cheek. He laughs as I rest the paper on the wall and sign on the dotted line.

There's another pause between us. These pauses get longer, and more intense, yet they're easy pauses. I'm happy in Gustav Levi's silences. The relief of making a decision is like the lifting of a weight. The frisson of anxiety that I might have signed my life away, done something disastrous, is like the flicker of a distant torch about to run out of battery. And easy to dismiss.

It's only till Christmas.

'Your work is marvellous, Miss Folkes, and you are going to make millions. I can't believe how lucky we are to have discovered you!'

As the lift doors start to close him off from my view, I realise that he's said exactly what I was praying someone would say to me. He truly is the answer to my prayers.

A satisfied smile, shining with possibility, spreads across his face and behind him an aeroplane cuts a swathe through the velvety evening sky as it starts its descent to Heathrow.

SIX

It's the tall dark mansion on the corner of the square, somewhere in Mayfair. The one the witches swerved past on Halloween night because they were too scared to bang on the knocker to trick or treat. The one he started to walk towards that night then changed course to walk me to that cocktail bar. The one that is now being battered by gusts of wind as a storm revs up and tips buckets of rain over me as I struggle up the hill.

I should have known that's where Gustav Levi lives.

What I didn't expect when he invited me to his house tonight to celebrate our long and happy association was that no-one would answer the door. I ring the bell and bash at the knocker for a few minutes, getting wetter and wetter, before the door swings open apparently of its own accord. I hesitate. It doesn't creak on its hinges, but it's pretty Hammer Horror nonetheless.

I follow a trail of bright lights set into the edges of the floor, the treads of the stairs curving up into the shadows upstairs, enticing me from the darkened, red-lacquer-painted hallway down another flight of stairs into the basement, and the second thing I didn't expect was that I'd find the man of the house in a vast, quartz kitchen wearing chef's whites and breaking eggs into a huge glass bowl.

'Ah, you found us.' He looks up at me with a boyish grin and starts whisking so energetically that he has to follow the bowl across the counter. 'And so we come back to the square where it all began.'

'Us?'

'My household. My underlings.' He waves the whisk vaguely. 'Usually you'll find all sorts of people coming and going here. But tonight it's skeleton staff, you might say. I've even let Dickson off tonight.'

'Dickson?' I look around.

'My chauffeur and pilot. Doubles up as my chef, too. But a man's got to find a way of relaxing when he comes home from running his empire and sealing deals with startling new talents he's picked up in the street. So I'm cooking tonight.'

To cover the sudden chill of awkwardness I walk around the kitchen making a show of examining everything. It really is state of the art, with several ovens of various sizes and at least six gas rings the size of hub caps on the oversized central hob. What did I think Gustav was going to be cooking? Toe of frog and eye of newt?

'So you didn't pick me at all. You live right here in the square. You were just taking a constitutional that night and happened to bump into me.'

He shakes his head calmly. I see what's different about him tonight. He's had his hair cut. It's sweaty with his culinary efforts, but it makes him look tidier, more formal, but somehow safer. And it means I can see his eyes clearly, and tonight they are very bright. 'Believe what you like, Serena. I picked you, as soon as I saw you.'

'You thought I was a boy.'

'*Touché.*' He grabs at the escaping bowl and we both start

to smile. 'But very soon you'll see that we're a perfect match. In fact, I can't wait to get started.'

'On the exhibition? Or on me?'

He allows himself a brief chuckle. 'Both. Although the exhibition I believe is nearly ready for lift off. It's the other part of the contract which is beginning to feel a little like the blind leading the blind.'

'The sex part, do you mean?'

'I love that you're so direct, Serena. Was I really that explicit?'

'You didn't have to be. You started off by touching me, remember? Very intimately. I took that as, I don't know, an introduction to what you have in mind?'

He puts down the egg whisk and rubs at his hair. Now that it's shorter it stands up in black spikes and makes his face look more open. 'I confess you caught me on the hop. Once I'd met you and seen the work stored on the camera, I wanted to do something to keep you here. Otherwise I feared that you would simply vanish into thin air. Or someone else would snap you up. So I thought of doing it this way. Making it personal as well as professional. Having said all that, I'm not sure I thought it through.' He neatly rips a huge paper bag and releases a cloud of flour. 'I think it's a case of suck it and see.'

I turn my back on him before he sees me blushing, and walk as calmly as I can to the end of the kitchen. The scraping of my feet sounds intrusive on the underheated floor. Through the big doors I can see, in the long thin moonlit paved garden, small trees and rose bushes in pots being bent and buffeted by the rain and rising wind. I lean my forehead on the glass.

I'm well and truly trapped in his web now. Gustav's designers and printers are working all hours. The pictures have already been selected for enlargement and framing, and the railings leading along the street towards the front door of the Levi Building have been cleared to display the publicity poster we've chosen for my exhibition. It will show the crocodile of mini witches caught by my camera on their way to the party, lit by the streetlamps and halted in their tracks by the little one falling over. In the next day or so that image will be developed, enlarged, elongated and fixed to the railings, the witches waiting in their various impatient attitudes under the melancholy statue for the little one to right herself.

'No going back now, Serena.' Gustav rubs the foil from a pat of butter round a couple of ramekins. 'We're on the slippery slope.'

'I like you barefoot,' I remark as he dances from what the chefs would call the *mise en scène* over to the fridge and back again. 'And I like those dark jeans. You were wearing ones like those the night we met.'

'I'm flattered you remember.' He stops buttering and whisking and looks down at himself. Holds the white apron out comically like Little Bo Peep. 'You like it rough, Serena?'

I bite my lip. He does too, biting down the shocked smile we share at the naughtiness of his remark. *Yes, I like it rough*, I think to myself. *Or I will when I try it.*

'The suit distances you, that's all. Makes you unreachable. Maybe first impressions are the ones that stay with us?'

He frowns as he ponders the question. Ponders me. 'I think I like you every which way, Serena. Though I'm glad the tomboy is beating a retreat.'

'I can be all things to all men. But yes. It's kind of fun, and kind of pervy, dressing as my cousin.'

He laughs lightly and turns to a tray on the counter. I nearly tell him I also prefer him with his arms showing, because I love his strong hands and what I know they can do, and his strong forearms with the ropes of muscle. But I say nothing.

'Have a drink,' he says. 'Shaken, or stirred?'

I pick up a glass of vodka martini from a tray on the

counter and once again relish the slow burn of it down my throat. I hold the glass up and watch how his movements sparkle and undulate through the clear liquid.

'Dip these nachos into the tzatziki. I'm willing to bet you haven't eaten anything today.'

I hitch myself onto a stool and drain the entire glass. Take another one. 'You'd be right. The cupboard is bare at Polly's flat. I had a sandwich at the gallery today. So what's this going to be? Pavlova? Mousse? Meringue?'

He moves the bowl along the counter to sieve the flour into the eggs. 'Double baked cheese soufflé, if you must know.'

I watch the way the muscles in his arms flex as he whisks.

He catches me looking. Stops whisking and holds the bowl over his head to check the whites are done. 'And if you're lucky, maybe a taste of my famous Coquilles Saint Jacques.'

'And for afters?'

'What my grandmother used to call wait and see pudding.' He dances back to the huge American fridge and brings out a bright berry coulis and some clotted cream. 'Where's my piping bag?'

I snigger like a schoolgirl. He looks at the limp, wrinkled bag in his hands, looking exactly like an oversized condom, and chuckles with me. His face is flushed from the heat of the kitchen. He's unshaven again. Yes. I like him rough. It makes his face shadowy and manly, makes his eyes bright.

He grabs a hunk of mature cheddar and starts grating.

'What's that cheese ever done to you?' I laugh.

'Just getting it prepped for the second bake. Timing is crucial. Hey, look at you,' he says suddenly, reducing the hunk of cheese to a few crumbs. 'You're soaked. What was I thinking? I should have got Dickson to collect you from the flat, but now you need to get dry. If you go up the stairs, as far up as you can go, you'll find a shower room and something to put on. It's the old attic. The previous owners claim it's haunted.'

I let out a nervous tinkle of laughter. 'I'm too tired for jokes, Gustav. You asked me to be at your beck and call, but you don't have to scare me half to death as well.'

'I didn't mean to. Some people find that an added attraction. But I'm hoping you will consider this your home.' He waves his grater in the direction of the stairs. 'And when you come down I have a little gift for you.'

I wander obediently through the big house. There's no-one else here. The skeleton staff consists of this mysterious man cutting and chopping and baking in his kitchen. And me.

The night gets wilder, pressing black and insistent against the windows as I climb the stairs, past closed doors, past low lights and pillar candles, soft music piped presumably from a central system Gustav is controlling from the kitchen. For the first time it occurs to me that all this melancholy magnificence, bought with the spoils of success, doesn't amount to a hill of beans if he has no-one to share it with.

The room at the top really is under the eaves, but the beams have been painted white as has all the old, distressed French style furniture. White muslin curtains stir slightly against the glass doors leading out onto a little balcony. On a large four-poster, like something Scarlett O'Hara might sleep in, someone has laid out a white silk negligee. Why does everyone think I should dress as a vestal virgin? Don't two years of active, adolescent sex with Jake count?

But I shiver suddenly as the rain slaps against the long thin window.

As I step into the warm spray of water in the little shower room attached, Polly's voice in my ear has changed to: *suck it and see. What's not to like?*

I am so ravenous and the jazz music playing in the background is so mellow that it feels perfectly casual and natural half an hour later to be perching barefoot against the quartz island in the kitchen devouring soufflé, warm bread, and cherry mousse. None of this strikes me as at all odd. That I'm eating supper in a strange house, wearing nothing but a white negligee given to me by a man I only met a few days ago. What else would I be doing?

Now softer music is playing throughout the house and Gustav has gone upstairs ahead of me and lit soft lamps everywhere. He has also taken off his whites and is wearing a soft blue and white striped shirt unbuttoned at the neck.

He waits for me solemnly as I come up from the kitchen to the ground floor and puts his hand in the small of my back to usher me into a little art deco cocktail bar off the hallway. The walls in here are of dark purple velvet. The chairs and stools are the same. It's like walking into the cushion of a giant jewellery box. Even the bottles crammed onto every available glass shelf behind the mirrored bar are filled with liquors gleaming in jewel-bright colours.

'Nightcap?' He holds out a champagne bottle. His face looks almost bearded in the flickering candlelight, and the wolfish air has returned. His black eyes are asking questions again. But despite our signed agreement, despite eating together tonight, even though he touched me, pushed his fingers into me so intimately to pin me down, to make his point, to stake his claim, I still don't know the answer.

'Just one, thanks. And the food was great. Who knew?' I walk a little shakily across the polished wooden floor, over the creamy rug, aware of the silk negligee clinging to my legs. Still sore from his fondling. Aware of his dark eyes trying to read me again. 'But then I ought to get going. It's quite a long way back to Gabriel's Wharf.'

'You're going nowhere dressed like that, *signorina*!' He twists the cork out with a pop. I was right. He is staring straight up my legs, directly at the place where he touched me. I perch quickly on the arm of the sofa and cross one thigh over the other. He chuckles. 'But I would love to see it. You, running through the driving rain in nothing but a petticoat. Hailing a cab on Piccadilly in the middle of a thunderstorm. Eyes huge. Hair streaming down like a waterfall. You'd look like a Hitchcock damsel in distress.'

I look down at my body. My arms and legs are bare, my feet are bare, like his, and the lovely garment shimmers, the spaghetti straps slipping down my arms, delicate silk catching the light from the sconces and candles and picking out the tremor of the fabric as I move and breathe, lingering on my curves. And oh God, the low light lingers now on the stiffening of my nipples. I am wearing nothing underneath after the shower, because I had nothing dry to wear.

I'm learning the different ways he looks at me. The businesslike stare, deadpan but flashing with interest and enthusiasm. The concentrated one of this evening as he shuts out the rest of the world and whips egg whites and cheese into an ambrosial fluff. There's another look, too. This one. The magician's sleight of hand, which changes him from a formal, polite, reasonably easy colleague or friend to a man harbouring deeper, darker intentions.

That's the one I glimpsed in the gallery, when he marked me, hooked me with his fingers. And that's the one who seems to be here now, standing behind the bar. The penetrating gaze that sends shivers of doubt, fear, anticipation, and excitement down my spine.

He hasn't laid a finger on me this evening. Hasn't so much as mentioned the pictures which have been framed today, especially the controversial Venetian ones which are bound to cause a stir when the show opens. He hasn't mentioned what else he requires me to do to fulfil the personal part of our agreement. Maybe he's lulling me into a false security, lulling me into forgetting that this is all a lot more complex than just being colleagues, with his soufflé and his easy chat, and now the champagne. Maybe soon he's going to demand the next instalment. And maybe I'm going to shock him by being totally ready, willing and able.

But for now I play his game, assuming nonchalance. I fold my arms. 'How am I supposed to get home, then?'

'If our Dickson was here, he'd take you home, semi-naked or not. He knows not to touch my property, however tempting. But as he's not, and I've had too much drink to drive you myself, you're staying here, Serena.' Gustav hands me a flute brimming with palest gold and reaches out to run a finger down my jaw. My eyes flutter at the touch. Surely he can see how I react to him even with the slightest contact? Surely he can see what he's awoken?

'But–'

'No more questions,' he insists softly, pressing his finger on my mouth in his familiar gesture. His eyes spark as my tongue flicks out to lick his finger. I know he's feeling the same clench of desire inside him that I am.

I reach up to take his hand, lace our fingers together. They are longer than mine, and stronger, and warmer, but somehow they fit so well. 'Gustav,' I whisper. 'When?'

His eyes blaze back at me as he swallows hard. He lifts our joined hands towards his mouth, brushes them over his warm lips. I try not to squeal with impatience.

Then he gently extricates his fingers.

'First we drink to celebrate! That first glass down in one go. And then another, I think, to quench any nerves.'

'I'm not nervous.' I keep my voice low. Hope it's seductive.

He clears his throat. 'Tomorrow we prepare for your private view, and we still have a lot to do. Tonight, I will try to answer your question, Serena. Starting with this.'

I do what he says. Drink the flute of champagne in one go, and it feels as if I could float off the floor. Then he hands me a little blue box tied with a scarlet ribbon.

'Open it.'

The box is empty. Or so I think. In fact there is a wisp-thin chain lying in a heart shape on the velvet cushion. It's a silver bracelet, so delicate it looks as if it has been woven by a spider. I take it out, turn it in my fingers. It's like fairy hair.

All the ease, mellowness, barefoot familiarity evaporates. I stand stiffly behind the massive purple sofa. The atmosphere has shifted yet again. Gustav Levi is behaving like a suitor of the most old-fashioned sort, but he's taking it much slower than he did yesterday.

I'm confused, and frankly annoyed. Right now he doesn't look like the same man who pushed me up against a window and put his fingers inside me, made me tremble and come like a bird in his hand. Made me want it again, and again.

Tonight he's a handsome, rich, successful host, enticing me into his house and flattering me. The next step I daresay will be him expecting me, demanding that I climb the stairs with him at the end of the evening and sleep with him. It's in black and white in our agreement. Well, the simple words are there in a little clause of their own at the very bottom of the document, below *50:50* and above our joint signatures.

Sex when demanded.

This is the whole reason my work will be hung tomorrow on the white expanses of Gustav Levi's gallery, splendid and stylish for its admiring audience, cajoled by my champion to open their wallets. It's how I will repay him for making my name known nationwide. Worldwide. It's perfectly simple, but now I'm here, in his house, in a diaphanous negligee, full of his food and drink, close enough for him to scoop me up and carry me off, I'm still not sure how it will work. I'm not sure he is, either.

How hard can it be? Polly would be rolling her eyes by now.

'It's beautiful.' I tentatively touch the bracelet. 'No-one has ever given me anything so exquisite before.'

Gustav takes the chain and winds it twice round my wrist. 'You've reached the age of twenty and have never been given jewellery?'

We both study it as he holds my wrist up in the candlelight. The bracelet fits perfectly. It's so light that once it's on I can't feel it on my skin. I notice that my name is engraved in a kind of Gothic script on a tiny plaque. I also notice that once the clasp has locked into place, I can't take the bracelet off.

'Never. No-one at home ever saw the point of jewellery. They saw it as extravagant and vain. I got pens, pencils, books, clothes for birthdays and Christmas, practical things that I needed. But nothing unnecessary or flippant or fun. Not even a watch. Nothing to make me look pretty. When I was fourteen my cousin Polly pierced my ears for me with a sterilised safety pin.' A sulky sigh escapes me. 'But until then I was never adorned.'

'In that case, I am thrilled to be the person breaking that chain of deprivation.' He keeps his fingers hooked round my wrist. My skin, and the intricate silver, are heating up under his fingers. 'This isn't just a gift, though. Not just an adornment.'

He keeps his eyes on me as he takes another chain from under the velvet cushion. This one is slightly thicker. He hooks it onto my bracelet and then unwinds it, like he unwound my hair the other day. With a smile creasing his eyes now, he walks backwards away from me to show me how long this second chain is, and then he clips it onto his watch.

'What are you doing?' I jerk my wrist, and the chain between us goes taut.

'It's more than jewellery, Serena.' He frowns and tugs it harder, forcing me to take a jerky step towards him. 'Think of it as a symbol. Here's the chain, joining us together. I know it's a symbol of captivity. Slavery, even. But I also like to think it represents an anchoring. You know, like the rope thrown over the side of a ship.'

I put my hand over my eyes, suddenly tired. 'All these symbols are making me dizzy!'

'Look at me, Serena.' He takes my hand away from my eyes. 'I want it to represent our binding relationship. What we've agreed. What we're going to do for each other. A silver handshake, if you like.'

I lift my hand to examine the intricate work. Somehow the chain makes my wrist and hand look elegant, swanlike.

'Isn't that when people say goodbye?'

'A silver handcuff, then.'

Suddenly there's a blinding flash of lightning. The flames in the candlesticks dip to one side and I bunch my fingers round my mouth to stifle my automatic scream. I count the minutes to work out how far away the noise is, but it's already here. There's the thunder, thick, fast and deafening, right above the house.

Gustav is in front of me, holding my arms. 'Hey, what's this? My young Amazon frightened of thunder?'

'Always have been. Since I was young. They always left me alone when there was a storm.' I realise I'm shaking.

'They?'

'We lived in a horrible house on the cliffs. Right at the very end of the country. It felt like the edge of the world. I was terrified of the storms, and they just shouted at me. I'm certain that thunder is amplified by all that water. Or that's how it sounded to me, anyway.'

He holds me close, just as I was hoping, and puts his mouth in my hair just the way I like it, strokes my bare arms, listening, pushing my hair off my face, until I calm down. The temperature has dropped like a stone with the rain still battering against the windows. There are goosebumps on my skin. My nipples are out like corks. I let him sit me down, shivering, on the sofa.

He fills my champagne glass. 'Your family were cruel to you?'

I take a long deep swallow, feel it seep through my veins, weigh the delicious heaviness in my head.

'They weren't my family. Not really.' I mutter, aware of the coarsening of my voice. 'He found me abandoned as a newborn, tripped over me actually on the church steps, and when no-one came forward to claim me they were allowed to adopt me, but they made a mistake. I was always the alien. They chose the wrong child.'

'They hurt you?'

'Sometimes. Nothing major. No broken bones, or Social Services, or A and E visits. Just a kind of cold, calculating neglect, punctuated by the odd kick or punch until I was big enough to fight them off.' I take another swig of cold bubbles. Blood singing nicely in my ears now. 'And then they just ignored me.'

'Until you could leave home?'

I nodded, staring over his shoulder at the black windows. 'I suppose I should thank them because it was because of them that I had these dreams, to escape the house, the village, to travel, to make real this fantasy life where I had adventures. So as soon as I could I did travel. Sometimes round England and Scotland, later round Europe. They practically shoved me out of the door, they were so glad to be rid of me. I came home occasionally for my things, to nick money off them. I never said a word. And then I'd disappear again.'

He is listening intently. The rain is pattering. The fire crackles in the grate. The bubbles pop and fizz in the glasses. The music has slowed.

'The only good thing they ever did was die. I was like Harry Potter living with the Dursleys.'

'The muggles.' His smiling eyes glint in the firelight. 'And you the little orphaned witch.'

'Yeah. But it feels great to be alone in the world, especially when you have some money. You can do whatever you want. And here I am, doing it. I want to relish every minute of it, Gustav.'

There's a slight pause as we think about the truth of my words.

'And so you shall, Serena. You look enchanting in that negligee by the way.'

I gasp at the unexpected quiet compliment. Tilt my head demurely. 'Glad my lord approves.'

'Bewitching. Now's the time, Serena. I know you're going to please me, very much.'

I lift my shoulder coquettishly. Thank the champagne. 'Your wish is my command.'

He takes a deep breath, as if daring himself. Runs his tongue over his mouth. 'Dance for me, Serena. Forget everything that's gone before. I want to see you move. I want to see your spirit. I want to admire you here in private. I want to see if a mere garment can change you into my dream woman.'

I fold my arms. 'Please, Gustav. I'll feel stupid. I didn't mean that kind of command. Why can't I just kiss you?'

He frowns and leans forward. 'Pretend it's not just me, if that inhibits you. Pretend your cousin and your friends are here. You're stepping out on stage.'

The volume rises in the speakers, a sultry Latin tempo with a wailing saxophone accompanied by a low, hypnotic bass beat. Gustav walks in front of me and there's the chain, looping between us as he leads me across the hallway into the big drawing room, where another fire is burning in the kind of fireplace you could roast a whole cow in. He goes to stand by it, stroking his dark chin like a forbidding Victorian patriarch.

'Will you dance with me?'

He shakes his head and sits back down on the sofa. Stretches his arms along the back. So confident suddenly, so sure I'll do what he wants. And I will. I want to. I want to make his eyes gleam with desire. I want to make the pulse in his neck race like a jack hammer.

I pause in the middle of the huge dark red carpet, breathing fast like a frightened animal as the thunder still grumbles outside. Gustav shifts in the cushions, his thighs slightly parted, so relaxed that the casual shirt untucks from his belt where he hasn't bothered to fasten the lower buttons, and I can see a sliver of stomach and a dark line of hair twining enticingly down into the cool jeans.

Remember what he's doing for you, Serena. There's no going back. This is the start of your new, colourful life. The one that you're going to relish. Remember how he makes you feel. How you wanted to stay with him in that bar. How he's gotten under your skin. How you even rejected the advances of that rich, cute American guy at Polly's party because this man had already taken possession of your mind.

I kick my legs out like a pony and start to pace up and down the floor like a matador, glaring at him. Gustav grins and lifts his glass to me in response.

'You look angry,' he remarks quietly, his eyes roving over me hungrily. His hair looks wilder than ever, pushed in damp spikes off his forehead. 'Like you're going into battle.'

'You made me talk about my family. It always makes me angry.'

'Anger's good. But forget them. I'm here now. That's all you need to know.'

'But you inhibit me.'

I tilt my chin so that the glare becomes seductive rather than sulky, then shake my hair round my face. My crowning glory. Rapunzel. I'm thinking mermaid now, not witch. A siren from another world.

'So like I said. Pretend. Think of all of this as a game. Then you'll realise how sexy that can be.'

He reaches above his head to dim the lights totally so it's only candlelight now. He doesn't see me glancing again at his stomach when he stretches, the shirt flapping open as if he's a schoolboy running late. The bare strip of skin that my fingers are itching to touch.

He settles back down, biting his finger now as he focuses on me. I let the music direct me, closing my eyes and rotating my neck until I'm dizzy. But dizzy's good. It makes me feel lightheaded, energetic, daring. An exhibitionist. Best of all, the centre of attention.

I edge the negligee upwards, revealing my ankles, then my knees, pausing as he continues to stare at me. Those eyes appreciate me. I lift the negligee up my thighs, my feet freer now to step apart and together while I run my hands over my ribcage.

A sudden, firm jerk on my wrist reminds me we are still linked, the nearly invisible thread joining us together. The thunder rumbles more distantly now, and the show-off in me takes shape. Let's see what happens. How long will it be before he comes begging. Preferably on his knees.

My hands wander down my throat, over my shoulders, then they're over my breasts, hovering an inch over them, tracing the soft outlines, the protruding little peaks, outlined under the silk and even the suggestion, the threat of touching triggers a sharp tug in my nipples, then another much lower down. My nipples scrape and catch on the silk. I run the tips of my fingers between them, squeeze my breasts briefly together, then flicker and tease down my stomach and down between my legs, holding my softness there for a moment, licking my lips like a stripper. Hands sliding down my thighs, pushing them open and closed.

As the music grows louder I accelerate my moves, bending

and straightening and sliding my legs further and further apart. This is a private dance, just for him, no audience. I'm not sure of the programme, what will happen next, but I'm turning myself on, that's for sure, dancing in my new negligee. My fingers want to creep inside to play, but I slap myself away.

'Don't stop, Serena.' He can't hide the animal groan of arousal in his deep voice. 'This is strumming all the right strings.'

My hair sways in front of my face, down my back, I sweep my hands down my body, cup the dampness growing between my legs. I pull the silk up so high that any further and I'd be totally bare to him.

He is leaning forwards, his hands dangling the champagne glass between his knees as he watches me, his eyes burning with desire but the rest of his expression so concentrated it's as if he's at the ballet. It's flattering, but strange. All I'm doing is prancing around his drawing room, really. Awaiting further instructions. The streak of warmth across his cheekbones, the working of the muscle in his jaw give away what's really on his mind.

The daring is like a pair of hands pushing, pushing me on. I go over to the sofa, bend over him, let my hair fall in a tent around our faces, tip his watching dark face up close to mine, then I push him back into the cushions and swerve away as I see the gleam lighting up his eyes.

I'm making it up as I go along, but I'm tired of dancing solo. I want him to join in now. I'm dancing as I assume he wanted me to dance, burlesque style but without the tassels and the props. I sway towards him, aware of how all my curves push against the shimmering silk.

I hold my hands out to him, wriggling and gyrating.

'Dance with me, Gustav. Let go. Hang loose.'

I twist away from him, dance to the other side of the room, crooking my finger like a Scheherazade. And at last I get my reaction. His mouth snaps open in a wicked grin and my wrist is suddenly pulled out in front of me so that my arm is straight.

'You're gorgeous, Serena. I could watch you all night. Maybe one night I will do just that. You move like a sea creature. But I want you over here now.'

He tugs at the silver chain, smiling wolfishly at his game, at this small but potent display of power.

I resist the pull of it at first. But as he goes on pulling, and it takes the strain; that spindly meshing of silver threads has the strength of a tow rope. So I let him pull me until I come to a halt in front of him again, still swaying slightly to the insistent music.

'I'm enjoying myself, Gustav. Dance with me!'

He shakes his head, holding the chain tightly in his fist, moves it from side to side so that my arm is forced to swing like a pendulum.

'That's what couples do. No, don't turn your lovely mouth down like that. Anything's possible, once we're used to each other, but for now we're still working to an agreement. I'm your patron. You're my protégée. What a patron does is take the protégée under his wing. And what protégées do is what they're told.'

I fold my arms and look away from him. Tap my bare foot impatiently.

He sighs deeply. 'Please would you kneel down, Serena. You've had the effect on me I knew you would. Look.'

I look. There's an unmistakable bulge in his jeans, straining at the dark blue denim. His eyes, glittering in the candlelight, half closed behind those thick lashes, are pulling me towards him as irresistibly as the chain.

'I've been in this parlous state, on and off, since I first set eyes on you. You probably guessed that by now.' He spreads his hands in a helpless gesture and we both stare at his crotch again.

'Hands and knees, you say? You want me to scrub the floor now? Surely I can do something else for you? Much more fun. Protégée isn't the same as servant.'

He laughs, so naughtily. 'Very true. How about slave? That sounds a whole lot sexier, don't you think?'

'Maybe. If you're Caligula.'

'Hmm. Very tempting, if it wasn't for the toga.' He jerks on the silver chain. 'So, what does a slave do when her master calls? She hears the command, and she comes, that's what.'

But I don't move. I can't bring myself to go down on hands and knees, lick his shoes, his floor, whatever it is he wants me to do. He jerks again on the silver chain. I'm so busy resisting that I stumble and fall towards him, half falling into his arms, but he catches me, stops me in midair before him.

His strong hands are brakes on my hips. I stare down at his silky black hair which seems to grow as fast as his beard. He's about to push me down onto my knees, his word being my command, but I don't want to do that. I fall against him, press into him, his face is against my stomach, his nose is level with my navel, his mouth so close to where his fingers were yesterday.

His breath is hot on the silk at the top of my legs. I'm soft and weak from the dancing, the music, the kiss of silk on my bare skin. I push myself towards him.

'Stay right there, Serena.'

He groans into my stomach. Such a primeval, sexy sound. My man, groaning because he wants me.

Then he pulls me slowly, almost thoughtfully towards him, his hands spread over my bottom to keep hold of me. He looks down with that questioning frown, why is he always so unsure, unwilling to let go? He pinches the fabric up between his fingers, right up, so that it's all wrinkled up around my hips and there's nothing between my naked skin and the cool air. I'm bared before him.

He reminds me of the hung-up, insomniac businessman in *Pretty Woman*. The scene where the escort girl comes downstairs late at night and finds him playing sensual jazz on the hotel piano. She sits on the top of the music stand, her legs on either side of him, rousing him from his apathy in the most obvious way possible, and as he pushes her silk nightdress up over her nakedness her toes start to play the keys out of tune.

I wriggle, press my thighs together. He slides his hand in sideways, and parts them.

The saxophone wails suggestively, up the scale, minor key, sad but sexy.

The way he's looking. Examining this part of me like a precious jewel, a long sought specimen. It's because he's so slow, so quiet, his lips working silently as if he's praying. It's as if this core of me is rare, precious, the Holy Grail, something he's somehow been denied. He felt it yesterday, but today he wants to see it.

It fills me with a hot, wild surge of womanly pride. There's nothing special about the way I'm built. But this guy's slow-burning, horny fascination is making me feel like the most special woman in the world. No-one's looked at me like this or made me feel beautiful like he does. Ever. Not even my face, let alone my body.

Jake looked at me because he fancied me. Loved me in his adolescent way. He looked at my face, my eyes. Very occasionally brushed my hair if I begged him. But he was young and he was in a rush, greedy, hungry for me. Desperate all the time to get his rocks off. But he never took time out to look at me in this reverential way, like I was up on a pedestal.

Let's face it. We were both young and hungry.

I lay my hands gently on Gustav's head, on his face, run my fingers down his neck to say yes. Not that I need to. I'm his servant after all. But he's right. The game is fun, whichever way you play it.

Gustav tips his head back to show me he likes my hands in his hair. I go on stroking him as he parts me gently with one hand. His lips are so close to my very core. He blows on the secret place as if blowing flames onto kindling laid in a cold grate. I wriggle invitingly. His fingers hold me open like a prize, wide open, unfurl me like a flower. One finger smoothes out each petal, making each part damp, then wet, as he touches it, and then his mouth is moving against me and he slides his tongue up me, like a cat, in one movement.

The kindling flares into life before I'm ready. I moan and shake uncontrollably, tugging at his hair. It's not just the one small sliver he's touched and inflamed. The wet slick of his tongue has licked right through me, embers catching fire. Literally to the roots of my hair, the tips of my fingers as the sensation shoots through me.

I gasp out loud, a really dirty, wanton sound, grasp his shoulders, tangle his hair in my fingers so that I'm sure it must hurt, and yank his face into me harder. He pauses. I loosen my grip on him, perhaps this isn't allowed, but I'm not letting go completely. And then he licks again, his fingers still holding me open, the exposure exquisite yet excruciating, I feel like one of those botanical drawings, every detail sketched by a fine pencil.

And by his warm tongue, licking again, his other hand fanned out over my bottom to keep me in place, keeping me pushed against his mouth and thank God he's taking my weight because my legs are buckling as he licks, and then his tongue flicks on the bud that's poking out rudely, waiting.

It's private, but it's no mystery. Certainly not to him. Shades of other women, other intimate kisses, make my desire all the fiercer. Gustav finds the exact spot and touches it with the tip of his tongue. It's an electric probe on me. I close my eyes to shadowy rivals because I'm starting to come now, grinding against his mouth, his fingers, his tongue, ripping at his black hair, squeezing my thighs round his face, falling heavily down onto him when it's finished, crashing onto the sofa as he slides backwards to catch me. I land on top of him and lie there, never wanting to move, listening to the slow, steady thump of his heart beneath me.

His voice is a rumble in my ear as he strokes my hair. 'That wasn't supposed to happen. You're supposed to be at my beck and call, not the other way around.'

I bury my face in his shoulder.

'I'll do whatever you want me to do.'

'Turns out what I wanted was to pleasure you.' He sighs. I can smell myself on his breath, just a faint tang. He's tasted me. 'So hot. So eager. Such a sexy woman. Not much tuition required here, at least not in the oral arts.'

'You make me sound like a tart.'

'Classy tart.' He chuckles. 'Lady, wildcat, virgin, whore. Whatever I can get.'

I bury my head against his chest. 'I've never behaved like that before.'

He pushes me gently up, makes me sit up so he can look at me. His hair is rumpled. His mouth is still glistening with my juices. I long to kiss it.

He picks up his glass though, and tosses the rest of the champagne down.

'You've only ever treated sex as a pastime to get you through those bored teenage years. With the one guy. Am I right?'

I shrug, in a very teenage fashion. 'I told you. I'm very inexperienced.'

He frames my jaw with his hand. I'm learning this is one of his favourite gestures. It means I can look deep into his eyes, see the way his brows move with his thoughts, the way his upper lip releases the lower before he speaks.

'Maybe you've blossomed very recently. Maybe you were plain as a pikestaff before. You'll have to let me see some photos. How could no-one else have noticed these slender coltish arms and legs, that tiny waist, those beautiful breasts, that amazing hair, your closed, innocent face. How has nobody ever snatched you up and carried you away before?'

'I've never been interested. And I'm no pushover.' I roll onto my side at last, still panting, my body still flinching with delicious surprise. This is easier territory. 'You've seen how I normally dress. It's easier hiding under unisex clothes.'

'And yet you undressed for that lucky boyfriend of yours.'

'Just the one. In the dark. Usually pissed. Always in a hurry.' I sit up and move away from him. That's not strictly true or fair, but none of it matters now. 'Where I live, by the sea, people look more at boats and rocks than they do people.'

'Well, I'm looking at you now, and I want you to look at me. What you've done to me. What you constantly do.' He pushes me down and off the sofa until I'm on my knees on the floor in front of him. His eyes burn urgently. 'I don't want to lose the moment. I'm not all poetry and compliments, Serena. I've just licked you to orgasm and it's my turn now.'

My breath catches in my throat as he pushes his shirt aside and unzips his jeans. He grabs my hand and pushes it inside his pants, pressing me onto the hardness waiting down there. He tugs on the silver chain and I lift it out cradled in my fingers, revealed to me at last. The second penis I've ever seen. A man's, not a boy's. Bigger, harder, curving up so majestically as it meets the air.

He leans back easily, moving my hand up and down the shaft so that it grows even more. 'See what you've done to me. Can you make a happy man very old?'

It's more of an order than a question, yet it also sounds like a plea. There's just him and me here. I could jump up now, simply leg it. Yeah, right. Out into the pouring rain. I could tell him to get stuffed. Yeah, and find my photographs out in the trash tomorrow morning.

'Teach me how, Gustav. I'm a quick learner.' I lick my lips to cover my naïvety, then realise how suggestive that must look. The answering gleam in his eye tells me I'm right. 'Teach me how to take you to heaven and back, just like you did for me.'

It jumps in my hand. He pushes my hand off to show me. I can't tear myself away. Why would I want to run from that? It looks like it would fit me so beautifully.

Gustav tugs the silver chain again, pulling me down again with a thump. I start by putting my hands on his thighs. Feel the tensing of muscles there. I stroke my hands up and down, up towards his groin and away. Is he afraid? And if so, why?

'Still your choice, Serena. That agreement can be ripped up at any time. And if you choose to stay here and do what I ask you, you'll find I'll sometimes be tough on you. That's how I've been used to operate, especially with women. I think you'll respond very well to it. I think you'll like it. I think you want to empty your mind sometimes and let your body be ordered about by someone who knows exactly what they're doing.'

'And if I don't?'

'Quite simply if you don't start by passing this one little test for me, the deal's off. Pleasure me now, like I've pleasured you, and I promise you we have some truly amazing times ahead of us.'

'OK. So quit the lecture.' I press my finger to his lips so hard it makes a dent. He tries not to smile at my cheekiness. But then something steely enters me. A new, cool certainty, that this is fine. More than fine. Being around this guy makes me constantly alert, constantly wondering what's happening next, and he's just shown me what a couple of swipes of his tongue can do to me. How the world can tilt in front of my eyes when he licks me. He thinks he's in charge, and yet he's also a slave to my new, feminine power.

Why would I run away from a master class like this? It's only a few weeks of obedience, after all.

I'm not going to let on that I've never sucked a man before.

I grip his legs harder, slide my hands right up to his groin. Now it's my turn to spread his legs a little. My face is right up against him. The heat from him pulses outwards. He smells so clean.

His glorious ready hardness springs forward in his lap. I lean forward. The soft rounded end bumps blindly against my cheek.

His hands come off my shoulders, slide under my hair. Yes. I have taught him something. If he touches my hair, I'll do anything for him. Look at me. I'm kneeling in front of my master. My master, at least until our agreement ceases and we walk away from each other.

To help me I think about what's happened so far. That curtailed cocktail, how I didn't want to leave him. How I obsessed about him all through Polly's Halloween party and couldn't get it on with a readily available American millionaire. How I nearly ran all the way to the gallery to find him after he called me yesterday morning. How distant and scary he looked in his suit, how good and dirty it felt when he took me with his fingers, us both standing by the window overlooking the river. What he's just done to me with his tongue. Cunnilingus. A fantastic old word I'll never laugh at again.

The rounded end prods at the corner of my mouth as if it has a life of its own. Gustav rests his head on the back of the sofa, half closes his constantly burning eyes, and for once that's a relief. His eyelashes leave spidery shadows on his face as it settles into something approaching peace.

I open my mouth and the most precious part of Gustav Levi slips smoothly into my mouth.

The silver chain is lying limp across the base of his stomach, catching in the triangular shock of black curling hair, like a decoration winding round a Christmas tree.

My heart is pounding. Sweat pricks under my arms. But I want to do this. And it's not so bad, is it? Think about what he did to you, what he'll do again if you're a good girl. My body twitches in lazy memory. There's still moisture slicked inside my thighs. He did that to me. I close my lips as the length of him jumps over my tongue. So long. So hard. His hands close over my ears so now I can only hear the thick pulsing of my own blood. I stretch my jaw wider.

This isn't just for him. This is for me.

He is hard now and huge, pushing into my mouth and shoving to the back of my throat and I realise that this cool, mysterious man is about to lose control of himself at my bidding. I try not to gag, ridiculously remember Polly telling me how it was done, demonstrating on a banana when we were on the beach one day, looking really filthy as she licked this curving yellow peeled fruit and pushed it right down her throat.

Guys love you to swallow, she said, biting the banana so that it almost squealed with pain. How I giggled and spluttered. If you swallow they'll be your slave forever.

When I next see her I'll be able to tell her I've done it at last. Or are we too grown up for all those confidences now? I'll tell her what she didn't tell me, that it only really works if you're falling for the guy. That's why I couldn't have done it for Toga Tomas. Or Jake.

I push the thick shaft back with my tongue, close my lips round it again, and start to suck it into the wetness of my mouth. As it gives a little buck, and starts to grow even more, so does the balloon of triumph inside me.

I'm getting wet all over again. Gustav's big warm hands are jammed over my ears, but stroking and tugging at my hair at the same time. He's stiffening and swelling as I suck. I don't know if it's my breath or his that is gasping and rasping with excitement now, but pride surges through me.

He thinks I'm his pet. But watch this. He's my pet, too. His obvious, thrusting pleasure is turning me on. I can taste him.

His hands tug at my head, up and down, moving my mouth up and down, he's a little more rough now, tangling and yanking at my long hair.

My mouth loosens, lips losing their tight grip. I start to bite instead, nip the taut surface, no idea how hard to bite or how much it might hurt.

He moans, his hands growing weaker, and elation surges through me again. Here am I, Serena Folkes, just up from the country, with my lips wrapped round one of the most powerful men in the arts world. I am the one making *him* whimper.

He thrusts deeper into my mouth. I will myself to exercise control for a little bit longer and start to fondle underneath it, the soft balls shrinking shyly as I encircle the base with my finger and thumb. The chain is tangled up between us. He's filling my mouth. He's pushing at the back of my throat and now he's forcing me down over the velvety surface.

I nip once, nip a little harder, then suck, my lips sliding up and down, and then he is jerking, pushing himself into my face, he's jerking against the roof of my mouth, blocking my throat, his fingers are pulling at my hair, pulling me away, pushing me back, and then he's groaning loudly and painfully, sobbing his control away. His life force is spurting and flowing. It's hot and thick, and alien. What did Polly say to think about when you were doing this?

Imagine you're dying of thirst in the desert. I open my throat and swallow every drop.

I kneel back at last, wipe my mouth quickly, and watch him. His eyes are closed now, so I can't tell what he's thinking. His throat bulges as he regains his breath, swallowing down the shouting excitement. His mouth slowly closes and he lies back, totally spent. I could watch him all night. The lovely man I've reduced to this exhausted heap.

Instinct tells me I can watch him but I can't kiss him.

Can't do anything except rest my hands on his legs, watch the pulse in his neck judder to a calmer rhythm.

After a few moments, his eyes still closed, he packs his subsiding erection away into his jeans then lifts his hand and finds my bracelet to unhook it from the silver chain.

'Will you leave me now? You can find your own way to bed tonight.'

I stop his hand on my wrist. 'Have I done something wrong?'

'No, sweet girl. I just need some time. Please.'

I want to sit beside him on the sofa and watch the dying embers of the fire in the enormous grate. But I get up obediently and watch the silver chain fall away from me and trickle against his leg, and as I leave he waves me away as if he really is a Roman emperor. I turn abruptly and walk into the chilly hall.

How can I sleep after this? How can he dismiss me like this after I know I've pleased him? I stop on the landing outside a set of double doors, churning with anger. I've a good mind to go straight back down and tell him to act like a normal lover. At least to talk about it.

I turn to grab the banisters. I'm ready to straddle and slide down them in my fury, and then I catch sight of it. The Rossetti painting he mentioned earlier. The model, Elizabeth Siddal I'm certain, is in typical pre-Raphaelite pose, doomed woman bathed in early evening light from a window outside which a river slowly flows. Her mournful eyes are turned upwards, cheeks and jaw pointing down, a mane of tawny hair falling over a green velvet medieval gown pulled slightly off one shoulder, candles symbolically blown out around her.

I calm down, looking at that. No matter where I go, I know that every time he passes that priceless picture, he will think of me. My hand comes to rest on the doorknob of his bedroom. Is he a collector? Has he more in here? But the door is locked.

I glance down at the hall, the flickering strip of light from the sitting room. He must be sleeping now. One day he'll take me into this bedroom, carry me over its threshold like a prize.

I run up those shadowy stairs to the little room in the attic, lit only by one lamp.

I feel light as a feather. I climb up onto the high four-poster bed and fall into the mountain of white cushions, running my hand over my lips, where I just tasted him. Down to the place where he tasted me.

Then, as the wind rattles insistently at the glass doors to try to get into my bedroom, I fall straight into a deep slumber as if tumbling off a cliff.

SEVEN

The girl solemnly lowers her face into the man's groin. I stand and watch her. I'm leaning against a warm, cracked wall. All I can see of the man are thick, muscular brown legs, hands pushing the girl's head brutally into him. All I can see now of her is the tension in her hunched shoulders as she grasps the stone seat he's sprawled on, her knuckles white, her knees on the stone floor and spread apart to take the strain, her toes curling into the cracks of the paved floor.

I feel dust come off the wall as I try to move away. There's a metallic rattle and my short progress is stopped. I'm chained. There are terracotta smears on my arms and hands, on my bare legs. I'm naked apart from a scrap of faded, torn cloth wound under my arms and again round my waist. My hair is coiled up on top of my head, and every part of me is dripping with sweat.

It's so hot.

In this low ceilinged, claustrophobic room the shade is impenetrable and black. The top half of the man is hidden in shadow. But it still feels like an oven in here. I glance outside. I make no effort to get out because I know I'm in a kind of prison. The sky was its usual bowl of bright blue when I walked here through the city earlier, but now, through one small window, I see that it's turned a dull, angry yellow, hanging low over Pompeii and scratched across with grey smoke. The ground is shaking and simmering as if we've all been set upon a stove. The air is choking hot. Hotter than I've ever known it.

A pair of hands grabs my wrist. I have a thick metal cuff on both wrists, joined by a stubby chain, and the person unhooks me from the wall and leads me by this chain out of this little chamber and into another one even darker than the first. I am pushed onto my knees just like the other girl. They scrape painfully on the stone floor. That was blood mixed with the terracotta dust on my skin.

As I fall against the ledge which acts as a bed, the whole world seems to shake. I'm sure I can hear people running and shouting outside.

But I can't move. I'm chained up again. Big, rough hands are on my bottom, fanning over it, wrenching the cheeks open. There could be more than two people in here with me, that's normal business, but I can see nothing and no-one because it's pitch dark in here.

I can only hear a kind of grunting, smell musky sweat, I can only see a strip of daylight on the floor, and as someone bends me further forwards and pushes something between my butt cheeks, nudging into the reluctant tightness of my bottom, it's a finger, no, two fingers, something else thick and hard, I stretch out to scrape at the strip of daylight and all at once it is gone and in its place the chamber is full as the yellow sky crashes right in along with grey clouds and choking piles of dry dust.

The pillows are pressing down on my head as I clutch at fragments of the nightmare. I fling them off me and thank goodness I'm not in the dark chamber of a brothel at the foot of Vesuvius but in a quiet attic in the middle of London. Far from the world being hot and yellow and about to erupt, it looks cold and grey out there and only good for staying warm in bed.

In the morning light this room seems bigger than it looked last night. I am dazzled by all the whiteness, the light flooding in framed by three arched windows. Hanging on the door of the wardrobe is a pale blue jersey dress I didn't notice before and a brand new pair of shiny brown boots. My caramel tweed jacket is arranged over the dress, the blue check picked out perfectly by the dress. I wash quickly in the little white bathroom and get dressed.

There is a romantic-looking balcony outside the window and although it's windy and cold out there I step outside to blow the cobwebs away.

Down below my window is the quiet square, and there's the sad statue on its plinth, poised for flight and gazing straight at me which is strange, because the other night he was positioned facing down the hill. Parked outside the house is a huge silver Audi four-by-four with a chauffeur standing beside it, built like a tank and uniformed to the hilt. The chauffeur glances up at me and taps his watch.

The exhibition is complete and ready for tonight's private view. The gallery looks superb. Better than any graduate show could ever hope to look. Slick, sophisticated, sorted. In the space of a few days my best images have been printed, blown up, framed and hung. The huge space at the top of the Levi Building is filled by my work. *My work!* I wish my dear old tutor was here to see this.

There are acres of whitewashed wall with meaningful clusters of mostly black and white photographs grouped according to theme or place. I have spent the day standing on a chair in the middle of the huge empty space of the gallery like Boadicea directing a small army of workers to group the pictures into themes.

Now each picture is labelled with the legend I had carefully stored on my camera and thought I'd lost. My name and the title of the collection – *Halloween* – are all signed in cool, lower-case font and they're the first things you see when you come out of the lift.

I've been home to the flat and chosen a long red sheath dress of Polly's to wear for the private view. It's pretty daring and vampish, a halter neck slashed between my breasts to the navel, then draped across the hips in the style of a Grecian goddess.

Gustav has been absent all day, but the instruction he's given the tall spiky lady from downstairs, whose name I now know is Crystal and who told me earlier that my jacket and dress and boots were not suitable for evening wear, is that I must appear in something extremely glamorous.

Crystal is here, too. Her guise tonight is as a waitress, hence her uniform of tight black skirt and starched white blouse. Dickson the chauffeur is serving drinks, too, in his shirt sleeves. He looks as if he'd be more comfortable manoeuvring machine guns rather than ferrying hors d'oeuvres. As the evening takes over, prompting lights to come on all over London, the three of us bustle about stocking up the temporary bar that has been set up by the window. Boxes of wine and champagne, trays of canapés have all materialised while I was back at the flat getting ready.

Across on the South Bank the theatres and restaurants and galleries light up one by one, and the London Eye slows to a halt. I take a picture of it, and of the gallery, and wish Polly was here to see this.

'Exactly as I would have designed it. Everything shown off to its best advantage. Good work, everyone.'

The lift opens like the curtains of some grand stage, and

Gustav marches out across the poured concrete floor, rubbing his hands against the cold. He seems to suck all the air in the space towards him, leaving everyone else stunned and waiting, like a row of night creatures mesmerised by oncoming headlights.

His black hair is slicked back like the Godfather this evening, making him look positively sinister and intimidating. Film-star bad guy, not low-life Mafioso. His charcoal pinstripe is cut slightly looser than the sharply tailored grey one of yesterday. My stomach twists and turns like an autumn leaf because I know what lies beneath that suit. What was deep inside my mouth last night.

Snared by sudden nerves I start stacking a pile of catalogues to hide the urge to go to him and as I do so the column of prices catches my eye. They have not been fixed to the pictures themselves and I gasp with greedy delight. Gustav has priced each of my prints at more than two thousand pounds. Some as much as five thousand. Not so expensive as to be off-putting, but way above anything a humble graduate could normally command.

'Good evening, Miss Folkes.'

He comes up to me and calmly, right in front of Crystal and Dickson and any guests about to arrive, snaps the chain from his watch back onto my bracelet. No-one bats an eyelid. Maybe that's because if you are at any distance you can't see the silver chain joining us.

'Good evening, Mr Levi. I can't thank you enough for this opportunity. The exhibition looks superb.' I lean back against the desk to look at him. He's tossing a small key up and down in his hand.

'As do you. I can't wait to see the reaction of all our guests.'

'What's that you have there?'

He holds the key up like a talisman, his black eyes

glittering wickedly. 'It's the key to my house. I want you to have it. I missed you when you left this morning.'

I gaze at him, my stomach in a knot. Remembering what we did to each other.

Polly would try and fail to keep a straight face if I told her. *You stayed over, but you didn't go the whole way? What's wrong with him? What's wrong with you?*

'It – it was a lovely evening, Gustav. Who knew you could cook like a dream?'

We smile secretly. *Who knew you could make me come like that, just licking me?* Yes, Polly. You'd be proud. Because I swallowed, just like you told me.

I glance across at Crystal and Dickson, polishing glasses and holding them up to the window. Above the lift the lights come on.

'The private view is about to start,' I stammer. 'Did you want to discuss anything?'

He presses me back against the desk so that the glass edge of it digs into the back of my thighs. His breath blows across my face as he pushes my legs open beneath my red dress, moves his hand gently beneath the material to the top of my thighs.

'Not discuss. Tell. I want you to come and live at the house with me. Starting from tonight.'

There is a flurry of voices over by the lifts. Crystal and the chauffeur glide about with trays of glasses. Music starts to play, echoing round the space like a night club. More elegant jazz, soothing the day away. Gustav clicks the key onto my bracelet and with a slow wink he moves away, tucking a few catalogues casually under his arm like a priest master about to deliver a sermon.

And of course, because we're chained together, I must follow.

Several people swarm over to me at his introduction.

Reviewers, mostly, magazine columnists, one or two other gallery owners. I have to swerve subtly as I greet them shyly, so the silver chain doesn't get entangled. Or snap.

Soon the entire gallery is full to bursting. Crystal has been positioned by the lift with a stack of catalogues, but now she glides up to me and Gustav.

'Already five sold!' She announces triumphantly, jabbing her fingernail at my catalogue.

'That's fantastic, Crystal!' I try to focus on the big bold ticks she's marked against the relevant items, then I stare round at the images themselves. Soon they will be adorning someone else's wall. My babies, let loose on the world.

'What a great way to start! Let's see if we can't shift a few more before the evening's out.' Gustav leads me back towards the window, ostentatiously holding his hand up for silence. I'm still dazed by this early success. I can see the silver chain winking in the sharp lights cast by the spots, but I don't know if anyone else can tell that I'm chained to him.

'Ladies and gentlemen!'

Gustav claps his hands and achieves instant, glass-tinkling silence in the room. He tugs at the chain so that I am even closer.

'I want to introduce you to Serena Folkes, a previously undiscovered talent who has, to say the least, been hiding her light under a bushel.'

There's a murmur of amusement around the room.

'It would be politically incorrect of me to admit, out loud, that it was her unusual fey beauty that piqued my interest when I bumped into her on Halloween night, so I won't go on about how gorgeous she is. A living, breathing installation in her own right!'

There's another murmur, and one or two press lift their big cameras and take pictures of me.

'Actually it was the subject she was stalking and working on that interested me, but then she left two of her cameras in my, ah, safekeeping for a night and I took the liberty of having a scroll through the other images still stored there. I realised that she was telling the truth when she told me she was a young professional starting out. A burgeoning talent, coupled with a fierce determination. But then, when I managed to persuade her to let me showcase her work and we'd signed the paperwork, I never dreamed what else she had tucked in her arsenal.'

He sweeps his arm around the walls, winking at the veiled obscenity, then everyone turns obediently to examine once again what I have put on show.

'I reckon I've stumbled on a gold mine here. I think you'll all agree that she marries stunning natural lighting and composition with sheer beauty and originality of subject. Her pictures all have the look of work that has been painstakingly developed in a dark room. And within the apparently subtle and delicate framework I think you'll be as astonished as I was when I unearthed frame after frame of these erotic images of people who thought they were alone, unseen. Those lovers. Those sunbathers. And the *pièce de résistance*, those nuns.'

A titillated titter ripples round the room.

'I'm sure you'll agree that this young woman, not twenty-one yet, doesn't hold back. I hope the way we've laid out the exhibition has led you on, that you've all been taken in by the apparent innocence of some of her work, particularly the Venetian convent pictures. She took these illicitly and they are breathtaking in their voyeuristic content.'

The murmuring hushes slightly. Several people push out of the crowd to look at the pictures he's pointing at, which they haven't seen before. I prickle with pride when I see the women raise their hands to their flushing cheeks when they see the content. The men shift their legs apart like cowboys, shove their hands in their pockets.

Is that a gun, or are you just turned on by my pictures?

'Perhaps instead of *Halloween* we should have called it *Flagellation*.'

Everyone is staring back at Gustav now. Those who aren't ogling my Venetian series. He really holds an audience, like one of those sham preachers who brainwash their congregation with sheer charisma. 'Anyway, I give you Serena Folkes. The girl with a great future.'

Gustav raises his glass to me, a strange new tenderness burning in his eyes. I raise my glass in return and smile, watch and wait for the answering smile, and there it is, transforming his face to stern beauty, and filling me with hot pride. I won't let him down. These influential people, celebrities, well known faces from the arts and fashion pages, even some academics and, best of all, two famous society photographers, have all come at his bidding because they trust his judgement. And now they're here to judge me.

I feel my wrist tugging slightly as he unchains it and moves away but I remain where I am by the window. I catch faint noises across the city. Something flapping on the roof of a building opposite. Leathery wings taking flight, the blood-curdling shriek of an animal hunted down, its neck snapped with one tidy bite. Probably foxes, vermin slinking about among London's rubbish bins, killing mice. Do foxes lurk near the river?

The flapping sound is a jubilant Union Jack left over from the Olympic summer, flying above the National Theatre. I'm so keyed up I swear I can hear applause from the audience.

And in here, the low heartbeat of drum, double bass and breathy sax from the speakers.

Venice is like that silver chain, tugging me back to its

watery secrets. I remember that night so well. Wandering through that maze of *calles*, so thoroughly lost, catching sight of this young nun scurrying out of nowhere. I dashed forward to ask her for directions but she was in such a rush that it turned into a mad chase. Eventually I followed her through a little gate in a long crumbling wall and when she vanished up a big stone flight of stairs I realised I was locked in for the night.

I tiptoed around the silent convent clumsily disguised in an oversized grey habit, but I couldn't get out, and then I found her again, her and her sisters, all preparing for sleep in their tiny, doorless cells. At first they were praying and then they took out these little whips and started hitting themselves on their bare skin, and that's what's on display now. My camera caught the technique my little nun used, a quick flick of the wrist to bring the tails down on her flesh. The sharp tipping of her head after each blow, the licking of her lips, the slow belly dance of secret pleasure.

'Say something,' murmurs Crystal. 'They're all looking at you, see? They expect you to talk them through it.'

'Gustav didn't warn me about this!' I hiss back, starting to sweat even in my flimsy dress. 'I'm hopeless at public speaking.'

Crystal hands me another full glass and starts to move through the crowd, who are starting to shift slightly. 'Who else is going to explain these very naughty pictures?'

'Good evening, ladies and gentlemen.' My voice is high and girlish, but when I look across their heads to find Gustav, I clear my throat and start again. 'Perhaps in fact we should have called this entire exhibition *Voyeurism*.'

I pause there, and the effect is fantastic. Everyone laughs warmly, glasses lifted to cover laughing mouths, but they are all focused on me now.

'Because that's essentially what photography is. Voyeurism.

Watching. In fact that's what Gustav Levi called me when he caught me photographing these little witches on Halloween night. A voyeur. And I don't think he meant it in a good way.'

There's warmer laughter, glasses waved jovially at Gustav, who raises his glass in return but keeps his eyes on mine. Is he expecting me to slip up?

'But I hope this exhibition shows my type of voyeurism in a positive rather than salacious way. Or at least constructive, artistic. Even arousing. If that's not looking for excuses.' I walk slowly along the wall towards the Venetian series to the accompaniment of more friendly laughter.

One guest holding a mini tape recorder puts his hand up. 'I don't know if you're taking Q and As?'

'Of course.' Wow. Where did this smooth professionalism come from? 'I want everyone to understand my work.'

'So I'm interested in your influences. They're obviously very varied.' The journalist taps his pen against his mouth. 'But I know everyone's dying for you to talk us in particular through these convent ones. These Venetian nuns in their cells?'

'Ah, yes. To be honest I was stunned myself when I walked into the gallery this morning.' I arrive at the series, firstly of the arched cloisters, then the chapel, then the stone staircase flanked by statues of female saints which led up to the nuns' sleeping quarters. The arch of the corridor, the punctuation of the little doorless cells. The ghostly figure, slightly out of focus, appearing in the first doorway. 'I mean, when I saw just how erotic the effect is now that they're blown up to life size.'

The journalist nods. 'That scenario, well, it's the stuff of pure fantasy, isn't it? Did you realise you were appealing to a male audience when you took these?'

'Male, female. I want to appeal to all audiences, obviously. Especially the one here tonight.'

I wave my arm around the assembled throng and again they laugh kindly. One or two cast suspicious glances at the journalist and I wonder if he's trying to wrongfoot me for some reason. Gustav has his head down and is writing something on a pad of paper.

I plough on. 'I studied the work of Helmut Newton, and I think you can see his sado-masochistic mannerisms expressed here, however subconsciously.' I flatten my hand on my leg and stroke it absently. 'These women are alone with their masochism. Their impure fantasies. But it's also a penance. They're obeying orders.'

'Would you say,' interrupts another woman, 'that such depictions are bordering on the pornographic, no matter how tastefully shot?'

'That depends on whether you think something occurring naturally in life counts as porn. I'd say it's a heightened and corrupted version of reality.'

'Even so. Those little whips they seem to be using, the flagellation,' coughs the woman, taking a noisy sip from her glass. 'How did you get such intimate pictures of such secluded, holy women?'

'If you've visited Venice you'll know that the nature of the place makes every nook and cranny there seem hidden and secretive, but I only stumbled on that convent by mistake when I got lost one evening. I followed this nun who seemed to be in a hurry, I wanted to ask her the way, but she disappeared through this little gate. I learned later that you can get inside the convent from the canal, too, but only if you have a gondola handy. And by then I had all the shots I needed.'

'Adventurous as well as talented,' someone else piped up. 'I can see you come alive when you talk about your travels.'

'My travels last year are what kept me alive.'

Across the river the inky black clouds scud across the sky.

'This was an enclosed order of nuns, you say?'

'There was no speaking to each other in there, let alone the outside world. Apparently once a year or so, they talk to outsiders through a grille.'

'So you never asked for permission to enter the convent, or spoke to anyone?'

'God, no. They would have chucked me out. It's a silent order, but they are still very – active.'

The journalist is biting his pen. The others are standing about like deer in the fens, waiting for more.

'Active? So what made you think there was a photo op in there?'

'The first thing I witnessed, hiding behind a pillar obviously, was a prostration.'

Several pairs of eyebrows rise questioningly.

'I think the nun I followed was a novice. One of the reasons I was able to get in so easily was that the entire community was gathered in the chapel to watch this initiation ceremony. Or penance. I couldn't linger too obviously to find out. No wonder the young nun was in such a rush. She must have been making her initial vows, or she could have been confessing to some heinous sin. Either way they were whipping her.'

Mouths drop open. Crystal is standing next to Gustav, her eyes wide with undisguised admiration. Gustav glances up at me, then back at what he's writing. Annoyance flares at me. Why isn't he paying attention?

'It was hard to see at first because they had this heavy incense pouring out of a large silver basket swinging back and forth on a silver chain. It made my eyes stream and I had to stop myself sneezing. Anyway, it was a beautiful vaulted chapel and in all these pews were rows of nuns, standing so still I thought they were statues. Then this young nun came out, there she is in that picture.'

All heads turn back to the pictures hanging there, at the soft-focus pictures of my favourite nun in her cell.

'She came in, dressed in a kind of thick linen nightdress. She lay down on the floor, flat on her face, and spread her arms and legs out like a star. The nuns were all singing, fingers telling their rosaries, and singing some sort of Gregorian chant. Some of them were stretching their arms up to the ceiling, others were stretching their arms out sideways as if to embrace something.

'I'll never look at *The Sound of Music* in the same way again!'

I allow a space for some light relief. I glance at Gustav who nods his head for me to carry on.

'Some lay down on the floor, too, but it was this new one who was the centre of attention, and then the Mother Superior – it was obviously her, she was astonishingly beautiful, but very tall and terrifying-looking, with an enormous crucifix hanging on her chest – she came and stood over the girl brandishing this long black whip. It was all pretty alarming. I wondered if I should step in, you know, I was worried it was some kind of black magic, not holy at all, but something awful might have happened to me if they discovered an interloper.

'I wonder what . . .'

I let the question hang in the air, remembering how my heart pounded with fear that night. How sick and dizzy I felt with that incense clouding the air in that chapel, how the chanting of the nuns grew louder in my ears. The sweat trickling down my back, gathering in my armpits, prickling in my hair. The stifling heat of Venice in summer. The stink of the canals penetrating even into that hallowed space. The sheen of sweat on everyone's skin.

'The Mother Superior planted her feet on either side of the little nun and folded her dress right up over her bottom so that I could see she was wearing these Victorian-type white bloomers.'

The journalist groans and snaps his biro in half. 'Pretty barbaric.'

'You and I might think so. But we all know that there are some people who do this for a living. For pleasure. And for these nuns it's an initiation process. Routine. The girl's face was shining with happiness. What do they call it when the saints in those paintings and statues look as if they are having an orgasm? Ecstasy.'

There is a really hearty laugh around the gallery.

'Did they hit her with these horrible whips?'

'You're obsessed,' someone else laughs at the questioner.

'I can answer that if you want me to?'

Everyone nods and cheers. Gustav is shaking his head in amused disbelief, still looking down at his pad. It's all so flattering. I'm tempted to confess what really happened inside me, the dark flowering of fascination when I watched those nuns. But I mustn't get carried away. I haven't the nerve to reveal now, at my first ever public show, how the shock of the public flagellation in the chapel turned to a twisted pleasure when I crept upstairs and saw the sisters continuing it in private. The swish and bite of those whips on snowy white skin. The answering bite and swish inside me as I hid watching in the shadows and my body tightened with anguished recognition.

I rouse myself. All those faces are so expectant now. Crystal's thin eyebrows are crescents of surprise. Gustav is looking at me from under lowered brows as if he's never seen me before.

'Well, the Reverend Mother stepped forward. She had to push up her sleeves and it was a shock to see human limbs under there, she could have been a robot, but yes, she whipped the girl's bottom. It was so loud. So sharp. The acoustics in there are designed for singing and praying, not punishment. So discordant in a quiet, holy place. I saw the girl's fingers clawing at the polished wooden floor, but she wasn't trying to get away. She kind of flinched under the blows and even though she wasn't supposed to make a sound I could see her lips mouthing "I'm a sinner, cleanse me Mother, please cleanse me."'

You could hear a pin drop. Later Crystal will tell me that it's a first. Probably a last. But the story of my private view revelations will run in the industry press for weeks afterwards.

'I didn't get a picture of that initiation ceremony, unfortunately. I was stuck by the door. If I'd started fumbling around for my camera under that stolen habit they'd have seen me. Probably got me on the floor and whipped me, too.'

I look round calmly, enjoying the eyes all fixed on me as if I have become some kind of oracle. I point at the next enlargement showing the young nun in her cell.

'And this is Sister Perpetua, later that same night.'

The heads turn to follow my finger, as if they are all students in a riveting lecture. Several cameras follow me. We all stare at the picture, the bony line of the nun's bare shoulder, the moonlight streaking the bars of the arched window across her spine.

'I've never told anyone this. But I did speak to this one. She saw me. I watched her standing in the room, her nightdress falling off her, and I watched her whip herself. The other, older sisters were doing it, but I didn't get many shots of the others, because she warned me not to. I saw them, though. There were no doors on the cells. No privacy. They just wandered in and out of each other's rooms if they wanted. It seemed to make them less inhibited, not more, like they knew they were being watched. And they were so wrapped up in what they were doing they probably wouldn't have noticed if I'd walked right into the cells stark naked and offered myself for a bit of punishment.'

'And did you?'

Gustav's voice cuts through the murmuring. He's folded his arms now. It must be time to wrap this up. Well, let him stew. I leave a deliberately dramatic pause, and lick my lips lasciviously. Crystal drops one black painted eyelid very slowly and winks at me. I don't know which is more shocking. My nun whipping herself, or a wink from the wooden Crystal.

'They were all far too busy seeing to themselves, to be honest. Flagellating the sins, getting the impure thoughts out of their heads, but this looked much more like pleasure than punishment. Pulling off their nightgowns to flick the switch across their bare skin, so white in the moonlight, a really sickening thwack against their tender flesh; I have tried to show here the marks they left on their skin. You can see how they tilt their heads back so sensuously, the little shimmy in their bare feet when the blows have landed. All positively orgasmic.'

My rapt audience waits for more. Only the first harsh flurry of what looks like snow pattering on the window disturbs the quiet.

'I stayed as long as I dared. Some of them went to sleep. But even the sleeping sisters looked restless, flailing around on those horrible horsehair mattresses. I wonder now if they were dreaming of their past lives, lovers, lovemaking, the lost sensation of naked limbs and bodies, sweat, tears, men kissing and touching them, maybe even other women. All denied to them forever. They can't all have been virgins in their former lives.'

'Did you ever find out where the nun had been?' It was Crystal this time. 'Surely it was forbidden for her to be running round the city?'

I shake my head. 'Sadly, no. I shudder to think what her

punishment would have been if she'd confessed to what she'd been doing, even to me. Intriguing, isn't it?'

'It's a shame you didn't manage to interview them all, as well as getting such graphic visuals,' murmurs the journalist, and others nod in agreement. 'Have you thought of a career in photojournalism?'

'Not until this moment, but you might have something there for the future!'

More laughter, but glasses are empty now and feet are fidgeting.

'One more question,' another man pipes up. 'Your plans for the future?'

Crystal has materialised beside me and I take another drink. 'Let's see how well I do with this exhibition, first! But yes, I'd like to do more people-watching. You'll see from this picture of the couple kissing in Paris that another influence is Robert Doisneau. His apparently candid shots were actually set up, but I would like to explore that idea further. Either catch people unawares, or ask them to pose for me.'

Crystal nods once, rubbing finger and thumb together to mime the making of lots of money.

I notice that Gustav has put away whatever he was working on and once again is dangling the silver chain up in front of him, letting it glint under the lights. I smile back, lift my hand high to show him my bracelet.

'And as I've already admitted to being a voyeur, I'm thinking doors and windows, open and closed, will be the theme for my next show. Walking down a street in the evening, spying at the life unfolding in the houses you pass as the lights are switched on. Lifts. Sliding doors. Sexiness, secrecy. One night I could be outside your house!' I raise my glass with a wide grin. 'After all, that young nun, and her sisters in their convent, they thought they were alone. They were dancing like nobody's watching.'

I smile round at them and Gustav and Crystal start to clap. The applause is brief but enthusiastic, and then I'm alone in the middle of my crowd.

I acknowledge a pleasing number of compliments as I move towards Gustav. I see a few people lining up by the desk, Crystal busy filling in a form on her clipboard.

What I haven't told them is that I stole one of the little flagellating whips when I fled the convent at dawn. I hid it underneath the habit when I slipped through the gate when the gardener unlocked it. I have the little weapon still, tucked into the bottom of my rucksack.

But there it has stayed. My dark secret waiting for the right moment. What would these smart Londoners think if I produced it now, whipped myself, right here, in front of them? Would it sell my pictures faster?

What if I reached up now to unhook my dress, let it fall away from me like the nun's simple nightdress? She untied it, standing in front of the arched window of her cell, and let it fall to the stone floor. I'll admit it. I wanted to step inside the cell, come up behind her and touch her.

What if everyone saw my breasts falling out of this sexy red dress, bare, the nipples shrinking under their gaze? All of them looking at me bared before them, performing my own photographs. What would Gustav say? Would it really, really turn him on?

I take another long sip of champagne. He is at the other end of the room, in front of the Halloween witches, and he wants me to come to him. I refuse to catch his eye. I'm not moving.

What if I had the whip with me now, exhibit A, stood with my back to them like the little nun did, what if I used her technique, right now, a quick flick of the wrist to bring the tails down on my bare shoulder? I know how it would feel, sharp and shocking, tight on one spot. I tried it later, back in my hotel. I would tilt my head back sensuously, as my young nun did, and the tickle would become tingling, radiating through me. Then I would flick it again. Everyone in this big room would be able to see the vicious tail cutting red across my skin, like a line of fire rushing along a trail of dynamite, but after a few moments the sharp sting would diffuse into intense, invigorating heat.

What if I touched myself intimately with the whip? I saw some of the nuns do it. The blunt leather handle, sliding down. The men in this crowd wouldn't know what to do with themselves. Their hands would wander into their pockets. Their eyes would be watering because they would want to get this load off. In fact they would want to do me, bare as I am in front of them, showing them the pale sweep of my spine, my thighs.

They would see my hand taking the length of thick woven leather, spreading myself open. These sophisticated city slickers would become voyeurs lusting for my pale skin striped with punishment. They would line up to take their turns with me. They want to put their hands on me, the same hands that have driven sleek cars or written cheques or typed emails or lifted espressos all day today.

My chattering audience is oblivious to my randy thoughts. But not Gustav. I'm certain he can read every iota scrolling through my mind. Every itch of my fingers. He's watching me as I stand there, soft and wet, beside the image of my young nun with her head turned sideways, moonlight a halo round her shaved head as she lowers her nightgown. Everyone here has been moved and impressed by my work tonight. Gustav knew they would be. And if he's that perceptive, can he tell how aroused I am right now? Does he know how hard I'm wishing all these lovely rich people would melt away and leave us on our own?

I realise what's changed since I took these photographs.

The girl on those travels had no-one waiting for her back home. There was a great big gap, over six foot tall, which had never been filled. No father. No brother. There was no man. And no home.

And now there's Gustav. Even if he is only for Christmas.

He rattles the silver chain, all the way across the room. It rouses me from my reverie. I can't tell if he's cross with me for giving too much away. Or is he pleased? His mouth is opening to say something but it's Crystal who reaches me first and taps her clipboard.

'Thought you'd like to know, Serena. Twenty-five of your pictures sold so far! Out of a total one hundred. I'm astonished. Well done.'

I thank her. At last I go to him, walking through the crowd, bowing and smiling like a queen as people stop me to congratulate me or ask me more questions about the Venetian series, or the kissing Parisian roof runners.

'A resounding success, Serena.' Gustav is momentarily alone beside a small photograph of a pile of pebbles and detritus I took on the beach below the house on the cliffs. He smiles as he pulls me right up to him and attaches the silver chain once again. He doesn't care who sees. 'A perfect example of team effort, I'd say. I saw. You conquered. Crystal says they're falling over each other to get their money out. Your work really is superb.'

'It's thanks to what you've done for me, Gustav. I'm overwhelmed.'

He frowns down at the silver chain. Winds it round his fingers like a cat's cradle. His dark hair falls against his eyebrow and I long to brush it aside. 'That remark has a dying fall to it, as if you're already saying goodbye. I was hoping just the opposite. I was hoping that you would use that key I gave you and move into the house tonight.'

I've wrong-footed him somehow. He's as surprised as I

am by the reaction tonight. I sense it's given me an advantage, if only a small one.

'How can we improve on all this, though?' I hold myself upright, watch his mouth working with his thoughts. 'How will my moving into your house change anything?'

'How simply can I put it? It's what I want, and that should be enough for both of us.'

His eyes snap back onto mine. Unwavering, as if he's stopped fumbling for an answer. He's got me where he wants me. So am I the answer?

I frown at him to cover my uncertainty. 'You mean our contract?'

'I was hoping we'd gone beyond referring to that. But yes, it's still in place if ever you're confused about what's going on here. Perhaps all this noise and chatter, this private view, is putting us on edge.' He pulls me closer. 'I'm talking about last night. Didn't you enjoy yourself?'

People are pressing round us. 'You know I did! It was amazing. You tasted me. I tasted you. I would have gone upstairs with you.' I want everyone to overhear, but I lower my voice obediently. 'But you dismissed me. So why do you want me to move in?'

'I don't have to explain my every move to you.' He narrows his eyes. 'But I'm saying my house is the only place I can have you truly to myself.'

A shiver runs down my whole body. I'm suddenly cold in my flimsy dress. The possessiveness in his voice is washing over me, pulling me towards him, weakening me. I'll do anything he wants. I've agreed to. But I have to put up a little more resistance first.

'I'm happy in Polly's flat.'

He pulls the silver chain hard so that my hands bang against his chest. 'I want you with me. I rattle around like a lost soul in there. It was only when you were there last night that I felt at home. That's what our agreement means. Or at least what it's started to mean. I'll go over it again, shall I?'

One or two people are hovering and I try to pull away. 'No need, Gustav. I understand you.'

'No, I don't think you do. I'm helping you professionally. So you must help me personally. We've already made a start, and that has made me want you more, Serena. There's so much I want to do with you, teach you, teach myself. I need you under my roof, where I can find you.' He tugs on the silver chain. 'Attached to me.'

'Not tonight, Gustav. Please? I'm exhausted. Exhilarated, but exhausted. Can you give me a couple of days?'

'And what if the exhibition is sold out in two days?'

I shake my head. 'You know it won't be. And if it is, then I'll give you those extra days in lieu.'

'Fair enough.' He refuses to show me his disappointment. He lets the silver chain go slack.

'I need to sort my head out, Gustav. And if I come to you, I'll need to tell Polly and pack up her flat, too.'

He nods silently. Why is there a plunging of disappointment in me at that? Does the perverse creature in me want him to beg, plead, take my hand, say something irresistible? Touch me, there, where he knows I melt? Yes. That's exactly what the perverse creature wants.

But instead he lifts my hand to his lips, brushes his mouth across it. His eyes are softer now, because I've said what he wants me to say. He half closes them as he breathes me in, then he unclips the chain once again and steps back.

'Two days, Serena. But after that you're mine.'

We stare at each other. I bite my lip, fiddle with a strand of hair. Why don't I just give in, let go? The security he offers is wrapped in danger, and that's why I'm playing hard to get. I welcome the danger, I think. It's the security I'm worried about. I want to make my own luck. Just when I've cut loose, in swoops another jailer to take me prisoner.

He gathers up the silver chain in his bunched fist and turns to speak to some waiting people.

And much later, when the crowd has dispersed and the gallery is locked up, when Gustav has gone without another word to me, and I'm walking away down the Strand towards Polly's flat, the realisation of tonight's quick success, the hard figures Crystal quoted earlier, it all hits me like a stone in the chest.

Sell another three-quarters of the display and sooner than blinking my time under Gustav Levi's wing will be finished.

EIGHT

When you are a child the house in which you grow up is impossibly large and menacing. Endless stairs stretch away to the shadowy rooms upstairs, corridors are too long to run along and get to the table in time before being shouted at for being late. The dark corners teem with unmentionable horrors because you're never allowed to turn on the light or they've removed the light bulbs. The shelves are too high to reach the sweets or books they've snatched off you and placed there as a punishment. The doors are locked. The windows stick and won't open.

I am standing for the last time in the house on the cliffs and it all looks shrivelled and pathetic to me now. Dirty, dark, ugly, and small.

'A unique location. That's what the buyers are after. I can't think why your family didn't extend the house, or think about running it as a business. This would have made an incredibly profitable bed and breakfast, or a hotel, almost as scenic as Burgh Island. That place is a roaring success, partly because you can only get there by foot, boat or helicopter. You know they filmed *Hercule Poirot* over there a few years ago? It's an art deco gem.'

The estate agent can barely contain his glee as he looks around the house of my childhood. The auction has taken place, and the highest bidder has paid well over the odds for it. Easily enough to buy my own flat. A house in the sun. My own gallery, even.

'They can bulldoze the rotten dump for all I care. In fact, I hope they do. It's riddled with unhappiness, like woodworm.'

I kick at an old box and as it disintegrates a pile of old exercise books tumbles out, the lined pages crammed with scribbles and drawings ripping off the spiral spine. I bend down. My old diaries. The ones that she found under my bed one day when I was at school and confiscated, screeching and slapping at me when I got home because on every single page I'd written how much I hated her. I'm surprised to see them here. Apart from anything else I thought the house clearers had got rid of everything. And she said she'd burned them. She even dragged me outside and showed me the bonfire he'd made, with my favourite books and jigsaws thrown onto the pyre for good measure.

I pick the books up and stuff them in my bag. I'll decide what to do about them later. To read them will be too painful.

'Well, I'm sure they will have the vision to develop this into a high-end, luxury destination for discerning travellers. And you, Miss Folkes. Well, you can expect a very healthy sum to land in your bank account any day now.'

'Thanks. I'm grateful to you for dealing with all this for me. But I mean it. They should pull it down otherwise they'll be haunted. Every brick, every cornice, every timber in this house is tainted.'

The estate agent glances at his watch then tries to hide the gesture by folding his hands across his jacket. He backs away from my mild lunacy towards the front door. I'm guessing he's itching to get back to the office to calculate his commission.

'You'll lock up, then, Miss Folkes? Bring the key down to the office when you're finished?'

'No. You can have it now.' I hurry after him through the front door. The key feels as if it's branding itself like stigmata into the palm of my hand. I toss it at him. 'I've finished in here. I'm just going to take a last walk and then I'll be along to sign the papers.'

'Shame they let it fall into rack and ruin like this. It could have been a fantastic house. You could have kept it as a holiday home for you and your children. Like something out of a Daphne du Maurier.' He bleeps open the door of his little car. 'These buyers will work wonders with this place, Miss Folkes. They're experienced in the trade. I just hope you can find happiness wherever you are now.'

Thank you, Mr Estate Agent. I hope that too. It's possible I've found it already, miles away from here. A fledgling happiness, cracking its way out of the shell.

I think about my life, how it's changed since I rode that train out of here. I call to mind my exhibition, resplendent on the white walls of that huge gallery space. The tall dark town house at the top of the garden square, the pretty French-style attic room waiting for me when I stop being so stubborn.

And towering over all my thoughts Gustav Levi, watching me, always watching me, and not just watching but touching me whenever I think about him, touching me secretly, under my skirt, or presenting me with a silk negligee, asking me to slip it on in the privacy of his house, let it drift down over my body, only for him to lift it right up, find my secret place, and lick me there until I shudder, owning me as he touches and licks and hooks me in with his fingers.

The estate agent throws his papers onto the passenger seat and buckles himself in, starts the engine, takes a call on his mobile.

I wait politely on the doorstep to see him off. The lady of the manor.

When is Gustav going to take me properly, no holds barred? When is he going to take me to bed or lose me forever, as they say in *Top Gun*? Arms, legs entwined like a normal couple as we move frantically together by candlelight. Is it ever going to happen, or is this always going to be an infernal game? Is he always going to circle me, hackles raised like a wolf, claws primed, but never pouncing? Does he really want me? When is he going to stop treating me like a cheap tart and *kiss me*?

When am I going to kiss him?

I watch the estate agent crank the car into gear and wave as he bumps and lurches with difficulty along the muddy, pot-holed drive leading back to the coast road. They refused to put tarmac down to make this track easier to negotiate, because they wanted to deter visitors. That's why visitors rarely came to the house. Even burglars couldn't be bothered.

I start walking in the opposite direction from where he's gone, sending up little stones and sprays of still rainwater from under my feet. My phone is silent in my pocket. I texted Gustav as I left Paddington this morning to say I would not be at the gallery because I'd been called down to Devon to wrap up the sale of the house. He hasn't replied.

I fear he's angry with me. It's two days since the private view and he expects me to be resident in his house. The key is here, on my wrist, on the bracelet I can't get off. Presumably if he's angry enough he'll call the deal off, even though the exhibition has been mounted. Always that threat hanging over me like the sword of Damocles. He's perfectly capable of ripping down all those pictures if I don't do as he asks. I envisage the gallery space adorned with my work the other night, the throngs of visitors, the fat cheques, the bright publicity, the glossy new clothes, Gustav Levi standing proudly in the shadows, architect of my commercial success.

Then I see a great hand from the sky coming down and snatching it away, feet stamping on it, me out on the streets in my horrible old clothes, the magic spell punctured, little match girl going from door to door with my portfolio.

Fine. I won't let that happen. So what is it that he's asking? What will he want me to do once I'm in the house? How can I ever repay him for the exhibition, for the party, for enabling the sale of a quarter of my pictures in the space of an evening? Does he expect me to repay him for the two portrait commissions that came in yesterday morning, along with all the glowing magazine reviews? Do I have to express my gratitude for everything he does, and if so, how? With my mouth? My tongue? My hands? My pussy?

I bunch my fists as I walk. Where did that word come from? That's Gustav's fault. It's what he does to me. He's made me this way. Obsessed. He makes everything zero in on that one small, closed, wet part of me.

And I've earned those commissions. It's my talent, my work, that they're commissioning. Not his. He's given me the platform. I've given him the blow-job. I allow myself a wee snigger.

What more is to come? Just a little light petting from time to time? Another thought stabs at me. Perhaps this goes much deeper, whatever happened in his past. Perhaps he's impotent or something? Is that what went wrong with his marriage? Did his wife mock him for his inability to perform, parade her lovers and her loving in front of him? Am I here to pander to what little he can manage? Is there a great rage in him as a result, which will rear up and hurt me if I don't please him? Am I to cure him of some awful affliction?

Is that my task, like the miller's daughter, am I to spin gold out of piles of straw before the exhibition sells out? There's always a time limit in fairy tales. Will he stamp his foot right through into the bowel of the earth like Rumpelstiltskin if I don't?

I rush off in the direction I've always gone, striding as quickly as I can, almost running through the scrubby rough grass, over the toe-stubbing boulders, the tripping roots. I want to run until I'm out of breath. I want to stop these whirling, confusing thoughts.

I'm high up on the cliff, the sea pounding the rocks below, and here's the little gate leading down to the beach. Another selling point the sales particulars will have trumpeted. The beach down there happens to be a little private cove belonging to the house. The perfect site for picnics, regattas, fishing, smugglers' caves, pirates. Games of cricket. Murder mystery weekends.

Yet I don't have one memory of playing on that beach with them or even sitting or walking there. Not a single sandy sandwich. Not one can of Coke or Mars Bar or apple carried down there in a wicker basket or plastic shopping bag. Not a rug on the sand, or arm bands, not a cold dip in the choppy sea, no-one shrieking with laughter and cold, rushing back over the pebbles to be rubbed briskly dry with a towel.

It was only ever me, or me with Polly on those rare occasions when she visited and the two of us came down here, swimming, smoking, even sleeping in the summer. Once I was a teenager old enough to go off on my own they didn't care. When Polly was here they'd stand and watch where we went, but when I was alone once I was out of sight I was out of mind. I could have drowned, been dashed against the rocks, and they would never have known.

I hesitate by the gate. There's a shrill, driving rain now, shrouding the house behind its own veil of mist. I could go down to the beach, but there's no point. I don't need to hide any more. In any case I'm not that tomboy scruff any more.

I've changed. I'm worrying about my clothes. I'm wearing some designer jeans and a white silk blouse nicked from Polly's rail, my caramel tweed jacket and blue scarf, and the expensive brown boots that appeared in that attic room in Gustav's house. I feel smart. I'm accustomed to feeling smart these days. I've brushed my hair into some sort of discipline and plaited it. Even the estate agent looked impressed.

Well, I'm a woman of means now, aren't I? There's the money that came to me when they died, mountains of it, how they would jump up and down gibbering like, well, Rumpelstiltskin if they realised how ignorant they'd been in isolating themselves, isolating me, and not making a proper will. And now there's the house.

Instead of scrambling down the path I lean over the gate and take a few shots of the Jurassic stone arch, the amputated limb separated from the cliffs by the relentless sea. It stands huge, craggy and alone, perfectly shaped, but it will always be a doorway to nowhere. I've taken endless pictures of the same scene from different angles, including from right underneath it when the tide is out, but it's going to be part of a new project I'm assembling. To symbolise my escape. Doors and windows both locked and unlocked. Open, or jammed shut.

Then I march on. If I have the energy this will take me to the other end of the village, and round to the pub, and the estate agent. Then back to the station and home. Yes, home. To London. To Gustav, if he'll still have me.

A shortcut will also take me through the field where Jake's caravan is. I can see it now, parked up in a slightly different place, away from the cliffs and sensibly in the shelter of a hedge.

I could avoid it and retrace my steps but that means going back past the house. I start walking, towards the caravan. No harm in saying hi, is there, if he sees me?

The caravan is even more rusty than I remember, but there are new curtains at the windows. Sprigged, small pink flowers. Girlie. Christ, already he's come over all domesticated. I get closer, and take a picture of the door. It's a door into what is really a glorified tin can, but it's a door nevertheless and once that door represented safety and warmth and fun. For a while.

I can hear music playing inside, and raise my hand to knock, but then a sound stops me. A girl's voice, a laugh, followed by a squeal. Hands slapping on the big window at the front of the caravan. Of course. What was I thinking? I'm not the only one who's changed. Jake has company.

I walk round to the window and peer through the curtains. And I see them on the pull-down bed, on the old faded duvet. They must have been in a rush to get down to it, because that's how Jake always is. His jeans and boxers are halfway down, just enough to free his buttocks before thrusting hard into the girl whose legs, also half clothed, are wrapped around his hips. Chipped stiletto shoes dangle off her feet which are neatly crossed, bouncing up each time he thrusts into her.

I remember the feel of that bottom. Smooth, hairless, the muscles bunching inside like fists. It always felt like an onslaught or a fight. A challenge, to see how hard and how fast he could do it once he'd learned how, sometimes waiting for me to come, more often shouting out as he came first, his hands roving briefly over me, down my sides, over my bottom, prising me open, no finesse but who cared about that? Always I was on my back just like this girl is.

She's kicking those stilettos off now, bringing her legs down, unhooking her knees and ankles, wriggling like a little fish from under him, and I wish I could tear myself away but I can't move now. She must be a gymnast or an acrobat because she spins in the air like a cat and although she's tiny she's strong enough to push Jake down onto his back. He lifts his hands, waggles them in playful surrender. He hated that with me. He hated me being on top when I tried it. He didn't like me looking like a cowgirl as he put it, but this one, she's pushing him down easily, poking one red talon into his chest as if she's just pressing the button on a jukebox.

I step back so they don't see me, but not before I've managed to take some shots of the shoes dangling lifelessly from her bare feet, her long red fingernails digging into his flesh. Her one red talon overpowering him. I'm a peeping Thomasina.

I can't help it. I know these shots will amuse me later, when I can get my camera out on the train. I sidle back to the window, and then I realise why he's letting her sit on top. Because her tits are tiny. They curve up in the air like dough rising in a cake tin, like those childish breasts of those Parisian prostitutes in Gustav's gallery, each topped with a raspberry.

She leans back so they jiggle pertly in the air. Jake's hands rest loosely on her hips, and she does all the work, head thrown back, yes, definitely a dancer or something nimble like that, eyes closed, red painted lips hanging open like a porn star.

I move away, leave them to it. He's over me, as I'm so over him. He deserves to have fun. I leave him with his new girlfriend riding him like a cowgirl in the rainy afternoon and walk on across the muddy field into town.

Now everything's wrapped up. I'm a wealthy young woman. After the final meeting I shake hands with the estate agent and head towards the station.

'Well, if it isn't Annie Leibovitz herself, gracing us with her presence.'

Jake emerges from the newspaper office just as I'm passing. He's dressed for an assignment. The same leather jacket, packed satchel bag slung round him, notepad and recorder in his hand. No wonder they were in such a hurry to get on with it, earlier on in the caravan.

'Hi to you too, Jake. Why do you say that?'

I press up against the window of the estate agent to get away from him.

He waves the local newspaper at me. 'You're the flavour of the month. Didn't you know?'

There's a short piece in the review section raving about the exhibition and a photograph of me at the private view, standing next to the Venetian picture, my head leaning back against the wall, my eyes shining flirtatiously at the camera even though I have no memory of the picture being taken.

'You're all over the press. A packed party for your debut exhibition at the Levi Gallery, I gather. What or who did you have to do to get that gig?'

I shake my head. Whatever I say will come out wrong. Especially the truth.

'Look, I'd be happy for you too, if you got a break in journalism, Jake. Why can't you just be happy for me? And why is it of such interest to everyone down here, anyway?'

He shakes open the paper and shows me the series of photographs which are part of the exhibition. 'Because we're in it! Or at least the cliffs and the beach and the village are. So it's our story, too.'

'And I've put you on the map.' I turn and carry on walking towards the station.

'Five minutes, Serena. For old times' sake. Surely you're not too high and mighty to give me five minutes?' He holds out his recorder like a microphone. 'How about an interview? Now that you're a sleb? *Local girl makes good.* For me, Rena? For the village. Get a few more grockles to spend some money down here, at least.'

'I don't owe this place anything.'

'Swallow your bitterness and think of the commercial gain.

You could sell these prints as tasteful postcards. It would be good for everyone. Come on. In here. Over your favourite chocolate icing cream bun.'

He holds open the door of the cafe. The smell of the coffee and the icing sugar is too much to resist. I shrug and push into the cafe in front of him, and we play at being interviewer and interviewee.

'Are you going to say anything about us in the piece? Any personal titbits?' I ask him, when we've exhausted a very short list of questions and answers. 'I mean, everyone knows that we were, you know, an item, but my love life is of no interest to anyone nationally.'

Jake pushes back the beanie hat he's wearing. He's cut his hair and it's much too short. It makes him look rough, and mean. Takes away what remained of his cuteness. I'm ashamed of myself for thinking it, for being the high and mighty cow he obviously sees, but I honestly can't recognise the clear-eyed, eager teenager he used to be.

'Hmm. What do you think, Serena? Should I give them all the lowdown on our sex life? How we popped each other's cherries in my caravan? How once I'd popped your cherry, you were like a bitch on heat? How you liked trying it on top?'

'How you still prefer the missionary position?'

We glare at each other across the chipped Formica table. A few people turn and look at us arguing over the condiments. Over the crumbs of cream bun left on the plate.

What do they see? In headline terms? *Handsome, rough-hewn local hack seen arguing with red-head city girl.*

'Still? What do you mean, still? We're history, remember?'

A week is a very short time in the search for fame and fortune.

'I saw you. An hour ago. In the caravan with your new tart!'

We gape at each other. The tea urns behind the counter hiss and steam. The small audience props their chins on their hands, turned fully round now to listen.

'I know the window is extremely grubby, but if you were watching closely, Folkes, you'd have seen that it wasn't the missionary position after all. She's very nimble, that one. Very flexible. When she rides me like that I come in seconds. I don't know what it is, special internal muscles, a technique learned in a Chinese massage parlour, whatever, but she's always gagging for it, she's brilliant at making me come. She's a sexy little thing. So much better than you!'

He jabs his biro at me like a dart, tips his chair forward on its front legs, and I slap him across the face. The silence in the cafe is equally sharp.

'My God. There's fire in that belly of yours. You're not jealous, are you?' He tips backwards, holding his sore cheek. I can tell he's trying hard not to yelp with the pain. 'You're the one who ran out on me, remember? You're the one who grew too big for her boots.'

'I'm the one who dumped you, yes. But that doesn't mean you can go around saying foul things about me. It's offensive. You hit a nerve. All that intimate stuff about what I was like in bed!' I clasp my hands together and shake my head to calm myself down. 'I shouldn't have hit you, and I'm sorry. But I'm not jealous. Get that into your head once and for all. I'm happy for you, Jake. You're a great guy, and she's a lucky girl. You and me, we're over. So let's leave our sex life out of it, OK?'

'Says the woman who's been creeping round spying on people!'

'Write what you like about me! Kiss and tell! There's no such thing as bad publicity, and sex sells, doesn't it, however kinky or sad? You know that better than anyone!' I fire it all back at him, then lay my hands flat on the table between us. Lower my voice. 'I'll just have to trust you.'

'That could be interesting.' He sticks the biro behind his ear and uses the movement as an excuse to touch his red cheek. 'There's always another tack. I could tell my own story, how I rescued you from your abusive parents? How the first time I saw you you were twelve years old, cowering outside the pub, in the rain, while they sat in there drinking like fishes?'

'Fish.'

'Or the time I found you sleeping on the beach, covered in bruises?'

I sigh and hold my hands up in exasperation. 'Perfect! A shameful stick to beat the new talent on the block. Why would you do that?'

'It's what they want these days. Misery memoirs. It'll add to your mystique, Serena. They'll sit up and take even more notice. And if you want to be really pretentious about it, it'll explain why so many of your pictures show the archetypal light and shade. Mostly shade.'

'You have a point, actually, but you haven't seen the half of them. The ones I took in Venice and Paris, they're really dark.' I narrow my eyes at him. Try a different tack. 'But you are right. You know me better than anyone, Jake. You know what lies behind those photographs. What drives me. I'm trying so hard not to be bitter and poisonous. I had no-one except you and your family to teach me how to be the opposite of them. So you also know how ambitious I am to fly above all that. You did help me, and you did rescue me, but when fate stepped in and took those bastards away, the world turned a little more, and I decided to get off. Please don't waste your life being angry with me.'

I push my chair back after my little speech. It's late. It's getting dark outside. Jake remains slumped in his chair, sweeping his recorder and his other things across the table and into his bag.

'Show's over,' he growls.

The other punters resume their drinking and gossiping.

I step out into the cold street, into the shrill column of air where the sea breeze and the wind from the moors always clash. I've been rude and abrasive to my first and only love, but I feel strangely liberated as well. Jake's a big boy. He can take it.

I wrap my blue scarf more closely around my neck and square up my shoulders to move on.

A leather-clad arm blocks my path.

'I didn't mean that. About you being no good at it.'

'At what? Photography?'

Jake plants himself in front of me. He looks down at the ground and shuffles in the kind of kicked-dog way he has when he's saying sorry. 'Sex. I was lashing out just then. Seeing you down here again so soon has thrown me, I guess. You've obviously moved on with your new life, your career and all, but I'm not quite there yet. I feel as if we've only just said goodbye. Anyway, just want you to know I didn't mean it about you being selfish in bed.'

I stop and button on my new blue leather gloves. 'This apology sounds good. I'm listening.'

He looks up sheepishly. 'I should have told you, bigged you up more at the time, but you were, you are, red hot. Despite the efforts of your family to crush you, you were like those flowers that come up again and again, even on a rock.'

I shake the hair out of my eyes and laugh. 'Never had you down as a poet, Jake.'

'Just hear me out!' He coughs awkwardly, still scuffing boyishly at the kerb. 'I won't get the chance to say this again. But you blossomed, Serena, and now you have the body of a goddess. Every inch of you. You were dynamite in the sack. I'll never forget that, and I'll never forget you.' Jake looks up, takes my face in his big hands. Thank God already the gesture feels platonic. 'Some lucky geezer is going to find that out about you very, very soon.'

Once again I'm on the train. He's not seeing me off this time. He's got an article to file. An ex-girlfriend to eulogise. A new girl to get back to, keeping his caravan warm.

And I've got a patron to please. He was proud of me at the private view. I know that much. I saw it in his eyes, in the way he introduced me, walked around the room showing off my work, watched me as I stood against the wall remembering that night in the Venetian convent. I'll tell him all about that when we're alone together. Every detail. Maybe I'll even take him back there to Venice, and show him.

When I get back to London he might tell me what he wants. And I'll do it, whatever it is. I'm desperate to get back to him. He has something he needs to get out of his system, maybe the ex-wife, maybe something else nasty that's lurking in his woodshed.

The train gets underway, the rumbling tug vibrating through the seat as it pulls us out of the station, out into the countryside, it thrums up my legs, right up into me, making me vibrate in time. I'll move in tomorrow. I'll get my stuff, and use this key. And then I'll set out to please him. How will I do that?

How about I arrange myself on my bed up there in the attic, ask him to bring me up a glass of water or a candle, let him find me stretched out on the bed, the white negligee half on, half off, perhaps pretending to be asleep but my arms stretched wide in welcome, legs a little open too.

He'll come into the room hesitantly because he'll be unable to leave. He'll stand at the end of the bed, breathing heavily as he looks at me. He'll come closer, and sit beside me on the bed. I'll feel the mattress give under him. My chest will rise and fall with my breathing; will I be able to conceal the fact that my heart is hammering? My breasts will rise and fall, too. He'll stretch out a hand and run it over my contours. I'll be able to feel the electricity in the millimetres dividing us.

The palm of his hand might brush the points poking sharply through the silk, and they will stiffen eagerly. I'll resist the temptation to smile, or lick my lips. I'll be the Sleeping Beauty. But inside I'll be melting.

I watch the countryside rush past, glance at my passengers. One or two are looking at me, but could that be because I'm looking smart today? Lashed by the sea wind and rain, bright eyed from the fresh air, but focused totally on what lies ahead of me in London?

What will Gustav do then? Will he rise and step quietly from the room, leaving me fuming with frustration? Or will he notice the dampness, close his hands over the swell of my breasts, shift nearer on the bed, a tiny fleck of saliva in the corner of his mouth, his face flushed with desire, pulse pummelling in his neck?

In the train I cross my legs, trapping my hand inside my thighs. My newspaper is open on my knee. Another review of my show. Under it I start to lift my skirt, slide my hand underneath as I plot and plan how to bring about Gustav Levi's downfall.

I will yawn and arch my back, let my arm drop over the bed, push my breasts up higher to be seen. Will he be able to tell that even in pretend sleep I'm aching to be touched?

Shift the tempo of my fantasy. How about if he was already on the bed with me, running his hands down my back, turning me towards him. What if I flipped up, like Jake's girl in the caravan, surprised him with my agility, pushed him down and straddled him?

'Do you like what you see?' I might whisper, pushing the

straps of my negligee down my arms, bending over him. 'My nipples are hard. I like them being touched. I like them being sucked.'

He will stare at them, take my breasts in his hands, this is torturing us both. He'll rub his thumbs over the nipples, and then I'll lower myself right over him and push them at his face, at his mouth, poke them hard so they slip between his teeth and he'll feel the leap of desire inside him as his mouth closes round them and starts to suck.

I am lying back in my seat now, my fingers stroking myself under my skirt. This fantasy is driving me mad. Jake was right, in a way. I am jealous. Not because I want him, or our old life together, but because I want someone, right here, right now, to call my own. And if that special person turns out to be Gustav, I know that nothing will ever be simple and straightforward again.

Why can't this train go faster? I rub my fingers faster under the newspaper, press my thighs together as the excitement builds and bursts and leaves me weak and breathless, and a little ashamed.

He'll suck until I come, and maybe then he'll call me selfish.

I close my eyes. One step at a time. I start to drift, away from Devon, away from everything.

A text pops up on my phone. *Come to me as soon as you can. I miss you.*

But it's not from Jake. It's from Gustav.

NINE

I like sitting behind this glass desk. When I'm here on my own it's as if these few hundred square feet of prime London real estate are all mine. The whitewashed walls are adorned with my photographs, and nearly half of the exhibits are dotted with red spots to indicate a sure sale. Already limited edition prints, posters and greetings cards are being rushed out for sale in our pop-up shop – and I've gone with Jake's idea to sell the Devon series as arty postcards in the village.

I am itching to go to Gustav like his text said. But I've managed to resist for another whole day. Something is telling me to play hard to get, just a little longer. Not withhold completely, because we have an agreement. Just not show him all my cards. How I sat on that train travelling away from my past, wanting to be with him, as he seems to want me. That silver chain permanently pulls at us, even when we're at opposite ends of the country.

A while ago Crystal glided out of the lift with a huge cup of Americano. Not polystyrene. A proper, French-style *tasse,* complete with tray and plate of chocolate HobNobs. She looked round the exhibition, nodded with satisfaction at the red dots stuck onto the frames. She is wearing a red trouser suit to match the dots today. But she didn't linger for a chat.

From here I can see the London Eye, Westminster Bridge and, if I crane my neck, part of the Houses of Parliament. I love the clear wintry daylight bathing my face. There's something serene yet life-giving about watching the river, this once disease-ridden artery of the city flowing ceaselessly past.

It's lunch time, and several potential buyers have wandered in. A couple are standing in front of my Halloween triptych. It's already been sold, but I drift up to them and tell them that they can also buy a special edition if they put down a deposit.

Next, a large group of photography students troops into the gallery. I watch them study the composition and lighting, and I really enjoy giving them a mini lecture on my technique. It's especially fun seeing their reactions as they see the Venetian series, look once, then take two, glancing at each other, as they see what the angelic nuns are actually doing to themselves.

At last the gallery is deserted.

I wander back to my desk and as I sit down I knock my bag off. A pile of old exercise books tips out all over the floor. My diaries. Covered in dust. The big print of a man's boot on one of them. Some ripped. Why on earth didn't she burn them?

I shouldn't do it, I know it'll be opening a can of worms, but there's nobody here and so I open one at random.

Today my calendar says it's my seventh birthday. I put a big pink heart around the day. I told everyone at school and they sang to me in assembly. Miss Joney gave me a packet of felt pens and was very kind.

When I got home I hoped there would be a chocolate cake with seven candles that I could blow out, but there wasn't. Not any sandwiches or squash. She was there and she threw the teapot at me. It was full of tea and it didn't hit me but the tea burned my hand.

She said the school had phoned her but it isn't my birthday and I'm a wicked little liar. She says I'm the only girl in the world who doesn't have a real birthday. I don't even have a real mummy or daddy. Nobody wanted me. When I was born he found me in a plastic bag when he was coming out of church. He was a vicar then. He's not a vicar now.

He was sitting there while she said all this new stuff. He sat in his chair, not looking at me or the teapot or at her, just looking at the floor as if he wishes I was down there so he could step on me.

I shut the diary and slam it back down on the desk. A red mist has come down over my eyes. Seven years thinking I belonged somewhere, belonged to someone, all shattered in that one moment.

A train clatters over Hungerford Bridge. The light is already fading. Try not to think of it, try not to remember, but here it comes. The paralysing sense of betrayal that lingered for months after that. Maybe years. They must have been relieved to get that off their chests. Someone could have advised them how to tell me the truth, but they never consulted anyone. I don't know how I coped, because I can't remember, and I didn't write anything in my diary for about two years.

This fading winter darkness reminds me though of the muffling boredom when I was a child, too young to get away. As the light faded, closing off the cliffs and the sea behind the darkness, I would stare out of the window as the night rolled in, with no-one to talk to until I got to school the next morning, nothing to do except read and draw sad pictures in my cold little room.

They're still hurting me, even though they're six feet under. Making me feel, again, like that piece of shit on the dirty kitchen floor. The one that had to mop up the spilled tea and shards of teapot and go to bed with no supper.

What did Gustav say about being besotted, blinded,

belittled, blamed? Well, they were the adults. I was the child. There's no-one else to blame.

The phone rings.

'There's something I want to show you, Serena. I think it's time. Can you shut up shop and meet me?'

'Where?'

'Are you alright? You sound breathless.'

I take a deep breath. Open a drawer to shove the diaries away, and something catches my eye. A hasty sketch on a piece of paper torn from Crystal's clipboard.

A woman's face. Big eyes. A swan-like neck. Face turned sideways, mouth half smiling, half gasping in secret rapture, an arm outstretched pointing at something. She looks like the pre-Raphaelite Rapunzel in Gustav's house. She looks like me. I recognise the long drop earrings I was wearing at the private view. Someone sketched me that night when I was leaning against the wall, remembering Venice.

'Are you there, Serena?'

'Er, yes.' The diaries topple on top of the sketch and without thinking I slam the drawer. Wipe the sweat off my hand, off the phone itself. Stare out of the window at the sliding river.

'I'm OK, Gustav. Just had a trying trip to Devon yesterday.'

'I missed you when I came to the gallery. Important business, was it?' He clears his throat. 'That ex-boyfriend hassling you?'

'Tying up loose ends, yes.' I can feel myself calming down as I hear his voice. My heart rate slowing. 'Ex-boyfriend hassling me? No. I was making sure I never need to go back there.'

'You still sound stressed, Serena. What's happened to that feisty mare with the tangled hair?'

Tears are welling up, obscuring my view of the river and the London Eye opposite. Goddammit. How does he do that?

Takes what I'm feeling, reads it even through the phone, processes it, susses it, even makes it rhyme?

'If I start telling you what's dead and buried, I would never stop.'

'I'm a good listener.'

'One day, Gustav.'

'Fine. So. You've looked at the figures? Crystal held the fort while you were out and she's shifted nearly half the pieces now. Your amazing delivery the other night has tapped into some kind of underground zeitgeist. I thought I had my finger on the pulse when it came to trends, no matter how off the wall, but the response to your masochist voyeur motif has hit the mainstream!'

'I don't know how to thank you.'

There's a silence at the other end of the phone. Rain is starting to hurl itself against the window.

'You can thank me by meeting me in half an hour,' Gustav answers at last. 'Indulge me by letting me show you something that will extricate you from all those memories once and for all.'

'In that case I'll bring my bags. They're right here. I'm coming to you tonight.'

'Leave everything at the gallery. I'll send Dickson for them.' I hear a quiet hiss of satisfaction at the other end of the phone. 'This will blow your mind. But if I'm wrong, you can walk out of my life with your head held high.'

He's waiting for me at an anonymous-looking house in Baker Street which has seen better days. Rain stains run green and brown down the facade, over the peeling plaster and cracked woodwork. It's almost opposite where Sherlock Holmes fictionally lived, in fact, and not far from the weirdness of Madame Tussauds. So much effort put into recreating the make-believe.

He is walking towards me. We are both holding umbrellas. As he sees me he picks up his pace, and I pick up mine. I can practically hear the swelling of violins in the backing track. He's wearing the red scarf again but the vampire-slayer's black coat has been replaced by a cool rain jacket. Underneath that he's wearing another business suit, black, almost funereal.

But despite the formal garb it's his face that catches me unawares. He looks happy. Slightly unshaven, with that rough, gypsy look that makes me want to touch his face. The cold air and the rain seems to have washed life into him. His eyes under the shade of the umbrella are bright and lively, and when he sees me it's as if someone has switched on a light behind them. He starts to smile. Really smile. As if he's about to burst into laughter.

I smile back uncertainly. We're still separated by a few yards. I look down at myself. Have I spilt something onto my jeans? Is my jacket buttoned unevenly?

'You look even more beautiful than when I last saw you. That sea air has blown roses into your cheeks.'

'It's the only good thing about that place.'

'You're where you belong now.' He lifts my hand and runs his lips slowly and sensuously across the back of it. It's that mouth I want to conquer. The softness of his mouth in that world-weary face has become my secret challenge. Soon I'm going to make him kiss me properly. French tongues. Everything. But for now he closes his eyes in rapture at the smell of my skin. Then, still slowly as if he's waking from a sleep, he opens his eyes, produces the silver chain, and locks it onto my bracelet.

Seeing him hook me up like that has become so matter of fact now. But the instant I'm chained to him, I'm anchored. He's strong, but so am I.

He pushes open the shabby front door and leads me inside.

The house is a museum. The musty, waxy smell tells me it's not lived in. The walls are all panelled in dark wood. The floors are polished dark boards, as are the stairs and even the ceilings. It's like being boxed up in an antique crate.

Our footsteps echo in the silence as we turn left through a set of huge double doors and enter a long ballroom.

'Christ, this is like the Tardis!' I exclaim, whirling round in a circle. The silver chain winds itself around me and I have to twirl anti-clockwise to unwind it. 'It looked like a kind of slum from the outside.'

'The wonders of Georgian architecture. City architecture in general, actually. Everything built to maximise the use of the space, and yet deceptive. Go up higher, if you're in the new world. Dig deeper, stretch backwards, if you're in the old country.'

He unwinds his scarf as he waits in the doorway of the ballroom. His handsome face, settling into calm as he's revealed to me properly once more. The knot at his throat is a peacock blue with a feathery design fading down the tie.

When I was about nine I came home with some gigantic feathers I'd found arranged in a circle in the middle of a campsite along the cliffs. It was winter, so the campsite was vacant. I thought the feathers were so pretty, the shimmering green and blue with the huge eye in the middle. I stuck them with Sellotape into a fan but when she saw them she screamed that I was a wicked girl who'd brought the evil eye into the house.

I start to walk down the middle of the polished floor. This room is also panelled, but the panels are hung with oversized black and white photographs in very contemporary plain frames. The far end of the room, which should traditionally accommodate a fireplace or an ancestral portrait, is filled entirely by an enormous flat screen.

'What you're going to see here should appeal to your

voyeuristic tendencies, Serena. And your secret taste for punishment. In fact, I'm banking on these images really liberating your mind.'

I plant my hands on my hips. 'You really think you know me, don't you?'

He bats his hand lightly as if I'm a moth. 'Half the glitterati of London reckon they know you, *signorina*. That's why certain erotica collectors have been sniffing round while you've been out of town.'

'Collectors? Cool.'

'Did you know that Ian Fleming allegedly possessed a collection of flagellation erotica? It was his wife Ann who was into it, apparently. She wrote him letters, begging for it. *I long for you to whip me*. Imagine the scandal of that. In the fifties and sixties. Whipping each other to a frenzy in their Jamaican paradise.' He runs his hand along the wall, rubbing dusty plaster between his fingers. 'So you see, punishment isn't only the stuff of dungeons and fetish clubs. Even the smarter echelons are into it.'

I pretend to look through a magnifying glass. 'Imagine. The collected work of Serena Folkes coming to light in centuries to come, unearthed in dusty antique shops and little galleries in the back streets of London or New York.'

'Or Venice itself. You didn't hold back, that's why they're eager to snap you up. You're out there now and every bit as daring as I suspected.' His face is wide with laughter, that pebbly rumble from the base of his throat as he unwinds his scarf. 'Hey. Don't look so appalled. Everyone has a dark side.'

'And you want to explore mine?'

'I want *you* to explore yours. It's time to place yourself inside the action for a change, with the aid of some wizardry. See if you want to participate, as well as watch.' He still sounds so relaxed, his scarf dangling round his neck, his coat open as he leans in the doorway. 'You'll see what I mean.'

The photographs show men and women dressed in marionette costumes dancing, feasting, or sleeping. Arms are raised in Bacchanalian delight, bodies are prostrate on sumptuous beds, or resting in poses too awkward for real sleep.

The composition is more stylised than my photographs. More technically adept, too, using studio lighting and exaggerated colour stains.

As I get to the furthest series I see that some subjects are not resting at all. They are being driven from sleep as an orgy is depicted, step by step. It starts with a couple, just like the figures in the *lupanare* frescoes, half-clothed. They are laying each other down on a big bed in a room styled like a Titian painting, with draped curtains, bowls of fruit, slave girls whispering in the corner.

Soon it's the people I'm concentrating on, not the composition. In the next picture the couple are kissing messily, pulling at each other's remaining garments, and in the next the woman is on her back and the man is pushing himself between her legs while other people gather round to watch, including the slave girls.

A familiar heat starts to trickle through my body. The same sensation assailed me in the convent. My eyes travel over the faces, the mouths, the hands, the naked bodies. I remember the nuns drifting round their cells, the shock of the first slap of knotted leather on their downy skin. But this is different, because the people in these pictures are acting, directed by the quiet eye behind the camera.

'Those nuns were alive and breathing, right in front of you. That's why you were turned on watching them.' His voice is soft, and caressing. I can hear it, but I'm barely listening. 'Let's see how these images affect you. They're more extreme, more adult, an even stronger story. This isn't a private dance, as you so aptly put it. The action involves more than one person.'

'No technological tricks here that I can see. Just very effective crowd control,' I sniff. 'But what's troubling you?'

I catch him glancing warily at the photographs.

'The trick is in the way this exhibition forces a response from the viewer. Just go with it. Take no notice. A goose just walked over my grave, that's all. This is about you, not me.' He holds up his finger as I try to protest. 'We're taking you way out of your comfort zone.'

He waves me on along the sequence. I decide not to query the peculiar way he slips into 'we' instead of 'I'. The scenes progress into a no-holds-barred orgy, beautifully composed and patently not simulated. This is sex by numbers. The hands, fingers, mouths, are everywhere. The women are open, the men are erect, they're all gymnastic in their positions, beautiful in their physiques. It's art, but it's unadulterated sex, too.

'It's artificial,' I remark dismissively. 'No comparison with the insouciance of my nuns.'

But the display is starting to work on me just as he said it would. The frisson of menace in the room accentuates the chill running through my own limbs. I come to a halt in front of one woman, her face contorted with abandon as she's groped and penetrated by two men. Not so artificial now. She could be one of those female saints in the Venetian convent's cloisters, in the throes of religious fervour. The same excited fervour invading me now.

'The next room will show you the punishment I was talking about. Flagellation brought graphically to life.'

I realise my hand is up as if to stop traffic. For once I want to shake Gustav off, be totally alone. I stumble to the end and turn right, and here is another, smaller room with another huge television screen dominating the far end. This is switched on and is showing an interior of some kind. Just an empty bed, in an empty room. I suppose anything passes for modern art.

The photographs continue to gallop round the room. Here is the same couple as in the last room, but the woman is on all fours now. She is wearing an ordinary-looking dress, but nothing else in the picture is remotely ordinary. For a start her hands are tied to the bed post. Her flowery dress is flipped up over her backside so that it is bare. The man is standing behind her, fully clothed, resting one hand on her rump. His other hand is holding a long thin switch. I'm willing him to get started.

'Did you ever try it? The whipping? Did you ever use that whip you nicked from the convent?'

Gustav is just behind me.

'How did you know about that?'

'I had a suspicion during your presentation. But I'm not entirely a mind-reader. We've been through your belongings at your cousin's flat and in the gallery. Yes, I know that's intrusive but I have to know everything about you, Serena. So. Did you use the whip?'

'Once or twice. But since I was called home from Venice it's never come out of the rucksack. At least, not until you rifled through my stuff.'

'You can get down off your high horse, Serena. No harm done. Now, take a look at this.'

He waves a remote control at the television screen showing the empty room. A woman, a different woman from those in the photographs, walks calmly to the bed. It is the same bed as in the photographs. It's all repetitive, a repetitive loop of perversion. I'm beginning to feel horribly claustrophobic. This gloomy house is hemming me in. The people in these photographs look hemmed in too. Cajoled. Diminished. But I am beginning to understand why they are feverishly delirious to be so.

The woman in the film takes up a pose on all fours, and spreads her knees. Then she looks directly at the camera.

Her jet-black hair is pinned up in its usual severe knot. She's wearing a high-necked white blouse and even a string of pearls round her neck. She grips the edges of the bed with long claw-like fingers, and lifts her bottom.

'My God, Gustav!' I gasp, turning to him. 'What's Crystal doing at an orgy?'

'We employed her to take part. This house, this exhibition belongs to me. I used to live here in the bad old days.' He keeps his eyes on Crystal as she starts to move. 'She used to be a model, and small-time actress. But most of all she was a muse for the guy who took these films and stills. And no, it wasn't me doing the filming. I was – otherwise engaged. See? Even though she's living another life now, in here she's immortal. Looped over and over for anyone who pays to watch. She's a permanent installation.'

'I'll never look at her the same way again.' My hands are over my mouth to smother a mad giggle. 'She was at my opening party, serving drinks, selling my work. She's still hiring herself out for this kind of thing?'

'No. She's my sales director now. Turned over a new leaf. We all have. But she'll be glad to know this film has opened your eyes.' He is very close behind me now, his fingers tangling in my hair. 'Shame, though. She would have been perfect in the role. She's so nearly nailed the Mother Superior vibe, wouldn't you agree?'

I giggle again. 'I could have lent her my whip.'

'You're getting it, my little ankle biter.' His hands are on my shoulders now, massaging them slightly. 'But I'd rather see *you* wielding the whip. No, don't deny it. I'm just drawing all the venom to the surface. Admit it. You skulked about in that convent because you wanted to get caught.'

'I told you, I was locked in.' My voice squeaks with embarrassment. He has me round the throat now.

'You wanted the sisters to catch you and drag you down

to the chapel to do penance in front of the entire congregation.'

I move away, afraid he'll discover how wet I'm getting. All fight drains out of me. I remember the sensations flowing like warm water as I hid in the shadows watching Sister Perpetua.

'All these sticky, wicked layers. So rewarding peeling them away.' He keeps his thoughtful distance. 'So you're ready to see Crystal's punishment?'

The answering jolt and thrill on my own skin is the same reaction as when I watched the nun's whip first biting into her soft white flesh.

'The further I travelled, the more I witnessed, the more I wanted to join in.'

'And that's why you're not taking pictures of flowers and kittens for a living. You're a gorgeous, inquisitive woman who's been starved all her life but what you've seen through your camera lens, look what it's done. It's made you blossom. You're ready to ripen, my exotic flower.'

His face has gone pale, his eyes dark and distant as if he's peering at a mirage. Soon I'll understand, but not yet.

'Exotic flowers don't grow in rural Devon.' I try a shy smile. Take a risk. 'But maybe they can be cultivated in central London?'

'Those monsters did a number on you and I intend to repair the damage.' The cloud clears from his face. 'Let's hope this next scene will be your catharsis.'

Crystal continues looking into the camera, her face white as a mask, her eyes black holes. Only her red mouth, with its strange little smile and snaky tongue, shows any kind of animation.

Someone else steps into the shot. Dressed entirely in black leather, including a cat mask. Dominatrix gear, black leather, studded collar. The figure is holding a thin black switch, like a riding crop, with a bunch of fine leather tassels dangling off it. I glance at Gustav. He is watching the video intently.

The rooms seems to shrink, the pictures and walls and ceiling sliding inwards as if to crush me, then spinning nauseatingly. I sway, nothing to grab on to. This isn't art as I think of art. This isn't soft-focus nuns in Gothic candlelit shadows, about to purge their sins on their own virginal skin. This is starkly lit domination.

Gustav wavers in front of me like a flame. He even splits in two for a second. I am afraid I'm going to faint. What's the matter with me? It's only a dirty home video masquerading as indie film. A bit of kinky behaviour, fetish dress, all up there on screen. Readers' wives, but more skilfully stage-managed, more convincingly acted. If I look closely, surely I'll see the joins.

Crystal spreads her arms and legs in a star shape. Sweat trickles down my back, in my hair, my armpits as I regain some focus. The black-clad creature plants its high-heeled boots on either side of Crystal and yanks her milkmaid skirt up to reveal her white bottom. Crystal is wearing no knickers, just black stockings. Her bottom and thighs glow in the dead lighting of the interior. Then the creature lifts its arm. No-one is uttering a sound. All I can hear is the sliced air as the leather-clad creature brandishes the whip so clearly that it practically lifts the hair from my forehead in its breeze.

There's a swish like a wasp's wing as the whip is brought down on Crystal's buttocks. The stroke rings out like a cruel gunshot and I run my fingers quickly over my own bottom. Her skin quivers under the blow as I gasp out loud. She is so skinny. She jerks involuntarily, showing a quick flash between her thighs, and I see her fingers clawing at the bed cover. My own fingers dig into my backside, try to quell the dirty excitement growing in me. But still she makes no sound.

'Don't you move, Crystal, or you get double.'

The dominatrix's voice hisses out of the film. Fills the room like the humming of a bees' nest. She leans down and strokes Crystal's butt cheek, where a livid red stripe has come up. I stroke my own bottom to soothe the imaginary pain. And still Crystal lies there as if she is in a trance. Remember, she's an actress. Or she's been doped. The dominatrix is stroking her on the one hand as if she is preparing a rare steak, but on the other she steps back and swipes the whip down a second time, squarely on the second cheek.

I squeeze my legs together as the dampness pricks up in excited response. On the screen Crystal flicks her head as her bottom jerks up again involuntarily. Again the frail flesh quivers under the blow, and again there is a tantalising glimpse of her sex as she bounces off the floor. My own is tightening frantically in response.

'Remind you of anything, Serena? These sounds? That white skin, scored across with punishment?'

As a third stroke comes down and the thwack resounds round the panelled room we're standing in, I could swear that instead of moaning or cringing in fear, Crystal actually lifts her bottom, as if inviting the stroke instead of recoiling from it. She moves slightly from side to side, kneeling up to lift her bottom higher into the air. As I glimpse the softness tucked between her legs, the quick slash of bright red as she wiggles her bottom, a spike of desire flashes through me and at last I recognise it for what it is. Clear, urgent, sexual desire.

I was aroused when I watched little Perpetua and her secret sisters. But this is like a hand reaching inside and physically shaking me. It's not Crystal I want, surely?

The dominatrix creature kicks at the back of Crystal's knees, so that she rises higher, thrusting her bottom, decorated now with three pink stripes, into the air. The dominatrix places the whip on the crack and for a moment I freeze. Is she going to shove the whip in there? Hasn't Crystal suffered enough? My own body clenches tighter still. I'm so close to feeling it for myself. I wriggle restlessly as the whip strokes Crystal's bottom almost tenderly. Yes, it would be tender as well as cruel. Sweet, as well as sour.

I wish I could see the dominatrix's face. Who is she?

The whip is in the air, swiping down once more onto the butt cheek. I sway along with the teasing of the whip. Four pink stripes on her bottom and now an audible groan escapes from Crystal, but she's unashamedly showing her pleasure now. She's fidgeting from side to side like a mare scratching herself on a fence. The blows have raised her beaten flesh into weals. One hand has come up brazenly between her legs and she is touching herself, just as I'm desperate to do, she's moaning as she waits for her mistress to strike her, her fingers sweeping up and down, her face tilted heavenwards as she sways, one long white finger going up inside, pushing in.

I can feel heat on my bottom, the thrust of the finger's invasion. It will hurt, I know it, but although I can feel the fear I want to be in the film now. I want to be in there with these people, I want to push Crystal aside, take my place in front of the mistress, feel those blows on my own soft skin and the heat and pain they will conjure up.

Her black eyes blaze and I read clearly what's going on behind them. She isn't cowed, or humiliated. Or if she is, she's loving the belittling. Being paid to reveal it. She's euphoric. She's loving those red, sore stripes on her. This is more than a job to her. They're battle scars. They've brought her to life.

My mouth drops open as she tips her head back, her eyes and mouth alight with pleasure. She lifts her bottom for more. I push mine back against the wall. It's like a foreign language being translated for me. It's all so clear now. It's not Crystal I want. I want to be playing her part.

Suddenly the picture freezes.

'Have you seen enough, Serena?'

For the first time since we met I've forgotten about Gustav. I can see my face superimposed onto Crystal's. She was tense and stiff when she lay down on that bed. Now she's liberated. Crazy Crystal. Surrendered Serena. No illusion. That was real. Every blow, every flinch and tremor felt real to me.

I press my hand against the frozen image on the screen. 'I could quite happily go right back to the beginning and see it all again. But then I might never leave! So no. Let's get out of here.'

I saw the nuns doing it, and now I've seen Crystal submitting to it. I won't be still, won't rest, until I've tried this for myself, and surely that's why Gustav brought me here today? To show me these films, these scenes, these people writhing with pleasure. To tease me, then invite me to try it. My own photographs, the little nuns hanging brazenly in the other gallery, have told him I have this twisted urge to watch and then to be tried and punished. He understood it before I'd even admitted it to myself. But I'm ready for it now. In fact, I'm practically ready to come. Euphoria rushes through me, heats my body, lifts my feet. I want to run as fast as I can. Jump as high as I can. I have to get him home, persuade him to do all those things to me.

Gustav has done what he set out to do. He's shown me what I need, what I want him to do next.

I jerk the silver chain tight, lead him quickly through the dark, panelled rooms. The twisting, groaning, gyrating bodies will continue silently writhing inside their fantasies, imprisoned joyously inside those frames forever.

At the front door Gustav lets me push past him.

'I don't want to talk. I just want to get home before these images fade. They've done something to me, Gustav.' I jump down the entire flight of steps, tipping my head back to the twilight. 'I've got this terrible itch I need to scratch. You can help me. That's why you brought me here, isn't it?'

He plays the silver chain through his hands like a fishing line, then gives it a playful tug. I jerk exaggeratedly back towards him, making jazz hands like a puppet. I'm grinning like the Cheshire Cat. I can't identify this new exuberance. I'm fizzing with a deep, dark energy.

His eyes burn with the tenderness I saw at the private view the other night. I'm the cat on a hot tin roof. As he starts to descend the steps it's my turn to yank on the chain.

'Remember your place, young lady.'

Still grinning at me he dances me right up to him with the chain. Our faces are so close. His mouth opening to speak, to smile, perchance to kiss?

His big silver car purrs alongside and he opens the door for me.

I climb into the back seat first, and then tug the silver chain again, urging Gustav to hurry up as he gets into the car after me.

'Take me home, Mr Levi.'

'Dickson? This girl has something pressing on her mind,' Gustav murmurs, rapping smartly on the window then sitting back, dangling the chain loosely in his lap. I challenge myself not to touch him, the whole way home.

'Yeah, Dickson?' I call out. 'Step on it.'

TEN

We're back in the tall dark house in the quiet garden square. Dickson has brought my bags in, taken them upstairs. Lit candles and fires around the house. Set out a meal of rare steak and roasted vegetables dripping in olive oil, and tells us chocolate pudding is in the fridge. Two bottles of red wine are breathing on the white counter in the kitchen. And then he's gone, and we're alone.

I'm wearing another dress that magically was waiting for me on the bed in the attic room. A vibrant purple number, velvet and medieval, very low at the sequinned bodice and cut on the bias so that it flares out from my hips and swishes round my bare ankles when I come back downstairs. I don't put on any underwear. Whatever I put on will be wet in no time. I'm still on fire and I've got to get this over with.

I eat the dinner as quickly as I can. We race at it like a couple of cavemen, tearing at the meat, tossing the vegetables into our mouths, wiping oil off our chins with the white napkins but then glugging red wine down our necks as if we're in the desert.

'Let the pudding wait,' I say, getting up from the table and leading him, with the silver chain, into the drawing room.

'I know why you showed me that collection today, Gustav. I know why you showed me Crystal being slapped by that woman. I didn't get it at first. But it turned me on, just as you predicted. And now I want you to do that to me.'

He stands in the doorway as I pace agitatedly around the room. He's brushed his black hair back and has changed into a soft cashmere sweater in the same deep purple as my dress with a white T-shirt underneath. His black jeans accentuate his long legs and the hips I long to feel grinding against me.

The silver chain tinkles and glints in the space between us.

'Part of the game is that you seek punishment. What have you done wrong, do you think?'

'You want me to play? OK. Bless me, Father, for I have sinned.' I squirm, clasping my hands together as if I'm in confession, winding the silver chain round my fingers, tight, so it bites white into my skin. 'I was brought up in a house full of hatred. All my life I was told I was a nasty little runt. That I was worthless, good for nothing. Even the woman who gave birth to me tossed me away in a plastic bag. Drip, drip, drip into my ear, day after day, year after year. But my way of coping was to stop listening or even speaking. I became a difficult child, a surly teenager.'

'Doesn't really count as a sin.' He steps closer, winding in the silver chain. His mouth has become dark with stubble. It would rub if he kissed me. 'More like a virtue. You were strong, Serena. You rose above those pathetic bullies. Why should I spank you?'

'I still need to do penance.' I pace from side to side, warm and fuzzy from the food and the wine, but still revved up from what he showed me earlier. 'It's the only way to delete them. Crystal was purged of her problems by that dominatrix woman.'

'You are a quick learner,' he interrupts quickly. 'Quick, swift punishment. So much more straightforward than years of wrestling with psychological warfare.'

'So do it, before I change my mind.' I shake him.

'You won't change your mind.' His fingers are digging into my arms. He's handling me so much rougher now. His piratical air is just the way I like him. 'I knew what you needed as soon as I saw the photographs in your portfolio. The nuns, the whipping. You confirmed it with your rapturous talk at the private view. I know what I'm doing, Serena. I can banish your demons once and for all.'

'But will it become an obsession?'

'For me?' He shudders. 'My demons are still out to get me.'

'I meant for me. Will I become addicted to it? Will I be like Crystal and beg to be whipped every time I feel I'm losing it?'

'If you do, it won't matter. You'll be with me, and I'll decide when and if you need punishing. Special perversions can always be saved for special occasions.' He picks a pin out of my hair so that tendrils fall around my face, tickling me. His eyes are dancing tonight. 'Crystal controlled her obsessions in the end and so can you.'

I sway slightly with the lightness of his touch. He curls the tendril round his finger. 'First, let's go over what those bastards did to you.'

'Do we have to?'

'Yes. It will heal you in the end.' He taps the end of my nose. 'I told you. We're exorcising your demons.'

'They made me feel like a freak, Gustav. Always telling me I was an outsider. The unwelcome little cuckoo. That I would never belong anywhere.'

'I thought you said they found you on a doorstep, and adopted you?'

'Yes, and they regretted it the moment I opened my mouth and started to answer back.'

His black hair falls over his eyebrows and this time I brush it away. 'But foundlings are supposed to be magical beings, aren't they? Like fairies.'

The silver chain is twined round both of us now. Joining our hands like a rosary.

'Goblins, more like.' I shrug. 'You'll understand more if you read my diaries. I left them in the gallery.'

'I know. Dickson found them. I warned you how intrusive I could be.'

'I should never have brought them back to London.'

I start smacking at my forehead.

'You spoiling for a fight, Folkes? Because that's exactly what you're going to get!'

He holds my hands tight to calm me.

'Let go of me! I need to punch something! I've been waiting all my life to let rip. I never could when they were alive, otherwise I'd have killed them both!'

'Then you'd be my murderess, as well as my temptress.'

He catches me off guard with his laughter.

'OK!' I shout. 'So how about I punch you instead!'

He ties my hands together with the silver chain.

'*As flies to wanton boys are we to the gods.*'

'What?'

'King Lear. *They kill us for their sport.*' He tests the tightness of the chain. 'It won't be me who gets hurt, Serena. But if pain is what you want, pain is what you'll get. I've seen this coming a long way off, and believe me, I can't wait to get my hands on you. It's going to do me the power of good, too.'

He ties my bound wrists to the legs of the oversized sofa by the fire so that I am forced to sprawl on my front, my face buried in the cushions.

'I don't see how tying me up and spanking me can help *you*.' I wriggle and kick furiously. 'This isn't how it's supposed to work! This isn't what I meant!'

'This is exactly how it goes.'

'No! I feel stupid. I've changed my mind!' I scream, kicking my legs out to try to catch him. 'I just need you to give it to me straight, Gustav. Why can't you just fuck me, like any normal man!'

The obscenity sears the air. There's an electrified pause.

'Believe me, Serena Folkes, I would give my right arm to do that right now. Hard, and fast, preferably, and rough as hell, to shut you up. I've wanted nothing else since I first set eyes on you. But there's method in my madness.'

'Shakespeare again!' My voice is muffled.

'I don't go about things like a normal man. In any case if I gave my right arm I wouldn't be able to do this.'

He tests the strength of the silver chain.

'Untie me and give it to me!'

He really laughs out loud this time. He leans on my legs to quell the kicking. He's heavy. I can't move.

'Such an unquenchable spirit despite everything they laid on you.'

'I don't want analysing, doctor. I just want some good hard loving!'

'As if you knew what that was.' His hands just press down harder. 'All this wild beauty. They were jealous of it. That was their problem. Or the woman was jealous. And they must have been frightened, too, because no-one knew where your beauty and spirit came from.'

'No more psycho-babble!'

He weighs me down with one hand on my velvet bottom. And then he slides his other hand under me, walks it down my stomach, lower, until his fingers brush through the strip of hair and feel the wetness of me. I stop struggling, as he knew I would. My thighs part eagerly for him, even though my legs are shaking. I tilt myself into his familiar fingers. They pause, then trace the folds, the soft opening.

'See how creamy you are? This always works to shut them up.' His breath so warm on my neck, my hair. 'You're such a horny little devil, aren't you?'

I groan hopelessly. 'Those bloody diaries. I don't want to remember that horrible house on the cliffs, or the girl who lives there.'

His response is to jerk on the silver chain again. 'We'll burn them on a massive bonfire.'

I am quieter now. His words are like gentle fingers, stroking my hair, my forehead. I want to curl into a ball. But I can't, because my hands are tied and he's leaning on my legs. I press my face further into the cushions.

'Go ahead, but if you want to know all about me you'll have to read them.'

We are both very still for a moment. There is music playing somewhere, violins, a melancholy cello. The wind is getting up again outside in the garden. Otherwise all I can hear is the snap of a stick in the fire, and the heavy ticking of the grandfather clock out in the hall.

'You'd give me permission to do that? That's very intimate.'

'Look at me. I'm lying here on your sofa. I'm tied up with a silver chain, and I'm not wearing any knickers. I've sucked you off, and I've asked you to have your way with me, and you've refused. Doesn't get much more intimate than that. Read them. I don't care. I told you, I'm not that girl any more.'

'You can't kill her off completely. She's here, with me.' His fingers comb through my hair, undo another pin.

His words are so strong, so comforting. I twist round to look at him. He's let go of my legs, and is sitting with his hands dangling between his knees, his handsome profile highlighted by the fire. I want him to put his hands on me again.

He taps his hands together. 'Time to put you in front of the camera instead of hiding behind it.'

'You're going to film me? What if I say no?'

He laughs, and starts to push my skirt up. 'Says the uppity little voyeur herself! You really are my girl. The gift that keeps on giving.' He leans over me and blows his laughter into my hair. 'You won't even know it's rolling. Are you ready?'

A drape of white cloth falls over my face and he ties it over my eyes. Then I hear the little pop of what must be stoppers coming out of little ointment bottles. Here come his hands again, pushing my dress up and massaging sweet smelling oils into my legs. He's being gentle, but the lotion is setting my skin on fire. I can almost hear it crackle like burning paper, and when he comes up to the space between my legs I screech out loud.

'What the hell? Is there chilli in there or something?'

'No more talking for now.'

He pushes my legs open and goes on massaging the cream right in, up and in. Every sense is magnified. There's the warmth from the fire down one side of me, the coolness of the room on the other, the heat and scent of these creams soaking into me and wafting perfume through the air.

I can see nothing but silky darkness. My heart beats faster. I'm not afraid. I'm powerless, and free at the same time. There's no more to be done, and it's wonderful. I am blindfolded and tied. I can do nothing to change what's happening.

I know he'd let me go if I screamed loudly enough. Or at least, I think he would. But I'm still totally at his mercy. And with the blindfold, everything else that has troubled me, my trip to Devon yesterday, reading my old diary, all the misery flooding back, the agitation I felt looking at those photographs, that film of Crystal, the euphoria when I realised that's what I needed, the secrets he has yet to tell me, it's all blotted out as well.

If I can't see you, you can't see me.

Hiding in the attic, under the stairs, the places they thought they'd looked, the stamping feet, the shouting voices, the broken toys. I was very good at hiding.

Gustav is silent. His long fingers swipe and wipe, the cream covering every fold and crevice until the whole area is alive and throbbing, burning bizarrely. I feel stoned. My head feels as if it's floating away like a balloon. Far removed from the rest of me, that's for sure, because all other senses are zoning in on that one secret part of me, sizzling like bacon, that bright beacon flashing a message. I'm here. I'll open up for you, Gustav, when you're ready. When you want me so much you won't be able to hold back.

He's stroking my bottom now. Slowly, resting his hand there, as if measuring his own hand print. And then with no other prelude, no warning, he slaps me there.

I can't see anything but before I've had time to compute what's happening I hear the rush of air as his arm goes up. I stutter with confusion but he slaps me hard on the butt, thrusting me forwards with the force of it, making me yelp. The yelp obviously fires him up, because he slaps again, on the same spot, and this time I can hear the sound of his palm landing on my flesh, the sizzling slap, and with it the stinging heat from the blow, and it sends a shaft of twisted pleasure through me.

That sharp whisk of air, then a handprint of fire on my buttock as it lands. The stinging goes deeper this time, radiates away from the original soreness, burns inside me, makes me twitch, I can even feel myself closing up tightly. The tentacles of pain touch me everywhere. I twitch and groan, unable to control my own reflexes now.

This is like someone else being punished in a muffled dream. So different from whipping myself feebly in that cheap hotel bedroom behind the Piazza San Marco.

'I've got your whip right here, Serena. Ready?'

'Yes! Give it to me!' I struggle at the chain round my wrists, but that just makes it tighter, the silver chain biting into my wrists.

I hear him testing the whip on the palm of his hand for a moment. Then it comes down on my other buttock and the pain daggers straight up me.

This could be on camera. Who knows, who cares? Everyone can see me lifting myself off the cushions and flopping down again. He laughs softly, whips me again, that quick, vicious whip lashing down again and again. I'm floating somewhere near the ceiling observing what is happening below. I can see myself stretched out like a sacrifice at the mercy of this tall, strong man who could easily finish me off if he wanted to.

But he's not killing me. He's curing me.

I've heard of people who like to be whipped. Men, mostly. Judges, politicians. Rumour had it that my tutor liked it. Until I saw those nuns doing it, before I tried it on myself, I had no idea what pleasure could there be in submitting to horrible pain. Why would you beg to be punished for some made-up crime, just to feed a fantasy? What pleasure could there possibly be in wanting to be hurt so much it would make you come? What was so sexy about smacking and being subjected to that kind of humiliation?

Well, trying it myself was nothing on this. The answer is blowing in the wind. Being handed to me by Gustav Levi. I am smarting with the lashes, my skin no doubt striped with thin red welts. I strain at the silver chain binding my wrists, trying to understand this degrading, nasty thrill releasing me from all that stress, the dark memories, trying to understand why the helplessness is turning me on so much, poking little fiery sparks of pleasure right up there between my legs.

Wishing it had always been this simple.

Another slap, stinging and hot on my rump, a bite sizzling

through me. And the strange thing is that I was waiting for it, and I welcome it. I want him to do it again, I want the shock of the slap itself, and the lovely after-glow. The turn on isn't just the heat and the pain, it's the anticipation, how it's going to feel, not quite knowing, here it is, the cold on my skin, the brand of five fingers, of the whip, then the hot smack, the blood and heat zoning in on one place to try to cure it.

And every time the blow falls, another piece of the ugly jigsaw smashes.

He is silent behind me, above me. He smacks the other cheek hard and this time the heat is prodding and probing everywhere, fingers of fire and pleasure feeling me all over, inside and out.

Once this is over I want him. Around me. Inside me. It's not the spanking I'm addicted to. It's him.

The rain is battering at the windows again. I want thunder and lightning. The elemental terror to add to the thrill of what he's doing to me, marking my white skin with his red marks of pain. His creature, branded.

There's something else above me now, not a hand, something flat and round comes slapping down on my bottom. I let out a kind of gabble of laughter. My confused mind tries to identify the instrument. A wooden spoon. Surely he's not hitting me with something he was using to stir the peppercorn sauce earlier?

I lift my bottom up in the air like Crystal did in the film. The wooden spoon swipes down again, landing accurately, on a different, pain-free spot each time.

Now I hear it clattering to the floor. Something flicks in the air with a whispering crack, like he's a circus master. A tie, or a rope. I cower, trembling with cold and anticipation. Every inch of my bottom is sore and tender. He brushes whatever it is, a ribbon, over the backs of my knees and down to the soles of my feet while I wait for the first hit. It flicks across my buttocks, comes down once, twice. It doesn't hurt any more. It sets me alight. There are spasms inside me now, deep between my legs, hungry spasms of pleasure and wanting.

He knows it. Because now he's pushing my legs open again, and bringing something up between them, right into me. It's a ribbon, and he starts to rub it on me. The friction is unbearable, rough and sweet at the same time, like rubbing flint on flint to make a fire. I bury my head in the cushion, taking in short gasps of breath, loving the lightheadedness. It's like hyperventilating a free, natural high. My already acute senses make everything bright and exaggerated, like a cartoon.

'My little dish of delight just lying there,' Gustav growls to himself. At last. A really bestial timbre in his voice. 'So why am I always denying myself?'

I wriggle eagerly. I want him so badly it hurts. The movement sucks the ribbon right up into me, and it rubs against the little bud that's jutting out, burning and begging for attention. He sees me writhe and makes the ribbon taut, rubbing it cruelly, harder and faster against my clitoris, and that's it. A couple of swipes and I explode, instantly, bucking crazily against the ribbon as all that pent-up frustration and anger pumps out. I rub against the ribbon, the cushions, the sofa, my bottom jerking frantically. I'm aware of how it will look on film, but I don't care.

I lie there limply until my senses reassemble and I start to feel acutely self-conscious. The dying spasms mock me, because they won't go away. I'm restless, wracked with brazen sexual desire. Oh, God, I want him in me, now.

Where is he?

Suddenly the storm is back, doing its best to shake the house down, break the windows, tear off all the tiles. Breaking the spell. Gustav is pulling off my blindfold now. He unties the silver chain, sits me up. He even rearranges the long velvet skirt over my knees.

He thumps down beside me. The flames reflected in his lustful eyes leap up in their candelabra and candle sticks, sending shadows careering around the room. His handsome face is shaded into canine planes and angles. This could be it.

The Adam's apple juts in his throat as he swallows. He leans closer, his eyes half closed, his face right up to my cheek. His nostrils flare as he breathes in the scent and sweat on my skin. His fingers come up and frame my jaw, and then he turns my head sideways, stretching my throat. His breath rasps hot, burning hot, on my neck. My pulse beats frantically as if hammering to get out. His mouth slides down under my ear, his lips dry at first, then getting wet as they linger over the spot. The tip of his tongue touches my pulse, like a little arrow.

He's gripping my arms unnecessarily hard. Can't he see that I'm not going anywhere? I'm his. I stretch out my hand and slide it up his thigh. Something tells me to move slowly and quietly. We are both panting hard, our breath mingling. I turn to him, push my hands onto the burgeoning hardness.

'I'm here for the taking, Gustav. All clean and new. Don't you want me?'

'Right now?' His teeth graze on my neck, his mouth moving against my skin. 'More than I've ever wanted anyone.'

'We fit so well together.' I press harder, to show him I want him. 'We're all alone. You're the boss. What's stopping us?'

The final crash of thunder is so timely it's as if someone is sitting out on the terrace with a bank of sound effects. But it's broken the spell. I shouldn't have spoken. I should have just touched him, made him putty in my hands. Because my words have snapped him out of his reverie. He picks up the little whip and flings it across the room.

'*She* is. Rearing her ugly head, just when I thought I'd banished her for good.'

The whip skitters against a glass lamp beside the fire and we both watch as the lamp wavers, totters, and then smashes onto the floor.

The silence is thick and suffocating. I daren't break it.

'I thought you and I were the same.' He rubs his black hair so that it stands up in furious spikes. 'Both been down a dark path. But I got it wrong. You lived your life as best you could, a lovely, healthy, feminine child who couldn't extricate herself. But I'm an adult who should have known better. I should have got out before it damaged everyone.'

'Who is this "she" who's done a number on you, Gustav?' I try to unfold his fingers from the fist. 'Is it your ex-wife that's freaked you out?'

'Margot is her name.' He jumps up and goes to pour himself more wine, kicking out at the little whip. 'Still contaminating everything.'

'Forget her. I'm here. You've saved me, Gustav. Histrionic, but true.' I stretch my arms out. That woman's name has scared me stiff. I have to reach him before he slips through my fingers. 'Let me count the ways. The exhibition. This house. What you've shown me. What you did to me just then. It's saved me from all the shit. So let me help you.'

'I can't let you. Watching you submitting to whatever I dealt you just then, the catharsis, the release, that was thrilling. But it's had the opposite effect on me.'

He can't even look at me directly now. Through the mirror he stares at me as if from the bottom of a deep well.

'It's my job to make you feel better.' I gulp back the tears. 'Let me please you in return.'

The silver chain hangs loosely between us. He draws it taut, like a surgical scar.

'I can't let you near me with that thing.' He tips more red wine from a crystal decanter into two big goblets. The muscle is working furiously in his jaw.

'Not the whip, then. How about simple tender loving care?' I shrink back into the sofa. 'Or perhaps you just want to be left alone?'

He shakes his head, handing a full goblet to me. He doesn't come closer. I take a sip, spilling a little on my leg. She's in here, alright. She's a shadow sliding in between us. The rain spits against the window, filling the long, heavy silence.

Margot is her name.

'If you want to help me, there is another way,' he bursts out, putting the glass down suddenly. 'Come to Switzerland. We'll get out of the city, breathe in some Alpine air.' His eyes flash back to life. 'I haven't been back there for more than five years. It's time to clear the house. Tackle those lingering ghosts. You can be my mascot.'

'There are ghosts in Switzerland? What about right here in Mayfair?' I glance about at the flickering candles, the huge yawning fireplace. The man standing there, tapping his foot as he waits for my answer.

'She's not here, Serena. If this house is haunted, they're not my ghosts. The day I met you in the square was the day I completed the purchase.'

'But you look as if you've lived here for centuries!' I think of the mournful portrait hanging on the landing. The glittering, fully stocked kitchen. The old furniture so at home in my bedroom.

'Like a wizened old vampire, you mean?' The etched lines in his face disappear as he smiles slightly. I can do that to him. I know it now. I can make him smile whenever I like. 'Nope. The new owner.'

'We are the same, you see?' I raise my glass to him before draining it. 'Both wiping our slates clean.'

'This house is my clean slate, yes. But there's unfinished business in Lugano.' He takes my empty glass from me. 'Let's go wrap it up.'

'So I'm a removal man now, am I?' I'm deliciously woozy now. 'Just one thing. If we go ghost-busting in Switzerland, what happens about my exhibition?'

'It'll take care of itself for the time being. Crystal can oversee any sales. And I've arranged some media interviews for you for when we get back. They're clamouring for you, girl. So what do you say? Will you come on another voyage of discovery with me?'

He runs his finger up and down the goblet, waiting anxiously for my reply.

'The two of us in your luxury retreat? Fur rugs and deep dark forests! What's not to like?' I stand up stiffly. I make sure he gets a good eyeful of my burning, red striped butt before the dress drops softly over my legs. 'Maybe we can get in some skiing while we're there if I can bend ze knees?'

'There's no snow so close to the lake,' he replies sharply, kicking at a log coming loose from the fire.

'Listen, Levi, whatever's eating you is not my fault!' I step over and lift my hand as if to strike him. He catches it in midair. 'Perhaps you should go to Lake Lugano on your own.'

'You're my lucky charm, Serena. You're coming with me.' We really are like weighing scales. The crosser I get, the calmer he becomes. He frames my face with his warm hand, tipping it up to his. 'Anyhow, Dickson has your passport. He'll fly us over tomorrow and open up the house. If that suits?'

'Your wish is my command. But there's just one problem.' I pick at the silver chain. 'The sleeping arrangements. There's this "he" who fancies himself as a shrink. I thought he was a Halloween spectre when I first saw him, but it turns out he's real.'

He smiles slowly, holding my hands now. 'Go on.'

'He's my Pygmalion.' I go on, keeping my voice low. 'He's very rich and he's sculpted me into a successful snapper. He's a bit mean and moody sometimes but he has these amazing fingers and dark flashing eyes, and this annoyingly mesmeric mouth.'

He puts his finger on mine to hush me and I nibble it in between my lips. Gustav pulls me closer as I suck the tip. Further down his sexy hardness is pressing urgently through his jeans, nudging at my dress. I hook my thigh around his for a moment. That tango stance again. I push his finger out of my mouth.

'He's touched me intimately, you know, with this very finger. But you see, doctor, that's where I get really confused. Offended, actually. Because he *still* doesn't fancy me enough to go any further. He gets hard. I've felt his erection. I've even sucked him off. But still he rejects me.'

He smiles quietly and unclips the chain.

'Oh, Miss Folkes. I told you in the beginning. *Poco a poco*.'

'There's nothing little about you, Levi. Oh, just loosen up and come to bed with me!'

'Patience, princess.' He marches me to the door. 'This is the famine before the feast.'

'You can trust me.' I wind my fingers through my hair flirtatiously. 'I'll be gentle with you!'

He laughs softly and takes something from behind the big vase full of winter roses on the mantelpiece. It's a mini disc from a camcorder. He waggles it in his fingers. 'I've seen what you're like when you're on fire, my lovely. You're every boy's wet dream.'

'Give that to me!' I yelp, failing dismally to snatch it as he dangles it high above my head.

'Not on your life. This is another bargaining tool. Or maybe I'll save it for private screenings. You see? It's not you, as they say. It's me. I can't be trusted.'

I stomp sulkily into the hall, praying he'll follow me and reassure me. But he doesn't.

'I'll get that film off you.' I turn at the bottom of the stairs, sweep into a sarcastic curtsey like the principal ballerina before the curtain falls over *Swan Lake*. 'And I'll have you in my bed before the week is out, Signor Levi, by fair means or foul. Just you wait.'

ELEVEN

The car leaves the quaint squares and pretty lanes lined with chic shops where elegant inhabitants glide about their well-heeled business. I peer through the rear window like a condemned woman as we head inland. Lugano looks right up my street. I could love a town that calls itself a city, one with palm trees, Riva boats and jazz festivals in the summer, and skiing, cable cars and lakeside restaurants in the winter.

'The guide book says *dolce far niente* is one of the mottos of Lugano, did you know? All of Italy thinks like that, actually. I think it means "so sweet doing nothing".'

'For lucky buggers on holiday, maybe. And technically we're still in Switzerland.'

The mountain-fringed lake drops away behind us, glittering with wintry sunlight.

'Why can't we linger a little longer? What's the rush?'

'Boss said to bring you straight here, Miss.'

The car labours doggedly up a narrow road squeezed on either side by colossal boulders. It turns under a high brick archway smothered in ivy, bumps over the cobblestones into the middle of a deserted yard, and stops. For a moment there is no sound but the ticking of the engine and the sharp whistle of the wind.

Dickson shifts round heavily, his broad shoulders and back making the leather seats creak.

'The chalet's still locked up and it'll be freezing up there. I have to get into town for some supplies.'

'Charming welcome. If I'd known nobody would be here I'd have asked you to leave me in Lugano to have a look around. At least I'd have some other human beings for company!'

I glare past the empty yard to the backdrop of navy blue mountains. I'd feel differently if Gustav was here with me. The city looks enchanting enough but those projections of rock dragging their bony knuckles against the heavy sky seem menacing rather than majestic. They promise avalanches to be buried in and ravines down which to plummet. Grist to the mill of experienced, show-off skiers like Gustav no doubt, but alien to dreamers like me growing up in the soft rain and undulating fields of Devon.

Sure, the cliffs beneath my childhood home had their own sea-battered grandeur. They had an uncanny siren call, too, luring hikers to venture too close to the edge. Polly and I used to dare each other to take that extra step across the smooth, layered outcrops overhanging the waves. We'd stub our fags out on the grey rocks and decide that mica schist, the name of their geological formation, would be a grand name for the girl band we were going to form.

'Well, I've delivered you safely. Now I need to get on.' Dickson's gruff voice butts in.

'Just wait, Dickson. It's bad enough that we didn't travel together, but why hasn't Mr Levi bothered to meet me?'

'Oh, he took the funicular straight up to San Salvatore peak soon as we arrived at Agno airport last night. He'll be on one of his climbing escapades I daresay, and checking out the weather. Typical of him to do in winter what everyone else does in the summer.' Dickson tugs back his driving glove to look at his watch. 'Not that he's been anywhere near here since – not for at least five years.'

He gets out of the car and opens my door. I step out and am nearly knocked backwards by the bitter cold.

Thank God Crystal kitted me out with all these layers of custom-built thermals, topped off with this *Dr Zhivago*-style hat and cosy quilted ski jacket. Before Gustav fled to City airport like a thief in the night, he obviously instructed her to supply me with everything I'd need to follow him to the Alps. He knows full well that all I have to my name are my caramel tweed jacket, scarves, some jeans, jumpers and T-shirts, and my beret. Oh, and all the clothes I purloined from Polly's flat, which are designed for fashionistas to trip between taxi and catwalk rather than piste and peak.

I was so sleepy when Crystal tip-tapped into my bedroom this morning and switched on all the lights that she ended up attending to my toilette as well, dressing me like a lady's maid.

'Spit, spot, Serena, you have a plane to catch.'

Her back was to the window and with the cold white light behind her I couldn't see her face clearly. Only the outline of her ramrod stiff back and today's beehive hairdo. As she wasn't moving or averting her eyes, I went ahead and slipped my negligee off.

'You actually said spit, spot!' I mumbled, hunched shivering and naked on the edge of the bed.

'Mary Poppins is one of my heroines. As is Lady Macbeth.'

'That would figure. *Out, out, damned spot.* Isn't that what she said when she couldn't wash away the blood?'

'Indeed. Both sticklers for cleanliness, you see?' Crystal gave a thin smile and picked up the first item, a rather sensible pair of all-encompassing knickers, from a neatly folded pile on the chair beside her. 'Now, don't catch a chill.'

I pulled on the softly clinging pants, which felt warm rather than seductive but still sexy, like a second skin. I tried to hide my embarrassed wriggle as she watched me. Then she handed me some amazing silk leggings which I could feel heating my skin as soon as I slipped this pair of perfectly fitting white jodhpurs over the top. Crystal glided behind me to fix them round my waist, then led me to the pretty art deco dressing table by the window.

I fiddled with all the brushes and bottles. She moves as if she's on casters. She seemed to have taken root in my room like a bodyguard so I decided to poke her for some information.

'Crystal, we don't really know each other, and you probably won't tell me, but there are so many questions buzzing around my head about Gustav.'

'Only one thing you need to know,' she trilled, picking up a huge silver-backed hairbrush. 'And that's that you should never play games with him. Either you're with him, or you're against him. He sees everything in black and white. No grey areas. Would you like me to brush your hair?'

I started. 'How did you know I love having my hair brushed?'

She lifted the brush and the sudden thought of her whacking it down on someone's bottom made me bite my lip, hard, to stifle a giggle.

'I didn't know,' she replied calmly. 'You might have thought it an impertinent suggestion.'

'Not impertinent. Friendly.' I settled back in the chair so that my head was nearly resting on her stomach. 'Go ahead, Crys.'

'Crystal.'

'I crave it, actually. More than that. It turns me on if, well, if a man is touching my hair. Gustav sussed that out from the start. I was starved of affection as a child, you see.' I glanced up at her in the mirror. Her beady gaze was laser-steady. 'No-one ever washed it, brushed it, plaited it, did anything nice to it when I was little. They hated my hair.'

'They?'

'The people I lived with.'

'Your parents, you mean? You can't say their names?'

I flattened my hands over my ears.

She tapped me with the hairbrush. 'You can't say Father, or Mother? Mum, or Dad?'

'Crystal, they weren't even my real parents. I was the wrong baby. My hair was the wrong colour. It symbolised everything that was wrong in that house.'

She made a snake's hissing sound with her teeth and laid one hand on my head as if I might erupt. 'They must have been blind. It's beautiful, like a waterfall of liquid amber.'

I shook my head violently, like a child refusing to eat carrots. 'They hated it. Their favourite punishment was pulling it or hacking it off.'

'Where were Social Services when all this was going down? Sounds to me like you were being badly neglected.'

'I was good at hiding things, that's all. But enough about me. Gustav is good at concealing things, too. His real feelings, anyway.'

'He has good reason to barricade himself in.'

I tried to relax, let my head move lazily against her as she started to brush.

'But that leaves the rest of us guessing. So if anyone's playing games it's him! Look. I know he likes me. I've made it as clear as I dare that I'm into him. I mean, how could I not be? It's not just the money, and the chances he's giving me, but he's got the kind of eyes you want to drown in, if only he'll let you dive in. Metallic one minute, melting the next. And his mouth. What would it be like at kissing, I wonder? You can never tell if he's going to swear or smile. What's with the grim, distant mystique?'

'He's deep, not distant,' Crystal murmured. 'But attractive, sure. If vampirical millionaires are your thing!'

I giggled. 'So what's the craic? We're lone souls who collided. And yet . . .' I made a throat-cutting gesture '. . . he's let me go so far with him and then – zip. Nada.'

'You didn't collide. He picked you.'

'That's what he says.' I bent my fingers into hooks and waggled them like a witch casting spells over a cauldron. 'But how could he know I'd be hanging round this very square on Halloween night? He'd only just moved in here himself!'

She lifted one thin shoulder. 'I sometimes think he has a sixth sense.'

'I don't believe in all that. He's just a voyeur, same as me. A spy. And now he's got me where he wants me, in his house, under his roof. I'm contracted to stay here until the exhibition is sold out. I'm contracted to, you know, please him whenever he asks. So why doesn't he ask? Why doesn't he take advantage?'

'He won't bare his soul until everything is absolutely right in his own mind.'

'Who's talking about his soul? I'm talking carnal knowledge here. Christ! Life's too short to be a perfectionist!' I snatched a pot of gloss, smeared it carefully over my lips. 'So is there something wrong with him?'

Crystal raised her thin eyebrows. She looked just like a wooden matryoshka doll, with seven diminishing Crystal clones trapped inside.

'As opposed to something wrong with *you*, you mean?'

'All in working order, as he well knows!' I glared at her, but it had no effect on her etched expression. 'Is he . . . how can I put this? Is he impotent? I know he's responsive to stimulae, but can he get it up? Did this ex-wife torment him to such a degree that he can't perform any more? Is that why he won't come on to me?'

'It's not my place to say.'

'That sounds horribly like a yes. I need to know, Crystal. You were part of the ménage here. I'm guessing it was no-holds-barred in the Levi household once upon a time.'

She shook her head and concentrated again on fussing with the curls at the ends of my hair. 'I assure you, young lady. Nothing wrong with him at all. Not physically. He's all red-blooded male.'

'I'm going to have to take your word on that. Mentally, then?'

'Nothing wrong with him up there, either. He's an intelligent, perceptive, savvy man who made some terrible choices. Sacrifices, too. You're right about one thing. That woman knocked the stuffing out of him. And when he ordered her to leave she lashed out in the worst way possible. Took the one person he loved in the world.'

'His little brother, you mean? How did that happen?'

The blackbird eyes glimmered over the top of my head.

'Not little, exactly. He was about your age by then. But she seduced him and brainwashed him. I'm certain of it. The original cougar, red in tooth and claw.' Her thin red lips opened slightly, then snapped shut again like a letter box. 'But that's forbidden territory. Gustav's Achilles heel. The day he tells you about that saga is the day you'll know he's letting you right in, Serena.'

'He's not dead, is he? The brother? Just tell me that much.'

'No, no. Alive and kicking somewhere on this earth, but I suppose you could say he's dead to Gustav.'

She was holding the hairbrush like a weapon and I had another graphic vision of her bringing it down on a soft, bare bottom. *My* soft bare bottom.

'Be very careful with him, Serena. You're the first, the only woman who has got this close since – for more than five years. Apart from me, but I don't count.'

'You do count, Crystal.' I leaned nearer the mirror to paint on some mascara, but kept my eyes on her. 'I've seen the video. Don't go all poker-faced. Gustav showed me the photos and movies in the house in Baker Street. I saw you being spanked by some dominatrix figure. You know my work. My scenes from a Venetian convent. So you know we're on a similar wavelength. I daren't ask Gustav, but who's the person in the fetish leather going at you with the whip?'

'I guess it's no secret. It would be easy enough to google the material if you really wanted.' The brush paused in my hair, then snagged on a tangle. 'It's Margot. His ex-wife. That was her sideline.'

'Some sideline! What was her mainline?'

'She ran a couple of boutiques. One in Switzerland and later she opened one in Marylebone.'

'What sort of boutiques?'

'Fashion. And then she branched out into accessories.'

We caught each other's eyes in the mirror. Hers were two black slits above her thin red mouth. Mine were huge with questions.

'Accessories. Right. Like handcuffs? Catwoman muzzles? Whips?' My hands flew up to my mouth. 'So how on earth did you get involved, Crystal? Were you friends?'

She picked up a vicious-looking comb and worried at a knot of hair until it unravelled.

'She placed an advert, about a year before the end of their marriage. Discreet demo model for the private shows she staged to encourage her more timid celebrity customers. Gustav was refusing to be part of the underground business by then, although he oversaw the filming of the installation.

Then the dreadful showdown occurred and she, and the brother, were gone.'

Down in the street we heard the melodic honk of the car horn.

Crystal's eyes glittered in the bright morning light flooding in from the three arched windows. The brush resumed its work and jerked my head backwards.

'Margot hasn't left the building, though, has she? She's still up here, getting in the way.' I tapped my head. 'I need to know what I'm up against.'

Tangle sorted, Crystal brushed so briskly that it hurt.

'You're up against a spectre, nothing more. But everything about her was toxic. They were a toxic mix. At first her, ah, hobby was only indulged when she was at the house in Lugano. But then her buyers and clients became international and started clamouring for more access, and so their home in Baker Street became the club. The punters loved the illusion of the respectable old English town house being the facade for all that debauchery, and that's why it was the obvious place to keep the collection even after they both moved out.'

I shook my head in disbelief. My hair swished like silk. 'No wonder it felt like a mausoleum.'

'It went to her head. She was the queen bee in that house. She paraded her obsession in front of him, cajoling and threatening him if he didn't join in. It got out of control. Mind games and bullying.'

'I don't understand why he would preserve it as an exhibition if it made him so unhappy?'

Crystal bent her head in agreement. 'I agree. I've tried to persuade him to sell it or just destroy it. But it's an investment. It still makes huge amounts of money. He's an entrepreneur, remember. Sees potential in the darkest of corners. Maybe he's holding it to use against her one day.

But it's poisoning him, just like she did. Women like that are very devious about the ways they wound and men are too proud to fight back.'

'I know all about what goes on behind closed doors. But in the end it's only–'

'Sticks and stones. Yes. But that woman could have cut you down at fifty paces with just a look, let alone words. And then finally when he did fight back she carried out her ultimate threat.'

'Ultimate threat? You mean stealing his brother?'

'His only remaining family. He'd cared for the boy since he was tiny.' Crystal stares at the wall above the mirror for a moment, as if the lives she's described are scrolling across it like an old cine film. 'But when she left, I decided to stay.'

I took the brush off her and stood up. 'So you and Gustav were lovers?'

She actually laughed, then. A surprisingly tinkly, musical laugh, like sleigh bells.

'Oh no, you're barking up the wrong tree there, my little lotus blossom! Men aren't my thing, even charismatic ones like Gustav!'

I wish she was here now. Cold and peculiar as she is, she makes me laugh. I am getting used to her being around; my maid, the kindly shadow over my shoulder. And how much light has she shed, in one short conversation!

'Come on, Dickson,' I am bleating now. 'At least let me stay in the car until he gets here. It's freezing, and I'm starving. It's been hours since you made me those smoked salmon sandwiches.'

'Yeah, he's told me what an appetite you have. That's why I have to go to the shops, Miss. The cupboard is bare.'

'So take me with you. I'll show you what grub I like.'

He takes his chauffeur's cap off and rubs his gloved hand

over his totally bald pate. There's the tattoo of a slender woman's leg, foot pointing like a ballerina, winding up the back of his neck.

'No can do. My orders are to leave you here, Miss. He told me you'd be fine. A tough nut brought up in the middle of nowhere, is what he said.'

'Marooned, more like.'

Dickson shrugged awkwardly. 'Just my instructions.'

'Do you know, Dickson, all I dreamed about when I was stuck in that house on those wretched cliffs was being in the middle of a city, part of a herd, hemmed in by buildings and streets, assailed by strange music, foreign languages, aromatic smells and exotic food. And being warm. Always warm.' I rest my hand on his bulky sleeve. 'Stay here and tell me your story.'

'Nothing to tell.' He brushes my hand off as if it's a speck of dust. 'I'm sorry, Miss. After I've bought the food I've got to check progress with the land agents and then I've the afternoon off. I do have a life, you know. Between you and me I've got a friend who works at the Alprose chocolate factory over the way. She's waited for me all this time, would you credit it? Then the boss wants me back on duty to sort out your dinner.'

I take a good look at Gustav's chauffeur-chef in this stark white light. Usually I only see the back of his head. Occasionally catch a glimpse of him in his chef's whites in Gustav's kitchen, tenderising meat and blending mangoes. Difficult to tell how old he is. Around Gustav's age, maybe. They've been together a long time, apparently, boss and manservant. Batman and Robin.

'I thought this was going to be a dirty weekend for me, too.' I scuff my feet grumpily, clapping together the beautiful leather ski gloves with a mother-of-pearl shimmer that Crystal has given me, trimmed with silver fox fur to match my hat.

'I'm sure he intended you to enjoy the view while you wait, Miss, you being artistic and all that. It's beautiful here. Look.' He waves his arm around the mountains surrounding the lake and the pastel buildings reminiscent of the islands of Venice lounging around the water's edge. 'Italian on the one hand. Swiss on the other. See that pretty church tower up there? That's the chapel where they were wed.'

'Don't want to hear it, Dickson!' It's almost a sob. 'Come on. What am I going to do in this smelly old yard if he doesn't show up?'

'You can ride, can't you? Horses, I mean?'

I glance around. So that's what this is. A stable yard. But most of the loose boxes look shut and bolted.

'Yes, as a matter of fact. I used to ride a lot in Devon when I was a kid. It was the only fun I was allowed to have. And that would explain why Crystal dressed me up as "Equestrian Barbie" this morning. But how does Gustav know that?'

'Perhaps the whip gave it away?'

I gasp and go bright scarlet.

Dickson chuckles and taps the side of his nose like a gangster. 'You don't think he'd invite any random bird to stay here, would you? It used to be his favourite place in the world. He hasn't shared it with any of the others.'

'Others?'

'You know. Floozies. Girls. Blimey, is that the time! I really must be going before all that lovely chocolate melts. My weakness, you see. Sweets. Chocolate.' He licks his lips.

'Mine too.' My breathy laugh is snatched quickly by the cold. I can't hear any hooves, or snorting, or jingling of bridles. His words are clanging in my ears. 'Bring me back some, will you?'

'Sure. But riding is the order of the day first. That's all I know.'

'You can't eat horses. Or fly home to London on one. I don't like it here, Dickson.'

'I daresay he's testing your patience, Miss Serena. And your stamina.'

I catch a light in his eye as he looks me up and down. What have the two men been saying about me? 'Either way you have to do as you're told. We all do. We're all marked.'

'Marked?'

He jams his cap back on. 'It means no-one else can have you. You belong to him.'

'I don't belong to anyone, Dickson!'

'You do. You signed your life to him, remember? We all sign contracts. That's how he operates, how he keeps his people in line. He learned the hard way never to trust.'

'Well, he has a funny way of keeping his side of the bargain, winding me up like a bloody puppet then rejecting me.' I push past him to get to the car. 'I'm not his property, and nor are you.'

Suddenly a blinding light flashes from somewhere. Dickson jumps straight into a defensive position, hands out in a karate block. The light flashes again in a kind of code, and Dickson gives an embarrassed cough.

'He can see us. He likes to take a powerful telescope with him on his hikes.'

I flick a V sign in the direction of the cable car station. 'Who's the voyeur now, Levi?'

Dickson salutes smartly. 'Message received and understood, Boss. Never disobey him, Miss. He can be fearsome when he's roused.'

'You're all just frightened of him.'

'No. We understand him. We know why he lost his mojo. We do what he pays us to do, he looks after us.' He eases his bulk back behind the steering wheel. 'But I tell you it's not worth disobeying him, or playing games.'

'Spooky. That's exactly what Crystal said.'

He crosses his fingers. 'We're like that, Crystal and me. Go back a long way, since the bad old days. And she's right. Once you're over the threshold, on the payroll, it's non-negotiable. And whether you like it or not he'll hunt you down.'

I snigger scornfully. 'My arrangement with him is different from yours. It's had built-in obsolescence from the start, because it only lasts until Christmas. Or until my last photograph goes.'

'Good luck with that,' he murmurs, adjusting the rear-view mirror.

I flounce round towards a low grey stone building on the far side of the yard where I think I can see a dim light glowing. Behind me, the car engine starts up again.

'For God's sake, Dickson! At least wait to check that he's actually coming!'

Dickson tips his cap in a suspiciously jaunty manner, slides the car out of the yard and down the rocky road towards the lake, leaving me hemmed in by the ring of mountains.

'The pair of you!' I yell uselessly, my words snatched by the wind as the brake lights disappear. 'Bloody bastards!'

The day's exhilaration is gurgling away like so much cold bath water. When I stepped aboard the sleek white jet this morning, saw the Levi font painted along its flank, and then Dickson jumped down from the cockpit like something out of *Top Gun*, I could barely contain myself.

My mood went lukewarm when Gustav wasn't at Agno airport to meet me. When Dickson changed from Tom Cruise to The Sweeney and guided the silver Lexus along the valley floor below the purple mountains, circled the calm cold lake with its colourful buildings crowding round the shore, then purred up this mysterious-looking road with the overhanging boulders and rocks, I assumed that any minute we'd get to a fairy tale castle with grey pointed turrets and Gustav would be bounding over the drawbridge to greet me.

Tepid is the word for how I'm feeling now, as the bracing air with its tang of glacier slaps at my cheeks.

Oh my God. My bags are in the car. Even my handbag. All I have with me is my camera. Dickson has to come back. This is just a tease. The test he was talking about. Surely he's not that mean, even if Gustav is.

A church bell echoes round the valley, reminding me that civilisation isn't so far away. Even the herd of goats just visible further up in the wood must have someone tending them.

I wander back through the arch and take some pictures of it from the forest angle, the ivy clinging to the brickwork for dear life. The black pine trees lean into the wall, dark green branches poking and grabbing, as if determined to break it down and take it over. But as I zoom in on a fragile-looking wild rose, I notice that the brick isn't as old as it looks. It's been recently re-pointed.

Dickson isn't coming back. Ten minutes have passed. There is only the occasional flap of wide wings breaking the silence, a woody crack as something heavy lands on a bending branch, and the whistle of the wind, but even the elements don't seem able to penetrate this dense forest. There's only the pervading cold and the metallic light glinting off the lake below as the afternoon draws in.

If this is some kind of sick joke then I am having a sense of humour failure. I have to find shelter. I push open the door of the little building and the dim light turns out to be an oil lamp burning in the corner. Someone has recently put a match to it. No. On closer inspection I see that it's electric. From the sharp clean smell I can tell that someone has recently polished all the tack arranged on racks around the room, bridles, saddles and martingales, gleaming bits and buckles.

In the darkest corner is an American Western-style saddle strapped to its own frame, broad as an armchair. It gleams with saddle soap and polish. I glance around. Nothing and no-one here. Just me and the wind howling round the building. And presumably somewhere up in the forest, Gustav prowling around with his telescope.

My elegant riding boots ring out in the empty tack room. The dim light outside is laced now with approaching mist. Any minute now it will lower itself over the landscape and smother us all.

I pack my camera away. The only place to sit is that comfortable-looking saddle. I climb up and sit astride it for a moment, taking care not to thump down on my bottom which is still sore from last night's punishment. I hold myself just above the saddle, my legs spread on either side of the wide seat. I start to rock.

The owners of the stables along the cliffs must have suspected something was wrong at home when I started hanging around for longer and longer. They might not have noticed the odd bruise, but they can't have missed the fact that I seemed happier talking to horses than to people.

I just told them that my family was busy, that they wanted me out of the house, and after a while the stable owners liked having me around, said I was a great help, paid me to groom and exercise the horses. I spent every weekend and all the holidays galloping across the cliffs or down on the beach, sometimes roaming as far as the moors, especially in the winter when the tourists had gone back to the city.

Sometimes they allowed me to sleep in the straw loft, listening to the horses and ponies stamp and snuffle all night. Was anybody missing me back at home? Who knows? Who cares?

Only once did I go home and ask for a horse of my own. It's there, in the diary. Yet another ugly fight.

You think we're made of money? You can do what you like when we're rid of you, but you're not bringing a dirty animal back here. Now go and wash all the stinking mud and fur off those clothes.

Looking back on that row, I wonder why they didn't just lock me up for the whole weekend as was usual when I'd displeased them. Why didn't they refuse to let me go to the stables again? They must have known how much that would hurt. How much I loved going there. But we struck such poisonous sparks off each other that they would rather have me out of sight, out of mind, than have me imprisoned in my bedroom, filling the house with my unhappiness.

My body wakes up with the rocking motion as I pretend to be riding. I lower myself gingerly, lean slightly sideways to take the weight off my sorest buttock. The leather feels warm beneath me, as if it has only just been lifted off a sweating mount. It creaks as if it's speaking.

Damn Dickson for abandoning me here. Damn Gustav for ordering him to do so. If he'd just hung around another few minutes, had the courtesy to wait until Gustav pitched up.

Outside, the wind wuthers round the corner of the building like a damned soul, rattling the stable doors and knocking over a bucket. My heart jolts in my chest. I'm certain there is no-one else here. No way of knowing how long Gustav will keep me waiting. I could die in here. I have no idea how big his estate is. Does he own the whole mountain? The whole forest?

I'm not threatened by any ghosts, but what if the real thing is here? What if Margot knows we're coming and is lying in wait up at the castle?

I wriggle down into the saddle and concentrate on the creaking sound it makes, just as if a muscular steed is trotting smartly along beneath me. I grasp the high rounded pommel at the front with one hand and the back panel of the saddle with the other and slide myself back and forth until the leather heats up with the friction and I start to vibrate with the heat. The smooth fabric of my jodhpurs slides easily across the leather, quickly growing damp with exertion and secret excitement. The smell of the leather grows stronger, mingled with my own sweet aroma.

I close my eyes, raising myself off the seat as far as the long stirrups will allow me so that the chilly air can get to me. Then I bang myself down onto the seat again, rubbing up and down the saddle, tilting myself so as to feel the heat more acutely, spreading my legs wider so as to press down on the leather surface and rub some more.

I start to quiver with excitement, driven on by the whistling of the scary wind outside. I am holding onto the saddle to support myself, fingering the high, rounded, phallic pommel. The shape of it is perfect for my private game, and before long the pleasure is growing as I gyrate against it.

'Did you know,' comes a deep voice into the dusty silence, 'that pommel means "little apple"?'

I half-groan, half-laugh at the interruption. 'So you've finally made an appearance.'

'The journey hasn't tired you out, I see.'

I can't look at him. I grasp the pommel, hunching over it as reluctantly I abandon my game.

'Would have been more polite for you to travel with me instead of running off in the middle of the night.'

'We're not joined at the hip, are we, Serena?'

'I thought that was what the silver chain was all about?'

'Yes. When I choose to attach it. Oh, I have it here, don't worry. But you're a big girl now. And Dickson delivered you safely.' Gustav strides past me. He reaches for a bridle. Despite his rough tone I can see the edge of his cheekbone rising with amusement. 'Right. When you've finished scratching your itch, are you ready for a ride?'

I blush furiously, turn to glower at him over my shoulder, and nearly fall off the saddle.

It's like a different man has just walked in, even though I can only see his back view. The only familiar item of clothing is the dark red scarf.

Gustav Levi, the well-built, pale, slightly reclusive businessman in Jermyn Street tailoring has been supplanted by a muscular, swaggering, unshaven horseman in unashamedly tight black jodhpurs, long black boots and a black high-necked Belstaff-style jacket. He looks magnificent. The ensemble makes him look taller, leaner, fitter, and much, much younger.

It's easy to imagine his body stripped of the black skin of fabric, his clearly outlined buttocks bare, the muscles tensing under my tentative touch, flexing under the skin, pulling back ready to thrust himself between a pair of willing thighs.

Wind your tongue in, Polly would say. *You're ogling the guy*.

I shove my finger into my mouth to keep from giggling.

'Loving the Equestrian Ken motif, Gustav. We match, see? I'm your Barbie doll, all in white. Madame Crystal has sent us forth dressed as two sides of a negative.'

'That's why I hire her, Folkes. She sticks to her brief.'

I wriggle into the saddle, wishing he'd turn round. If Gustav's jodhpurs reveal his fit physique, then every dip and curve of my soft, lazy bod will be on display, too. Let's see if he is similarly inflamed by lust when I present myself for inspection in all my snowy splendour.

My teeth nip my finger harder than I intended and the tiny jab of pain flares deep down between my legs. It was definitely worth flying over half of mainland Europe to catch an eyeful of Gustav Levi in tight black jodhpurs.

I can't take my eyes off him as he runs a cloth over the tack. The black hair falling over his eyes, the sequence of muscles rippling through his body, the inviting curve of his bottom, the fine bulge of muscle in his thighs, the strong jut of his knees as he lifts the saddle off its moorings.

What did Crystal say about him? Deep, not distant?

But is he goading me? Is he parading in subtle yet skin-tight clothes to tease me? Crystal would tell me not to be so ridiculous. She'd retort that these are the requisite protective garments for horse riding. Slim-fitting, but supple. And she would be right. Nevertheless I intend to feast my eyes because this is as close as I'm going to get to seeing my lord and master naked.

He turns to face me, the saddle in his arms, his mouth open as if he's about to say something. His black hair has caught on his eyelashes. I long to sweep it away so that I can see how bright his eyes are, what's going on in those black pools, how steadily they are staring at me. His face is pale, but there's a strong growth of dark stubble chiselling his cheeks and chin and making him look more devilish than debonair.

My hand feels automatically for my camera. I want to capture Gustav's new rugged, restless energy. My Alpine Zorro.

I take a quick shot, because he's standing so still. I play back the image to make sure it was in focus and there he is, a modern-day musketeer staring at me in the same mesmerised way I've been staring at him. I glance at my trapped specimen, and then at the real thing. His black eyes are half closed with what? Attraction? Amazement? His wide lips are half smiling, biting back an exclamation of what, admiration? Or amusement?

A fine specimen indeed.

I swing my leg over the saddle rack and jump down.

'I'm not sure my bottom will take a rough ride after last night.' I smooth my own trousers and tug the puffed jacket down. 'And I don't see any steeds.'

He laughs softly and saunters towards a far door, kicking it open. The air whistling in from the yard behind us is bitterly cold, but when I stump after him I find myself in a bright modern corridor of loose boxes. Brightly lit, centrally heated, and smelling cosily of straw, oats and equine sweat. Grey and chestnut and black noses poke over the doors, waiting for attention. I pat each horse as I pass, but it's the Arab chestnut mare with the huge Bambi eyes who draws me back.

'This one's my favourite.'

'Her coat matches your hair,' Gustav remarks from inside the furthest stable. 'And she's pretty jumpy like you, too. But go ahead. Take your pick.'

I lean on the door to watch him as he saddles up his big black mare. My nostrils prick at the familiar smell of linseed oil freshly brushed onto the horses' hooves to make them gleam. There must be a groom somewhere. Did he or she see me rubbing myself on the saddle just now?

Gustav strokes his horse as he buckles up the girth. His hair shines like silk in the dull light pooling in from the high window. I can't resist peeking at his butt again, craning to look at his crotch in those tight breeches, and there it is, the tantalising bulge pushing against the zip.

A brief memory hits me. Gustav the other night in his candelit house, lying vanquished and groaning on the sofa as I sucked him.

And then my horse shakes her head and stamps her hoof, and the memory melts.

Gustav emerges from the far stable. Pets and their owners. It's true. The high cheekbones of the highly bred horse, the majestic curve of the nose, even the over-long eyelashes and glossy mane are all an equine version of him.

Gustav eases a sugar lump into the nibbling lips of his horse.

'You're sure you know one end from the other?'

'I never had my own mount, but I spent most of my teenage summers around horses. But you know that about me already. I even used to help break one or two young ones. So yes. I know what I'm doing. You just watch me.'

He hands me an armful of tack and narrows his eyes in challenge. 'Great. Let's get going, before it gets dark. It's going to snow tomorrow, it'll fall right down here and by the lake, so we won't be able to take the horses out again.'

I don't move for a second. We stare at each other in the warm building buffeted by an increasing wind. Face to face, alone, just as we were in that London square. How far away that seems now in time and space.

His eyes have a feverish glitter and he's practically bouncing on his toes with an eager energy. I know I should be infected by it, but I'm disorientated by everything. Part of me is withdrawing, curling up defensively inside me.

I see to my horse and saddle her up. Typical of Gustav Levi to be relaxed in a place where the rest of us are constantly jumping at our own shadow.

'Put this on. Got to keep you safe.'

He steps up to me and removes my warm fur hat and gloves and stashes them in a black leather rucksack slung round his shoulders. His dark eyes are alive with fiery light as he plonks a very unglamorous helmet on my head, tugging my hair away from the strap, smoothing it down my back.

He fastens the chin strap carefully, running his finger underneath it to check the tension, my skin as sensitive there as if it's been scalded. My mouth parts a little, and so does his. His tongue runs across his lower lip as he traces the swell of mine. Back, forth, his finger moves towards my mouth as if to enter it, pauses. I can feel saliva gathering as I hold my breath. We're millimetres apart. His white teeth bite down as he nods.

'Perfect fit.'

Despite everything that has gone on between us, despite the fact that we've been alone together several times, done intimate things to each other, talked about intimate things, despite this unaccustomed breezy cheerfulness, I am suddenly rigid with shyness. It's like a shell forming round that snail's curl of doubt.

The stark afternoon is lighting up the whites of his eyes, the sheering bone structure of his face accentuated by the weekend bandit's beard.

And the mouth. The usual grim lines are relaxed into a sensual fullness. Oh, he's still so beautiful. And yet he won't kiss me. I know that now, and worse than that I know why. He's brought me to this beautiful setting, for this weekend away, but there is another presence here. How can I feel relaxed in the very place where he lived and loved with Mad Margot, the same woman whose mention still has him pacing and cursing?

This is the place where her perversions developed into a thriving profession. Where all those debauched parties and antics occurred. Where Margot reigned supreme. What am I doing here?

I'm his protégée, that's all. He's brought me here to sort something out in his own mind. Or, as he said, as a dogsbody to help him pack up some old mementos.

'Just one more thing, Folkes.'

His voice is so quiet, so soothing. He's holding out a pair of soft leather and woven riding gloves. I refuse to meet his eye this time as he pulls my hands out straight in front of him. But the skin inside my wrist quivers just the same when he circles it then separates the fingers. My body tightens just the same when he eases the leather fingers over mine. His breath tickles my face as he twitches the gloves tight. The sensations are all the same as that first night in the square, and later in the bar of Dukes Hotel when he dressed me up to go out into the cold.

'Have I told you how good it is to see you here?'

I shrug wordlessly. He hooks one finger round the silver bracelet and pulls me closer to him.

'Takes your breath away, doesn't it? The mountains, the lake, the horses. You don't have to speak. God, we all spend our lives banging on, don't we? Being here suits you. You've a real bloom in your cheeks already. It means a lot to me that you came. I can't wait to show you my favourite spot.'

I glance quickly at him, astonished that tears are pricking my eyelids.

'Thanks for inviting me,' I blurt quickly, and turn towards my horse. For the first time he is reading me all wrong. 'But let's not bother with talking. Let's get out there.'

I place my foot in the stirrup and swing easily up onto my horse, remembering not to thump down too heavily on the spine of the saddle. Yes. This feels right. Some good hard exercise to get the blood pumping. A good night's sleep in the mountains. Make my excuses and go back to London tomorrow. Hard sell to finalise the exhibition. Onwards and upwards.

I grip the reins. I get it now. I'm some girl he's picked up who has surprised him with her talent but he's basically enrolled me to further his own profile in the art world. A cute chick he can amuse himself with when he needs to take his mind off his troubles. Someone wet behind the ears he can practise a little light spanking on to keep his hand in. But who isn't good enough for him to kiss.

'Right. Let's see what kind of horsewoman you make then, Folkes.'

The world looks different from up here. It all comes flooding back. The powerful beast between my legs. The flicking forward of the ears, the dancing legs, the skittering of her hooves across the cobbles as I check my stirrups. The rocking and creaking of the saddle. And I can't ignore how unutterably sexy my companion looks as he strides over to his mount.

Black clad, black hair falling over his face as he strokes the black mane. In another life I'd have done anything for him. But he's not mine. He never will be, no matter how cute and clever I try to be. So what if Gustav stops in his tracks at the sight of me astride the Arab mare? I know I look good. What else is new?

'Lead on,' I cry brightly. I'm forced to straighten my spine, and as the horse strides out my body tilts in response, bottom sliding on the saddle and breasts thrusting forwards with each step.

Gustav vaults nimbly on board without bothering to use the stirrups. He looks me up and down with frank delight, eyes lingering on my breasts, my hips, my legs, before nudging his horse in front of me.

'You look stunning up there, Serena. Majestic. The warrior queen, born to ride.'

'This is me at my best.' I trot up beside him. 'And you don't look too bad yourself.'

His black eyes flash wickedness under his glossy hair. He clicks his tongue and I'm still trying to harden my heart as we trot briskly out of the stable yard and straight up a bank into the dense forest.

'Wait for me!' I call, but he ignores me, pressing his horse into a gallop up a well-worn path and disappearing round a corner.

When the horse's tail flicks out of sight I squeeze my chestnut mare into a gallop to follow them. The man in black on his black horse flashes in and out of the trees, in and out of the shadows, into brief oases of daylight, hooves muffled on the pine needles. I have to concentrate at first to get into my horse's rhythm, thighs screaming to grip the saddle, bottom tensed up into a half standing position, but then I catch up, I'm right up behind Gustav as he crouches over his horse, his hair streaming in a similarly glossy mane, his hard, muscular, squeezable butt held up in the air like a jockey.

And then we are neck and neck, very dangerous on the rock-strewn pathways, so close I could flick at him with my whip if I had one. I laugh out loud at that. Whips in London, whips in art galleries and echoing mansions, but not here, in the great outdoors, when you're actually riding.

His long fingers in tight black gloves are curled on the reins, controlling his horse as we race. The blood is pounding through me now, beating in time to the drum of hooves. I am determined to overtake him, but he keeps pace with me. On and on we race, the going getting tougher because it's steeper, and stony. We're on the mountain, now, but the peaks recede as if laughing at us.

Up high in this forest the trees press together, cramped as a crowd of people straining to watch a street performance, pushing at us as we gallop neck and neck, twigs grasping at my arms, swiping with their spiky, thorny branches as if to drag us off our saddles.

All at once the light opens up, the tunnel of trees becomes sparser, they fall back as if to make way, and then we burst onto a rocky plateau flat and bright as an arc-lit stage. The horses clatter to a halt just as I realise that there's a mere few yards of shiny granite between us and a sheer drop. It's not the ravine I was thinking about earlier. There is simply a void of air between us and the mountains on the other side of the lake. The ground seems to have been sliced away by a giant pair of shears.

Gustav walks his horse a few feet closer to the edge, just as Polly and I used to do on the cliffs. The hoofs clatter noisily, slipping on the frosty surface.

'For God's sake stop pissing about, Gustav!'

'I'm flattered you're concerned for my safety, Serena, but I know this terrain like the back of my hand, and so do the horses.' He laughs, settling his hands on his saddle. His legs are so long in those black jodhpurs. So relaxed as the toes rest in the stirrups.

'Just feast your eyes on all this splendour, Serena. This is one of my favourite vantage points. I used to walk or run or ride up here to get away. To think. To plan. You see? We're almost on top of the world.'

The peaks are that much closer, it's true. The illusion is that they're at eye level, that I could reach out and tap their outline. It's as if the earth was in a rage when it forged this landscape, punching its way as high as it could out of the plains, aiming for the heavens, fighting itself into these muscular fists of jagged rock to separate territories and make a statement.

We mere humans and horses can only stand and admire and grip the ground. The clouds of our mammal breath are wispy imitations of the weighty clouds up in the massive bowl of sky, but for now we are part of the landscape too.

'See, there's snow on the high points above us.' He is turned sideways. He points over the deadly drop. He looks like a Sioux chief surveying his prairie. 'It'll be coming further down by nightfall tomorrow. You can tell from the light. We won't be stranded at the house but we won't be going out on horseback again. To ski we'd have to go over to St Moritz or Como.'

'You know I'm a beginner at skiing?'

'You'd give it a go, though, wouldn't you, my gutsy girl?'

I shrug to distract him from my reddening cheeks. If he's a big chief, does that make me his squaw? 'Maybe. But I don't know you well enough to risk making a clown of myself.'

'Anyone less like a clown I can't imagine. And you do

know me, Serena. Better than you think. Certainly well enough to let me teach you to ski.'

I stare at him. Where are the words when I need them? He has this way of taking coherent thought and rubbing it out before I can articulate it. Do I know him? I know his face. I think I could reproduce every line, every eyelash, every shadow now, if you gave me a pencil and paper. But can I interpret the commentary behind those black eyes? I'm not so sure.

When I don't reply he sighs. 'Well, we may not have the time. My priorities for this visit are to get the house cleared and sold and off my hands.'

I can hear the harsh chord of bitterness as he speaks.

I clear my throat. 'So tough for you, when you so love this place.'

'This particular spot, yes. She's killed my affection for the house and the land. Oh, I'll still manage my investments from here. And maybe I'll buy another property over the border in Italy. A ski lodge, maybe. What do you think? Or a house on one of the other lakes.' He squeezes his knees to urge his horse a couple of paces nearer the edge. I stifle my squeal of horror. 'But this is the last time we'll ever set foot or hoof on this part of the mountain.'

'We?'

He is turned from me now, his hair hiding his face, and doesn't respond. I decide it was a slip of the tongue. This setting just proves how far removed his life really is from mine. There can't possibly be a 'we'. Can there?

I follow his glance. Far below us the lake is a smooth looking glass. I can see one or two of the slim ferry boats spitting their white triangular wake over the water. The tiled Lombardy roof tops glow red as the sun retreats. The mountains become shadowy silhouettes as it drags its train of fire behind them, leaving embers of shredded pink cloud.

I am sharing Gustav's love of this amazing vista. *We* are sharing it.

I turn my horse across the plateau, hoping he'll follow me. The mountain rears above us. I tip my head back dizzily to see the summit. It's been obliterated while we've been up here, the dark grey clouds anxious to dump their load of snow. I'm just about to aim my camera at the sunset when I see, tucked in a little grove and surrounded by an incongruously twee picket fence, a little white Bavarian-style chapel, its elegant spire adorned with an iron cross. The one Dickson pointed out to me earlier.

That's the chapel where they were wed.

TWELVE

I try to halt my horse, cursing under my breath but even though I tug on the reins she ploughs on. The chapel is closed, the high doors bolted, the arched painted windows shuttered. But I can just picture them, Gustav and Margot Levi, newly married, emerging from the wooden interior to a shower of confetti and well-connected applause, he dark and victorious in his morning suit or perhaps a traditional Swiss jacket, she with features and colouring I can't decipher, but nevertheless stunning and smug and dancing along the path in a beautiful white dress, one hand holding his and the other clutching a sweet bunch of white edelweiss into which she mock-shyly dips her nose.

The pain of the image winds me sharply as if someone has kneed me in the stomach.

'No wonder this is your favourite location, Gustav. But I've suddenly gone off it.'

He turns from his reverie. I see his face like the sky transforming from thoughtful to thunderous. He kicks his horse over and grabs the reins of my horse.

'Forgive me, Serena. Of course it's not the church that draws me up here. I barely give it a thought, and nor should you.'

'You married her in there, Gustav. How can I ignore that?'

'Ten long years ago. I was a different person then. Blind, clueless. Now I'm seeing clearly and that's thanks to you. Five years ago I was divorced. Serena, don't look at me as if I'm gabbling in a foreign language. Everything was different then!' He shakes the reins, and my horse stamps her foot, jolting my balance. 'None of it applies any more. You've got to believe me.'

'I don't *have* to do anything! It still happened. You still married her. It all feels horribly real to me!' I can't help it. I'm shouting, and angry. 'Oh, let's just get back.'

He drops the reins and backs his horse away, lowering his eyes. I can see the muscle working in his jaw as his face goes tight. But I'm too upset to forgive him. I'm too furious with myself for giving myself away, for being gripped by this fresh fist of jealousy just when I thought it was safe to go back into the water. Or up the mountain.

Gustav clicks his teeth and the horses' ears prick up. So no apology then. With no sign from me my horse quickens into a trot. Their hooves ring out smartly on the hard plateau as we turn our backs on the little chapel and the fading sunset. We barrel back into the darkness of the forest, and then Gustav lowers himself over his horse's neck and kicks her into a gallop. My horse copies. There's nothing for it but to adjust my seat, grip with my knees and press myself down low into the saddle as we swerve and rush break-neck through the trees, through the tunnels of spiny trees, slithering down the vertiginous narrow paths, leaping over fallen branches.

Gustav's steed is faster, and soon he's several corners ahead of me. Sobs of panic escape me as my horse stampedes after him. It's getting dark, and now the ground is descending ever more steeply. I am just beginning to tire of gripping on for dear life when far ahead Gustav swerves through a curtain of ivy and vines and vanishes.

'Hey! Gustav! Wait!'

I gallop through the curtain. My horse rears up and whinnies as she trips over a huge twining root. We are in a coppice overhung with branches like a tent. All sounds, including hooves, are extinguished in here. It is curiously warm and sheltered. The fading light can't penetrate.

I think I see Gustav's horse flickering through the stark winter shadows up ahead, obviously knowing perfectly well which way to go. They disappear from view. I try to kick my horse to go after them, but she wheels round and stops dead, lowering her head so suddenly that without warning I shoot down her neck, over her ears, and onto the hard cold ground. My ankle is twisted awkwardly underneath me.

It hurts like hell. I didn't hear a snap, but I remove one boot carefully, knowing I must do that in case the ankle swells.

'This is all I bloody need!' I yell to the elements as I roll my sock down and see the blooming palette of blue and purple, the flesh bulging already around the ankle bone. I burst into tears.

There is only the strange, dry creaking of the trees accompanying my furious weeping. That same church bell tolls the next evening hour, and my naughty horse stamps and snorts. At least she hasn't run away. She is investigating some bright green shoots over on the far side of the copse. The wind has died down completely which sheds an eerie silence over everything. The twilight has nearly closed in.

I hold myself very still, hugging the ground. Logic tells me that I'm not totally lost. That only happens in nightmares, or horror films. The horse will know her way home. But then again, she might only understand German instructions, or Italian. She might take me further into the forest. Or bolt with me down to the lake and gallivant with me in front of all the sophisticated Swiss residents sipping *Glühwein* in the cafes.

The first time I was lost like this I must have been about five years old. Why they brought me up on Dartmoor, climbing the craggy outcrops around Hay Tor when it was threatening snow, I have no idea. The adults were always too far away. I remember running and tripping to keep up. I was wearing wellies with no socks. Why no socks? Did they expect me to put them on myself? Did they give me a few seconds to do so, sitting on the bottom step of the steep dark stairs, then get impatient with waiting and bundle me into the car anyway?

The wellies were too big, and rubbed the skin on my feet into blisters. I fell over, into some kind of bog. I was knee-deep in mud. I knew I'd be in trouble for messing up my clothes. And when I got back to my feet everyone had gone. There was nothing to be seen but the looming crags, like broken bones sticking up out of the bruised skin of the purple moor, and a couple of bad-tempered-looking wild ponies.

'Wait for me!' I wailed, but my childish voice was a kitten's mew in the huge open space. Like I'm doing now, I held myself very still. I crouched underneath a huge stone with my knees up to my chin. If I sat still enough, nothing bad would happen because nothing bad would see me. On the other hand, no-one would find me either.

There was no relieved crying out and comforting arms when they found me. Only furious voices, accusations of being slow like a little worm, and a smack on the back of my legs.

After that I learned to do it deliberately. Run away and hide from them, and wherever possible find my own way home. Eventually they stopped taking me out anywhere, even if it was for a day, sometimes a night. I preferred the empty house.

I am doing it now. Sitting very still. Not hiding exactly, but weighing up the relative safety of dying out here of cold and starvation, or being found and bawled out for injuring the horse.

I'm not sure I can put weight on this foot, either. I try to move it and it twinges.

Now fear is replaced by anger, and I force myself upright, holding onto the nearest tree for support. The horse glances up at me. She is fine. And there are no bones sticking out of my bruised skin. It's not broken after all. But it's badly twisted.

I click my teeth at the horse. She chews disdainfully, her eyes pitying over her working jaws. Rage surges through me in a tidal wave. What is Gustav playing at?

I'm about to scream for help when I sense rather than hear hooves drumming nearer. Twigs crack, leaves rustle, and at last Gustav hurtles back into the copse, stopping with a dramatic rear up on the hind legs like Clint Eastwood galloping into a dusty town.

'Serena! What happened to you? We'd gone miles before I realised.' His hair swings rebelliously across his face. He looks even more like a rampaging bandit.

'No you hadn't. You left me behind on purpose.'

He jumps off the horse, sweeping his hair back off his face. He looks as if he's fighting back a smile. A few moments away from me seems to have restored his spirits.

'Well, I could have noticed sooner, admittedly. I mean, if you got lost in these mountains you would never get out alive. But you looked so strong and sure I forgot that I was supposed to be looking after you.'

'I *am* strong and sure if I know where I'm going. I can outride you any day. Just don't disappear and make fun of me when it's getting so dark.'

'Take it as a compliment, Serena. I don't treat you as my guest any more.' He takes out some more sugar lumps and feeds his horse. I watch her thick black lips nibble at his gloved fingers. I know that his eyes are on me. 'I thought we could work up a sweat. I wanted to put clear water between us and that awkward reminder.'

'Awkward reminder?' I snap. 'You were rubbing my nose in it. Come and look at the cutesy chapel where I married my wonderful wife.'

I fuss with my sore ankle. He walks across the gloaming. There's that insouciant swagger again, the slight sway of his slim hips, the macho yet gymnastic control of his walk which is totally different from the reined-in stride of the man back in London. The tight breeches and boots make him move in that sinuous way. My eyes are drawn again to the muscled contours of his thighs in the black fabric, my gaze dragged towards his enclosed crotch. Is the bulge there bigger than before?

Am I ever going to wind my tongue in?

Gustav steps over me, apparently unaware of how close his groin is to my gawping face. He gives my horse some sugar lumps, too. His long fingers in their black gloves move over her nose to stroke it thoughtfully.

'Not cutesy. Not wonderful. Not rubbing your nose in anything. But I should have been more sensitive.'

'So much for seeing clearly at last.'

'I wanted to share my favourite view with you, that's all. If I'm honest I wanted you by my side when I drank it all in for the last time.' He closes his eyes and leans against the horse's forehead, his black hair mingling with her chestnut forelock. Her huge eyes blink down at me as if asking, you any idea what he's banging on about? 'I'm glad you were there.'

'Well, I'm not glad,' I snap. 'It *is* a stunning view. But it's your view. Your history. Your house. Your past. Your wife. Not mine.'

The horses chomp on their sugar. Mine pushes cheekily

at Gustav, so unexpectedly that I hear his teeth bite together as her bony forehead knocks him. He rubs his cheek, already coming up a livid red, but he barely flinches.

'Should I be flattered? I mean, that you feel hurt? Jealous, even, or am I wide of the mark?' His voice is low, almost as if he hardly dares ask the question. A spot of blood trickles from the corner of his mouth where he must have bitten his tongue. 'Do you really care about me that much?'

My insides churn, sharing the anxiety I can see burning in his eyes. The furrowed emphasis of his thick eyebrows casts a shadow over his face. He's still unaware of the blood smeared on his lip. I so want to wipe it off for him. I'm so afraid of all this. I'm so afraid of what he's doing to me.

I take a breath, wonder if my eyes are reading his correctly. Wondering if he can read mine.

'You brought me to Switzerland to help you. But seeing that chapel, feeling like a tiny dot on this vast landscape, I can't be any use to you.' I struggle to wring the words dry of emotion. 'And I feel a long way from home.'

He senses the wetness on his lip at last and wipes the blood, staring at it gleaming red on his upheld finger. 'While you were working yourself into a froth about some stupid chapel, I was thinking how ready I am to find a new view, Serena. A new horizon. One that we can enjoy together. I was just about to say so when – I'm sorry. Yet again I've handled this episode badly.'

My horse swings her head up at the same time as I do. She is obviously equally astonished at this unheard-of apology.

'And what's more you should discipline your horses better!' I yank off my helmet and let it bounce across the ground as I brush mud and leaves off me. 'She threw me off. Admittedly I'm out of practice, but she bucked. There was nothing I could do. I'm bloody livid with you, Gustav. And to cap it all I think I've twisted my ankle.'

'*Mea culpa*. Let me take a look. Let's see if you can put weight on it.'

He offers his hand. I hesitate, then let him pull me to my feet. Our hands are sexless in the riding gloves, but they still conduct the heat between us. I'm level with his darkly stubbled chin, his mouth, half open, tiny spotlets of blood on his lower lip.

He takes his red scarf off and wraps it round my neck and shoulders to warm me. I'm stunned afresh by the tenderness in his eyes, in the gesture. I also realise I'm shivering with shock and pain.

'Another apology, even if it is in Latin!' I mutter. 'Why can't you just act like a normal person for once in a blue moon?'

There are red flashes in his cheeks, and not just where the horse bashed him. Anger, remorse, or the bite of the wind? He leans back against the tree and folds his arms.

'Ah, that's more like it. The rude girl I know and – the stroppy girl I met on Halloween night who thinks nothing of hurling the odd insult at her master.' He lifts up my gloves. 'The master who holds her future in his hands.'

'We both signed that agreement, remember?' I exchange sulky looks with my bemused horse. 'I've delivered my work. I've let you tie me with that silver chain. I've given you as much pleasure as you'll let me. You're still bound to honour your part of the bargain.'

He turns my face towards his serious, pale features. So close, so close. His dark eyes are blurring as he tugs me closer, a coal-like gleam. That mouth, oh, that sexy, half-open, mocking mouth. 'What am I going to do with you, Serena?'

We half-stumble against the tree trunk. Our bodies are pressed against each other now, the smooth fabric of our jodhpurs such a flimsy barrier against the fierce heat. I can feel every stretch of muscle in his rangy limbs. Every push of his male response against my stomach.

The closeness of him stops me thinking straight. I push my mouth up against his.

'You could take me, right here, al fresco against this tree. How about that? Show me you're a real man,' I murmur dirtily, coiling my arms around his neck. I remember my conversation with Crystal, when I asked her if there was something wrong with him. What was her answer?

'Ravish you in the open air?'

I am reflected in the black depths of Gustav's eyes, the desire flaming into life as he takes hold of my hips, fans his fingers over my bottom to yank me, grind me against him. Our lips are practically touching, breath panting. The kiss of life.

'Yes. Your *droit de seigneur*.'

He chuckles deeply. 'I like it. My wicked wench. Have you any idea how savagely adorable you are right now?'

'That's because you've made me so angry!'

'No. It's because you want me, Serena. You can't back-pedal when you've just made such an outrageous suggestion. I love that you're an open book. A volume of stubborn sexiness. And what did Oscar Wilde say? *I can resist anything but temptation*.'

'So why resist?'

'My woodland nymph. Look at you!' His voice is rough now. 'I knew it would suit you. A vigorous bout of riding. Still so touchy, but you're in your element out here. You're on fire, if that makes sense in sub-zero temperatures.' His body is pressed so hard against mine that I can hardly breathe. My legs part slightly to invite him in. 'Why don't you try lording, or ladying it, over me?'

'If you would only stop talking.'

I flatten one hand over the front of his jodhpurs, pause for permission, start to fondle the obvious, solid shape throbbing there. I expect him to rear away, slap me off, hiss some cutting word of rejection, but this is our new verb. Ladying. I've tasered him. I can see every rippling muscle in his exposed neck now that I have his scarf. He is swallowing, his Adam's apple jutting. I can see the thick black bristles peppering his strong neck. That familiar fast pulse pushing at his skin.

Then his mouth opens again, I'm making him breathless, but he remains quiet, just nudges himself harder into my softly stroking hand. I'm being impudent now, taking a risk, but he doesn't resist. I watch his mouth struggle open as he gasps softly.

So I do it some more, relish the pulsing hardness growing under my touch. He reaches down and twines his fingers with my roving hand, urging it to work harder and faster.

'What was that you said about working up a sweat?' I murmur, moving my lips against his.

Oh, what was Crystal's reply to my question?

Gustav closes his eyes, lets his warm mouth travel across my mouth, across my cheek, down my jaw, and then with a gentleness that makes me moan he lifts my hair and kisses my neck, my throat, under my ear, where my own pulse is pounding.

I arch my throat under his mouth, shuddering as his lips tickle and tantalise the tender skin. I'm so damp now.

The bitter wind is whipping up my blood at the same time as slowly freezing my skin.

My white jacket rucks up as we rock more insistently against the tree, the weight of him rubbing my bare back against the rough bark and thrilling me with the brief scrape of pain. Gustav's free hand edges in between my legs.

He is nibbling on my neck, moving down to my collar bone, his tongue licking, his lips sucking. My breasts swell with longing under all that clothing. I ride on his hand, push against him, every part of me singing hopelessly with desire and desperation. My legs are shaking from the ride, the stress, the insistent pain in my ankle nagging, distracting. I can feel his breath on my neck, his restless fingers leaving mine to open my jacket now, his breath as ragged and hot as mine.

Nothing wrong with him at all. Not physically. He's all red-blooded male.

He is going for the zipper of my jodhpurs. I start to scrabble with his trousers, too, but it's impossible in these gloves. We're in too much of a rush. He takes the tab of my zip, starts to undo it, and then my ankle gives.

I stumble sideways, moaning in pain as my leg loses its strength and jerks from under me.

He stops what he's doing. We both stop. We are staring, wild-eyed, open-mouthed, our hands still poised over each other's zippers. His dark, hypnotic eyes.

'Gustav, I – oh, God, my ankle!'

Pain shoots up the tendons in my foot and the back of my leg. I'm torn, so torn. All of me throbs with cold and wanting, but the ankle is seizing up now.

Gustav straightens, smoothes my hair back. Watches me attentively as I bite my lips with pain. Whatever we started has finished for now. He tidies my jacket over my hips. He takes his time. Still so tender. Then he kneels down, yanks the gloves off with his teeth.

'Let's take a look.' He cradles the sore, discoloured foot in his long, bare fingers. His black hair falls over his face as he examines my ankle. I long to stroke it. 'No wonder you're in such a state. This looks nasty.'

Nasty or not, I could still come with that one touch of his fingers on the arch of my foot. I rest my head against the tree. I look past Gustav's dark head, avoid the temptation to tangle my fingers through his hair, to push his face against the part of me that he knows is still aching for him, because the moment has passed. I blink up at the dark grey sky glowing orange from the lakeside city below.

The bony fingers of the branches around us have calmed down as if they are also waiting to see what he will do next.

For a few more precious moments Gustav Levi is focusing on me. The brittle mask is torn away. The constant demands are gone. He's far from the phone calls, the people, the ghosts. For a few minutes more it's just the two of us. But the kaleidoscope of this last hour or so, the cold clarity of the air, the rush of blood as we galloped side by side, the stark reality of that chapel, the pain in my foot, all of it has been shaken into place.

I stammer into the silence. 'Please, Gustav. Either bind up this ankle and get me back up on the horse, or get me to a doctor.'

'Come on, Hiawatha,' he murmurs at last, moving away as if his legs are made of lead. The shyness creeps back as the distance lets in the cold. Fragile, and foolish, is how I feel now. Weak, cold, and defeated.

He takes my horse and walks it over to his. Those gorgeous long, strong legs, that were measured up against mine just now. I am still weak with wanting, weak with all of it. Slowly we push through the curtain of ivy and there we are, ridiculously, come full circle and right back in the stable yard. No wonder my horse stopped dead.

Gustav ties up the steeds, wolf-whistles through his teeth for the invisible grooms, and helps me over to the Lexus which is once more parked by the archway.

'How about a quick spin down into Lugano? You won't be doing much hiking with that ankle, so why don't I treat you to a hot chocolate by the lake?'

I'm suddenly overwhelmed with tiredness and confusion. I ease my aching foot into the car. 'Hot chocolate is just what the doctor ordered.'

We drive down the road, past a couple of cosy-looking bistros. Gustav tells me they are called grottos because they used to be carved from caves in the hillside.

It's not long before we're approaching the immaculate promenade lit by the glowing bulbs of streetlamps. He drives along the edge of the lake for a while, navigates some corners, then brings us out onto a quiet stretch of bars and restaurants. He parks outside a particularly pretty bar illuminated with fairy lights, its wooden verandah glassed in and heated for the winter but suspended over the flat, black water. As we walk slowly towards it I see a boat house full of polished wooden boats hauled up, waiting for the summer season when they will roar across the water once again looking like something Gregory Peck would drive in *Roman Holiday*.

We take our seats by the windows. The mountains sprawl around, listening in. Night drops round us like a blindfold as soon as we blow on the huge, creamy mugs of chocolate sprinkled with cinnamon.

'What a day. This is going to sound crazy,' he remarks when the waitress has withdrawn. 'But you have never been so irresistible as you were just then, Serena. Still my wild child, but scared, in pain, and oh so angry.'

His face is boyishly open tonight, still flushed from our lustful encounter against the tree, fresh and lively. He thinks he's got it made.

'I'm not your anything.'

'You are. You nearly were just then. You got me worked up like some kind of horny teenager! Perhaps it's a good thing that we didn't – that wasn't exactly the setting I had in mind when I drew up that contract. But we're off-piste now. I'm trying to tell you how captivating you are. You always have been, you little sprite. Your photographs are magical enough, but it's you that grabs me.' He takes the silver chain out of his pocket and clears his throat. 'It's you.'

I take a sip of chocolate. The sugar hits me immediately and decisively. 'I thought I was just another scared, pained, angry woman. You prefer us vulnerable, don't you?'

'Yet again I've expressed myself clumsily.' He frowns down at the silver thread. 'Because that sounds as if I revel in causing you pain.'

I look across the lake. The rocky outline against the star-punched sky resembles the shoulders and hips of sleeping women. 'You did last night. When you whipped me.'

'That's not fair. *You* were revelling in that pain. Not me. But if you'd asked me to stop, of course I would. I did that because you wanted it and because every stroke was liberating you. Perhaps you still don't fully understand what was happening.' He strokes his chin for a moment before calling for the bill and counting out crisp Swiss francs. 'You were the very opposite of vulnerable.'

'I'm not talking about me, now, Gustav. I'm talking about another thing that's troubling me. The others.' I give him my arm to help me up. 'The floozies.'

'Floozies? What on earth kind of cheap nasty word is that?'

'Damsels in distress, then. Tarts. *Petites amies*? The other women you've ensnared over the years. The pain is one thing. But you certainly like them pathetic and disposable.'

He takes me roughly by the arm and we stumble too quickly and awkwardly out onto the wooden verandah. The lake is wreathed in lacy mist. The lights from the buildings sway and sparkle on its surface. My words scatter like marbles into the freezing night.

'Why do you do this, Serena? Rake over all these dead coals? You're like a terrier with a bone. And you've got me so wrong. But perhaps that's my fault for being so goddamn inarticulate.'

He sighs and reaches into his leather rucksack. What's he getting out now? A gun? My little whip? But he removes my mother-of-pearl gloves with their fur trim, waggles them in front of his face. Automatically I put my hands out for him to ease the gloves on. He smiles at the unspoken familiarity. Gently, as always, he slides in one finger at a time, pausing, tugging that one down, running his own fingers between the gaps, turning my hands over to button the fur cuff and make sure it all fits.

It would be so churlish to relinquish this sweet ritual. How can I, especially when it is going to be so short-lived?

His black hair blows wildly in the unkind breeze coming off the cold lake. He pushes my gloved hands down into the pockets of my white jacket. For a moment he is brushing my stomach, wandering over my hips. So close. Come closer. Inside me an answering jolt of desire even as I'm struggling with it. Even as he turns away.

'You don't have to explain,' I mutter, pulling my arms tight into my sides as we start to walk down the windy promenade towards the car. 'Men have needs, even you. You need women, and sex – just not with me, that's all.'

'So who was that flame-haired girl I was grappling with just now, tempting me to take her al fresco against the tree?' He stops again and grabs my stiff, unfriendly arms in a vice-like grip and gives me a shake. 'Was she a figment? Just one of a long line? Oh, I wish you'd shut that pouting sulky mouth of yours for just one minute!'

Now it's his voice ringing out over the water. A smart group of people all wearing dark green or navy Loden coats turn towards the commotion. Gustav calls out something in Italian which makes them laugh and wave. He marches me swiftly on then stabs his key at the car to open it.

I flinch at the emotion in his voice, allow myself a secret shiver of triumph that I've scratched more than his surface. I limp towards the car.

'I thought you were different, Serena. But like every other woman on the planet you've just managed to trick me into sounding crass, twisting the conversation to put me in the wrong.' He wrenches open the passenger door. 'Look. I was open with you. I told you from the start that since my marriage there have been – other females. Arm candy, some. Gold diggers, mostly. But the reason none of them remained in my life and certainly are not here in Lugano is that ultimately they didn't do it for me. Sorry. I know that sounds arrogant.'

'Yes. It does.'

He really can read my mind. Or at least my face, even out here, in the dark. But now I can't read his.

'They considered me cold, careless and uncommitted. And they were right.'

I wait for him to hand me into the car which he does with cold chivalry, and we drive away from the lake in silence. I'm relieved when we only drive up the mountain a short distance. The boulders and trees melt away and all at once we've arrived.

This is as far away from the grey turreted Colditz I imagined, with iron eagles guarding the ramparts and a spiked moat repelling invaders, as Polly's bright flat is from the grim house on the cliffs.

Because welcoming us with great open squares of flooding warm light and glimpses of roaring fires spilling woodsmoke from stone-built chimneys is a huge wooden chalet raised up on pillars the size of great American redwoods. Wooden gables and eaves and traditionally carved balconies sprout joyously from every angle, but they are the ornate frame to a super-chic structure with vast glass windows and doors. Tucked beneath the baronial front door is the garage, opening slowly to admit the car and displaying snow skis and water skis hanging on neat racks along its walls. And under what must be the main salon is a glass-walled wine cellar with rows of wine bottles.

Best of all is the blue glint of a steaming infinity pool

partly laid half in the grass bank overlooking the lake and glittering with frost, and partly disappearing inside the basement of the house.

Gustav hands me over to Dickson who hoists me into his arms and deposits me, slightly over-emphatically, onto one of the enormous white sofas in front of the fire. They both fuss about finding footstools and compresses. Dickson disappears to chop and baste and finish preparing a huge roast, which he carves and lays on a tray. A haunch of venison with vegetables baked with rosemary and thyme and other aromatic herbs I've never tasted before, followed by a treacle pudding big enough to do yoga on, all washed down with gallons of ruby-red wine. I remember my manners and thank them both, but otherwise say nothing.

When Dickson retires, Gustav takes up his favourite position beside the wide wooden mantelpiece, jabbing at the logs with a long iron poker. He's taken off his jacket and is wearing a black sweater which hints at the broad chest and flat stomach beneath. I slide my eyes away to stare into the dancing flames and let them blur into dancing feathers as I half close my eyes. As soon as I do that I can feel the exhaustion washing over me. He continues the conversation as if we haven't left off.

'Yet again, I'm sorry. I'm to blame for mucking about and galloping off earlier. For misreading the situation. For imposing my selfish needs onto you. You were scared and hurt and you needed me. Being needed by someone is different from having power over them, and far more alluring, and I'm a fool for not recognising that. I'm a fool for not recognising *you*.' He takes the silver chain out of his pocket. 'You're the one who's got under my skin, Folkes. You're the one I want by my side, as I said before, particularly now. Particularly here. And then when this is all done, those new horizons I was talking about.'

It's all too much for now. Who knew that a sore foot could affect an aching head? So instead of holding out my wrist for him to hook us together I pull the big fur rug right over me and settle myself as far back into the corner of the sofa as I can. I turn to stare out at the plunging mountain road leading back to civilisation, the winking lights of Lake Lugano spread out like a welcome mat below.

'It's so much white noise, Gustav. The idea was for me to come to Lake Lugano to help you with the ghosts, but I still think you're all locked in here together.' I start to shiver suddenly. I assume it's the cold, and the pain in my foot, and the delayed shock. 'I'll always be the outsider. I'm not the woman you need, Gustav.'

'I didn't say need. I said want.' Gustav holds the silver chain up to the light and watches it sparkle between his fingers. The light dances on his face, all sharp planes and deep shadows now. The chain has never looked so pretty, and so flimsy. 'But you know what? I think the ghosts have already fled.'

He looks down and I look up at the same time, and our eyes lock. His eyes are soft dark pools. The hard glitter has gone. The fever has gone. I think I can read tenderness there. Even pleading. But if his ghosts have fled, mine seem to be stirring sluggishly from wherever they are buried.

I lie there on the sofa, under the rug, the wind buffeting the windows and agitating the fire. I wonder if Gustav can see the weight of sadness in my eyes. He's never looked so handsome, and so elusive.

'Only you know that for sure,' I shrug wearily. 'As for clearing out the furniture or whatever you needed me to do, I can't be much use to you with this sore foot, can I? So I may as well go home tomorrow.'

Gustav comes and sits next to me. 'You're not going anywhere, my headstrong little filly. We're so close to the end now.'

'The end?'

He turns back the rug and picks up my wrist. He moves to clip the silver chain onto my bracelet. I know his eyes are burning on me but I resist the urge to stare back at him. Instead I close my own eyes, shaking my head.

I wait for him to attach it despite any resistance from me. It's his prerogative after all. It's our agreement I'm refusing to honour tonight. I must be making him angry. But the silver chain no longer feels like a safety net to me, or an anchor. It's becoming a shackle.

It falls limp and untethered across the rug. He drops it, and leaves me to sleep.

THIRTEEN

I'm tapping crossly at my phone. I want to speak to Polly. I need to tell her where I am, and why I'm here. I want to tell her I've woken up in an extraordinary bedroom which would resemble a sultan's harem if it wasn't for its pale pine walls and ceilings. The Italianate buildings of Lugano are hidden by the bristling barrier of dark green trees that populates Gustav's estate, creating the illusion that I am holed up in a very glamorous gingerbread house hidden in the forest, the crisp Alpine vista of violet mountains painted on like a box of Lindt.

I'm alone in my chocolate box chamber. I want to share all this before it fades. I need to hear Polly's voice. Her opinions. Her conclusions about all this. Maybe I can even cadge a visit to New York for Christmas. I wait for the tone. But what do you know? Up here in the idyllic mountains there's no signal.

I toss the mobile onto an upturned barrel carved with the faded words *Tre Api Merlot Reserva*, which serves as a bedside table. I lie back on the huge square pillow. No rush. I'm reclining on a kind of low-slung, carved teak bed the size of a raft. Emperors and opium smokers would sprawl on a bed like this to indulge their vices. It's draped in wine-coloured velvet and scattered with tasselled and fringed and sequinned Moroccan bolsters, and cushions which are soft to the touch. They sparkle and reflect the clear blue daylight. I feel like an empress, despite the frustration and isolation of last night. I stretch luxuriously, and realise I'm wearing a nightdress I've never seen before.

'Hello? Anyone here?'

It must be late morning. Behind gathering clouds the pale yellow sun is balancing on the highest peak on the other side of the lake. There's nobody here, and I'm glad. I want to be alone with my thoughts as I gather my belongings.

Except that my white jodhpurs and thermals have disappeared, along with the Louis Vuitton bag packed with clothes suitable for mountain walks and fireside dinners. Hiking Barbie and Dining Barbie.

All I have in here is my camera, my useless phone, and a shell-pink nightdress with spaghetti straps.

I swing my legs out of the bed. My body jumps and buzzes with life. Must be the reviving mountain air. I stretch out my arms and legs curiously, checking for flaws, for signs of someone manhandling me, but there are no scratches or bruises other than the slight stiffness and the violet hue still staining my ankle.

Did thc two men undress me together? Peel my winter clothes off, layer by layer revealing inch by inch of my bare body? Did they reach out to run a finger over my cheek, shoulder, trace the curve of my breast, run up inside my thigh? Did they grow hard looking at me, dare the other to make a macho remark about the sleep of the innocent, or did they deny the bulge in their trousers?

My hands slide between my knees, up the soft inside of my thighs as the fantasy takes hold. Was that chocolate cup doped to knock me out? Or the *Glühwein* we drank back here? If so it's had a medicinal effect. I haven't felt this clear-headed for years.

Did they have their way, the two of them exploring me with tongues and fingers, and other parts, forced to be stealthy so as not to wake me, both so horny as they tasted the Sleeping Beauty in front of the fire?

Or was Dickson dismissed to his quarters or down to the lass who lives by the lake so that Gustav could drink in the sight of me? Did he glance about for prying eyes, check I was still sleeping, then lay me down on this Moroccan divan, open me up carefully and gently, ease his hardness inside, feel my warm softness closing round?

My head falls back as my fingers accompany my thoughts, push urgently inside the space that's so empty, so ready to consume. I remember Gustav's deep, dark eyes penetrating mine.

The solitary satisfaction is too petty, too brief, and it swiftly evaporates. I compose myself, bat away the lingering frustration, pull my hair away from my hot face and secure it in a tall tight bun on top of my head. I swathe myself in an embroidered shawl shot with green and gold threads that's been left at the foot of the bed. I feel like a gypsy flamenco dancer as I pad through the open door to investigate.

I'm nearly knocked backwards by the dazzling light from the glass-walled corridor leading to the main salon. Someone has lit a fire, which is burning merrily. On the other side of that space, down another corridor, I follow the smell of coffee into a pine kitchen lined with sociable leather banquettes and bristling with stalactites of copper cooking utensils. I lean against the warm blue and white tiled wood burner as I fall hungrily upon the plates of pastries and fruit.

The quietness in the chalet solidifies as mist and fog closes in. I must find my clothes and handbag and the wherewithal to make my escape. Far below I can see the oblong of swimming pool, steam still curling into the air to repel the cold.

When I'm sure Dickson is out, I slip off the negligee, wrap a huge towel around me and limp down the stairs to plunge into the glittering water. The room is like a sauna, but I swim out through the glass doors into the garden kicking all the stiffness and stickiness away, the warm water steaming around me as the dark grey fog drops down like a thick curtain.

The mountains have disappeared. I can just about make out their majestic, strong outline, forming a guard around the valley and the lake. I lie on my back in the water, the tip of my nose freezing, the rest of me warm as a bath. The chalet looks down at me, so many unexplored balconies and rooms. Just as I turn onto my front to swim back into the house I fancy a shadow crosses behind one of the huge windows. Surely a cloud reflected, or a big bird flapping home through the fog.

Suddenly I feel an urgency to get out of the pool. Get out of here. It's all so beautiful, so warm, so luxurious, and yet it's all so alien. It's not mine. This slice of potential heaven belongs to him. And to her. Never will it belong to me, and in any case I don't want it.

I realise when I get back up to the salon that the ministrations of Gustav and Dickson last night combined with the cooling effect of the swimming pool this morning have made the swelling in my ankle go down. I'm left with a dull ache but can easily have a good snoop around before I leave. I slip on the negligee and shawl and come to the foot of a wide wooden staircase, lit by the glass dome above and ringed by a wooden gallery. I've never been able to resist a staircase ascending into the unknown. Just as I couldn't resist the lure of the stone staircase in that Venetian convent, flanked by its ecstatic saints.

The gallery opens at the far end over the salon with its

carved fireplace still burning with sweet-smelling pine logs. This chalet is like a stage set. You could be having a *tête à tête* with one person and someone else could eavesdrop from above, or burst into an aria.

I decide to retrieve my camera. I may as well conduct my own little travelogue, otherwise Polly will never believe my story when I take her through every detail. But near the top of the main stairs I notice an alcove leading to another, narrower set spiralling up to another floor. Something, or someone, is driving me on to explore.

Unlike the other locked doors, the one at the top of the spiral is fashioned from studded iron like a prison cell. It swings open. I step inside a long thin room which presumably extends the width of the house. It looks like a theatrical props store room. There is a brass bed in the corner hung about with tapestries, a couple of free-standing fringed lamps and a dressing table, but it all looks staged rather than cosy. Instead of a wardrobe there are garments hanging from the kind of metal rail you'd find in the stock room of a retail store.

Margot ran a boutique, didn't she? Fashion. And accessories.

There is no other furniture. The other three walls are simply mirrored, with chrome barres bolted on as if for dance exercises. There are no generous windows embracing the valley below. Only a few skylights set into the pitched ceiling which is also mirrored. When I flick on the switches, intermittently placed black chandeliers send out a dappled, swaying light answered by a low red glow from the standard lamps by the bed.

I pad across the bare wooden floor, aware of the creak of the boards and the goosebumps rising sharply on my skin as the cold permeates. I wonder why Dickson hasn't bothered to put on any heating up here. I shiver in my flimsy nightdress. I'm Goldilocks tiptoeing round the house of the Three Bears.

Despite the bone-crunching cold there's the eerie sense in this room that someone has just got up and left. I notice a head-shaped dent in one of the pillows on the brass bed. The sheets and old-fashioned eiderdown are flung back and crumpled. Above the bed is a row of hooks from which various whips hang. I recognise the long black whip the dominatrix used on Crystal in the video. It makes my little nun's whip look like a stick of candy floss.

Even more intriguingly, on the dressing table are several oversized bottles of perfume and a scattering of lipsticks and mascara. Crumpled rolls of cotton wool are smeared with lipstick and face powder. I limp over to look more closely. The bottles are all different sizes, but one of the perfumes is the same one as I wear: Eternity.

I half expect to find the portrait of Dorian Gray propped up against the wall. Except that I still don't know what Margot looks like.

Ghostly fingers tiptoe up my spine as I spin round, looking for other clues. Why haven't they emptied this room? Is the house so big that they forgot about it? Is this the room Gustav intends me to clear? Is he preserving it like a shrine, make-up and whips and all? Or keeping it for when Margot returns?

On the brass bed various items of underwear are splayed out, arranged like a taped crime-scene figure, outlining where the body was found.

There is a black basque, unlaced. I shuffle over and finger it as if it might bite. It looks hard and shiny like the carapace of a scorpion but when I touch it I realise it's made of very thin latex. I hold it against myself in front of the mirror. It seems to mould itself round my contours.

The house is so silent. I shiver, and try to put the basque

down, but it seems stuck to me. I glance at my face in the mirror. My expression shocks me. I am smiling, my teeth glinting in the half light, and my eyes are half closed, strips of green like a cat. My tongue whips across my lower lip. I feel horny, a kind of sick, sudden uncoiling.

I've never worn anything as daring as this. Surely a quick try-on won't hurt?

The flimsy negligee and shawl slither lifelessly to the floor. My white breasts fall heavily forwards, nipples shrinking sharply in the cold, and I shiver with pleasure. The cold makes me super-sensitive all over. Puckers up my skin. Goosebumped and tense, every touch is as sharp as a scratch, every lick of air a smack. I fit the two cups over my breasts, hooking the corset tightly round my ribs to keep it in place. Even though it fits like a glove, I lace it tightly as well. Now I can hardly breathe. My breasts ooze over the rigid whalebone top, puffing in an effort to gain oxygen. The reflection in the mirror is very white, and very still. While the real me is fidgeting to get used to the tightness of the garment, my reflection is simply staring.

And then it hits me, as if I didn't already know. I saw this same basque in the video. The dominatrix whipping Crystal was wearing it. Margot's skin has been sealed inside it, just like mine is, and now it's trying to squeeze the life out of me. I'm the challenger. I must be more voluptuous than Margot was because the basque is too tight. If she wore this contraption while entertaining her guests and clients no wonder she was permanently hyped up and hungry for trouble.

There are other aromas. Surely Gustav didn't sleep in here last night? Is that why the bed is rumpled? Would he sleep in the bed of a woman he claims to loathe?

But the stark image that rises as I stare at the bed is of the two of them clinched together. Margot and Gustav making the beast with two backs, her thighs open, gripping him like a lioness, riding on top of him. Her back is to me. I'm guessing she had long black hair. Or maybe she always wore that leather mask when having sex. But Gustav's long legs are kicking out underneath her as she straddles him, as she brandishes the long black riding crop above her head and smacks it down onto whatever part of him she can reach, whipping him into a frenzy.

Jealousy stabs so hard that I clutch my side in pain. Each time I take a breath, my breasts heave and my nipples prod at the tight seam of the corset. My movements have slowed down, as if I'm wading through molasses. I stand there in the swaying fractured light, watching my nipples flip over the edge and stiffen as they meet the cold air. I lick my finger and rub each one, making them wet and cold with saliva. As I start to pinch them my body sets up an answering, heavy pulse. The corset squeezes the breath out of me until my ears sing.

He'll be back soon. I should unlace myself. But before I do, why not use these clothes to test him, once and for all? Why not see if Gustav has been telling the truth? See if it's true that he wants her erased from this house and from his life?

I start to spin about in front of the mirror, lurching on my weakened ankle until I am dizzy. I come to rest in a raunchy pose. The corset squeezes me like a fist. This is no fancy dress. This is the uniform of a professional whore trained to give and withstand pain.

My hair is still pinned into the kind of severe cornet that Crystal would favour. My face is dead white, my lips colourless and my eyes are hard and staring. The corset makes me look war-like, yet debauched. Gustav's warrior princess. Let's pile it on. I pick up a thick leather dog collar studded with spikes, and buckle that round my neck.

His reaction when he sees me will be the proof I need. This is my one chance to get rid of Margot for good. Replace her with my own irresistible self. I allow myself to preen in the alien outfit. Big breasts, waist pulled in unnaturally tiny. Face deathly pale. What would Crystal say? What would cousin Polly say if she could see me cavorting like a burlesque dancer in another woman's bedroom?

I am naked beneath the basque, my nipples dark red and sparking painfully with the cold, my white thighs pressed together in fake modesty. I look like Rapunzel, the prostitute staring out of the photographs of the Parisian brothel.

The wind rattles the window above me. I prowl about the room looking for more fetish gear. When I move I swivel my hips stiffly, all the natural suppleness reined in. I pull on a pair of elbow-length lace opera gloves. And there's another pair of long rubber gloves arranged on the bed. Not gloves. It's a pair of black leggings.

I have to roll these on like stockings. The stranger in the mirror looks like me but moves and acts like someone else. Now I can't get them off. They are stuck fast. My own nervous sweat makes a kind of glue. Too late I realise she would have used talcum powder or Vaseline or something to stop them sticking. The rubber squeaks and pinches, forming a kind of membrane.

Instead of shedding my skin, I am acquiring a new one. What does that make me? A snake? A chameleon? A butterfly regressing into its chrysalis? The reincarnation of Margot?

The crotch of the trousers is cut out. At the back, my buttocks are totally exposed. Like wearing skin-tight cowboy chaps. I continue to stamp around the room because moving is easier. The front and back openings of the trousers are linked by a rubber thong which runs like chicken wire between the two and starts to chafe me.

Now I am a mannequin in a specialist magazine. I'm the conquering dominatrix.

I touch myself down there and flinch. It's sensitive as a scald. The squeezed lips are turning a livid dark pink while the rubber twangs at the little hairs.

Why didn't I go the full Hollywood wax? Polly swears by its clean nakedness.

One more item to go. A pair of patent thigh boots are practically doing the can-can to attract my attention. I pull these on over the leggings with great difficulty. My ankle protests as I try the teetering heels, but I ignore it. Walking is virtually a sex act in itself. I try tripping along like a geisha, then loping mannishly with splayed legs. Whichever way I walk the tight thong shaves away at me. There is no slack. Each time it cuts, the string slices into the soft groove.

The window rattles again. I have no idea what the time is. The chalet seems shrouded in permanent semi-darkness today. The cold air on my breasts and shoulders is a mean contrast with the salty sweat steaming up inside the rubber.

One thing missing. I root through the make-up scattered all over the dressing table, paint on some grey glittering eye shadow then choose a dark purple lipstick the colour of a bruise. I twist back the black lid, the lipstick's knob-head emerging crudely.

I smear it over my mouth, breath clouding the mirror. My hand is shaking so much I veer over the edges, making my mouth big and uneven as if I've been punched. I touch some stripes of colour onto the soreness throbbing below. It feels so good, the cool stickiness running over me like a tongue. I'm painting myself like a savage going into battle.

What would Margot think, seeing me in her bedchamber, dressed up as her, smearing myself with the same lipstick that once coloured her mouth?

And then I hear the rattle and bump of a car driving up the rocky road below me, and the slamming of a door.

Holy shit. Oh, help. Help!

There is nowhere to hide. I'll skulk in here but he'll find me soon enough. There's nowhere to run. Because I can't run. This gear is so tight it is threatening to cut off my circulation. I can only stand here and brazen it out.

Gustav's boots march into the hall and into the salon. His footsteps, the jangle of his keys, the clearing of his throat, everything echoes round the chalet.

'Serena? Where are you lurking?'

He marches into the kitchen quarters. Is Dickson back, too? Are they discussing sauces and marinades and spits?

Yet again I wish that Crystal was here. She would know what to do.

I tweak and wrench at the rubber, panting with fear and humiliation. All I can do is stick to the plan. The test, remember? I want him to find me like this. I need to know what he will say, what he will do. I stand with my legs apart and my hands on my hips.

I've been expecting you, Mr Bond.

And then his feet on the stairs, clump, clump, various doors unlocking down the corridor. Another pause. I scrabble frantically at the trousers. In the mirror my face is still that deadly shade of white, the green eyes a sickly flicker as if there is a pilot light where my pupils should be. These pouting lips are the colour of crushed blueberries.

At last the footsteps stampede up the spiral stairs.

'Margot?'

An anguished sob escapes my throat. 'No, no, no. It's me!'

'Serena! Thank God! Serena!' Gustav bangs open the metal door so hard that it takes a chunk of plaster off the wall. He stammers out my name, over and over, then stops dead.

It's been said so many times. But Gustav Levi really *does*

look as if he's seen a ghost, what little colour he had in his cheeks draining totally away. His eyes sink back into their sockets. His hands drop down limply by his sides, his fingers twitching as if he has just been shot.

'But what the bloody hell are you doing in here?'

I suddenly feel stupid. And very, very sorry. I try to speak but it's as if someone has gagged me. The lipstick glues my mouth. I know I've done something very, very wrong. Either I grovel, or I brazen it out. And in these clothes, there's only one way to behave. Like the woman he just shouted for. Like their owner.

Legs akimbo, hands on hips. Toss my head. Look down my nose at him.

'Looks like you caught me playing dress up.'

My voice is rough, as if I haven't used it for a long time.

The atmosphere in the space between us crackles with menace.

'This isn't a game. When will you learn? I thought this room was empty. This vile crap should be long gone.'

His eyes are wide and staring, his black hair sticking to his forehead, and he's breathing hard as if he's run all the way up the hill from the lake. His nostrils flare like a cornered animal's. I notice he's shaved himself clean this morning. It makes him look stern and hard. He's stretching the silver chain taut between his fists.

I look down at myself, the skintight rubber. The nipples poking out like missiles. Lipstick messy all over my mouth. Back at his horrified expression. My body as a weapon.

Margot's body.

'I don't believe you want it gone. It was all laid out here, awaiting the mistress of the house.' I point at the clothes, the bed, the whips. 'It's the same equipment she uses in that film, right?'

His eyes snap with livid red fire. He seems to have grown

in height and width. He's filling the space between us. 'Who told you that was her in the film?'

'Crystal told me. She also told me that house in Baker Street is where you used to live. No. Don't be angry with her. She's a good friend to you. I peppered her with questions, and she told me about Margot, what she did for kicks. But what I need to know is, why is this stuff all still here, Gustav?' My voice is shaking. 'Is this a trick? Am I some kind of bait to get her back?'

I sway on my high heels, and the movement rouses him.

'Just take that filthy rubbish off,' he hisses, taking one long step towards me. His fists are still clenched. 'You have no idea how ridiculous you look.'

His black brows are over his eyes like shades. Deep grooves gash the sides of his mouth. I don't think 'ridiculous' covers it. Horror, dismay, disdain are closer to the mark.

'I would if I could, but it's welded onto me.'

'Take it off, Serena, or so help me! What's happened to that sweet, smart kid?'

Without realising what I'm doing I snatch the black whip off the hook, watch in sick delight as his face contorts.

'Maybe she's not all she seems! Maybe she's all twisted up inside. Maybe she's been, what did Crystal call it, so badly *neglected* she's beyond redemption!'

Gustav eyes the whip. Clenches his fists. 'This isn't you talking, Serena.'

'How do you know what's going on inside here?' I bash at my head with the handle of the whip. 'You've known me for five minutes. Just tell me the truth for once. Put me out of my misery. Does seeing me dressed in her clothes turn you on? Would you like me to thrash you? I'm not a fool, Gustav. I know you don't want me. But do you still want her?'

Those black eyes of his, boring into me. A black mist descending over us both. He struggles to get a grip on what's going on here. Is he daring me to challenge him, or is he too shocked to move? Have I overstepped the mark? I grasp the post of the bed for support. I'm forced to move like a stripper. Something wicked and dark is sliding through my veins. Is it her he sees, or is it me?

'You stupid, stupid girl.'

He wrenches the whip out of my hand. Then he pulls off one lace glove, hooks the silver chain onto my bracelet and ties it quickly around the brass bed post.

'Bend over, you little slut. If the only way is to thrash this gibberish out of you then so be it. Again and again, until you beg for mercy.'

'Let me go! It's me. It's Serena! When will *you* learn that I'm not your precious Margot?'

'Don't you dare mention that name!'

He shoves me between my shoulder blades so that my face is squashed into the satin eiderdown. Kicks my legs apart, and before I can take a breath he's brought the whip down on my exposed buttocks, so swift, so sharp that I can only gasp in shock.

'That feels good, doesn't it? Admit it!' His voice is low and guttural like a dog.

I twist on the bed, yank at the silver chain. 'Yes, alright, yes! It feels fucking great! Do it again! I'm a bad girl! Whip me again!'

The whip fizzes through the air, quivering like an arrow before it makes contact with a fresh piece of my still tender butt. The heat of it spreads through me, probing me and again, so weird, there comes after it, in a kind of calming wake, a sense of cleanliness and peace.

Is this how Margot's clients felt? A sense of penance and absolution, like those Venetian nuns felt? Or was it a perverted, kinky, never-sated addiction?

Gustav doesn't speak but thwacks the whip down on me

once, twice, three times more, watching me twist and groan with each smack.

'Enough, Serena? Have those demons fled?'

'Demons?'

I hear him smack the whip down on the palm of his hand. 'Whatever or whoever possessed you to come into this room and dress up like that. But it has to stop. The whipping. It all has to stop.'

But as soon as the whipping stops, the clothes start suffocating me again. I struggle round onto my elbows.

'Yes, yes, all gone. But Gustav, please–'

He pushes me back onto the eiderdown and unwraps the silver chain from the bed post. He seems calm, spookily so, but he hasn't finished with me yet. He links the chain to the other wrist, then runs it between the two posts above the pillows so that both my arms are wrenched up over my head.

'I told you I'd had enough so you can let me go now!' I kick out furiously, but every movement makes the boots tighten on my sore ankle, the rubber snag on my skin, the whalebones dig into my ribs. Excitement knots with panic behind my navel.

He shakes his head, breathing hard, then swipes everything off the dressing table onto the floor, perfume bottles smashing and releasing sprays of musky, overpowering fragrance, necklaces and bracelets and earrings clattering and breaking, diamonds and pearls flying off their strings.

There's a flash of lightning through one of the skylights above us, the yellow light illuminating the yellow fury in his eyes. Another flash shows me the pair of scissors he is now brandishing like a dagger.

I scream and wriggle, the silver chain biting into my wrists. 'Don't hurt me!'

He flings the whip down on the bed then he's over by the metal rail, cutting all the garments hanging there until they're reduced to rags of leather and lace. Then he rips one of the sheets from under me and throws it onto the floor, bundles the clothes, the jewellery, the broken perfume bottles, everything onto the sheet.

'They're killing me! These clothes. I can't breathe, Gustav!'

He straightens, panting hard, then he kneels on the bed, pulls my hair off my face, yanking my head up close to his.

'Can I trust you to stop this now?' He flips at the collection of whips hanging on hooks above the bed, knocking them off one by one. 'Has Serena come back to me?'

I nod dumbly. He bends each whip over his knee and snaps it in two.

Then he's at my feet, yanking the boots off and throwing them onto the pile, ignoring my squeals of pain when he lets my sore ankle drop. He pins my legs down under his knees and tugs at the rubber trousers. But now he can see that they are welded on. The body heat has made superglue of my sweat. He can't even get a grip. His fingers just slip off. My blood is sluggish as it struggles to circulate. My nipples burn. I am deranged with lack of oxygen. Every laboured breath makes the corset tighter.

Pain has finally overtaken pleasure.

The emotions inside me are like unravelling wire wool. Fear at the anger in his voice and the tightness of the silver chain imprisoning me on Margot's bed. Submission, because he's caught me doing something wrong and he's enraged. Relief, because he's here, taking charge. Lust, because there's animal fire in his eyes. Creeping despair, because I don't know who he sees.

He starts to cut one rubber leg then the other, slicing as if he's ribboning courgettes. Thunder crashes the clouds together, percussion drumming in the sky. My ribs are pushing uselessly against the corset to get air into my lungs. The bed seems to be bucking. The room jumps every time lightning strikes.

I stop straining against the silver chain, even though it's biting into my wrists. I let my arms rest on the crumpled pillows under my head while the rubber, the thong, the whalebones work my body to a froth. I lie still because there's no juice left.

There's a glint of metal in the air, and then he starts cutting again. The scissors run across my stomach. I go rigid as the cold blade snips against my skin, travels up my ribs, my spine, back over my breasts and hips until the corset falls away at last. As my body expands and settles back into its proper contours and air fills my lungs again, the tattered ribbons of black rubber fall round me like strips of dead skin.

'I promise all the nonsense is finished, Gustav,' I whisper, yanking at the silver chain imprisoning my wrists. My nakedness feels too exposed. I try to close my legs. 'But you need to let me go.'

'Never!'

Gustav is hunched over me, pale and angular, his mouth slightly open, teeth glinting. He looks like he's ready to sever my jugular. He reaches under my neck and starts to unbuckle the dog collar, but then he stops. His eyes hold that impenetrable blackness again, his Halloween look. The only sign of life is the beating pulse in his neck.

No wonder. He has a naked girl spread-eagled and helpless beneath him. If he's all man, as Crystal assured me, this will be one temptation too far.

He leaves the collar on. I come to my senses and start to wriggle and kick. Quick as a flash he tugs me further down the bed so that I'm right underneath him. The silver chain goes taut and I can't move my arms at all. My bare breasts curve into the air, rising with my frantic breathing. The rigid red points of my nipples are impossible to ignore.

'You're mine, Serena. You're not going anywhere.'

'Tell me, just tell me!' I suck in more breath and kick my legs out in desperation. 'Is it Margot you still want?'

'Don't you *ever* say that name to me!'

His voice is a deadly hiss echoed by the wind whistling round the chalet. He doesn't take his eyes off me. He runs his hands over my stomach, my hips and thighs, digging his fingers into my flesh, pressing right through the skin to the bone, runs them up the tendons at the top of my legs which scream with tension as I try to close them.

'Answer my question!'

'That name is like a dagger.' He leans down to snarl his mouth against my ear. 'What I saw just then was my worst nightmare.'

He doesn't blink. It's as if he's never seen me before. His face is streaked red with lust. He wrenches my thighs open, one hand cradling my chin in a gesture that would be tender if it wasn't also forcing my head back down on the pillow. What's he afraid of? That I'll lunge up and bite him?

The dog collar must still give me that evil vamp look, even though the rest of me is stripped bare. One band of studded leather can make me look like a slut. I'm turned on by that, and so is he.

I'm hypnotised by the distance in his burning eyes, as if he's at the far end of a very long tunnel.

The passion flares in his face then seems to settle, as if he's reached a long overdue decision. Is that a warning, or an awakening? Perhaps it's lightning reflected from above. Then I hear it. The swift unzipping of his jeans.

I kick and struggle against the silver chain as his hand moves downwards. He's so powerful. He's pinning me down with one hand. Taking hold of himself with the other.

Sex as punishment. This should be the answer to my prayers.

I'm damned if I'm going to show him how much I want him despite everything, despite her, despite it all. It's this ferocious desire that's consuming me. I twist about with a new strength, tortured by the surge of dark energy still coiling inside me.

Thunder rumbles outside as I try to bend my knees for leverage to kick him off, and that's when the lightning zig-zags across the skylight and I see his face in sizzling clarity. His hair is thrown back. His eyes are burning, his mouth a cruel line. He's looking at me as if I am his deadliest enemy.

One more superhuman effort to rouse him from this stupor, remind him who he is with. I kick out with my leg and he suddenly catches my flailing leg, holds it akimbo in the air and then slaps me, hard, on my buttock.

I squeal and writhe as the sting finds its mark and the renewed sharp heat follows, radiating and spreading through my body, melting my defences. And then I catch sight of myself in the mirrored ceiling above. The white flash of my flailing leg, the stretch of my bound arms.

The dark shape of Gustav leaning over me, his shoulder blades sharp through his black shirt. He spreads his strong thighs to keep mine open.

'I won't let you go! I won't let her take you away from me!'

He keeps hold of my leg, slaps me again. I wriggle and struggle, taking furtive glances at the reflection above me, and perversely the more futile the resistance proves against his iron grip, the more I'm fired with strength and energy.

He watches me intently, his fingers gripping my leg. As soon as I gather more strength to kick out at him, he slaps me hard and each time his arm goes up and that smack lands on me, my resistance translates into wild, wanton desire.

A final slap and my bottom bounces off the bed. He's too quick for me, too strong. He grabs my ankles and hooks them round his hips. My arms are tied tight. Nothing else I can do. I'm raised like an offering.

And then he opens his fingers to display what he's got for me.

In his free hand, extending from the shy V of his zipper, the big beautiful length of him. Made hard by the sight of me dressed as a dominatrix whore, the whore stripped bare. It worked like a charm, and now I'm the subdued sex slave. I've no more fight, pretend or otherwise. There is a phrase trying to assemble itself in my head to explain the calmness overtaking me as I surrender to him. To treacly languor. And now he's here, pushing inside me. He finds me wet and ready. Lust is forged in the furnace of his eyes. I tighten my legs around his bottom and give in.

This is where he should be.

I venture one last look up at the ceiling, see how our bodies are poised. I'm shy of my own reflection. Briefly I wonder how that reflected pose would look in a photograph, the black jeans, black shirt, black hair of my lover contrasting with my white legs wrapped round him.

I focus on him again. Our eyes are locked together. He's watching. Always watching me. No words. I grip tightly, wait, wait, and then he propels me into that lovely movement. Slow, slow, fast, faster, our bodies meshed together.

A faint chill ripples through me. Is this as it should be, though? Is he seeing me, or her? Someone else? Am I an object to him, the dotted line on an agreement? Something to be used, now that it's all coming to an end, now he's got me where he wants me?

He falls forwards onto his hand. He lifts me higher with the force of his passion, the silver chain biting and gnawing my wrists as our bodies battle. His fine features are more beautiful than ever, even as they start to blur. His black eyes, narrowed and steady, the mouth working silently. My eyes half close, my head falls back on the pillow. Waves wash over me as I try to understand what I've just read in his face.

Gustav Levi is calm for the first time. A ship that's been hurled by the storm into harbour. He's where he wants to be. He is finally inside me, taking full physical possession. Fucking me. He increases his pace, thrusting once, twice more, his pleasure, my pleasure, this wonderful new calmness and belonging, then as the storm crashes over us, over the chalet, battering at the mountain, we come together.

He collapses across me, his face in the pillow next to my shoulder, his body heavy, crushing the air out of me, but I don't care. I am just relishing the heavy thump of his heart against mine, the rushing of hot breath against my shoulder, the slow relax of his limbs as our breathing, and the storm, subside.

I run my lips over his cheek, but he shakes his head and rolls away from me. Now the crisp closure of his zipper sounds so bitter and final. Shutting me out again. Not only that, but now that his warmth is removed I start to shiver, outside as well as within. The storm has given way to hail now, white stones crashing onto the skylights like someone chucking gravel to attract attention.

There are all sorts of things I should say now. Things he's never heard before. This is my chance to find the right words to make him mine.

But what I actually say is, 'My wrists are hurting.'

He kneels up quickly and unties the silver chain, his face troubled again. He rubs my arms as he releases them, running his finger round the inside of the bracelet where it has been branding my skin. I can barely move my arms. They are stiff and sore with all the tension, the straining to escape, welcoming yet fighting the sexy struggle.

He remains hunched above me, shaking his head. I let my hand fall onto his back where his black shirt is sticking with sweat. Trace the shoulder blades, the bumps of his spine. The inflation of his ribs as he tries to calm his breath.

A residual, satisfied moan escapes me.

'I'm a monster. You see?' He moves away from me, running his fingers over the silver bracelet before standing up. 'All I ever do is hurt people.'

And then the lights go out. The room is plunged into frightening darkness, only a few squares of sickly moonlight coming through the ceiling and gleaming on the wall of mirrors.

Gustav wraps the Spanish shawl round me, gathers me into his arms and runs from Margot's chamber of horrors, down the spiral, down into the big warm salon. He drops me onto the big sofa with the fur rugs and I roll helplessly into the deep cushions, the shawl tangled around me as he lights banks of church candles with a gas taper.

'That's better. Much better.'

As each wick springs into fiery life the hardness leaves his eyes. Those long lashes are half-closed, trying to hide whatever fondness or farewell has replaced the fury.

I'm so stunned, so sated. Every sinew feels stretched and strained with post-coital exhaustion. So thorough. So bone-deep. I feel so womanly, so meaningful, so equal to him now. I know the meaning of rough now, and he can be as rough as he likes. I'll always want more. I welcome the danger, the threat, and what else did I expect from him? To be handled like a snow-white virgin?

He stokes the fire. I watch his lean body, the black jeans clothing that beautiful manliness. The black shirt untucked, still sticking to his back, showing me the muscled torso beneath. The jeans still half-zipped.

The thunder outside has calmed a little, but over the mountains thick clouds scud erratically about the sky like horses stampeding across the moors, not sure which way to go.

'Serena.' He clears his throat and comes to sit on the coffee table in front of me with a bottle of Merlot and two glasses. His head hangs. 'I'm sorry.'

'Don't break the spell, Gustav.' I look away from him, out over the lake. I'm scared I'm going to cry. 'Sorry means you wish that hadn't happened.'

'Yes. No. You're so beautiful, Serena. You blow my mind, and you deserve better. I had no right to take it out on you just then, but any hint, any shade of that woman and I'm possessed all over again. You've seen my true colours. Being forceful with a woman is the only way I know. And that is my true confession.'

He's staring down at his glass of wine, but his lips are curling as if he's tasting something nasty. I drink from my glass and relish the blood-warm Merlot seeping through me.

'You didn't force me. I'm not a fragile little flower, Gustav.'

He puts his hand up to hush me. His eyes are searching, always searching. 'I want to try to explain it to you if I can, and then never speak of this, or her, again. This is how we lived. She seduced me like Eve with the forbidden fruit. If Eve was a witch.'

I'm trying to understand. 'Like the Snow Queen of Narnia seduces Edmund with Turkish delight.'

'Exactly. Except that I was an adult. If I wasn't so hooked I could have stopped it. I became this brute. *Her* brute. All harmless at first, the insidious poisoning you don't even notice. Same as any drug. I was this cocky young man about town when we met, she was the sexy older woman. But she wouldn't let me touch her without all the paraphernalia. She taunted me that it was the only way I could turn her on. I know now that that was her fault, not mine. But I was only flesh and blood, Serena. I was enslaved.'

He winds his fingers so hard around the glass I'm afraid he'll break it. I look away from him, over the pretty lights sparkling beside the lake. The clouds have thinned now and a wedge of moon is peeking out between two low crags on the other side.

'Our lifestyle became our drug habit. Her demands were like those medieval racks, always turning, always tightening the pressure. More equipment, more participants, more pain, becoming professional, bringing it into the house despite her promises, then the exhibitionism, finally the filming. And I ended up as an extra.'

I hold my glass out. 'I can't imagine you doing anything you're not totally in control of, Gustav.'

'I was a different man then. That's what addiction does to you.' His face is hollow with strange sadness. 'Oh, you wouldn't have been able to tell from the outside. I was a stone or two heavier, maybe. More pompous. Ruthless about building up my business. In fact work was my saviour. But behind closed doors all was chaos. That's why I've become such a control freak.'

I take another deep swallow of wine.

'How did you end it?'

'Someone else ripped the wool from my eyes.' He rubs his eyes, leaving his eyelashes matted. 'My brother was the one ray of sanity. He kept me focused. He gave me the strength to put an end to it. But then he saw things in that house he shouldn't have done. Maybe you can guess what things. He was disgusted. His respect, his love for me nose-dived. She pounced. Poured pestilence in his ear. It all backfired.'

There is a long, long pause. I remember Crystal's words about his brother being his Achilles heel. Being brainwashed. What did he see? Gustav whipping Margot. Or worse. Margot whipping Gustav. I feel sick. I can't ask about it. Not now.

I kneel up against the back of the sofa and rest my chin

on my hand to stare out at the serene scene spread out beneath us, so different from the turmoil up here.

'And the others? The other women? Were you a control freak with them, too?'

'You make me sound like some kind of stud. There were only a couple, and they didn't hang around for long.' He laughs bitterly. 'But yes. No-one could handle me.'

I remain staring out of the window, watching the stormy sky settle down. Trying to make sense of his words.

'Enough now. It's me who should be saying sorry. You brought me here to help you, but I'm afraid I've made it worse.'

'No you haven't. You couldn't make it any worse. But what you have done with all that play-acting upstairs is deflect me from my immediate plans for this weekend. I was going to take you out to my favourite wine bar.'

'Sounds good.'

'Maybe later. The Bottegone del Vino can wait. There's something else I want to sample much, much more.'

He slides off the coffee table, comes to sit on the sofa behind me. He reaches up and pulls the pins from my hair so that it tumbles round my face, then he starts to stroke it over my shoulders, down my back. I can't see his face but my skin shivers under his touch. I pull my thighs together tightly because the ache of desire is starting to throb all over again.

'I was furious with you when I saw you standing in her room of pain, I can't deny that, but your disobedient, crazy, naïve actions have chased it all away.' He runs his hands under my hair, finds the dog collar and finally unbuckles it. You could say he's unbuckling my last defence. 'In fact your curiosity has done me a favour.'

'Has it killed the cat?'

He winds my hair round his finger and tugs my head

backwards. 'You're my breath of fresh air, Serena. Don't you see? You're the only one who can handle me. And look how I've repaid you. By smacking you, and ravishing you.'

'I only ever think of you as a true gentleman, Gustav.' I rest my head in the palm of his hands. 'Whatever you do to me, however you do it, I'll love it just the same.'

His hands stroke the skin under my hair and then I feel them plucking at the Spanish shawl and slowly peeling that down my body. He pauses, waiting for me to cover myself again, but I don't resist. I want to be bare before him. I feel his warm, damp lips running down my spine, and I tilt my head back, stretch my arms along the back of the sofa, sending him my message.

I mean every word. Take me.

He attaches the silver chain to my bracelet and I hold it up to the firelight to see it sparkling as it joins us.

'Did you ever give this to anyone else?'

'Never.' He flips the chain as if it's a harp string. 'It's unique. Yours and mine.'

Then his hands part my thighs, stroking up and down the soft skin there, up into the secret places where he's been before. First his fingers. Then the rest of him. He owns me. I shiver with renewed pleasure. His breath is hot on my hair. He is nibbling and biting me, his morsel. It's easier not looking at him. Like being blindfolded. I can feel everything that more intensely for not seeing.

Outside the world is hushed because snow is finally falling. As his fingers wander over my hips, peeling the shawl right away, I watch the snow forming a ridge on the balcony rail as if barricading us in.

Gustav bends me over the back of the sofa. The cushions press into my chest, making my breath more shallow. He's moulding me again, Pygmalion manipulating life into his statue. He pulls my hips towards him, echoes of that earlier roughness, fits my bottom up against him and oh there's the shape of him, he's so hard again, he so wants me too. My body is crushed against the cushions as I feel his heat behind me.

'Did you ever do it like this with anyone else?'

I laugh softly at the echoing question. 'Never.'

I push my bottom towards him, so wet, so eager, the brazen hussy in this house of hussies. He pushes forward to meet me. I feel him hot and hard between my thighs. Beating with heat, edging into me from behind. My first time. Jake and I weren't what you'd call adventurous. Just lusty, and energetic, and impatient. He never took me like this. What Polly would call doggy-style.

My knees buckle beneath me. Gustav's hands are rougher on me now as he holds me and fits inside and starts to move, but I'm learning to like the madness and the urgency, I like the way he decides how he wants me.

He pushes in deep, so deep. His hands dig into my hips. I wish I could see his face. I wish I could drown in his eyes as we start to move together. I wish I could kiss him.

I judder forwards as his hardness fills me totally, pushes to the centre of my body. He propels me, pulls me back against him, our bodies joined, and then he's going faster, and my body is gripping him, and we have a new rhythm now, hard, fast, but somehow calmer. I arch sensuously against him, tensing to lock every sensation tight inside me as I recognise the hidden phrase that tried to reveal itself to me earlier, the first time. I can put it into words now. As he comes explosively, shooting an answering wave of ecstasy up inside me I moan with delight and then slump forwards, carrying him with me.

He's fitted inside me, but I'm the one who's come home.

He rests on top of me for a few moments, his weight almost unbearably heavy and hot on my back. His cheek comes to rest against mine and, still fitted together, we look out of the huge window. Our pale reflected faces are side by side in the glass, his eyes black and glittering beside my wide green, still unbelieving stare.

'Serena, Serena, you're the only one after so many desolate years,' Gustav murmurs as he pulls away. I stay very still. I can feel stickiness on my thighs as he wraps me up again in the Spanish shawl. 'My Halloween girl.'

The moon has unpicked itself from the crags and is sailing free, white and proud in the sky like a Chinese lantern.

FOURTEEN

'So warm. Like a freshly baked baguette.'

That's what he whispered in my ear at some half-lit dawn time this morning, breathing into my hair, his moulding hands roving gently over me, his lips on my neck, my spine, my cheek. Not the rough, blank-eyed Gustav I've known before. This was a gentle lover who seemed intent on exploring every part of me until we were both satisfied.

My mission, should I choose to accept it, is to show him I'm equal to any punishment he cares to inflict on me. But also to teach him how other mortals live and love without props and weapons.

I sensed that I was back in my own harem bed now, not on the sofa in the salon, and then I was dimly aware of him lifting my arm to wind the silver chain round my wrist. Probably just leaving it loosely looped round to remind me. I remember him turning me over onto my stomach, handling me like new dough, his hands on my bottom again, spreading me open, my body lifting to him.

I shivered in my slumber, waiting to feel him enter, come right up inside me, filling me with his hot hardness. I wouldn't wake up completely, though. I didn't want to leave this dream.

But in the end he didn't do it. His hands and mouth, rough with morning stubble, drifted off me. The duvet dropped over me again, soft and warm as a cloud. Perhaps all of it was a dream. He left me lying there and I fell asleep again, full of sex and questions.

I want to talk to him about what had happened. I want to chew over it all day, all night, pick apart every detail until there's no doubt left, get past the delicious brutality upstairs while Margot's abandoned belongings stood around watching. Go over the calmer roughness in front of the fire which has left my skin glowing and sore.

And then when I'm fully awake, when he's told me everything I've waited my whole life to hear in his solemn, deep voice, when I'm certain that it's me he wants, then I'll ask him, order him, to take me in his arms and do it to me all over again.

The light is harsh on my lids because the snow has stopped falling and the clouds have rolled away. I sit up and see that the scenery has turned into a picture postcard. The mountains are tamed by capes of white. Even the pointed trees are less gloomy now that their contours are blunted by the snow.

Gustav has driven over the border to Milan on business this morning, and he told me he'd be gone all day. I wish I'd gone with him now. I can't remember if he asked me. Dickson should be around somewhere, sweeping out Margot's room of pain. But there is no sound anywhere in the chalet.

Right. In that case, I'll do it. That's what I came for. I'll get up, and clear away every last vestige of her.

As I roll over to get out of my big Moroccan bed, I realise that it wasn't all a dream. My body is aching and sore, inside and out, but it feels good.

Gustav has locked the silver chain to my bracelet and padlocked it to a hook by the window but this is a different chain. It's much longer than the other one, lying in loops and coils on the wooden floor and even when I walk out into the wide corridor it barely unravels. He's left me with a long enough rope to roam all over the house, though not enough to get down to the swimming pool for a refreshing swim.

Nor can I get properly dressed. Not unless I was Houdini, climbing in and out of my own sleeves. So it's back to the shell-pink negligee and fluffy socks.

I grab some coffee from the kitchen and after a brief internal argument where the senseless rails against the sensible, I brace myself to climb the spiral stairs to Margot's room of pain. The agreed reasoning is that I might get a signal up there, so I take my phone with me. Tooled up with my little piece of protection. My heart is juddering wildly as I push at the iron door.

What am I afraid of? That she'll leap out and strangle me? I half hope it will be locked, but the door swings open enough to show me that the chamber is totally stripped. Nothing remains of her presence but the bare bones of skylights, mirrors and barres. One day a family of ballerinas or gymnasts will enjoy this room as it should be enjoyed, with no knowledge of the previous troubled owners, or the visitors paying good money to don masks and dog collars, to be whipped and belittled by the mistress of the house.

I wind the silver chain several times round my wrist to avoid tripping over it as I descend to the landing and am drawn to those amazing huge windows framing the magical scenery. The road leading down to the town beneath the heavy boulders is still deserted. If it wasn't for the awful memories that haunt every corner of this house, surely Gustav would want to keep it? And if he can't bear to, perhaps he could buy another one on the far shore of the lake, or over on the Italian side?

I wriggle with pleasure. I could help him locate a Tuscan

palazzo. Or scout out a villa on the Ligurian riviera, over the border from Nice. This house is stunning, but yes. It has to go.

I press one of the music system buttons that are set into the walls at random intervals to enable the chalet's inhabitants to control music and ambience wherever they find themselves. Incongruously The Gypsy Kings strum into croaky Latino guitar ballads. I decide it's Dickson's choice. Gustav is more of an Astrud Gilberto or Stan Getz man, all vocals and sax wailing about lost love. Mahler if he's feeling classical. All dark and brooding.

But this music infects me. I practise a few flamenco moves in front of the window, stamping my feet and clacking imaginary castanets, then I try my phone again. I could really use a long chat with Polly. We've emailed briefly about the success of my exhibition, but she is too bound up with New York and Pierre and her job to be more than cursory. Anyhow, still there's no signal.

I amble along the galleried corridor, kicking lamely at the various still-locked wooden doors, trailing the silver chain. Gustav still hasn't shown me his own quarters. Every room was locked yesterday, but he must have opened them up this morning otherwise how are Dickson and I to pack up, which is after all why Gustav brought me here? And now we've, you know, become lovers, surely I'm allowed to treat this place as my domain? Surely I'm allowed the freedom of the chalet?

The gallery flies over the salon and tapers into one last dark corridor. Fixed to a tripod at the far end is a long brass telescope. Its great round lens faces the great outdoors. I smile to myself. Gustav's voyeur habit revealed. My secret bird watcher.

I settle against the eyepiece, adjust the dial to get the white blur into focus, and then train its sight along the lake as if aiming a gun. Dickson was right. It's very powerful. I pull the focus from the far mountains to this side of the lake, follow various flags with the Swiss red cross along the shore, and locate a rocky landing area away from the town where a boat seems to be moored. A couple are standing near the boat. I decide to focus closer, and when I make out their faces I squeal with surprise.

It's Dickson with a blonde woman, and he looks dejected. His bullish head and shoulders are bent in defeat while she wags her finger at him, her face bent right into his as if she's angry. They seem to be having a stand-up row, and then suddenly he grabs at her clumsily and kisses her.

Eww. Think I'll leave them to it. I flip the viewfinder shut. There is one more pair of enormous carved doors that I haven't tried. This must be the master suite. It overlooks the side of the chalet so instead of a panorama of the lake and the far mountains, the view from here would run straight through the trees and away along the valley like a sideways glance.

The silver chain tinkles quietly on the wooden floor as I pause. Gustav still has the power to scare me if for some reason he came home and was displeased to find me here. A nugget of doubt knocks in my chest. Look how furious he was last night when he found me in Margot's chamber of horrors. But then look how sexy and violent he became.

I shiver with pleasure, push my thighs together, run my hands over my sore bottom.

That was bad enough. But what if there's something even more forbidden behind this door?

The door opens silently and as I step inside my bare toes nudge against something soft. I kick at it, screeching. It feels like a small body, like skin and bone curled against my foot. But it's Gustav's leather rucksack, half open, his familiar red scarf curling out of the top of it like a welcome. I wonder if he left it for me to find, a reassuring sign that he's always near.

I chuckle softly and step further inside.

At first there seems to be nothing in this huge space. Only Alpine light. In fact it looks more like a gallery than a bedroom, but there is on my left the largest, most glittering quartz bathroom I've ever seen, illuminated by tiny star-like spotlights set into the ceiling and shining with chrome pipes and radiators fixed to the tiled walls. There's a shower head the size of a hub cap hanging like an oversized sunflower at the far end.

There are no towels. No soap. No toothbrushes or shampoo. But there, glinting by the hot tap on one of the two dry unused basins, is a single silver cufflink with the initials *GL* intertwined. My ribs contract. A gift. A token of love. This must be his bedroom, because that's where you would keep your jewellery.

I glance into the main space. It's furnished by light from the far glass wall. There's no punctuation of chairs or night stands or lamps. No marital bed. No chair. No rug. No drapes. This is the best room in the house, the master suite, but it's empty. No traces, thank God, of the master and the mistress sleeping, living and loving in here.

Signor e Signora. Herr und Frau. Mr and Mrs Levi.

My stomach growls for some of Dickson's creamy scrambled egg. There's nothing in here even for the nosiest of snoopers. But then I wish with all my heart that I'd never ventured this far.

Because as the snowy daylight sharpens the interior into focus, another pair of eyes catches mine.

Dark eyes. Black. Long, narrow eyes set far apart, almost oriental in the way the thickness of the upper lid weights the gaze before tipping up mirthlessly at each corner. Eyebrows, plucked slightly too thin, Polly would say over-Botoxed, and arched disdainfully.

A new chill crawls through me, even though the eyes aren't real. They're charcoal.

And there's her name, in flowing script. *Margot Levi.*

She's on every surface. Smudged in pastel, washed in watercolour, slathered in oil on canvas, sketched in pencil or crayon, sheets and canvasses overlapping, plastered everywhere, on the ceiling, covering the floor. My feet are treading on her. It really is a kind of warped, twisted art gallery. And I'm outside, looking in.

This is the opposite of the portrait of Dorian Gray. The Margot Levi prowling the planet somewhere outside this chalet, outside this ring of mountains, may age, go grey, her skin may one day ridge into wrinkles, but the woman glued into this room will never change. She will never die.

This is a shrine, even more than the room of pain. This is like one of those Russian chapels where holy icons sorrow at your sins, stare mournfully above glass boxes containing their own fossilised relics.

But Margot is not sorrowing. She's celebrating. And no wonder, because the initials of the adoring artist are inscribed on every faithful depiction. Gustav Levi, her besotted husband, has made this documentary of their married life, created a collage as a permanent memorial.

Why is she still here?

The eyes glare over a bare shoulder. They tease from a pornographically open-legged pose, every crevice and shadow and stray hair. The eyes burn above a mouth blowing a kiss or sucking on a finger or the rounded handle of a plaited whip. They even wink above hands joined beatifically as if in prayer. Here she is brazenly naked, wrapped round a tree or sprawling on a rumpled bed. There she is rigid in her dominatrix outfit, legs splayed in the crotchless leggings and laced basque which Gustav had to cut off me yesterday.

Margot's bewitching face, unmasked. These are the oriental

eyes and blow-job lips, the pixie chin, the black hair, the hands, the nipples, the body that thrilled him, enthralled him, continues to arouse him. This display is the proof that he never wants these memories erased.

Next to a babyishly bright picture of her skiing, her hair streaming out from under an emerald-green hat, there's a series of her whipping herself, the stripes stark across her skin. Then whipping an anonymous upturned bottom. Then she's outlined in bold black strokes as she grasps a bed post, the bed post upstairs, opens her legs, and thrusts the whip up herself.

My Venetian nuns. No wonder he loved my work. It was the perfect re-enactment of all his fantasies. An unwitting tribute to his past life.

Compared with this unalloyed worship, the sketch I found in the gallery was a derisory scribble. A scrap destined for the trash. Touching, but hollow.

You're the only one.

How did these modelling sessions end? Did he throw down his pencils, hard and hot for her, kneel before her, his hands on her, his mouth kissing, sucking, biting? Did they consume their rough, grunting lust right where I'm standing? Or did she tie him and whip him till he whimpered?

I gasp in pain as the grinding sexual jealousy overwhelms me. I'm the reluctant voyeur in the forbidden room. I shouldn't be here. I'm a trespasser in Bluebeard's castle.

You're the only one.

In the cafe by the lake, in front of the fire last night, he said such tender things. Brought me so close to loving him. But it was all a pile of crap. I'm just a foil, squirming bait to tempt her back, a snippet of solace until she comes to heel.

I never had a snowflake's chance in hell. What do I know of love? How did I ever suppose that a man like him genuinely wanted a scruffy upstart like me? How could the ignorant ginger pony with the over-ripe bod compete with the exotic Swiss panther who still possesses her ex-husband?

The gypsy music has stopped. Everything starts to jostle and blur. I stagger for the door and am confronted by the only photograph in the room. Margot in a wedding dress. She has a face now, and she's dipping her long, sharp nose into a pretty bouquet of edelweiss just as I envisaged, staring over the tiny white flowers, making sure the photographer's lens never leaves her.

My toes catch against the black leather rucksack, jarring my ankle. Gustav's red scarf is a lolling mocking tongue now. He can't keep away from her. He was in here last night, this morning, worshipping and confessing. After he touched me.

After we *fucked*. Language you understand, Mrs Levi.

No wonder he was so incandescent when he caught me in her clothes. It was sacrilege. It wasn't me he was seeing. It will always be her.

I slam the door behind me. The silver chain snakes away, back down the stairs, and I follow it to the salon like the thread leading Theseus from the labyrinth.

I pace about in front of the cold dead fire. My body still glows, no matter how hard I try to forget. I can still sense him in me, revel in the warmth of his body pushing my ribs hard against the back of the sofa until I can hardly breathe. The hard urgent sliding of him, my body settling round him like a possessive fist, totally belonging, then our rocking together, faster, faster, his fingers digging into my hips to keep me anchored, my hair over my face, catching in my eyes, the moon high in the sky quietly watching.

I can't bear it. He did all that with her, and so much more. They had years. I've had days.

Instead of the sweet-salt juices which eased Gustav's

journey into me last night stinging tears are trickling out of my eyes, washing him clean away.

I pace over to the window. The road is still empty, but for how long? Gustav is gone till nightfall, but Dickson could be back any time. He could even be bringing the estate agent and hopeful purchasers with him. What on earth would they think of the wraith wandering round the chalet in a pale pink nightdress, trailing a silver chain?

Far below on the steely lake I can see a boat coming in to the shore, delivering anoraked people to the same promenade where we drank hot chocolate the other evening. The sparkling white and blue of the holiday scenery mocks my despair.

And so does the silver chain binding me like a dog on a lead. I yank at it, but the bracelet just bites into my wrist. Then I spot the iron poker Gustav uses to stoke the fire. I seize it from its hook and run back into my room, thread the chain from the padlock out onto the balcony, lay it down on the balustrade and bring the poker smashing down again and again. Chips fly off the wooden rail and the blows echo round the valley, but the chain is unbroken.

I stop for a moment, ignoring the madness and the cold. I dart back inside and attack the hook where the padlock is hanging, and suddenly, miraculously, my weapon knocks the hook clean out of the wall, bringing a jagged chunk of plaster with it and leaving an ugly gaping hole. The force of my swing back catches my fist grasping the handle of the poker against my temple, but I'm too fired up to notice or care.

What will he do when he sees what I've done? Will he freeze with fury or roar with anger, fly round the chalet looking for me, howling like a wolf, shouting out my name? Or will he just come to a halt, understand why the silver chain, or at least his part of it, is broken?

I roll the silver chain up as best I can round my knuckles

and start searching for my missing clothes. I run through the chalet, back to the lovely warm kitchen, through to the laundry room, why didn't I think of it before? And there they are, the bag that Crystal packed, my *Dr Zhivago* clothes all neatly folded. I dress clumsily, shoving the padlock and the loops of silver chain into the pocket of my white jacket, hoist up the bag. May as well nick the Barbie outfits while I'm at it.

And air-head Barbie is my new persona, because it's only now that I realise I have no money, no passport. Not even a phone signal.

No matter. I'm out of here, even if it means walking back to London.

I zip up my jacket, shove on my Cossack hat, grab a huge Danish pastry. I consider writing a note and sticking it to the huge American fridge. But I'm all out of words. Gustav will know how devastated I am. He knows what I said, what I whispered to him last night when I was at my most vulnerable and exposed. He knows where he's taken me, the false path I've eagerly followed.

I've broken our contract, Gustav.

So sue me.

I push open the big wooden door and breathe in the crisp mountain air. I step gingerly down to the driveway, my ankle dragging. How can such a beautiful place be so tainted? How can one woman have so much toxic power?

I've made it as far as the road leading down to the lake when the silver Lexus glides round the corner, and brakes. I can't see the driver. I stand motionless in front of the bonnet, empty of thoughts, drained of action.

'Miss Serena?' Dickson gets out of the car and leans against it, folding his arms across his massive chest. 'What are you doing out here in the snow? And what's that mark on your head?'

‘I took a poker to it.’ I whisk the padlock out of my pocket and dangle it in the air. ‘I’m escaping.’

He comes towards me and takes my arm. ‘I don’t think so. Mr Levi will kill me if I let you go. He’ll kill us both.’

‘Don’t be ridiculous. He needs to wake up and smell the napalm. He’s got us all fooled.’ I shake him off and point up at the chalet, towards the master bedroom. ‘He’s still obsessed by that woman. This place is still as haunted as ever, but not by me. He’ll see that soon enough. I bet he had a rendezvous with her in Milan. They’re at it like knives right now!’

Dickson snorts. ‘You’re talking absolute and total bollocks, if you’ll pardon the expression, Miss.’

‘Go ahead. Swear like a trooper. There isn’t language obscene enough to cover it,’ I snap back. ‘She’ll be back in residence by the morning. I’ve seen the shrine he has up there, Dickson. Intimate portraits of his precious wife all over the walls.’

Dickson smacks his gloved hand against his mouth. ‘Sod it. You weren’t supposed to–’

‘I may be out of my depth, I may be far from home, I may be naïve, but I’m not stupid!’ I am shouting now, and it feels great. ‘I know an expression of true love when I see it.’

Dickson shakes his head. ‘You can only know that if you’ve felt true love yourself.’

‘A philosopher as well as a chauffeur now, are you?’

‘I’m not your servant, Miss Serena, so I don’t have to take that from you. There was a task Mr Levi gave me to do, and I didn’t do it. But you still don’t get how far off the mark you are.’ Dickson clears his throat. ‘Hell will freeze over before that woman sets foot on the same continent as Mr Levi.’

‘Ah, yes. The dreaded secret. The final betrayal which nobody will talk about.’

Dickson glances at his watch. 'After everything that's been said and done between you and him, I thought you'd have realised how he feels.'

'Said and done?'

'Like I told you before. Mr Levi has never brought another woman to this house. Let alone–'

'Let alone what?'

'He has never let his defences down like this. Let his passions run away with him like he did last night. You've unlocked something in him.' Dickson fixes me with his pebbly grey eyes like an interrogator. 'Make no mistake, Miss Serena. I know everything that goes on. That's part of my job.'

A flurry of snow drops off a tree and lands on the road between us.

'Well, stick your job and stick your boss and his evil wife. She's his problem, not mine.' I step towards the car and realise my feet are numb with cold. 'I need you to take me to the airport.'

'Even if I was allowed to, how are you going to get back to London with no money and no passport?'

I can see Dickson's mouth twitching back a smirk, and I fume with anger.

'You're going to get them for me, Dickson. He can't keep me prisoner. I'm going to wait here, and you're going to crack open the safe or wherever he hides his valuables. Then you're going to drive me to the airport.'

'Like I said. I'm not your servant.' He stares boorishly back down the road towards the lake. At the base of his neck, just above the stiff white collar, I notice two fresh teeth marks, reddened and bruised. 'More than my life's worth, Miss.'

I can feel my energy ebbing away. How soon the happiness has soured. Everything in Gustav's world is extreme, and these two days have broken me. My eyes are sore from crying.

My ankle's sore from falling off that horse and tripping over Gustav's bag. My body is aching from unaccustomed punishment followed by forceful, passionate sex. And my heart is snapped in two.

'Or I could tell Mr Levi about your little visits to the lass down at the Alprose factory when you're supposed to be fulfilling the tasks he gave you.'

'You're bluffing.'

For a brief moment I am Dickson's enemy, caught in the sights of his rifle, his eyes pure venom as they stare down the barrel. It was a stab in the dark, but my aim was true. There's a long pause while we each choose to break all the rules.

'She's blonde. I saw you through the telescope, arguing. But she's the bird who gave you that love bite.'

Still glaring at me he reaches into the car and brings out a pair of pliers. Without a word he snaps the silver chain off, right by my bracelet, throws the pliers back into the car, and stamps up to the house to get my passport.

As we accelerate round the corner a few minutes later and speed down the road towards the lake, either the wind or some wild animal up there in the mountains behind the chalet unleashes an unearthly howl.

FIFTEEN

I am lying on a wooden sun lounger on the deck, staring across the bad-tempered English Channel. I could be on the Titanic, plying towards its doom. The island is even hewn in the rough shape of a cruise ship. But actually I'm on terra firma.

If I turn my head ever so slightly I can see the windy cliffs where I grew up. In fact, I can see the house itself. The grey sea stretching between us forms a kind of moat, but this island hotel is not the fortress. That house is no longer the enemy. It holds no fear for me now. I've grown up.

I rub at the blanket covering my knees like an old lady and sip at the warm drink the waiter has just brought me. Push away the memory of drinking hot chocolate beside Lake Lugano, Gustav sitting opposite me, his face burning with exertion from our horse ride and the passion that I didn't recognise at the time. The passion that turned out to be, if not false, then certainly fleeting.

It's daft sitting out here in the cold like an invalid but I'll enjoy the peace for a few more minutes while Jake and the photographer set up in the glittering period bar behind me.

As well as mist, the house on the cliffs is shrouded in

scaffolding and jaunty blue tarpaulin. It looks belittled up there amongst the sheep droppings and the bracken, like a forgotten Christmas present. But some time in the spring the building works will be finished and a shiny new gastropub with rooms and a seaview restaurant will be born.

All my life I've stared across the sea towards this grand old hotel riding its rocky steed over the waves and dreamed of being rich enough to stay. Its shabby art deco facade has been gradually restored by the painstaking new owners. The stucco stained with rust and verdigris has become shimmering white. Agatha Christie books have been filmed here, and it's world-renowned as a luxury retreat. There's even a helipad further up the slope for the celebrity guests and below me, on the far side of the island away from the mainland, the hotel has its own private smugglers' cove and rowing boat.

I can feel the cobwebs unpeeling themselves and floating away as I drain my cocoa. But the dragging grumble of heart-ache remains.

'We're ready for you, Rena.'

Jake crashes through the glass doors behind me, interrupting the silence with voices and clinking glasses and his own brand of noisy intrusion. I feel a hundred years older than him.

'It's Serena now.'

I rise stiffly from my lounger, drop the blanket, and let them lead me into the bar and over to a wicker chair by the white grand piano. I think I'll milk the invalid thing a little longer. After all, I do feel physically drained. All I've done since getting here from London is shuffle from bar to bed to breakfast. I could easily think myself into a fever if I really wanted.

'This interview will be a piece of piss,' Jake jokes with the bow-tied barman, who wears the bored expression of a *Punch* cartoon and is brandishing a cocktail shaker. 'Serena Folkes and I were childhood sweethearts.'

I open my mouth to – what? Protest? Why? It's true, isn't it? They're all looking at me expectantly so I change my pout to a smile and cross my legs. I'm wearing a pale grey cashmere tunic pinned with an oversized silver flower brooch which I found folded in tissue paper in the bag Crystal packed for Switzerland, and some white skinny jeans. On my feet is another pair of fluffy white socks. How did she know I'm at my most comfortable in socks or bare feet?

'Our relationship is purely professional now, though, eh Jake? That was the deal when I agreed to the interview. No dirty linen.'

'No kiss and tell?' he smirks. 'Shame.'

I accept the blood-red cocktail someone hands me and the cool liquid knocks away the comfort of the cocoa. Jake can be snide if you're not alert to his tricks.

'We've both come a long way from student photographer and trainee hack. Now we're both being paid for what we love doing best.'

'Yeah, though what I used to love doing best was getting you into that caravan.'

'Jake!' I glare at him as the others titter awkwardly. 'Have you never heard that over-worked phrase "moving on"?'

'Fine. Fine. Just be grateful I've got the clout to persuade the paper to pay for your trip to Devon. You're a hard woman to get hold of these days, Rena. Who knew your old boyfriend would have to jump through hoops with your new man's personal assistant to get this piece?'

Jake gives a kind of gangster's flick of the wrist and straddles a chair opposite me, the back of it up against his stomach and his legs spread on either side. His blue jeans are too tight. His thighs bulge through the faded material. He's obviously been working out and I can't deny he looks good. Briefly I recall him naked in the dull afternoon light struggling through the dirty windows, jumping off the messy bed in the caravan and yawning, his youthful erection, aroused by me, still jutting out at right angles. He'd make a good life study, the ripple of his muscles, the taper of his torso.

I swing my sore ankle and get a handle on my thoughts.

He still looks like a lad, but a bulked-up lad. His shaved hair has grown a little, the fair curls bouncing gratefully back. Cute enough guy.

But he's not Gustav. He's the opposite of Gustav, a Labrador next to a greyhound. I long to feel the silkiness of Gustav's black hair under my fingers, the slide of his stern mouth over me. The man who manages to be far sexier than Jake even though I've never seen him totally naked. Perhaps *because* I've never seen him naked. But I've felt his hot touch, seen the black glitter of warning mixed with desire in his fathomless eyes, his strong fingers digging into my hips, opening me up to him, his hardness possessing me so forcefully that days later I'm still aching.

And then I see Margot, her black eyes mocking and triumphant. I see the two of them in the master bedroom suite at the chalet, her on top, waving her whip, Gustav's hands spread over her bottom to urge her on as she rides him.

I realise I've closed my eyes. Someone is pushing the hair off my sweaty face. I tip my head back longingly. Gustav is here, stroking my hair.

But it's the make-up girl, up close and frowning. 'You've gone a sickly green, Serena. Are you alright? And what's this bruise above your eye?'

'Silly accident with a – with a tripod.' I look past her at Jake. 'Listen. I appreciate the expenses. The train. The hotel. The publicity. All that, Jake. But I'd also appreciate it if you keep any crude comments under control. And no reminiscences in the by-line when it goes to print.'

Jake tugs his forelock and whistles under his breath. 'When did you get so high and mighty, Rena Folkes?'

The make-up girl hides the bruise with foundation and smothers my face in powder and blusher.

'I'm just trying to be the consummate professional.'

He sniggers. 'Sure. But you know and I know that there's a wildcat under all that cashmere who hasn't had it in a while. Probably not since our last one-night stand. A sex kitten just waiting to bust out.'

The make-up girl giggles and blushes.

'Oh, you're wrong about that, Jake. I was rogered rigid, as you would so charmingly put it, just a couple of nights ago.'

He rubs his hand through his hair. I know what that means. He's getting a hard-on.

'Who's the stud? Your rich patron?'

I lift one shoulder nonchalantly. 'Could be anyone. London's a big place. I'm just not *your* sex kitten any more.'

'What a great way to start an interview.' He flips me the finger. 'You need to look lively, Rena. Want to be nominated for this year's hottest new talent to watch, or not?'

'Guys, guys, this ex-lovers' tiff is all very entertaining, and it's sure brought some colour into our heroine's cheeks, but high tide is rising out there and I want to get home,' murmurs the photographer from somewhere behind the potted palms. We've forgotten all about him. 'Can we just get the shot, please?'

I straighten up, let the jumper's boat neck fall softly down my arm, twirl the hair that the girl has just tonged into a ringlet, dangle my half-empty cocktail glass in the other. But inside I'm thinking, oh, where is my lady's maid when I need her?

I turn straight to the photographer and give him my best smile.

'I'm ready for my close-up.'

'So you've done a runner?'

Crystal had barely blinked when I walked into the gallery, straight from the airport.

'I don't want to talk about it, Crys.'

'Crystal. You are aware that you've broken the contract by coming back to London without him? Do you have any idea what Gustav Levi is like when he's roused? And I don't mean "roused" in a good way.'

I moved around the walls, touching my pictures again. Even happier to see that the red 'sold' dots had multiplied.

'Yes, I've seen him roused. But I had to get away. The place freaked me out. She's everywhere, Crystal. Her equipment. Pictures of her. His drawings, plastered all over their bedroom like graffiti.'

'I'm astonished. He swore the place was fumigated and whitewashed years ago.' Crystal glided up beside me. 'None of that makes sense.'

'Listen, I don't have time to linger. He might catch me.' I stepped away, but she was by my side like Peter Pan's shadow. 'Can we just talk about sales, Crystal? He'll want me to pull out of the exhibition now I've broken the silver chain.'

'The silver chain?'

'You've seen it. It's more than a gift of jewellery. When he hooks it onto my wrist it becomes our symbol.' I rubbed anxiously at the bracelet. 'Please, Crystal. No questions. I daresay he'll tell you everything once I'm gone.'

'You bet he will. Just don't let a ridiculous misunderstanding jeopardise your career before it's even started.' Her eyes remained fixed on me as she ran a black-painted fingernail down the catalogue. 'Right. There's not much left to pull out of, in any case. Only nine more pictures to go. So no way can you back out. Not until it's finished.'

'I can't be near him, Crystal.'

Just then my phone bleeped into life.

Hey, babes, am jetting in at end of week for brief stopover. Styling someone on X Factor then free for fun. You up for getting loaded at the flat then going out on the lash?

I stared at the text as if it was in code. My darling cousin. She's coming all the way from New York and I can't face her. I'm bailing on her. Worse than that. She'll see that I've nicked her clothes and disappeared.

Sorry, doll. Photo assignment out of town. More notice next time?

'How easily those fibs come, don't they?' Crystal took the phone out of my limp hand and studied it. 'But in a way it's true. You are required out of town. We've been contacted by several outfits wanting you to come and work for them.'

I kept my eyes on the curved monochrome back of my little Venetian nun.

'Such as?'

She flipped over the sheets on her precious clipboard. 'A fashion design studio. A travel company. A hotel chain opening up in Venice. And the developers of a gastropub near Bigbury in Devon.'

I glanced up and her round button eyes were already latched onto mine. 'That's where I used to live.'

'I know. They know. They're the people buying the old Folkes residence. That's why they want the *Bleak House* series.'

She glided away calmly and tapped at an unsold series of sea and sky views framed by peeling, weatherbeaten windows and treated with chemicals to look like old postcards.

'Ah. The house on the cliffs.'

'Tell me about it.' She kept her eyes on the photographs. 'That's where they neglected you. Bullied you, no doubt. Hurt you. Where they cut off your lovely Rapunzel hair.'

'Yes. But eventually there was nothing but silence in that house.' I realised I was pulling the bracelet hard against my wrist bone. 'Apart from my diaries, and my dosh, those pictures are the only record.'

'But why take photographs of a place with such awful associations?'

The bracelet was really hurting me now, but it felt good. I took a step towards Crystal.

'All my life I've used cameras to make sense of the world, to bring light into the darkness. If that doesn't sound too precious. When I became more skilled I could shape objects however I chose, manipulate or even distort them. I needed to boil that house and everything in it down to bricks and mortar. A shell.'

'Reduce it, like one of Dickson's sauces.'

Crystal cocked her head and ran her fingers over the photographs, tracing the rotten window frames, the nails sticking out of the damp walls, the dry, waving grass glimpsed outside.

'That box of moulded plastic was my shield. That tiny window was my eye. It shrank everything to a seven by five image, or a six by four. A thumbnail. I took one solitary picture of those people through the kitchen window. I was outside, looking in. They were sitting motionless at the table. No food on there. No drink. No flowers. Just the two of them, staring not at each other, not at me, but at the floor. I went away and printed the shot then came back to rip it up in their faces.'

'I can't imagine you being so venomous, Serena.'

'You see? I'm a bad girl.' I stood close beside Crystal. 'That was the last time I ever saw them.'

'You're not bad. Mixed up, maybe, and who could blame you?' Without looking at me she uncurled my fingers from the biting bracelet. 'You made something artistic out of something ugly. Pity they've been earmarked, actually. I love them. Those breathtaking views. That arched rock in the sea. The spray flying up against the old bent tree.'

The calm, airy way Crystal described the house on the cliffs somehow diminished it, ironed out all that historical pain like a carpenter's plane smoothing away splinters.

'Was the house really teetering on the edge of the cliff?'

I nodded. 'Deliberately deceptive, those perspectives. But my life *was* vertiginous.'

'Plenty of beauty in bleakness. My favourite kind.' She tapped my silver bracelet with its tiny dangle of broken silver chain. 'I'll have signed prints of those, please, Madam, if I can't have the originals. So. If they follow through with the purchase that will leave four photographs unsold. Oh, and they've asked a local reporter to interview you. In Devon. As soon as you can manage it. I'll book the train ticket and a couple of nights at Burgh Island Hotel whenever you're ready. You could use the fresh air.'

She tied a silk scarf printed with blousy flowers tightly round her throat and buttoned on a pair of red leather gloves. Picked up my wrist. Glanced more closely at what remained of the silver chain.

'First the Alps. Now the sea. Go ahead and book it. I ought to get back to work, Crys.'

'Crystal. And what better way to get back to work than getting out there? Selling yourself. Promotion. Publicity. Some R and R while you're at it.'

'How did you know I've always wanted to stay there? And isn't it very expensive?'

'I'll run it past Gustav later. And why Burgh Island, you may ask? Didn't I tell you that Agatha Christie is another of my heroines?'

I laughed. 'OK, Crys – Crystal. But I wish you could come with me.'

She lifted her hand as if in benediction. 'I am holding the fort here.'

'After that I'm going to disappear while I still have the willpower.'

She turned her palm upwards like a traffic cop. 'Whoa! Back up a minute. You're going nowhere. You have other press interviews back in London next week. Remember this is ultimately about you, not Gustav.'

I felt as if I was imploding. 'Just don't tell Gustav where I've gone.'

'I don't know where *he* is at the moment.' She twisted the fragment of silver chain in her red leather fingers. 'Dickson phoned me. The chalet is locked up now. The estate agent has the keys. I know Gustav had business in Manhattan, so maybe he's over there.' She hesitated and then tilted my chin so that I was forced to look at her. 'I've warned you before. There's no reasoning with him. That woman left him raw, like an open wound.'

I let out a snort. 'Well, he has no intention of suturing it.'

'You're wrong. It's all he ever thinks about.'

'All he ever thinks about is her?'

'Being healed. He knows he has to move forward. He must reckon you're the one to do it, otherwise he would never have got involved with you. Drawn up the contract. Or taken you to Lugano.'

'Oh, Crystal, we got so close. Everything felt strange, but perfect. And then I found all these pictures. She's not history at all. She's in our faces, and always will be.'

Crystal tipped her head on one side. A wise blackbird, considering our foibles from a high branch. Her beak opened, then snapped shut again.

'If you leave now, you might never see him again.'

She switched off all the main lights, leaving only select spots to illuminate the photographs.

'I'll take that chance.' I pressed the button on the lift. 'Why leave those lights on? No-one's going to be able to see into the gallery, let alone study the individual images. Unless they're looking through a telescope, or flying low into Heathrow.'

'Or a cat burglar,' Crystal mused, following me into the

lift and handing me my overnight bag. 'They run all over London at night, you know, leaping from roof to roof when we're asleep.'

The interview is over now and Jake and I have to laugh as we stand on the deck outside the bar and watch the photographer and the make-up girl stumble in panic, laden with bags and boxes, down the awkward stone steps towards the jetty.

'They could have waited for the Range Rover,' Jake chortles, pointing at the car park over on the mainland. 'Once the tide recedes the hotel would have sent that over for them. But let's see how they get on with the sea tractor.'

I shiver in the wintry breeze. The ancient-looking sea tractor labours across the high water towards the island to deliver what looks like a single passenger.

'Although why you'd want to leave all this incredible luxury in such a hurry beats me.' Jake picks the blanket off my arm and wraps it round my shoulders. 'Especially when all you've got waiting over there is a measly old caravan in a field.'

'Oh, diddums. No-one keeping it warm? At least you have a place of your own. I don't have anywhere to go after this.'

'I thought you were staying at your cousin Polly's?'

I shake my head, watching the figure on the tractor. It's wearing a red jacket. I can't tell from here if it's a man or a woman. Whoever it is stands very still as the vehicle trundles through the water. My eyes sting in the cold air. I blink and look back at Jake. 'For now. But I'm leaving London soon. Maybe I'll travel again.'

'You need to put down some roots if you're going to make a success of yourself. Not keep running.' Jake fixes the blanket under my chin. 'There you go.'

He pulls me close. Instinctively I lean against him, a flower yearning towards the sun, towards the boyish warmth of his body all zipped up inside that leather jacket and promising comfort, fun. Simple, unvarnished sex. We can argue, we can fight, we can hurl insults, but he's right. I was his sex kitten once. And he was my stud.

'How about I stay here with you tonight? I could show you a trick or two I've learned since you left. I'd let you do whatever you like to me. I'd even let you go on top.' Jake's mouth is hot against my hair. 'Waste of an antique walnut-inlaid queen-size bed to have just one lonely woman sleeping in it. How about one more shag for old times' sake?'

Before I can answer Jake is lifting me up onto my tiptoes and kissing me. His lips are warm and wet, his tongue trying to push inside my mouth. I wonder if I should like it. I wonder if I should respond. But I don't like it, and I don't respond. My lips are cold, and dry. I let his mouth move on mine for a moment, then push him away.

'Sorry, Jake. It's just not there any more. I don't want you. I don't fancy you. How many times do I have to tell you?'

He spins away. 'Frigid little prick tease.'

'Don't be so foul. All I did was let you hold me for a moment, and it was nice. But that's all.' I lift my arms, smack them down against my sides. 'I'm not frigid, Jake. There's someone else, that's all. Just accept it.'

He snatches up his own bags and stares at me, his mouth still open, his cheeks flushed from the wind, that moment of re-awakened lust and, presumably, embarrassment at my rejection.

Behind him the sea tractor is slowing down from its already snail-like pace, its oversized wheels and canopy making it look like less like a pirate ship and more a kind of wonky Wild West wagon.

'I accepted it was over weeks ago, you idiot. It doesn't make you any the less beautiful.' He snatches up his bags. When did he become so poetic? 'Infuriatingly so.'

'Be nice about me in the interview, Jake?'

'You're a damn fine photographer, even if you are a bitch. Of course I will be nice.' He jumps like an agile goat down the stone steps towards the jetty, yelling one final message over his shoulder. 'Piss off and have a nice life.'

I open my mouth to call after him but my voice dies in my throat.

Because the figure now standing on the jetty as the others push past him and clamber on board the sea tractor for the return journey is not wearing a red jacket after all. It's a man wearing a red scarf, and it's Gustav.

It seems he climbs the stone steps in slow motion. Despite everything – my anger, my jealousy, my confusion – my heart leaps in my chest. No matter how hard I've tried to hate him, none of it has worked. I can't let on, but as soon as I set eyes on him I realise that I've missed him every second we've been apart. He looks so handsome in his black jacket and jeans, every feature so clear, so dear to me, hair whipping around his unshaven face, his black eyes gripping mine. His mouth, curved in a smile. He carries nothing but the leather rucksack and what looks like a long bulky roll of wallpaper.

'You look like the French Lieutenant's Woman all windswept up there,' he calls as he comes up to me. 'Tell me I'm not too late, Serena.'

I hesitate as he takes my hand. I should pull it away, but I'm immobile. He frowns at the silver bracelet with the little sliver of silver chain hanging off it. Flicks it with his fingernail. The broken chain is all that's left of the brief lightning flash that lit up our lives. Then he lifts my hand and kisses the soft skin there, his lips pressing gently.

The full lower lip. The redness of the blood running beneath it. The pulsing beat in his neck above the red scarf. I snatch my hand tightly back inside the blanket, running my fingers over the dampness he has left.

'Too late for what?' I sigh after a moment, because he's waiting for my answer. Behind him the tractor starts its slow, splashy journey back to the mainland.

'Do me the courtesy of looking at me, not him. Hell. I see that I am too late. You don't have to explain. It makes sense, actually. You and he look good together. You're the same age, for God's sake.' Gustav slices his hand in the air as if severing it. 'There's no fool like an old fool.'

'You're not a fool. You're not old. What are you talking about? The same age as who?'

The passengers have already turned away to face Bigbury and the rest of their lives. Jake is leaning against the rail of the tractor, arms folded across his chest. From the way his head is bent, and hers is lifted, I can tell he's chatting up the make-up girl. I have to smile.

'You see?' groans Gustav, smacking the bulky roll of paper down on his hand. He doesn't see what I see. 'You're smiling at him. And why not? Why wouldn't a hunky young man like that want to grab you and keep you? Look at you! You look amazing today. Every time I see you afresh something has changed.'

And every time I see you I want to come.

Even though I know I should be sombre and solemn before his obvious distress I can feel the smile still playing on my lips, hardening into satisfaction, because Gustav Levi is standing here in a state of disarray. Well, that's nothing to what he's made me feel. As I bring my eyes back to his sombre face I realise that with all his clumsiness Jake has just done me a favour.

'Are you jealous, Gustav?' I start to walk across the lawn, away from the hotel towards the rough steps leading down to the little cove on the far side of the island. I'm keeping it calm. I have to, if I'm going to survive this. But inside my heart is pounding. 'Because I don't think you have any idea what jealousy feels like, otherwise you wouldn't have left that gallery of horrors at the chalet for me to find.'

I know he's watching me as I walk away from him, still in my socks, across the wet grass. The way my hair prickles on my neck tells me he's watching me. The way that my body pulses and aches to have him near. I don't know how I'm going to achieve it, but I want to make him suffer. And the easiest way, the way that affords me the best protection, the one I learned from the cradle, is to be the ice queen herself.

'I've never felt jealousy until today.' He's right up behind me. 'But they're right when they say it's a green-eyed monster. Trapped on that ridiculous charabanc in the middle of high tide and I saw that whippersnapper kissing you, your beautiful hair blowing round you both. You were in a world of your own. So yes, I was jealous. Am jealous. It looked like the real deal to me.'

I stop at the top of the little cliff that plunges down to the hotel's private cove. So easy to tumble. I remember the Agatha Christie film that was shot here. Wasn't a body found on this little beach, dressed in an old-fashioned twenties bathing suit?

'As real a deal as your portraits of Margot? The ones I saw plastered all over your bedroom at the chalet? The wedding photo? The intimate ones? The sultry ones, all keeping her close? The ones drawn by a besotted husband who can't let go?' My voice veers up into hysteria. 'Peculiar kind of exorcism, when the spirit surges back stronger than ever!'

'Be quiet for just one moment.'

Gustav pulls me roughly, holds me close up to his shadowed face. We glare at each for a moment, then he kneels on the ground at my feet. I flinch away.

'No need to grovel, Gustav.'

'Are these the pictures you mean?'

He unrolls the paper and spreads it out on the ground. He weights it with a pebble at each corner. Margot's black eyes stare up from various torn shreds of paper. I fold my arms and sulk out to sea.

'A few fragments of them. So why bring them to me? To rub salt into the wound like you did when we went up the mountain and found the chapel? To show me everything she is, and everything I'm not? I knew you were made of stone, Gustav, but I never dreamed you'd be so cruel. How much more do you want to hurt me! Why don't you take your poxy collage and leave me alone!'

It's out before I can stop it. The strength and heat of it.

And he sees and hears it. Even if he hadn't come to know me so well, he'd see everything written on my face. Everything crying out in my voice.

'I don't want to hurt you, Serena. That's the last thing on earth I want to do!' He jumps up and grabs my arm. 'I don't blame you for running away after discovering these. I certainly don't blame you for rushing back to your old love. I've tried to explain, but I'm obviously useless with words. So all that's left is to say I'm sorry.'

I can't hear him. All I can see are those mocking, repeated eyes which were bad enough on the walls of the chalet, but excruciating now that he's brought them all the way to Devon.

'By bringing these bloody portraits of your wife to taunt me even more?'

'Ex-wife. Wife who ripped the heart out of me just as I managed to rip these pictures off the walls after you'd gone.' The heat from his fingers sears through the blanket, but I keep my eyes averted. I'll drown if I look at him. 'Serena. You weren't supposed to see these. Dickson was supposed to steam them off the walls years ago. He was supposed to redecorate the room as well but instead he was sneaking down to the lake to tup his *Fräulein*. Add springing the safe to his list of offences, giving you your passport, stealing money from me. My God, he's in deep shit.'

My head snaps up at his unaccustomed swearing. 'You knew about the *Fräulein* at the Alprose? But I used that as blackmail to force him to get my passport!'

'I thought you knew me so well, Serena. But have you forgotten?' Gustav's sombre eyes stir with something I recognise. Restlessness. Justified triumph. 'I know everything, about all of you.'

'My lord and master.' I sketch a mock curtsey, and then jab my foot at the pictures. 'But what infuriates me, what hurts, is that you couldn't keep away from that bedroom. Admiring your handiwork, no doubt. Praying to Saint Margot.' I'm on a roller coaster here, and I'm not sure how to get off. I swallow. 'I saw your rucksack in there. And your cufflink.'

'The cufflink I can't explain. It must have dropped there a long time ago. But the reason I went up there? To get my telescope. The rucksack I can also explain.'

He lifts it off his shoulder and pulls it open, starts to draw something out.

'What now?' I snap, shifting my feet angrily. 'Something tells me I'm not going to like this.'

'You have to see it. We have to do this together. And then you have to listen to me, Serena.'

As he kneels down again, right in the centre of the top picture this time so that he scuffs and rips Margot's face, I look down at him, at the silky black hair grown longer, at the eyelashes curved in concentration over his taut, pale cheeks. His big hands digging about in the bag.

My heart melts just a little, the first icicle sliding like a tear off the iceberg. Gustav Levi is stricken, that's for sure. He's come all this way, found me out here on this island in the middle of the sea kissing my childhood sweetheart, and I'm wondering if he's lost his way.

Still kneeling he pulls out a bunch of exercise books and tosses them down on top of the portraits.

My voice is low and harsh. 'What the hell? Those diaries are secret, and they're mine. And I never want to see them or read them again!'

'And nor shall you. You seem to have forgotten, Serena, that we still have an agreement, even though you've breached it by running away from me. You are still mine. Which means that all your belongings, everything you have left in my house, is mine.'

I kick out again, aiming for him this time, but Gustav swiftly catches my foot and pulls the sock off, damp and muddy now from the grass, knocking the breath out of me with surprise.

'So you're still claiming me. I'm supposed to take whatever you throw at me, good and bad. As if that farcical set-up in Switzerland is of no consequence?' I'm forced to put my hand on his shoulder to balance as he keeps hold of my foot. 'Is that why you are here, Gustav?'

'Claiming you? Yes. I couldn't have put it better myself. But let's use your language, Serena, for a change. Not mine. I came here to apologise and to try to persuade you to come back with me.'

He puts my foot on his knee and strokes it. I can't explain how sexy that gesture is, this small undressing. His big hand cradles my foot as it emerges from the sock, and he encircles it with the warm grip of his fingers. He's kneeling at my feet and yet he's the strong one again, like Sir Walter Raleigh throwing his cape down for the Queen.

I hear from far, far away an imaginary snort from Polly. *A bit over the top, isn't it? Knight in shining armour? Remember this is the guy who made you fall for him while he's still enslaved by his demented wife. Who won't even kiss you.*

Polly. Oh Polly. What a lot I have to tell you. And the first thing is that nothing about Gustav Levi is over the top. Everything is calculated. Whether he's doing business, or making love, or breaking your heart.

'Don't want to get these any dirtier, do we, if we're going to go down on the beach? Crystal chose them very carefully for our weekend in Lugano to keep your feet warm.'

Gustav puts my bare foot down carefully on the grass and picks up the other one. This time his hand wanders up my ankle. The shivering ripples from my toes up to the top of my head. How does he always make me feel so naked?

'I don't want to go onto the beach. I want you to go back to London, and I want to go back to bed.'

'Bed. What a fine place to be right now. With you.'

I hold my breath. His voice caresses me. Every part of me sharpens in response. The two of us, in bed. How would that be? Him up behind me, thrusting and hard, whispering into my hair.

'Don't tease me, Gustav.'

'You want that too, don't you, Serena? The last time I saw you, you were bare and asleep in your bed in the chalet. So beautiful. Flushed, a little bruised. Lovely. Leaving you that morning was the hardest thing I've ever done. And the most idiotic and dangerous, I now realise.'

He plants my second foot beside him. Pats it gingerly as if it might rear up and kick him. When I don't move he scrunches up all the scraps of paper in a parcel around the diaries, stands up with his bulky load, and strides over to the steps carved into the little cliff. He stares down at the cove.

'Gustav! Not as idiotic or dangerous as jumping into the sea!'

Oh, God help me, but he's so gorgeous. He flips round in surprise. He could be a pirate swinging aboard a ship to wreak havoc. His black hair flips across his face.

'Jump? Never in a million years.'

All I can see is his mouth, half open, half smiling.

The shivering excitement slows. I may have just given myself away, but this is still the mouth that has never kissed me.

We search each other's eyes as the wind buffets us. I wonder what he sees? A professionally made-up woman, for one thing. Thank goodness for Jake and the interview. At least I look pretty damn good for once even though I'm shrivelled inside. Let's hope seeing me as a sophisticated woman makes it all the harder for him to say goodbye.

My stomach twists with unhappiness, decades of it, and tears suddenly blur my vision.

'These pictures aren't meant to goad you. I've brought them here to show you the truth. I've admitted that I was completely besotted with her once. I've also promised you that spell was broken years ago. But you never seem to hear me.' He wraps his arms around me, pulls me against that warm, strong body that has grown in strength and stature in these weeks. 'So when I got back to the chalet and found you'd gone I was devastated.'

'I couldn't stay in that house a second longer,' I sob, crying openly now. 'I couldn't be near you if I couldn't have you.'

He presses his finger on my mouth, tipping my head back. He is staring right into me, tenderness softening his features. I let his finger push at my mouth, scrape against my teeth. Let his other hand creep up into my hair.

'When I calmed down I sat down and thought over everything we've talked about, your past, the way those people treated you when you were a kid. How did they become so rotten and loveless?'

'I made them like that.'

'No, no, no! How could you? You were a baby. A child! An innocent, angelic child!' He squeezes my face between his hands and gives me a gentle shake, his black eyes roving intently as if trying to memorise me. 'God help me, if those monsters weren't six feet under I'd wring their necks myself. But despite everything they threw at you, here you are, a butterfly, a tough, curious, adventurous, creative, sensitive creature.'

'You've really worked me out.' I can't see him because my eyes are blurred with tears.

He shakes me again. He wraps his arm hard around my shoulders again and pulls me so that his chin rests on the top of my head.

'Maybe that resilience comes from somewhere even huger than you or I can comprehend. Your real parents, perhaps.'

'Not now, Gustav. Please let's not go there now. One day, maybe.' I press my hands over my eyes. 'Anyway, since when did you become my therapist?'

He laughs softly and flourishes a big white handkerchief out of his pocket like a magician. 'Since I dug out your diaries and read every painful entry so I could know you better. Yes. Unforgivable and intrusive. You can beat me about the head with a blunt stick if you like.'

He dabs the hankie at my nose.

'So, doctor, what's your diagnosis?'

'That your unhappy life has killed your trust, just as my nasty past has killed mine. Is that fair?'

I nod. 'So how do I learn to trust again?'

'It's my job to guide you. Baby steps. Your phrase. First of all we're going to make a pyre and burn everything.'

He lets go of me abruptly and strides over to the cliff, descends a couple of steps towards the little cove.

'The hotel will be furious,' I croak, waving my arm helplessly back at the looming white facade. I can barely stand up without him, it seems. 'Bonfires on the beach like a couple of hippies?'

He steps back up and takes my hand, pulls me down the steps after him.

'The manager is fine with it. Hippies, tycoons, nymphs, all sorts. But to be on the safe side I emailed them for permission.'

I stumble down the steps after him. The cold steps on my bare feet, and then the shingly wet sand of the little cove feel strangely pleasurable.

'You think of everything, Mr Levi!' A laugh escapes me as he starts to arrange the papers and diaries into a conical shape on a flat piece of rock.

He lifts his head and looks back towards the coastline where the tractor has offloaded Jake and the others.

'Not everything, it seems.'

I bite back the denial. Let him suffer like I'm suffering.

He takes a silver lighter out of his pocket and sets it to the bottom of the heap of papers, and boosted by the sea wind and the dry rock the fire leaps in an instant into golden flames. Margot's black eyes blaze as the paper curls round, then her face disintegrates into black crisps. Having devoured Margot the flames turn their attention to the stubborn diaries, lapping and licking like greedy tongues, dismembering them like yellow fingers.

One book flips open to reveal lines of childish handwriting. Both Gustav and I lean forward, despite ourselves, but the only words we can decipher before they crumble to ashes are: *one day I'll fly away.*

Gustav and I stand there for a long time. The flames crackle as if they're laughing, blow sideways as if they're dancing.

'Do you believe me now? That she's gone?'

I nod silently. He moves up beside me but doesn't touch me.

'All the tests I had planned for you, all the ruses to keep you at a distance, you kept overcoming all the obstacles like an Olympic hurdler!'

He looks down at me and smiles. How can a smile look so tragic? He tips my chin up, brings his face down to mine. Breathes me in, like I'm his favourite perfume.

'Whatever happens between us, I meant every word. Every word in London. Every word in Switzerland. All that nonsense about ghosts. You were the girl to banish her. I knew it already, but the minute I saw you in that hideous room of pain, dressed in her ghastly armour, your gorgeous face all distorted with her make-up and that awful confusion in your eyes, I thought she'd ruined everything all over again. I had to thrash her out of you. But you'd already chased her away. You'd taken her place.'

'If all that is true' – I use every ounce of willpower not to touch him even while the blood is fizzing in my veins, oblivious to the cold. I need to retain my position of superiority for a while longer – 'why didn't you make it clearer? I thought you'd grown fonder of me. Fancied me, even. God knows that night in front of the fire was so magical! But I never know for sure what's going on in this head of yours.'

'Comes from years of not communicating with anyone.' He shrugs wryly. 'Why else do you think I commit everything to documents? You can't argue with the written word. What I meant to tell you that night was that you are the only one after all these desolate years who has' – he bashes at his heart – 'fixed this. I don't know. Unlocked me. You don't even know it. But your femininity. Your talent. Those eyes. That hair. That attitude. So normal. You get more beautiful every day.'

I flick at my hair. 'Thanks to the newspaper's make-up girl.'

He glances towards the sea. The tractor is trundling up to the jetty.

'No, Serena. It's you. Inside and out. It's always been you.' He winds a ringlet of hair behind my ear. 'And talking of make-up girls. That reminds me. Your personal maid Crystal tells me the show is very nearly sold out, so soon you'll be free.'

I bow my head, look at my cold toes making dents on the sand. Where will those feet take me next?

'But there are a couple of commitments back in London. The interviews?' He takes another step closer to me. 'That was the arrangement, Serena. If you won't come back for me, come back for them. Keep it professional, if you prefer. Whatever else is going on here, whatever dreadful harm I've done to open up this chasm between us, just focus on your own success for a little longer. I wish I could ask you to start again or at least wind the clock back a couple of days.'

'To when? When you were inside me, Gustav? Shall we go back to that point? When we were lovers in front of the fire and you made me feel like queen of the moment, as if I was totally yours? We fitted together like hand and glove, do you remember? You were hard, and fast, and it was fantastic, I never knew it could be so good, and I thought it would never stop. Can we go back to that moment, when I wasn't your business accoutrement but your–'

'My Halloween girl. Yes.' His eyes spark with the surprise I intended. The flush in his cheeks matches the bloom on his mouth as he moves a little closer. 'What are you saying, Serena?'

I still hold myself away. 'I'm scared to say it but if not now, then when will I get the chance?'

'I'm the one who's meant to be doing the talking. I'm the one who came here to see if I could win you back,' he groans, pulling me towards him. 'Everything we've done and said since that first Halloween night was leading to that magical moment in front of the fire. I realise that now. And I blew it.'

I shiver more violently now. He wraps his jacket around me. The red scarf, too, loops around my neck and back around his like it did out on the mountain. We are joined, our bodies pressed up against each other. Too many clothes. Too many layers separating us, stopping the heat spreading each into each.

The waves crash restlessly against the rocks.

'So you didn't see her in Milan that day.'

His profile goes dark. That receding of the eyes into shadows, the hardening of his mouth. I've said something wrong again. He shakes his head. 'Watch my lips, Serena. She is dead to me. I never, repeat never, forgive wickedness or betrayal.'

I swallow hard. 'Will you tell me what she did to you? How all that adoration turned into abhorrence? The final nail in her coffin, I mean?'

'The line between love and hate is less than a hair's breadth but once it's crossed there's nothing left. Don't look back. Was it Orpheus who looked back, and destroyed everything? Except that he was trying to save Eurydice.' He closes his eyes as if waiting for the guillotine. 'My ex-wife is beyond saving. She took my brother from me, still has him for all I know, but more than that I can't tell you just now. Not yet. I won't let her destroy us by talking about her.'

Crystal warned me. Maybe the time will never come.

I force my voice to lighten. 'So. Milan?'

'I went to Milan on business, and also to get something special for you. Dickson knew my plan. He should have explained. It might have stopped you running away.'

I cock my head sardonically. 'What was this something special?'

'Perhaps you'll never know, now.' He smiles sadly and strokes my cheek. 'He's a lucky guy.'

I frown as I feel the spray on my cheeks. 'Who?'

‘The guy you were kissing just now. Jake.’

I close my eyes and try to twist away from him, but Gustav holds me closer, tugs my hair so that my head tips up to his. We stare at each other for a long time. My tiny reflection in his black eyes. The tipping air and sea around us. Everything, everyone, miles away.

‘That was a genuine kiss,’ he murmurs after a while. ‘Go ahead and deny it.’

‘I *am* denying it. That wasn’t a genuine kiss. Let me show you how to make things absolutely clear without words.’ I put my hands on either side of his face, feel his cheekbones sharp, the stubble grazing my palms as I rise on tiptoes. ‘*This* is a genuine kiss.’

I do it. I press my mouth onto his softly at first, then as I feel his lips give, his arms go tight around me, I press harder, slide my tongue along his lower lip, and he responds at last with a low groan, gently and sensuously, holding himself back, and all the more tantalising and sexy for that, until we are kissing properly like lovers in a movie, the camera panning round us as we taste each other properly for the first time, kissing, smiling, gasping, as the cold waves creep up the beach to take a good look.

‘Oh, God, Serena,’ he moans at last, running his fingers over my mouth to smooth away the wet. ‘I’d give anything to go straight up to that hotel room of yours right now. Something happens to you when you’re outside. You light up. It’s extraordinary. It was the same when you were galloping beside me in Switzerland. There’s something supernatural and untamed about you.’

I take a risk and run my hand down his stomach, further down to feel what it is he wants.

‘So what’s stopping you coming to bed with me right now? I want that too. More than anything. I want to do it again and again, like proper lovers. It’s a waste of an antique walnut-inlaid bed to lie there alone,' I quip, biting my lip at the echo of Jake's naughty suggestion.

Gustav groans, tipping his head back in frustration.

'I can't stay. I have to get back. No, don't be angry with me. I'm not toying with you. How could I, after you've confided in me today? I do have a meeting about New York. I was going to drag you back to London with me but I want to be absolutely sure you're coming back of your own accord.'

'Drag me all you like, Gustav. I'll follow you to the ends of the earth.'

'No. One more test, for both of us. It's a habit I might learn to break, but there's something in me that forbids me to take what I want without being one hundred per cent sure I deserve it.'

'You were pretty sure the other night. You took me when you wanted me then!'

'Yes, and it felt absolutely right. But I regret the way it happened. The state of mind we were both in.'

'I'm in my right mind now.'

He holds his hands up, then folds them tight around me again. 'Yes, but I'm going to blame you for being such a beautiful temptress. No. Much as every sinew in me is urging me to stay, I'm going back to London now. My mission is accomplished. You stay here and relish the luxury. Crystal made a good choice when she purloined those funds from the company account, although she, like Dickson, should really be looking at a P45!'

'I know you don't forgive easily, or at all, but you'll forgive Crystal, won't you? She was rooting for me, even though she broke a confidence by telling you where I was. And so was Dickson.'

'Dickson? He deserves to be sacked.'

'You couldn't manage without them, you know you couldn't,' I reply confidently. 'And nor could I.'

'And none of us can do without you.' He takes my hand and leads me across the beach, leaving the heap of ashes behind us. 'Come back to London tomorrow morning. Enjoy your last night of solitude. Because after that I won't be letting you out of my sight. We'll start again, my *signorina*. Let's see this thing through to the end.'

The tender words are music to my ears, apart from the open-ended, enigmatic minor key of the word 'end'.

He leads me back up the steps, picks up my socks and puts them in his pocket, strides on over the wet grass to the terrace and leaves me there.

'What was the special thing you went to Milan for?' I ask, desperate to keep talking even while he's backing away from me.

'Come back to the house in London, where you belong, and you'll find out.'

And then with one final kiss of my hand he runs down to the jetty where the sea tractor is waiting.

SIXTEEN

I still have the key Gustav gave me. It was still on my silver bracelet. And it's a good thing, because he wasn't home when I let myself in this evening. He hasn't even left a note.

But Dickson has. In a surprisingly elegant italic scrawl, he has told me the master wants me to dine well and not to wait up.

I try the door of Gustav's bedroom on the lower landing, but it's locked. The excitement that has propelled me all the way from Devon today is still there, but it's mixing now with that nagging voice of doubt I can never seem to silence. I go over everything he said at Burgh Island. That's all I can hold on to. Until he's standing here in front of me, until I can touch him again, I don't belong.

I lie on my bed in the attic room and stare through the arched windows. The moon is like one of those puffballs you see swelling in damp undergrowth. I reach for my camera and from my prone position take a couple of shots. Zoom in as far as my Leica lens will allow, right into the acne scars on its surface. The twigs from the little plant on my balcony are like fingers tapping at the window.

As I roll over to put the camera back on my table I see

Crystal's neat carry case on the floor, packed with cosmetics. She came here earlier this evening with the prints of the *Bleak House* series, and asked me to sign them.

'You can close that chapter for good now, Serena.'

'Yes. I've got all of you now. An odd lot, granted. Very eccentric. A bit like the Addams Family!' I guffawed loudly. 'Oh, don't look so cross, Crys. Come and do my make-up for when Gustav gets back?'

'Crystal.'

She opened up this big carry case and balanced a couple of round containers of colour on the tips of her fingers. With a thin smile she painted two round red spots on each cheek. I looked just like her, in fact, with the two round spots painted directly under each of her two round eyes.

'Wipe it off and do it more subtle,' I laughed, slapping playfully at her. 'I don't want to look like a barmaid.'

She pursed her lips tight as a button hole and held a lock of my hair in very hot tongs till it started to smoke.

I watched the tendril bounce out of the tongs in a beach-babe-style wave.

'You know, you've changed since I've been here,' I remarked, feeling like a princess. 'You look a little softer, for starters. You don't pin your hair so tightly that it looks like it's being pulled out, root by root. Maybe you've put on a little weight? Munched too many of Dickson's cheesecakes?'

Her mouth twitched reluctantly. Even her lips, still blood-red, looked plumper.

I miss her spiky presence now. I don't actually know where she lives, although she is often here. Perhaps she floats around this house at night, watching over us.

I pick up her big blusher brush and flop onto my back. I stroke the brush down my throat, down between my breasts. I am wearing the lovely negligee Gustav gave me my first night here. The one I danced in. Why didn't I just go ahead like Scheherazade and seduce him that night? He's a man, after all, not a mirage.

I run the brush over the fabric to see if the soft bristles can penetrate. They aren't sharp enough, but the sensation is just as pleasurable, and my skin gives a little quiver.

No need to close the shutters or draw the muslin drapes. I glance over at the balcony. The darkness and silence are spooking me tonight. No-one can see me up here. Unless they are one of Crystal's cat burglars.

I pour out a glass of red wine from the bottle I've nicked from Gustav's cellar. Dutch courage, if he ever comes home. Maybe he'll be angry. I hope so. I want him roused. I've seen what he's like when threatened, or cornered. I may not want that violent reaction every time, but I want to make something beautiful happen between us. Something that is only ours. No-one else's.

I lie back again. So restless now. Where the hell is he? Maybe I should have gone out with Polly. She should still be gallivanting somewhere. I grope about but can't find my mobile phone. She'll want to summon me to whatever bar or club she's in.

Loser! Staying in with just a paintbrush for company!

The wine, the bright moonlight and the soft Miles Davis music makes me dozy. Mustn't sleep. The grandfather clock down in the hall wheezes, starts to chime, then for some reason thinks better of it.

I flick the blusher brush up and down my neck. It's quite thick, with a sturdy handle, but the bristles are soft as kitten's fur. I twiddle it like a cheerleader's baton before taking the handle delicately between finger and thumb. I touch the bristles to my leg and flinch when they tickle. How I long for Gustav's fingers on me.

I squirm as my skin tries to resist the hairy touch. I flatten the brush over my thighs, sweeping it down to my knees and back again as if painting myself, brush further up the insides of my bare thighs. I wriggle as my hands and the brush start moving of their own accord. The negligee rides up as my hands move about.

I remember how Gustav pushed it up, over my thighs and hips, how he studied me in the candlelight the first time he invited me here, and how he bent forward and licked me right here.

The brush flicks it, ruffling the neat cluster of curls. I let the brush explore.

There's a tiny creaking sound. Nothing new there. The whole house creaks, especially at night. But I notice that one of the three glass doors opening onto the balcony has swung ajar. The little tree in its big terracotta pot scratches again, as if trying its luck. I should close the door against the draught, but instead I close my eyes and rock back into my soft duvet, dancing about on my bottom as the music murmurs around me and the paintbrush strokes faster and faster up my legs, over my stomach in circles, and down again, straying away from where I want it to go, the part of me that's yearning and burning for attention.

This is what a cat burglar would see. Stop him in his tracks. Make him stand there with his swag bag, his coil of rope, maybe a weapon or two, crouched in the attack position, dressed all in black. My head starts to sway and I play my tongue across my lips. It makes me feel sexy like a starlet. I rotate my hips on the cushions, thighs moving further apart as the brush plays.

I am only flicking and stroking, but with each stroke of the brush my hips rock more wildly. I slide both hands between my white thighs and part my legs, wider and wider, all the time imagining Gustav here with me, remembering his tongue, the feel of his hands strong and rough on my hips and thighs, pulling them open.

Remembering the promise of it. The thought that we had all the time in the world.

He talked about addiction to that life with Margot. I push away her shadow. Well, I think I'm addicted to Gustav. That's the madness keeping me here. Why I'll keep flipping back to him like a boomerang no matter what he chucks at me.

There is another scraping sound, and I glance at the window. The breath catches in my throat. Be careful what you wish for. Because somebody has decided to answer my prayers. Or maybe realise my worst fears. Either way I'm not alone with this make-up brush after all. Someone is out there, watching me. A man, all in black, standing on the balcony.

His mouth is moving. Is he demanding something? My money or my life? I'm not stopping now for anyone. I bend my knees, relax into the pillows, close my eyes. The brush travels to the top of my legs, up over my smooth mound. The bristles pick up the tight curls, and I sigh out loud. Wonder what he is thinking.

It's not Dickson, and it can't be Gustav. Why would he break into his own house? My fingers waggle over the soft patch, I try to keep them back, try to tease for a moment longer, but the foreplay with the brush and the idea of the man watching are irresistible. I burrow in, crowd my fingers in for a moment. Everything is exquisitely sensitive and exposed, visible to the man outside and anyone else for that matter, no doubt about that, but my legs are aching now. I hear the moist kiss as my lips press closed.

Let him look for a little longer. Did he see what I was doing? Did it make him stiff? Or scare him off?

The brush starts again. Up and down, the bristles bending softly into my contours and making small circles round the emerging bud. My fingers follow the brush, probing until either the brush or my finger, I can't tell which, scrapes that hidden kernel. It blazes into life and starts to throb.

I wriggle again, really into this performance now, throwing myself backwards as my fingers guide the brush, or rather the brush guides them. I ache with suspense as the brush dips delicately. I gradually increase the tempo until like an electric shock the brush hits its mark again.

Why isn't the man crashing in through the open window, finishing the job off himself?

Figment of my imagination, that's why, and if he isn't, then the security in this house is better than I thought. In any case I can't stop now. The brush works furiously until I raise my buttocks off the bed, knees flopping wide open as I moan in private frenzy.

My hair tumbles across my face as I come, blocking out the room and the moonlight and the motionless presence out on the balcony. The CD goes back to the beginning track. The warmth of the brush on me and its friction subside. I open my eyes blearily. The grandfather clock downstairs clears its throat again. It was my imagination. There was no-one there. Time to sort myself out. My face floods with heat, contrasting with the cold, and I draw my legs slowly together. Then I stand up stiffly and wander to the window. Bang my forehead wearily on the glass. 'I don't know whether to laugh or cry.'

'Either option would be appropriate.'

Gustav steps through the window, wearing a black leather jacket, jeans and biker boots. He casually pulls off a black woollen hat which has left his hair slicked over his head. Then he starts to unzip one of his black gloves for all the world as if I've just invited him in for tea and cucumber sandwiches.

I move away from him, stand back against the window, the glass cold on my back.

'Forgot your key?'

He nods, looking me up and down with undisguised lust flickering in his eyes.

'Yes, as a matter of fact. Sent Dickson back to the gallery to check.'

'So he still has a job, then?' I laugh. 'You could have rung the doorbell.'

'I did, my darling. Frantically. You obviously didn't hear it. I was worried you might not be here after all.' He chuckles and picks up the brush. 'But you were obviously otherwise engaged.'

I tug at the flimsy negligee. Feel traces of moisture seeping through.

'So you thought you would, what, scale five floors of sheer London brick and leap over my balcony like Spider-Man?'

'Batman's more my style. More of a dandy, don't you think? And it's not your balcony any more, Serena. You're moving rooms tonight.' He unbuttons the neck strap of the jacket and cracks his neck to ease it. 'Thought I'd use my old free running skills to get up here, actually. I could have waited for Dickson to get back, but I wanted to get into my house. I wanted to get to you as soon as possible.'

I smile and go to sit on the bed. This is like treacle flowing over me, this new Gustav with the fierce face and the soft words. 'You're talking about parkour, then. You're a *traceur*.'

He takes off the other thick glove. Stretches his long white fingers. Clicks each knuckle thoughtfully. So no weapon, but he could easily have been out wringing the necks of foxes. Or burglars. When is he going to come and sit beside me, here on the bed? I press my knees together, bone against bone to stop me leaping at him.

'How do you know about free running?'

I examine my fingernails. 'I've given it a go, as a matter of fact. In Paris. I fell in with a group of free runners near Notre Dame and climbed up onto a roof with them. I came to a sticky end, unfortunately. I nearly broke my elbow.'

'Horses, rooftops. You little urchin. You should take better care of yourself.' He goes to sit on the white rocking chair in the corner. 'And you should close these curtains, Serena. Anyone with climbing equipment and evil intent could have seen you. I could have been up to no good.'

'Promises, promises.' I smooth my hands up and down the goosebumps on my arms. 'Maybe I want you to get up to no good.'

'This is my house, Serena. You could have been courting real trouble disporting yourself like that for all the world to see.'

I feel reckless and tired. 'So. How did you really get up onto my balcony?'

'I am serious about the free running. I'll show you one day. But I'm too rusty to risk it just now. Which is why I climbed up the fire escape. God knows but I have to think of health and safety in a house this size, with you lot leeching off me day and night.'

He unzips one of his heavy biker boots. Then the other. *Honey, I'm home.*

He sits back in the chair and stares at me. I follow his lazy gaze down my body. My negligee has fallen back down to cover my legs with reasonable modesty, but where it clings the dampness is clearly visible.

'What am I going to do with you? A half-naked Serena pleasuring herself without me. Though even the thought of that makes me horny. You are wilful, rebellious, disobedient–'

'And bestselling. Didn't you know? We've only got four more pictures to go.'

I kneel down in front of him and pull his boots off. Throw them with a thumping clatter across the room. He grips the arms of the chair tightly. Very slowly I start to peel off his socks, too.

'A tough week, Gustav?'

He laughs. 'A tough month, if you must know. It's this damned woman I've met. She's wearing me to a husk.'

I get up abruptly and walk to the bedside table. Pour out some more wine and hand it to him. He holds it up to the light, smiles at me, and then drinks it. Wipes his mouth with the back of his hand like a ruffian.

He looks beautiful sitting on the chair in my bedroom. The stoniness in his features softening despite his best efforts. A flush of colour in his lean cheeks. His hair long and glossy, the blackness of his eyes deepened by his burglar's clothes.

'Can I take a photograph to remember you by? The moonlight suits you. Makes you look younger somehow. It must be your natural lighting.' I lift my camera, all my movements very slow, as if he might vault back over the balcony at any moment.

He remains in the chair, rocking very slightly and holding the glass of red wine. This is me at my best. Stepping round the room, stepping round him, framing and clicking. Trapping him forever in my little glass window.

'What do you mean, remember me by?'

'Well, the show's nearly sold out. Technically I'll be free to come and go as I please.'

He picks up the brush I've just been playing with and strokes it under his nose. Heat surges through me, through my body, up into my face. He can smell me on the bristles.

'Your heart won't let you.'

I remain standing, but I'm cold now. 'We've fulfilled most of the clauses of the agreement in principle. And I'm grateful for your faith in me, the gallery, and the room here, and your contacts and your help.'

'You have no idea.'

He leans forward and takes my wrist. There's a new silver chain, glinting in the moonlight. He hooks it onto my bracelet.

I'm hooked onto him. He tugs hard on the chain and as I stumble towards him he scoops me up into his arms and carries me out of the room, down the stairs, past pre-Raphaelite Rapunzel, then he kicks open the double doors of his own room.

This is like falling through the looking glass. I haven't changed or gone crazy, like Alice. This isn't a nightmare, or even a dream. I'm still Serena Folkes, the girl in the nightie who has this terrible addiction. But in this moment Gustav has carried me into my new life.

He throws me playfully onto the huge bed which is pushed up against the enormous windows and then goes to stand by the wall opposite. An oblong of light edges in from the landing, but apart from that the room is in darkness.

A tiny spotlight pings on to illuminate a framed picture.

'You asked me why I went to Milan. I carried this all the way out there from London and then decided to frame it properly. I was going to give it to you in Switzerland.'

It's the sketch he did of me at the private view, small but perfectly formed. It's been set in the centre of a wide pale green mount and a beautiful silver frame. Instinctively I glance round the room, up at the ceiling. The other walls are totally blank.

'That was the first drawing I'd done for five years.' He gestures round the room before coming to sit beside me on the bed. 'Maybe one day your face will fill all these other spaces.'

'Just one picture's enough, Gustav.'

I nod quietly, my heart banging in my chest. He switches the light off again and he's right here beside me. We're in his room, on his bed. All I can do is sit as prettily as I can in my sheath of silk, try to ignore my nipples pricking up with the cold, the dampness seeping still between my thighs.

'I think I'm falling for you, Serena.'

He winds his fingers through my hair, tugging me towards him. I let him pull me closer. My stomach clenches with terrified excitement. The heat is beating off him. His eyes smoulder with lust, not anger. His mouth splits into a grin, gradually, as if it is out of practice. All at once he pushes me back onto the bed, my wrists trapped easily in his hands as he snaps the silver chain onto the bed post.

'You don't need to tie me. I'm not going anywhere.'

'Old habits.'

'Tell me more about the woman who's wearing you out.' I jingle the silver chain playfully, throw my arms back over my head.

He chuckles, and runs his fingers down the inside of my arms where they're outstretched, making them tingle. 'I wasn't aware I was missing anything or anyone in my life, but I realise I was. There's a big hole sculpted for her when she's ready to fit. She's impossible. Beautiful, talented, wilful, rough round the edges. Slippery, like an eel. And much younger than me.'

He makes the silver chain tighter around my wrist. The little bite in my wrist thrills me.

'Is she your prisoner?'

'I just want to make sure she never runs away again.'

I wriggle and lie back. The lamb to his slaughter. Little Red Riding Hood. He tugs off his jumper and shirt. I see his arms, sculpted and muscular, and at last I see his torso. Naked. His chest is broad enough to sleep on, tapering to that slim waist and sexy hips, just a strong line of black hair running from his solar plexus over his smooth, flat stomach, wandering like a tease down into his jeans. Skin so pale and vulnerable yet warm and muscular from climbing onto balconies and carrying country wenches down stairs.

He opens his arms, inviting my admiration like a showman, then he falls back onto the bed, runs his fingers greedily over me again as if he's just discovered me under the Christmas tree, over my skin, down over the negligee, over my breasts, lingers over my nipples till they harden in response, then his hands move on down along my thighs.

'And she has this amazing hair. Long, and lustrous, like Rapunzel.'

His lips are in my hair, running across my cheek. My mouth meets his, so warm, such a lovely fit, his body so warm, too, heavy as he continues to stroke me.

Our tongues curl round each other, more suggestively than before, then his mouth moves away down my throat. His fingers pull the negligee aside, baring my breasts, and he kisses them too, reverently and softly. My nipples are instantly burning for him. I can't help it. I moan and arch my back towards him. I've waited for this forever, it seems.

And there it is, oh God, his tongue, flicking across my nipples, circling them, his lips nibbling briefly on each sore point before his mouth travels on downwards. I can't do anything. My hands are tied above my head with the silver chain. It feels so good, lying here helplessly like this, unable to do anything, direct him, guide him, pleasure him even, other than lie here and be the feast he will enjoy again and again.

'Please, Gustav. Fuck me. I can't wait any longer.'

I open my legs and stretch them on either side of him. Pause. Don't want to scare him off. Then wrap them round the back of him and pull him close to me. He glances up at me, his mouth wet from kissing, then he walks his knees back up between my thighs, so pale in the moonlight. He strokes me again, down my throat, over my breasts, down over my stomach. I hold my breath. His touch is so tender.

'Enough with the talking.'

He is leaning over me now. I know his face so well. The half close of his eyes as if the lids are too heavy, when he's aroused. The pushing forward of his lower lip when he finally releases it, as if eager for a kiss.

'I want to touch you all over, Gustav. Will you untie the silver chain? I promise I'm not going anywhere.'

He grins. 'You can't leave me, anyway. Not while I have some rather incriminating footage in my possession.'

'Footage?' I wriggle anxiously.

'I have cameras in this house, remember? Mostly switched off, actually, but that night when I thrashed you with the little nun's whip, it's all on film. You wouldn't leave without securing that, would you?'

I squeal and kick at him. 'You bastard! Blackmailing me!'

'You're mine, young lady!' He laughs, and slaps me, hard, on the bottom. 'I can hold you to ransom for as long as I like!'

We wrestle, hard, my struggle getting weaker as he weighs me down with his hands. My head flops back at last, with one last yank at my shackles.

'You like it, don't you? Our silver chain? Being tied like this really turns you on.'

I lie there, waiting. He lowers himself slowly over me. Unzips his jeans. And there is my prize.

Dear God, I thought this moment would never come. It was hard and brutal the other night. We were both gripped by fury and fear. But tonight? Tonight I want the luxury of taking a good look. I'm rapidly becoming unable to live without it.

So. Stay still. Don't break the spell. We're facing each other this time. His fathomless eyes. His sensuous mouth. He's going to do it this time like a lover. Gorgeous, powerful, weird, wonderful Gustav Levi.

In the window the moon has slipped sideways on its way towards morning, as if averting its eyes, or ceding us some privacy.

The weight of him on my legs pins me down. I hitch my

hips invitingly, see his jaw tighten as he bends his face down to brush his mouth against mine.

'Thank God you're here,' he murmurs hoarsely.

I pull him into me, my legs strong and determined, and at last, at last his stomach is going tight as he starts to push inside me, little by little, he's so hard and hot. My body encloses him. My legs wrap around his hips and we tussle, he's strong, resisting, I'm determined, pulling, my body wants him deep, deeper inside me but still he's testing himself, testing me, holding back for as long as possible, and then we're rocking and tilting together, the pillows soft against my back, my bottom lifted off the bed as he pulls me with him.

This is normal, hot sex. So normal. My man and me.

His dark head is steady above mine, eyes black coals burning. It's the face that has been uppermost in my mind for the last month.

A thump and clatter down in the hall. So Dickson has found the key.

'Ignore him, Gustav. I'm here. Look at me.'

Gustav settles into a kind of trance, still staring at me, his fingers stroking my sides as if he's tuning a harp. Then he takes hold of my hips, lifts them easily towards his strong, lithe body. He starts moving again. He starts to push. He's just inside me. I move with him. It's all so natural.

Of course he's focused. Gustav Levi doesn't do anything by halves. He doesn't alter his slow, sexy rhythm. We are moving together, in time with the heartbeat of the jazz music. My legs grip tighter as he pushes further, further, he fits so perfectly, I'm loving this so much, I want to moan and thrash, and pull him and kiss him and bite him.

But I don't. Not tonight. I show him a woman who can remain silent and submissive.

I keep my eyes on him, take a good look before the moonlight slides away completely. He's filled out, somehow, like a ravenous man who has finally eaten a square meal. There's no spare flesh on him, his muscles are chiselled by some kind of workout he must be doing, but I like that he's bigger, stronger, than when I first met him. His arms ripple and flex with new muscles.

I'm his square meal. His nourishment.

I must have moaned just then, because suddenly he shifts, leaning close. I arch my back again, I'm so impatient now. Does he want my yearning breasts?

To my astonishment he reaches above me and unclips the silver chain, releasing my wrists, spreads his hands under my bottom and flips me like a pancake up towards him. We are upright now, face to face, nose to nose, like medieval saints praying on a tomb. I am straddling his knees. I feel so young like this, so athletic and free. I love that he's playing with me, experimenting with me. And I love that he is still fitted deep inside, angled right up to the hilt.

We pause for a moment, breathing fast into each other's faces, taunting each other to see who will move first, testing ourselves to see who will crack and give in to this incredible moment.

His lips are moving silently as if he's counting himself in, or praying. He pulls his haunches back and so do I. He's not gentle. He slams his hips into me and I buck back at him. We pull back together, arching in rhythm as if rowing a boat, slam back so hard that we shudder with the impact of bone on bone.

His black eyes bore through me. I want to shut mine, but I fear he might vanish if I do. *I've shut my eyes so you can't see me.* So I keep staring back, not blinking, as we grind and pause, so solid, filling, fitting me perfectly. My body grasping him like a tight glove.

An unearthly groan rumbles in his throat. Is this a first for him, too? This perfect fit? His body tenses up again. I ease myself across his thighs, no sudden movements to startle him or break him out of his trance. My muscles tighten around him, this I remember, this I can do, this I want to do, over and over, until I'm the world's expert.

His hands loosen slightly on my hips as his face softens. We are totally enclosed in this circle of moonlight. So gentle, compared with the last time. So real. Just the two of us. He's totally mine, and I'm his. Body and soul.

At last it's me he's seeing. Nobody else. His eyes glitter with fresh fire as he renews the rhythm, faster, faster, meeting me in a spiral of excitement until his expression grows dark with the effort of holding back, and then there's no need to hang on any more, here is his release, his eyes blazing with sheer ecstasy, his gaze never leaving mine as my own climax rushes at me and I fling my arms round his neck and cling to him as if I'm drowning.

Downstairs the clock finds its voice and strikes three.

SEVENTEEN

There are two photographs left unsold. The buyers of the house on the cliffs have confirmed their purchase of the Devon series of sky and seascape seen through battered window frames.

Proud as I am of those naïve efforts, it's a weight off my shoulders to know they will soon be gone. That house as I knew it will soon be gone. My photographs will provide the local colour.

I am jittery and nervous today. I'm trying to marry my professional pride with the new-found harmony I hope I've found with Gustav. Two nights ago he swung through the window like the man from those old Milk Tray adverts, and fulfilled every private dream I've had since I arrived in London.

But now that the night is over, our first full night together, and even though he made love to me again before he left for yet another business meeting, I'm still tortured, now that we're parted, by a nervy exhaustion I've never experienced before. He said he'd never let me out of his sight, and yet I don't know where he is. I know I should be concentrating on this show and what happens after it closes, but I can't get last night out of my head. The peaks of ecstasy followed by the calm quietness, his touch waking me to do it all again, my tongue on his skin, tasting him, his on me, exploring a new place every time.

All of that has made me a fulfilled, happy woman. All that, except the remaining dilemma. He hasn't said what happens between us when the exhibition ends. When we can terminate the contract. I want to sell, make money, be successful, but I don't want to have to cut loose from him. Ever again.

I wish I could speak to Polly, but she's not answering. Probably on the plane back to NYC.

When Gustav left it was so early in the morning that a milk float was humming across the square, rattling its bottles and crates. A group of schoolgirls with long legs and short socks pushed through the gate into the garden and didn't seem to be in any hurry to get to school. They stopped under the statue and stared at something on their mobiles, their faces lit by the light box of the screen. It could have been the stage set for a London musical. Any minute I expected a flower seller and a gaggle of chimney sweeps to tap-dance out of the wings.

The two remaining unsold pictures are totally unconnected with each other, which I thought would make them harder to sell. And now I don't want them to sell. Because what will happen then? Where will I go? How will I decide which of the many flowering avenues to take?

Crystal has handed me a clutch of portrait commissions from private clients, some of whom live as far away as the States.

One of the remaining pictures is the first I ever took with this little silver Lumix camera. I saved up all my Saturday job money and bought it on my seventeenth birthday.

That birthday was the turning point. It was the day Jake

kissed me for the first time, outside the camera shop. But they had followed us into town, and saw us kissing, and hauled me back to the car, Jake running after them shouting and swearing and eventually being arrested by an off-duty policeman. They drove me back to the house on the cliffs. Why did they keep dragging me back to the house if they hated me so much?

That birthday I grew up overnight. The man who said he was my father was getting sick then, and didn't have it in him any more to hit me. He stood in the doorway to the kitchen, smoking the fags that swiftly killed him. The woman went for me like a harridan, pulling out handfuls of my hair. My ugly orange hair, as she called it. I waited for her to stop for a moment, and then I punched her in the face.

You'll never amount to anything. We know that, and you know that. No-one will love you. No-one will employ you. No-one will want you. You've always been a wicked, selfish girl with ugly orange hair, and now you're a violent slut as well.

The picture is one I took in the shopping centre just after I bought the camera, Jake urging me to hurry up, and just before they came up and caught us kissing. It's a picture of a very long, empty escalator, shiny and grey, the parallel lines like receding railway tracks, sliding endlessly upwards, up to the next level, up towards the glass ceiling, to the sky and clouds shut out above. It's entitled *Stairway to Heaven*.

The other picture remaining is a self-portrait in monochrome that Gustav had enlarged to almost monstrous proportions. It hangs on the wall so that it faces punters when they first enter the gallery. It's a close-up of me wearing my black beret. My face is white and my lipstick looks almost black, but my eyes are staring slightly away from the lens, into the future. It's been used as a thumbnail for some of the publicity material, but that's it. So a tricky ask. Why would anyone want to buy that?

'You've fallen for him, haven't you?'

Crystal and I are sipping our double-strength Americanos and eating doughnuts at my desk in the gallery, looking out at the Christmas lights twinkling through the afternoon rain on the grey river outside and the slow circuit of the London Eye. I've been reading through the catalogue of my work, each piece crossed off neatly by Crystal as sold. It's like reading a diary of the last month. I can remember when each picture went, who it went to, and what had happened to me that day, or that night. What Gustav had said, or done.

I glance sideways at her. 'You a mind-reader amongst your other talents?'

Gustav isn't the only one who has changed physically. Since I first saw her dominating the reception area downstairs Crystal has altered her image dramatically. Her hair has finally been unpinned, and is in a dead straight flapper-style bob. The flowing maxi dress has been replaced by a red mannish trouser suit complete with silver tie, pin, French cuffs and fedora.

Well, we've all changed. I wonder if even Polly would recognise me now. My scruffy jeans and hoodies have been ceremoniously disposed of by Crystal. I have become incapable of choosing anything to wear without her say-so, and today it is a bunny-soft white cashmere dress, lined with satin, draping off my shoulders and clinging to my legs.

'You don't have to be a mind-reader to see what's been happening,' she answers crisply. 'It's like you were both starving, and someone has stuffed you with several square meals.'

I gasp in disbelief. 'You *are* a mind-reader! That's exactly how I thought about Gustav. But it's not a hugely romantic description of what love can do.'

'We all need square meals, Serena.'

Over on the other side of the gallery the lift doors swish open.

Gustav steps out of the lift slowly, speaking quietly into his phone, apparently unaware of where he is. Now I know what people mean when they say the heart leaps. Mine is ready to fling itself out of my chest.

Crystal nudges me with her sharp elbow, and I nudge her back.

It's like time has rewound. He's wearing the overcoat he had on the night we met. The same thick red scarf wound round his neck. His usually pale, still face is animated. Almost hectic. My leaping heart argues with my anxiously clenching stomach.

He finishes the call then studies the exhibition for a few moments, putting his finger on each of the red dots as if detonating them. Stepping back to look at the pictures as if he's never seen them before.

At last he turns. And the broad smile that warms his face when he sees me, lifts his mouth, his eyes, his brow, his cheeks, even his hands, is like the sun coming out after a long winter. He dangles the silver chain as if ringing a concierge's bell, and I come to heel.

'Crystal,' he calls, as he calmly clips the chain onto my bracelet and leads me back into the lift. 'I think we'll be winding this exhibition up tonight. The last two pictures are reserved.'

'Hey! Why talk to her about it? Why not me?'

I tug grumpily on the chain but he yanks it, and me, up close to him. 'I had to give her some kind of instruction, didn't I, to keep her occupied while I ravish you? The only reason I'm here is because I'm going to explode if I don't have you right here. Right now!'

I giggle nervously, glancing round the lift with all its

mirrors. I lift my hands and pull his face down. 'I'm yours whenever you want me, Gustav. Why don't you take me home right now?'

He runs his lips over mine, eyes half closed, brushing sensuously, instantly turning me on yet always, always holding back a little, doing his thing of breathing me in like perfume. 'No time. No time. I have to be at the airport. And I've just come from putting the house in Baker Street on the market.'

I blink. 'That's pretty radical, isn't it?'

'It's down to you, Folkes. You've opened my eyes.'

'I think Crystal might have tried to persuade you to get rid of it?' I murmur tentatively. 'We've had a chat about it.'

He strokes my face calmly, winds my hair round his finger. 'It earns me a fortune from the sado-masochist hunters with nothing better to do with their money, but I still have to divide the spoils with Margot. I want to chop off that final connection. It's like mainlining poison. I should have disconnected that artery five years ago.'

We stare at each other in silence. His face is calm, and serious.

'And in a couple of hours I'm leaving for the States.'

'You're leaving London? But you said you wouldn't let me out of your sight!' I drop my hands and step away from him. 'What will happen to us, Gustav? When will I see you again?'

He punches a button and the lift stops. We're up on the top floor but the doors don't open.

'At the weekend. I won't tell you exactly when. But let's not waste time talking now, Serena. I want you so badly, I can't think about anything else. Do you want me?'

I squirm against him hungrily. 'God, you know I do. All the time!'

He spins me round and pushes me down. 'Forgive me if I hurt you, Serena. I'm going to blame you. You make me like this. If we were at home, in bed, I'd be gentle, so gentle, I want to worship you as you deserve, as you're trying to teach me, but there's no time, no time, and oh God you make me feel like such a brute!'

'Do whatever you want and be quick about it!' I growl back. I fall onto my hands and knees. I let him manhandle me. Because this might be the last time. The illogical remnants of fear, so hard to shake off, still grip me. That he might not come back to me. But then the logical voice drowns out those fears. Of course he'll come back. I know now that I am the chink in his armour. The light in his darkness.

'Close your eyes. Imagine we're somewhere beautiful, not stuck in a seedy lift.'

'I don't want to close my eyes. I want to see you.'

I stare at him, hanging above me in the mirror. And that's the moment when I realise I love that face. I love him.

'Even if I do go away, I can't bear the idea of anyone else having you.' He kneels down behind me and starts to push my dress up over my legs, my hips. His breath is hot against my hair. 'Nobody else. I want to mark you somehow as mine.'

'We have the silver chain?'

In the mirror his dark eyes flash at me, and he nods. The silver chain is our own not-so-secret code. He loops it loosely round my neck, and then goes on pushing at my dress. The soft cashmere whispers over my spine, raising every hair on my skin. I shiver as he pulls down my knickers, lets the cooler air skim my bare bottom. The zip on his trousers rips down. Pure excitement prickles through me. I'm wet already, my knees trembling and weak. I can't wait to feel him, his fingers, his hardness. Any part of him is a taper to my flame.

His fingers move over my butt cheeks and ease them apart and I brace myself because I know what's coming. Something new. I'm ready and willing. I'll do anything he wants, because I want it too. I can see our reflections, our faces, my kneeling body, his big hands on my hips, moving in the stark light. I don't feel low down kneeling here. I am elegant. Poised, my white skin in the white dress, my hair waved and fiery around my eager face. I'm kneeling, but I'm not bowed. And he's not bearing down on me like some kind of rutting stud. He's holding me safely in place.

'Any which way, Gustav. I'm your lover today, even if it's the last time.'

I do bow my head then, because tears are burning my eyes.

'You talk too much, Folkes. Don't even think. It's easier that way.'

I give in to him. Give in to everything. When those last two photographs go, my career will be launched. But this part of my life will all be over.

He smears something cool up between my cheeks, and I subside into a kind of trance. This should feel crude, degrading, but it doesn't. Gustav's fingers on me, the cream, the slow, deliberate way he is rubbing it in as if anointing me with some kind of balm, is soothing and tender. That's how things are between us now.

The cream is warm now, as if he's heated it, and now his fingers open the way, and his hardness is there again, that lovely hardness, that lovely stiffness, probing at the private opening which closes like a fist against the intrusion. But he pushes so gently, it feels damp and welcoming there, and he is long and smooth, pulsing with warmth. My man.

I tip my bottom up higher without thinking because it feels sensational.

'My darling little whore, inviting me in,' he breathes, tickling my neck. 'What have I created?'

I rub my cheek against his hard cheekbone, and giggle softly. 'Yes, I'm inviting you in. I want to please you, Gustav, so that you can never let me go.'

He starts to push between my buttocks. My hair swings across my back as I arch myself a little more and he takes hold of it so that the roots tug gently at my scalp.

He groans and nudges inside my private space, pausing, pushing again, entering with a little pop, waiting again, and then he's right inside, a tight fit, and we start to move. I rock on my hands and knees, wanting to scream out loud with dirty excitement. His hand is underneath me, cupping me, supporting me, and I rub against it, matching his rhythm behind me as we move together, opening that tight part of me to let him in, no clenching or resistance, just gripping him in there, chasing the hot tangle of pleasure way up inside me, his balls going tight as his pleasure rises, he's thrusting now, sensations are sparking and radiating through me, how dirty can it get?

Gustav accelerates his rhythm, ramming into me. Not so gentle now. The fighter is back. Our breathing is hard and fast. There are voices somewhere, people who need the lift punching the buttons, and we both laugh softly even as we rock faster and faster, urgently, and then he's calling out my name in a broken sob, and I love him, and I fall back, squeezing him inside me until he stops moving.

His hands drift off me and I pull my dress down over the stickiness. I reach over and zip up his trousers. He tugs the silver chain and pulls me close to him. He pushes my hair off my hot, flushed face and looks at me serenely for a long time before nodding slowly.

'You and me, Serena. Sometimes it feels like dynamite. I'd like to have you in every single corner of London that means something to me. Every restaurant, every bar, every park bench. I'm so hungry all the time. I don't know how I lasted nearly forty years without you.'

I hold my breath. 'So tell me what's going to happen to us, Gustav.'

He punches the button, and the lift doors open. A crowd of people are standing there, clutching phones, briefcases, and extremely puzzled looks.

'I'm away to New York now but meet me here on Friday evening. OK?'

So there's no time to say any more.

EIGHTEEN

The gallery has been stripped. The brightness from the window and the bare walls dazzle me as I step out of the lift. I wanted to wear a dress today, I wanted to dress to kill, but Crystal has styled me in an immaculately tailored white trouser suit, the twin of her red one, with a silk flower in the button hole, low-cut silk camisole, high heels.

It's Friday evening, but Gustav isn't here. And all the photographs have been carted away. All except the last two.

'You never said it was being dismantled today, Crystal!' I run around the gallery, banging at the bare walls as if somehow that will bring the photographs back.

'Gustav's orders. The pictures are all sold, so we need something seasonal now.'

'A Christmas exhibition? Hardly his style, I wouldn't have thought?'

'We're not talking Santas and elves if that's what you mean. He'll find a whole other face to fit the Christmas spirit, you can be sure of that.' She takes out a hairbrush and starts on my hair with her habitual one hundred strokes which got forgotten this morning. Her mouth is spiky with kirby grips. 'He's always been infuriatingly restless. He wants to move on. He's had it with London for now.'

'The man who tires of London is tired of life. So where does that leave me?"

'Only he can answer that one. But you've both done extremely well out of it. Your first ever show's a sell-out, Serena. How many artists can say that? You've learned so much on the job. So. Has he given you your cheque yet?'

We are distracted by movement at the window, and watch in astonishment as the sky tips snow over the city.

'No. And I don't know who bought the last two pictures, anyway.'

She combs my hair into a high ponytail.

'You're going to miss him, aren't you?'

'Like hell. But don't tell him I said that.'

'I think he already knows.'

'I wish he'd give me a clue about what happens next, then. I don't know if we've become genuinely close, or I've just thawed him a little.'

My fingers wander to the silver bracelet.

Crystal pats my hand. 'He's never given anyone anything as pretty as this. It's an intimate gesture for him. And the silver chain? Pretty, but kinky.'

I blush and twist the bracelet round my wrist. 'We're supposed to be permanently attached by it. And symbolically or otherwise, I can't actually take it off now even if I wanted to.'

'Only he can unlock it, you mean?'

'All I know is I don't want to say goodbye to him.' I pick up my embroidered pashmina and fling it round my neck.

'So find a way to keep him, darling.' She arranges the pashmina around my head for a moment, making me look like a nun. 'The oldest trick in the book. Women have always snared their man in the most obvious way. So do it your way, next time. Not his.'

I blush harder. 'What do you mean? What's in your crystal ball today, Crys?'

'Crystal.' She's changed her image yet again today. Her hair is half up, half down, in a kind of artfully loose geisha girl's roll, to go with her antique golden kimono. She ties the wide, obi-style belt more tightly round her tiny waist and trips round the desk in her geta shoes to study a new list of figures. 'Use your assets, that's all I'm saying.'

'How can I, if he's not here?'

I stand in front of the self-portrait, lit by its single spot in the huge expanse of empty wall. I follow the curve of my face and shoulders in the photograph. I took that in the railway station waiting room, just before I caught the train to London. The red spot in the corner of the frame catches my eye.

Who would want to buy a picture of me?

The lift doors open and my heart does that skipping, lifting thing. I deliberately remain in front of the picture. If I turn round he'll see it written in my face.

But it's not Gustav. Several burly blokes I've never seen before wearing blue overalls and plugged into iPods stagger out into the gallery carrying huge misshapen parcels which look like cadavers wrapped in bubble wrap.

'What are you doing? What have you got there?'

'Setting up for the next show, Miss. Sculptures made out of recycled coat hangers, or summat like that.'

I hurry to the desk to check who bought the last photograph. But there are no details of the buyer of the *Stairway to Heaven* and my self-portrait.

I glance at the figures on the balance sheet, minus the final sale, and the reality of my success heats me stealthily from the feet upwards. I am rich. No doubt about that. Even minus Gustav's hefty commission, I am now a very successful, very wealthy young woman.

Right back at you, everyone who said I'd amount to nothing.

The phone makes me jump.

'It's for you.'

Crystal hands it to me.

'Serena? Have you cleared out of there yet? We need the gallery space for the new exhibition.'

'My pictures have all gone, yes. All except the last two which are still here, waiting for their buyers to pick them up. What's going on?'

'I meant your personal items. Everything needs to go. The entire gallery has been sold.'

Gustav's voice is gruff and brisk and snatched away by traffic and voices and the outside world. I glare at Crystal, who shrugs a little shamefacedly at keeping this bombshell from me. I have to delay for just a little longer.

'Where are you?'

There is a pause.

'Bring the envelope with you.'

'What envelope?'

Crystal hands it to me.

'I'm over at the London Eye.'

I have come to think of this as my own private stretch of thc Rivcr Thames. I've captured it on my camera at all different times of the day and night. Now snow is scudding thickly sideways as if a giant is blowing it, turning everything in its path to monochrome.

My eye follows the river westwards towards the elegant wheel. I imagine him standing there, tall and dark in his coat, his hand raised in the air as if he is drowning. The thick red scarf wrapped round his neck the only slice of colour.

'You can't see me, but you have about half an hour to get across to me.'

I bang my forehead against the glass, still holding the

phone. 'What am I supposed to do? Swing across the river on a trip wire?'

'A cab will do for now.' He laughs, a low, melodious sound I've never heard before. He doesn't share his laughter with just anyone. Maybe it's going to be alright, after all. 'But one day I'd like to see you fly.'

He is standing like a sentry beside an empty, waiting pod. The rest of the London Eye is swathed in snowy swirls now, but this pod is brightly lit, belching out warm air, and furnished with a comfortable-looking low-slung seat set with champagne and chocolate truffles.

He ushers me inside and with a kind of princely bow hands me a glass of champagne.

'What goes around, comes around,' he murmurs enigmatically, as the doors seal us into our bubble.

I'm consumed with shyness. So is he, perhaps, because we are silent as the Eye rises slowly. From up here we can make out the gallery along the other side of the river, its huge riverside window lit brightly. The self-portrait is still hanging in there, alone in the expanse of whiteness unless Crystal has told those delivery men to take it down. They will have deposited the new exhibits and disappeared by now. Crystal must have gone, too. Serena Folkes's oversized face will be the only sign of humanity in there.

'Not even I could have predicted how quickly this exhibition would sell out. Something in your work hit the mark, Serena. The zeitgeist.'

It is getting warmer in the pod, and I am blushing like crazy. I unwind the pashmina from my neck. The silk of the camisole under the jacket is still cool where it lies across my skin, but it's beginning to stick to my back and under my arms. My new boots click nervously on the floor.

'I'm thrilled about the last photograph selling, but I didn't want the exhibition to end so soon, Gustav.' I look at him, but I'm not sure he's heard me. 'Our arrangement, I mean. I'm not ready to go it alone.'

He is staring out of the window, this time downriver towards Tower Bridge, his glass tapping against his chin. The snow is so thick now that it could be night time. It's as if someone has dropped a white cloak over us. Landmarks and lights and shapes are muffled.

I get up and walk to the opposite side of the pod.

'This is going to feel like a very long ride if you're not going to talk to me, Gustav.'

We are floating in the sky now, over the spires and rooftops of London.

'I forgot to put this on you.' He is beside me now, tall and warm, lifting my coat off. He flings it onto the bench then takes my wrist to snap on the silver chain.

'What's the point of chaining me up now? I'm not going to jump out of the window,' I remark a little coolly.

He nods, turning his mouth down a little sheepishly. 'I admit it was meant to look like a lead at first. Me Tarzan, you Jane. Master and slave. Patron and protégée. And we've been all these things together, haven't we? But it's become redundant as a restraint.' He threads it through his fingers thoughtfully. 'Maybe it was more of a security chain for me.'

'Well, it's none of those things any more. I can hardly be chained to you when you're vamoosing to New York, and I'll be–'

'Where would you like to be?'

His voice is soft, like silk in my ears, chasing away the awkwardness. He walks over to the bench, the little chain tugging me with him. He takes off his own coat. The chain goes taut but I stay where I am.

'Not Devon. It won't be the same here in London, if you're

going away. My heart is set on returning to Venice, but first I have new commissions to honour.'

'That's what I like to hear. You'll need a new venue, of course, when you collate your next exhibition.' He pats the bench next to him, pulling on the chain and smiling. 'You have some new material?'

My feet are aching, unaccustomed to standing about on high heels. I sit down obediently.

'If you must know it's all about my new family. The Levi household. Windows and doors. I have some pictures I took at the chalet. In your house in the square. Dickson cooking. I went into the garden the other evening and took pictures of him and Crystal peeling vegetables through the steamed-up windows.'

'Domestic bliss. Except Crystal tells me you've likened us to the Addams Family.'

I blush like a schoolgirl. But he is laughing. He taps the tip of my nose. 'Which makes you, who? Morticia or Wednesday?'

He pulls me onto the bench and we straddle it, face to face. Our favourite position. He slides me closer, pulling off my jacket. My skin rises in goosebumps, tingling in response. The silk of my camisole shivers over my breasts. My whole body yearns towards him. I put my hands on his long legs to steady myself.

'Who bought the last two pictures, Gustav? Did you bribe someone to buy them so it would all be over and you could go on your way?'

His head is bent in concentration. He strokes the silk slip almost absently where it clings to my breasts, stopping just above my nipples. I hold my breath. *Touch me there, oh please, touch me there.*

He stops touching me, and picks up the white envelope.

'You'll get a lovely surprise when you find out who your

last buyer is. But what does it matter who bought them? Have you seen how much money you've made?'

'*We've* made.'

I open the envelope. There is a cheque in there, and another envelope.

'You haven't taken your commission, Gustav! This is the full amount!'

'I'd like to take it in kind. My *droit de seigneur*.' His hands are moving over my neck, squeezing slightly, feeling the pulse there. I stare at his fingers, moving so close to my breasts. 'You haven't forgotten that was part of the deal? Your idea, not mine.'

'Oh, that's so good,' I breathe, my head empty of anything sensible.

He strokes my breasts. My hardening nipples tell him everything he needs to know.

'Did we set a limit on how many times we could do it?'

He deftly unpins my hair and it tumbles down my back. He lifts a strand to sniff it.

I shake it off my face. 'Not as such, no. I would have done it every night, every day, every which way, if you'd only come to me sooner.'

'What a pathetic fool I am,' he whispers. 'Scared of my own shadow.'

'Yes, you're a fool. Because now it's too late. The clock has struck. Cinderella's time is up.'

A fidgety warmth is inside me, tightening, making my knickers damp. I push closer into his hands. We are at the top of the wheel's ascent now. The glass dome is blanketed with snow.

Do it your way.

I take hold of the silver chain and pull him towards me. My breasts are big in the magical snowy light. I pull his sweater off, neck first, like he's a schoolboy. He has a checked shirt on underneath. With his black hair ruffled he looks like a rock star just come off stage.

London is spread like a feast beneath us. The river is a silver path leading east.

The touch of his fingers on me just now, on my breasts. My nipples aching for his fingers, his mouth, his teeth, his tongue.

'If this is goodbye, then the least you can do is kiss me again.'

He doesn't move. I take his face, run my fingers down his lean cheeks, over his jaw, down his throat. I lift up my wrist to show him the bracelet, and slowly wind the silver chain in, round and round, until our hands are joined and our fingers interlink. He looks at me all the while. Questions are careering through his mind, I can tell. A running commentary to translate, going over his past, analysing our time together, regretting what we didn't do. Foreseeing what comes next.

Sod it. I pull his face to mine and kiss him. Slowly and oh so carefully. I won't let him pull away. If he tries, I'll just pull him back. Our lips press harder and more urgently, swelling with excitement. Our mouths open to each other, wet and warm, breath rushing faster as our tongues push inside, entwine and taste. Our hands are clasped tight within the silver chain.

We're halfway down. The snow has practically obliterated the city.

The wheel is still turning, carrying us slowly to the ground.

A series of small fires has been lit inside me, like beacons flashing messages from one army to the next. But I can't decode them. If this is addiction, I want more of it. I want more kissing. I want more of Gustav. But the messages could simply be saying, *the war is over.*

I know he feels the same. Not only from the hardness of him pressing urgently against me as I hook my legs over his, but because it's only when the doors of the pod slide open that he stops kissing me.

We stand up, pull our jackets and coats on, fling our scarves round our necks, all the time staring at each other like sleepwalkers, blushing and breathless. We carry the bottle and glasses, and uneaten chocolates, out into the cold.

London has disappeared behind a still falling sheet of snow.

We walk slowly across the bridge to delay our return to the gallery. The lights in the building are all off except one, and even through the snow we can still see my huge, sombre face.

'Who bought the last two paintings, Gustav?' I ask, shivering violently as we get to the other side and approach the building along the street. He stops me in the darkened lobby where Crystal used to sit.

'We're going up to meet the last buyer now. But first, open this.'

As in all the best finales it is an air ticket. I gape at it, then at him.

Has that internal commentary of his finally been translated, and is it all going my way?

'I bought the self-portrait of Serena Folkes.'

Hot tears prick my eyes. 'I should have known! So where are you going to hang it?'

'Well, there are plenty of blank walls in the house here.' He flaps the ticket in my face. 'Or if you come to New York with me you can choose where it goes in my new apartment.'

I fling my arms around him and kiss him, full on the mouth, all the way up to the gallery in the lift. And he kisses me back.

Now I know where I'm going, and who I'm going with. But then Crystal's voice echoes down the brief corridor of time we've had together.

The day he tells you about that is the day you'll know he's letting you right in.

The lift doors open and we step out into the corridor now full of crouching, leaping metal sculptures. A couple of unexpected live figures are in the gallery, too.

'Hey, babes! Look at you all sleek and cool! Rocking this *Star Trek* vibe!'

It's Polly, standing at the desk by the window with her arms outstretched. Crystal stands very still beside her like a sentry, looking straight at Gustav with an odd, blank expression. Something is flickering in her eyes, but I can't tell what.

I rush over to Polly and give her a hug. 'I didn't realise you were still in town, Pol! And guess what? I'm coming to New York!'

'Unbelievable! Maybe now I'll be able to get hold of you more easily. You've been off the radar for weeks!' She unbuttons her purple suede and silver fur Afghan coat and looks Gustav up and down as he kisses her hand. 'Hmm. If this is the reason you stood me up I'll let you off the hook. Just my type, too!'

'Hands off! I've been preoccupied, to say the least.' I'm bouncing with excitement. 'And look! My first show sold out!'

'Yes, I know, darling, because apparently I was the very last buyer. We bought that one. The *Stairway to Heaven*.'

'We?' Gustav frowns as he leans to switch off the Anglepoise lamp. He runs his finger down the final list of buyers. 'I only have Polly Folkes here.'

'Well, he lent me the money, because he's richer than me. You are way too expensive for me these days, Rena. Where is he, anyhow? Honey? How long does it take to find a couple of champagne glasses? Come out here and say hi!'

Pierre steps out from the office kitchen carrying a bottle of champagne. He's even more handsome than I imagined, now that he's unmasked. Tall, broad, well dressed. And those eyes are even darker and more glittering than before.

'Hey!' I cry, opening my arms to give him a hug. 'I didn't recognise you without your mask.'

He smiles and opens his mouth to speak. Catches sight of something over my shoulder. And stops dead.

Gustav hasn't moved. Crystal takes the glasses, but they rattle in her hands. She looks as if she's been taken suddenly, terribly ill. She's translucent with dismay.

Polly and I look at each other. The men are frozen, open mouthed, horrified.

'Gustav?' I put my hand on his arm. Even through his coat I can feel the muscles flickering with tension. 'You said this would be a lovely surprise! You knew Polly was the other buyer. So why are you standing there as if you've seen another ghost?'

The two men take another step towards each other, but no more than that. They don't extend hands for a handshake, arms for a hug. You could cut the atmosphere with a boning knife.

'Hello, Pierre,' says Gustav, his voice cracking uncertainly. 'What's brought you back?'

'I found this in my car.' The younger man holds up a business card and runs it along his darkly shadowed upper lip. 'Hello, big brother.'

Read on for a taste of what happens next, taken from the second book in the series, *The Golden Locket . . .*

'That night.' She starts to speak slowly, as if in a trance. 'Well, Pierre couldn't hack it. He saw them at it. He tears upstairs, shouting the odds, packs his suitcase. Gustav doesn't come after him, that makes Pierre even more furious, there's a deathly hush, and then it's Margot who's rushing into his bedroom, stark naked except for a ripped shirt.'

I lift up a gleaming sliver of salmon and force my hand to remain steady as I put it in my mouth. At the next-door table a group of guys are glancing across at Polly and me. They must be able to hear what we're saying, especially the words 'naked' and 'ripped', because they keep whispering amongst themselves.

'So she's taken off all her leather gear so as not so scare him. All the better to seduce little brother,' I remark through my mouthful of salmon. 'So? No great shakes. That's what she's good at. Pierre's a good-looking boy. You know what they're like at that age. Always hard, and always grateful.'

She manages a weak smile. 'Maybe. But you're missing the point, honey. His was a lad's world of pubs and rugby and his home had become this dark realm full of strangers filming each other copulating. Not only that but his adored big brother had lost the plot with all this sadomasochistic bondage or whatever you call it. Pierre feels *contaminated*. And then Margot's flinging herself at him, begging Pierre to rescue her, take her away with him.'

Polly stops then, goes very pale again.

'Don't tell me any more if it upsets you.' I push her plate across the table. 'You need to eat.'

'And you need to listen.' She chews obediently on a piece of steak, and then another. Then she lays her fork down. In unison we drain our beer and she signals for another. The guys at the table nudge each other and smirk.

'Pierre says it's the sexiest thing that has ever happened to him. Sexier than anything I've ever done to him.'

Polly's face is stricken as she speaks. The guys at the neighbour table are agog. I gulp. My throat has gone dry.

'What did she do that was so sexy?'

'That's the weird thing. Nothing special. Just, all the ingredients; the trauma, the timing, the fact that it was forbidden. His brother's wife. A winning formula. Here's this femme fatale, a sophisticated, sexy older woman, she's been living under the same roof, just along the landing, and here's Pierre, a red-blooded young bloke, the observer who's feeling left out and yet he fantasises about her year after year, when he's in bed at night, takes himself in hand under the covers because no little flopsy can match up to his sister-in-law. He drives himself mad, jealous of his brother, wanting to see Margot naked, wanting to collide with her coming out of the shower, all wet and slippery, the towel unravelling. Yep. He told me all this.'

We stare at each other for a moment. We are both holding our knives and forks in the air like spears, the food not quite reaching our lips.

I gulp. 'God, this really is too much information.'

She jabs her steak at me before popping it into her mouth.

'There's more. He used to hear her moaning in Gustav's bed and it drove him up the wall with frustration.'

My sweet salmon hash threatens to find its way back up my throat. She may as well have stabbed me with her knife and fork. Cold sweat prickles under my hair. 'Stick to the night in question. Please.'

'Yes, your honour. So now the tables have turned, Margot's the damsel in distress, crying and sobbing on his bed, tearing at her hair, tearing off her shirt, she's so terrified of big bad Gustav, and Pierre goes to comfort her, and she pulls him down on top of her, and Pierre's burning for her because just the sight of her in the doorway in this ripped shirt, her long bare legs, everything sweaty and ripped and dishevelled has turned him on and she wastes no time, she's got his trousers off, and her hand is wrapped round him, she's wriggling about on top of him like an eel and bingo!' Polly slaps her hand down on the table, making the cutlery rattle, and our ear-wigging neighbours spill their drinks. 'She's banging him senseless.'

'Bingo,' I repeat faintly. My mouth has dropped open. I daren't look at the next table. It seems that half the diner is now listening in, but perhaps that's just my heightened sensitivity. I try to cough, but my throat is blocked. 'Pierre fell for the oldest trick in the book. Ever heard of Eve? Salome? Delilah? Scheherazade?'

Polly stabs another piece of steak with her fork, and a little blood runs out of it. She lifts it up in front of her mouth and studies it. Her eyes are chips of blue glass arrowing at me.

'Pierre was shagging his brother's wife. Graphic enough for you?' she hisses quietly. We all – me, the guys at the next table, the waitress bringing their bill – we all watch Polly as she pops the steak into her mouth, the flexing of the muscles in her jaw as she chews. 'And the coup de grace? The bedroom door was wide open, so who do you suppose walked in and caught them in flagrante? Talk about a fearful symmetry. Anyway, hell was unleashed and Gustav chucked them both out. And that's when I told Pierre to shut up with the story-telling. I didn't want to hear any more.'

I smash the remains of the salmon hash on my plate. Our new beers arrive, droplets of condensation running down their smooth glass sides. I lift the glass and lick moisture off the side.

'The only good thing is that it's all out in the open now.'